PRAISE FOR FREAK CAMP

"Beautiful, painful story about two boys and the world they inhabit. This is a story about monsters, both the kind that lurk in the dark, and the kind that stand out in the open and pretend their souls aren't as black as the monsters they hunt. …It's about a friendship so strong that it's heartbreaking and life-affirming and painfully beautiful. This is the story of Jake and Tobias and the world they inhabit – it's not an easy journey to take, but once you begin the journey with them, you will never want to let them go." *–review from Tammy on Goodreads*

"Hauntingly good story. Toby and Jake become real to you as soon as you meet them. You feel for them, hurt with them and hold onto them to the very end. Worth reading over and over." *–review from Ginger on Amazon*

"Powerful plot matched by tight prose. Gripping world building and characterizations—the prose feels fresh and taut without being too self-consciously stylistic and precious about it. A pleasure to read—despite the horror of the situations in the book. Strong arc that stops at a satisfying place—but also leaves me really, really eager for the next part of the series!" *–verified review on Amazon*

"While the subject matter can be horrifying . . . this book is incredibly well written and the ending is so satisfying. . . . The plot may make you think of or draw parallels to some real life atrocities going on in America right now, the primary narrative is truly redemptive, and their triumph over unfair adversity is as American in nature as any other arc out there. Highly recommend it." *–review from S. Brannan on Amazon*

"Freak Camp comes from a place of recognition that the outside "real" world is a reflection of the battles we carry inside each of us. This series has started off with quite a punch—it's real and upsetting and purposeful—there is no gratuitous torture or abuse "for the sake of it" in these pages. Rather, the characters Tobias and Jake respective childhoods and traumas are very much relatable for those readers who have experienced—albeit not concentration camps—similar circumstances in their lives, especially in early childhood. Moving forward, not allowing the pain to consume you: I am excited for the promise of a better tomorrow in Part 2!" *–review from RW on Amazon*

FREAK CAMP

Thank you for buying this A MONSTER BY ANY OTHER NAME paperback.

For bonus Freak Camp stories and early access to the rest of the series, sign up for the monthly Freak Camp newsletter at **freakcamp.com**

The sequel FEAR is available now!

FREAK CAMP

BOOK 1

A MONSTER BY ANY OTHER NAME

LAURA RYE
BAILEY R. HANSEN

First edition. February 1, 2023.

Published by Laura Rye.
www.freakcamp.com

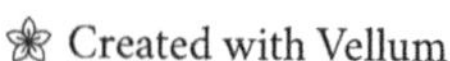

CONTENT NOTES

A MONSTER BY ANY OTHER NAME is a series about trauma recovery, not just trauma. However, Book 1 (FREAK CAMP) is the part of the story when the trauma takes place.

Scenes in this book include graphic violence, abuse and neglect of children, sexual and physical assault, torture, institutional dehumanization, and reference to domestic violence causing a miscarriage. Please always put your mental health first.

None of these dark scenes are written for entertainment, but rather as the framework for a journey of love, healing, and recovery.

Readers may choose instead to start with Book 2 (FEAR), which is also written as an entry point to the series. FEAR and the rest of the series do not contain any of the graphic content described above, though there are references to those past events. You can find FEAR at freakcamp.com or books2read.com/fearfc

This series is a hurt/comfort story to the max: for every ounce of hurt, there will be a pound of comfort down the line. Happy ever after guaranteed.

For all the children who have been locked in cages.

PART I

CHAPTER ONE

SEPTEMBER 1990

THE GRAY CONCRETE walls of Freak Camp weren't as tall as Jake had expected them to be, considering all the monsters held inside. He craned his neck to look up at the razor wire on top as his dad, Leon, stopped the car before the guard post.

"Hawthorne?"

Jake looked over, surprised to hear their real last name. The guard bent over to squint through the car window, looking curious and skeptical.

Dad stared back, implacable. "What's it to you?"

The guard shrugged. "Didn't expect to see you around here. Thought you steered clear of the ASC."

"There a problem with my hunting license? Unless you changed the rules in the last hour, any licensed ASC hunter has access to the FREACS facility."

The guard still hesitated, his gaze moving to Jake. "You got a license for the kid already?"

Dad snorted as Jake glared. "Like the Dixons never bring their kids here. Don't bullshit me. He's with me, and he can look out for himself."

With a final shrug, the guard stepped back and waved them through. Jake smirked, sitting back. Gravel crunched under the Eldorado's tires as they rolled forward into the small parking lot.

Even this far north in Nevada, the late September heat stifled the air as they walked from the car to the heavy metal door, where they paused under a camera for a beep that allowed them to enter.

Following his father, Jake stepped through the spirit-detection scanners, across the pentagrams, and gripped the silver-and-iron turnstile to push through into the lobby. He tried to look like he'd been there before, that this was all routine, as they headed to the reception desk with a grim-looking middle-aged woman stationed behind a reinforced plastic screen. Really, it had only been in the months since his tenth birthday that Dad had let Jake join in a few hunts instead of leaving him alone in the motel or with a babysitter. Well, sometimes his job was only to guard the Eldorado while Dad went after the vamps inside the warehouse, but that was still a really important job. Jake knew how to use the radio to call for help if things got ugly.

And now Dad trusted him enough to bring him into *Freak Camp*. Jake was more than ready to see real monsters in the light of day and not just the aftermath at midnight in a trashed house.

Dad wrote their names into the register, and the receptionist pulled it toward her to scan them, her eyes widening. "Mr. Hawthorne. Is this your first time visiting FREACS?"

"Suppose it is."

She looked at Jake. "We don't usually have minors loitering in Reception, but he could wait here—"

"No," Dad interrupted. "He's coming inside with me. No use sheltering him. As long as you don't have the inmates running the show." His tone was scornful, a challenge.

Her mouth pursed. "Certainly not. Well, this is not a situation that's arisen before, but ASC leadership leaves it to parental discretion. I'll call a guard to escort you in."

———

VICTOR TODD HAD BEEN WORKING at FREACS for less than a year, so he still found himself tagged for grunt jobs like escort duty. When he heard the summons over the walkie-talkie, he rolled his eyes and left his patrol of the Workhouse to head for Reception. At least the chance to give a tour to a jaw-dropped, barely-eighteen hunter could break up the monotony of the week, he reflected as he punched the code to open the security door.

The door swung open to reveal a grizzled middle-aged man, face as hard as the most experienced guards and hunters Victor had met. As he stepped through, a young boy jumped after him, his own gray-blue eyes wide and scanning the yard before them.

Victor took their measure, then cleared his throat. "Welcome to Freak Camp. I'm Officer Todd, and I'll be your tour guide today."

The man didn't look away from his cool study of the camp. "Hawthorne."

Victor did a double take. The boy beside Hawthorne imitated the man's posture, feet apart, one hand resting on a short-sheathed knife strapped to his jeans belt. This was Sally Dixon's son? No one had caught a glimpse of him since his mother was killed in the Liberty Wolf Massacre six years ago. His father had disappeared with the boy before the end of the funerals.

The kid couldn't yet be in junior high. He looked about the same age as Victor's youngest cousins. The only weapon they could handle was a baseball bat—though they'd be scary with one—and Victor would go to work bare-ass naked before he let them set foot in here.

With effort, Victor refocused on the man before him. While his son was a mystery, Leon Hawthorne was a legend among hunters and those within the Agency of Supernatural Control. He was a man who went alone, with only an ax, after monsters that other hunters tackled in groups, armed with machine guns.

"This is your first time here, is that right?" Victor asked, and Hawthorne gave a short nod. "Well, welcome to America's number-one most secure and only facility for housing supernatural creatures—whatever monsters under Timmy's bed we can drag out and haul here. I'm sure you've heard a lot of nicknames, but the official name is the Facility for Research, Elimination, and Containment of Supernaturals. Built and named five years ago by Director Elijah Dixon, founder and head of the ASC—"

Victor broke off with a cough, realizing he was talking about Hawthorne's father-in-law and the boy's grandfather. Neither of them looked at him, but Victor thought the grim lines around Hawthorne's mouth and eyes tightened.

Victor said hastily, "Let's start with Building A, the one you just came out of. That's Reception and Administration. If you want to book one of the dozen standard interrogation rooms there, you get to them through Reception. Administration is the other half of the building and takes up the whole second floor, but you'd only go in there if you got an appointment with Director Dixon. Now, this way." Victor gestured to his left, and the Hawthornes fell in behind him on the packed dirt path.

"Building B has the mess hall where we feed our monsters, with an infirmary wing if we've got a reason to keep a sick monster alive. Next up, Building C. That's the barracks for the main population of low-level supernaturals—your vamps, werewolves, witches, shapeshifters, all other basic, human-presenting freaks." Victor glanced back to see the Hawthorne kid, eyes wide, trotting a little to keep up with his old man. "There's Building D, the Workhouse, where we keep our monsters productively employed making all the salt rounds and hunter PPE you can find. Course, some of them find themselves allergic to the ingredients, but that's why we've got gloves."

In the middle of the compound, Victor stopped, pointing ahead at two looming, windowless buildings made of the same iron-reinforced concrete as the outer walls. "That's Building E, split between Special Research and Intensive Containment. IC is where you find the nastier freaks: your djinn, wendigos, or any other monsters that want to make trouble. Only specialized personnel allowed in or out, or hunters if they've done the paperwork. Special Research is where we take freaks for special interrogations." Victor didn't elaborate.

"That's where I'm headed," Hawthorne said.

So far, Jake found Freak Camp pretty disappointing. There were no monsters clawing and shrieking at each other in the yard, no groups of guards fighting to subdue a vampire or werewolf, or something stranger yet, something Jake had never seen or heard of before. Maybe not today, but someday, he'd face down a freak that even Roger had only read about in all his books.

The yard was quiet outside the buildings, but as they passed the Workhouse, he saw a few groups of prisoners dressed all in gray. They looked human, though of course he knew that didn't mean anything. Plenty of monsters were good at looking human.

They were digging a trench with plastic shovels. As Jake passed, they looked up, eyes flickering over Jake's dad and the guard, and then they turned away, hiding their faces. Jake smirked, skipping forward to catch up. Even monsters here recognized his dad.

As they approached the chained, electrified gate leading into

Special Research, Officer Todd stopped, looking back at Jake. "Uh, you want the kid to wait outside?"

Leon followed his gaze. "Sounds good. Jake, I need you to stay out here."

Jake planted his hands on his hips. "But Dad, I can—"

"Jake. Not today."

Jake stopped, dropping his arms to his sides. He trusted his dad with every bone in his body, as well as any other bones they might come up with, but he didn't have to like it. At least if Dad said *not today,* that meant *someday,* and that was okay, he guessed. Someday, when Dad knew Jake was really ready to join him in the hunt as a full partner, Dad would let him know.

He sighed loudly, but all he said was, "Yes, sir."

A smile cracked Leon's face, and he patted Jake's shoulder. "That's my boy. I'll be gone for . . ." He turned to the guard. "How long do these things usually take?"

"That depends on how—" Todd glanced down at Jake. "Depends, sir. Anywhere from half an hour to a few."

"Well, probably won't be so long today. Jake, I'll be back in an hour, give or take."

Jake nodded. "Yes, sir."

Dad looked back at the guard. "Watch him for me?"

Todd appeared taken aback. "Sir, I don't know that that's a good—"

"Jake knows not to poke at the monsters. Just make sure he knows where to stay out." Leon's mouth quirked again. "My boy's no idiot. He knows to keep his distance. And he's not going to pull any boneheaded moves in this place, will you, son?"

Jake rolled his eyes, whining out, "*Dad.*"

"One hour."

"I'll be here, sir."

"Good." Dad moved forward to the gate, where Todd did something complicated with a keypad and a large lock, twisting it open. Without a backward glance, Leon Hawthorne stepped through the gate to Special Research and disappeared inside.

As THE GATE clanked shut behind his dad, Jake found himself alone with the guard Todd, who eyed him like he had never seen a hunter before.

Or maybe, Jake thought proudly, he'd just never seen a *Hawthorne* before.

Finally, Todd cleared his throat. "So, kid—"

"Jake," he corrected. "My name's Jake. Is Todd your first name?"

The guard blinked at him. "Nah, it's Victor. So, Jake, what are you interested in?"

Jake gave Victor a look that said *How stupid are you?* He tapped the knife in his belt. "I'm a hunter. What do you think I'm interested in?"

Victor gave a huff of laughter. He looked around the yard behind Jake, then crouched down toward him. "Wanna see the baby monsters in their playpen?"

Jake felt a leap of excitement. "Sure! Wait, you guys got baby monsters? I thought they were always just adults or dead things that were killing people."

"Oh yeah, there's baby monsters. And they're just as fu—as messed up as the big, scary monsters. All right, this way."

The guard led him back down the path, cutting across the yard of packed dirt, past a pair of posts jutting into the sky with manacles attached to them. Next to the Workhouse, they approached a fenced-in block of bare earth. Inside were clusters of kids, ranging from younger than Jake to some who looked like they might be in high school if they were outside Freak Camp.

Jake stopped, disappointed again. They all looked ordinary,

no different from kids he saw on playgrounds, except this wasn't a playground, and no one looked like they were playing. He looked up at Victor skeptically. "These are monsters?"

Adults had tried to jerk him around in the past, and he liked to make it clear that he wouldn't put up with crap from anyone, even if they were older than him. The only adult he trusted implicitly was Dad, because Dad always knew best and wouldn't lie to him.

But the guard looked sincere, though amused, like he was helping a fellow hunter correct an elementary mistake rather than messing with a stupid kid. He nodded. "Don't be fooled if they look weak and innocent. Didn't your dad teach you how some monsters can look just like us?"

Jake scoffed. "Course he did. He taught me everything. I just thought you'd have them better tied up or something." He hadn't thought that at first, though. He had thought they just looked like kids. But he wasn't about to admit that to a man who dealt with monsters every day.

Victor grinned. "No need for that—they're well-trained. You got nothing to worry about. You could even walk in and poke at them with that knife you've got in your belt, and they wouldn't even snap back." He mimed swinging at someone with his billy club.

"Seriously?" If someone poked Jake, he'd do his best to break their fingers. He'd have thought that monsters would try to rip his head off at least.

The guard waved him on. "Don't believe me? Go ahead, try it." His tone added *I dare you*, but in a friendly, easy way. The guard might think Jake was just a kid, but the man wouldn't want him in any kind of real danger. After all, if he let Jake get hurt, then he would have to answer to Leon Hawthorne, and Jake knew—like he knew the purr of the Eldorado on endless roads, the recoil of a shotgun, and the smell of burning bones—that Dad would crush anyone who ever hurt Jake.

Jake walked forward, neither slow nor fast, and the guard opened the gate for him. It was a simple chain-link fence, something that Jake could probably have kicked down if he put his mind to it, but it marked a boundary of a place containing more monsters than real humans. He walked with his head high and hands open, confident, ready to draw his knife at a moment's notice—like Dad walked. Jake was a hunter, even if he was young, and no monster had better underestimate him.

But the monster kids didn't seem interested. A couple glanced up at him, eyes flickering over his hands and knife before moving away from him, but most kept their focus down. Now that he was closer, Jake could recognize some as monsters. Kid vampires—some of them maybe centuries old—had unnaturally pale skin flaking from the Nevada sun, and iron muzzles like supersized braces kept them from opening their mouths wide enough even to bite a finger. Shapeshifters had telltale neon-green tags flapping from their arms, while those with some kind of mind-control powers had a T brand on their forehead to indicate the danger. Two werewolves had silver buckles on their collars.

Everywhere Jake looked, he saw the same kinds of monsters that he and Dad hunted. These looked sad and defeated, but the danger in that space still made the little hairs on the back of his neck stand up. He couldn't see any of them looking at him, no matter how fast he turned, but he could sense their attention, the hunger some of them must have had for his flesh or blood or pain.

That awareness made Jake twitch, but it settled him too. He had seen all these monsters before and knew how to fight them. None of them would take him by surprise today, not like Mom had once been surprised.

Jake was almost ready to turn around, to leave the enclosure and wander around as much of the rest of the camp as he could, when one kid leaning alone against the building glanced at him. It was just a flicker of his eyes, but it made Jake freeze.

He couldn't tell what kind of monster the boy was. He looked . . . ordinary.

The boy was pretty small, maybe six years old, with buzzed-short hair and skin reddened by the sun. He was so thin that Jake could have picked him up over his head, and his gray camp clothes hung off him like he had gotten a set meant for a much bigger child. He didn't have tags on his collar, or the muzzle, or the brand. Nothing to tell Jake what he was.

That wouldn't have been so unusual—a couple of other monster kids also had no distinguishing marks—but what made Jake hesitate was that when he looked at the boy, Jake couldn't see any kind of threat in him. No hatred, no hunger, no loathing like he felt from the other monsters, even when they tried to hide it.

Jake glanced back at the guard, wanting to ask what was different about the little kid, but he changed his mind. Victor was grinning at him and mimed poking again with the club. The look on his face was nasty. Jake felt like the guy was daring him to do something stupid.

But Jake had never been afraid of a dare.

He marched over to the kid, stopped a couple of feet away, and glanced back at the guard. Then he looked at the younger boy, who was hunching in on himself, carefully not looking at Jake.

Jake raised a finger and poked him twice on the shoulder.

The kid tensed, his shoulders rounding a little more, but when nothing else happened, when Jake just stood there and waited for his reaction, he looked up in surprise. He had bright, clear hazel eyes that looked huge in his thin face. They made him look like some kind of startled bird.

Jake and the monster stared at each other for a moment

before the monster seemed to realize what he was doing and dropped his eyes.

Jake felt awkward. He was always awkward when he actually wanted to talk to someone. He was fine with a cover story—like Dad always gave him when they went to a new town, a new school, along with a new name and a new reason Mom wasn't with them—but he had trouble just being himself.

"So," he said, and stuck his hands on his hips. "What kind of monster are you?"

The kid looked up, then back down again quickly. "Unidentified, sir."

Jake frowned. "I'm not sir. Sir's my dad. You can call me Jake."

The monster boy raised his eyes, blinking at him. "Jake," he said, and then ducked his head. Jake wasn't sure, but he might have caught the edge of a smile. "Yes, s—Jake."

Jake felt like the kid didn't quite get it. Like he thought that Jake was just another substitute for *sir*. "Jake," he persisted. "It's my name. What's your name?"

The monster took a quick breath and held his hands straight at his sides. "Eighty-nine U I six seven zero three," he said, rapid and flat.

Jake scoffed. "That can't be your name. That's a number. What do people call you?"

His eyes flickered up again, and he hesitated before answering, "Tobias. Becca calls me Toby."

If Jake didn't know better, he'd have thought that the monster boy was shy. It was weird even thinking of him as "monster boy," because he seemed like any other kid. Nicer than any other kid, actually. Other kids usually didn't stick around this long just talking to him. They wanted to know how he fit in the food chain of whatever new school or town he was in, and that was it. Jake spent half of every first week—and sometimes there wasn't a second week, if Dad managed to piss someone off, or the hunt wrapped up—proving that he was at the top, untouchable, in whatever social order already existed.

But it looked like Tobias didn't mind sticking around, even after figuring out where they stood.

"Toby," Jake repeated. It was a strange name for a monster. "So you're unidentified? What does that mean?" He reminded himself that he wasn't talking to a kid. He was talking to a monster. Toby had probably done something awful, like eaten someone's dog or something. They didn't just lock little kids up in Freak Camp because someone pointed at them and said they were a monster.

"They don't know what kind of monster I am yet."

"But what did you *do*?" Jake leaned forward. "All monsters do something, have some kind of power."

Tobias shrugged his small shoulders, eyes back on the ground. "I don't remember."

It must've been really horrible if Tobias couldn't even remember what it was. Maybe he had woken covered in blood and screaming. Maybe every stuffed animal in an arcade had caught fire all at once when he was around, or he'd stabbed someone, or something.

But every time Jake tried to picture Tobias in those scenes, it didn't work. It was impossible to imagine this shy, jumpy kid doing anything monsterlike. It didn't help that the longer Jake thought about it and didn't say anything else, the smaller and more dejected Tobias looked, like the conversation had been as cool and unusual for him as it had been for Jake and he didn't want it to be over.

"Don't worry about it," Jake said at last. "It's fine if you don't remember. Do you have a lot of friends? I mean, monster friends?"

Tobias shook his head. "I have Becca. But a lot of the others . . . We're all freaks, but I'm *really* . . ." He trailed off and shrugged.

"Becca says they don't know what to make of me. Are you a hunter?"

Jake puffed out his chest and put his hand on his knife. Tobias cringed back, ducking his head lower. "Of course I . . . hey, wait, it's okay, I ain't gonna hurt you. I mean, you're a contained monster, right?"

Tobias nodded.

"And you don't want to hurt anyone, right?"

Tobias nodded again, so hard and fast that Jake could see the collar around his throat rubbing over his ear.

"So we're good." There he went again, saying something totally ordinary that filled Tobias's face with surprise and a hint of wonder.

Jake was used to thinking that he was a pretty cool kid, but that was an opinion shared mainly by himself and no one else. But every time he said something that was even moderately nice, he got one of those looks that made him want to keep being friendly. Jake glanced back at the guard, but Victor wasn't paying attention to him, focused instead on a few monsters in a corner standing close together.

"Let's sit down," Jake said, and that smile on Tobias's face caused some pretty awesome feelings.

"What do you do here all day?" Jake asked when they were settled against a wall, still in sight of the guard but far enough away that Victor couldn't listen in on their conversation. "Do you have to learn and stuff, or do you just walk around all day and, like, play cards?"

"I learn!" Tobias sounded almost defensive, if someone could be defensive without raising their voice. "I can read anything."

"Whoa, really?" Jake wasn't a big reader. He *could* read, he wasn't an idiot, but this kid might've been in first grade if he wasn't a monster, and Jake had a feeling that reading hadn't been his strong suit when he was that age. "What kinds of stuff do you read?"

Everything, apparently. Biology, geography, and folklore. General history, as well as specifics on monster attacks leading up to the Liberty Wolf Massacre. Tobias even had some knowledge of non-supernatural animals. Tobias had started cautiously, listing off books and subjects in a monotone, but as Jake sat and listened, he talked more rapidly, more eagerly.

"Do all the monster kids learn this stuff?" Jake asked.

Tobias shook his head. "I help Becca in the library. That's where we're assigned. She used to be a librarian before she got caught and came here, so they tell her to do research for the scientists. She's really good at it, and she's teaching me too." He glanced at Jake, who could almost see the proud smile in Tobias's eyes, though it hadn't quite made it onto his face yet. "The library's where they keep all the books," he whispered, as though that was a secret that shouldn't be passed around to just anyone.

Jake laughed. Tobias looked nervous for a second, then relaxed. Jake wasn't laughing at him, but in amazement that he was hanging out with a six-year-old monster boy who was explaining libraries, and he wasn't actually bored out of his skull. Talking to Tobias made him almost want to go check out a library himself.

"Could I get some of these books?" Jake asked.

Tobias nodded. "Sure you could, you're a hunter. Hunters get whatever they want. But . . ." He bit his lip. "If you take them away, then I won't get to finish them. So if you could wait a little . . ." Tobias abruptly looked horrified. "N-n-not that I'm t-t-telling you what to do, I'm just saying that I would m-m-miss them—do what you want. I'm just a monster, don't listen to me."

"Don't worry, Toby, I'm not gonna take your books. I'm sure there's other copies at some of the libraries I've been to." Though Jake wasn't sure of that. Some of the books that Tobias had listed sounded pretty rare, and Jake didn't know that most public schools would carry them. But he wasn't going to tell that to Tobias, who had looked so upset at the thought of Jake taking away his books.

"You've been to other libraries?" Tobias gaped. "You mean there's more than the one in Administration?"

"Toby, there's *hundreds* of libraries. One in every school I've ever been to—and I've been to a lot of schools—and at least one in every town." Jake told him about his last school, where he had hung out in the library just because the kids were all dumb and not worth talking to. He had read eight Goosebumps books because there had been nothing much else to do. He had pretended that it was research, but most of the stories sounded made up. No way civilian kids would ever be that smart and badass around monsters.

"I mean, I've never been to summer camp, but no way it's anything like Freak Camp, and the cops never help like that." In real life, Jake knew, cops only ever got in the way or got there too late to help. That's what his dad said.

Tobias tilted his head. "What's a summer camp?"

Jake groped for an explanation. "It's a camp you go to, but only like, for the summer. You stay with other kids in a cabin and tell ghost stories, and during the day they make you do arts and crafts and sh-stuff." Even though Toby was a monster, it felt weird to swear in front of him. Toby didn't look like a monster, he just looked like a little kid, like the ones Jake saw sometimes being pushed by their parents on the swing set across the street from his school.

Toby blinked at him. "And then where do you go?"

"Back home. And to school. Um." Jake realized this might not be as easy to explain to a monster kid as he'd first thought. As smart as Toby was, he didn't know about libraries. Maybe he'd never even seen a TV show. "Anyway, you gotta know there's no such thing as monster counselors."

"What's a counselor?"

"It's . . . um . . ." Jake glanced at the guard outside the chain-link fence. "Never mind, forget it. It's not like I've been to summer camp either. So yeah, that library wasn't half as big as the one at my third-grade school in Amherst . . ."

Tobias listened like he'd never heard anything half as cool in his life. At one point he rocked back and looked up at the sky, too amazed to sit still any longer. That was when Jake really noticed the collar, imprinted with the 89UI6703 ID number in iron figures.

"Does that hurt?" Jake motioned toward his own neck.

Tobias blinked at him. His eyes looked even bigger and more innocent up close. Jake didn't think monsters' eyes were supposed to look like that. "Does what hurt?"

"That." Jake reached toward him but stopped before touching the leather. Tobias hadn't reacted, just watched his hand.

"Oh." He dropped his gaze and scratched at the collar. "Sometimes. I've had it for a while, so I don't feel it much anymore."

Jake frowned. "Does it ever come off?"

Tobias shook his head.

"Not even when you shower? Or sleep?"

He shook his head again.

"Huh." Jake picked at the ground, not sure what else to say.

"Jake!"

Jake jumped to his feet, seeing Dad on the other side of the fence, waiting for him. He hastily brushed off his knees. "Sorry, gotta go."

Tobias looked up then, gazing straight into his eyes. "Will you be back?"

Jake stopped, startled. "Yeah," he said, with a rush of certainty. "Yeah, I'll be back. I'm old enough now, and Dad said we'll probably have to come back here now that he's found something. I'll come back and see you, Toby."

For the first time, Tobias smiled. It was a small, hesitant

thing that vanished almost as soon as it appeared, but it made Jake feel oddly proud.

"Jake!"

Without another word, Jake turned and ran back to his father.

"Sorry, Dad," he said when he reached the gate, breathless more from surprise than the short run. "I lost track of time. How did Special Research go?"

Dad glanced at Victor, frowning. The guard scanned the yard, looking anywhere but at the Hawthornes.

"Fine," Dad said. "It went fine. What were you doing, talking with that monster?"

Jake blanked. He had no idea what he had been doing with Tobias. But he had liked it, and it had made him feel better and more useful than anything since his last hunt. But there was no way he was telling *Dad* that. "I'm researching too. Getting to know monsters so I can recognize them later, you know?"

Dad frowned, but Jake could tell that his mind wasn't on their conversation. It was probably on whatever he had been doing in Special Research, whatever new clue he had gotten about Mom's death.

Jake didn't really know why Dad was still obsessed with Mom's death. Sure, it still hurt Jake, still hurt like blessed salt in an open wound to think about how she wasn't there anymore and would never come back, but she had been gone most of his life, and everyone in the country knew the monster that had done it was dead.

Everyone knew how Sally Dixon had died because it had been caught on TV during the Liberty Wolf Massacre. She'd been called the first casualty of the new War on the Supernatural, though that wasn't really true. Some Secret Service guards had gotten mown down before her.

Jake knew there was a statue of her in Washington, D.C., but he and Dad had never visited. He wasn't sure if he ever wanted to see it.

Dad had kept them safe from the asshole Dixons and all the other nosy people in this stupid country ever since. That was why they used fake names everywhere they went.

Except for today, when they'd finally come to Freak Camp.

So he understood hating the monsters, but he didn't know what Dad was trying so hard to find out from the creatures inside Special Research.

But he didn't need to know now. One day, Dad would know that Jake was ready, and then Dad would trust him with everything. They would hunt together, and no one would be able to stop the Hawthornes. No one would be able to sneak up on either of them.

Walking out of Freak Camp beside Dad, Jake acknowledged that that day was probably pretty far in the future. But he smiled as they reached the Eldorado and he climbed into the shotgun seat. At least now when he was bored, he could think about Freak Camp and Tobias.

TOBIAS COULD BARELY CONTAIN himself until that evening, when he saw Becca leaving the Workhouse with a group of other monsters. He knew better than to run to her, but he walked quickly, weaving between the monsters until he reached her side.

"Becca!"

She glanced down at him, touching her fingertips to the back of his head.

"I met a real today," Tobias whispered. "He told me to call him Jake!"

Like all the monsters in Freak Camp, Becca's face didn't change much, but Tobias could usually tell what she was thinking. He saw surprise followed by alarm, and his excitement shrank into almost nothing. Meeting Jake hadn't felt like something dangerous, but Becca knew much more than him.

She stepped out of the line forming into the mess hall, and Tobias moved with her. There were rules for who went first, and Becca and Tobias were usually near the end. He was in the back because he was small and unidentified, and Becca was there because she was a witch. That was why she only had one hand.

Becca frowned at him. "Where did you meet him?"

"In the yard. Victor let him in the playpen, and then he talked to me."

Becca's frown deepened, but she glanced around them and straightened up. "We'll talk later."

After she went inside, Tobias counted to fifteen before following. He approached the slot in the wall, and a bowl slid across the steel counter. Tobias took it and found a seat on a bench with the other monster kids. None of them ever talked much, and Tobias was used to eating in silence, as quickly as possible, before someone else grabbed his food.

Tobias glanced in his bowl for just a moment before bringing it to his mouth. It didn't taste like anything, which was all right, and there was nothing hard that needed chewing.

As they finished, each monster stood and pushed their empty bowl through a second slot to the monsters on cleaning duty. Then they left the mess hall, most heading to the barracks to rest before curfew, except those that had more work duties. Tobias followed the ones going toward the barracks.

The barracks were two long buildings with aluminum siding and roofs. Each had only one door, and the locks were on the outside. Only the guards were allowed to touch those locks. Inside were two rows of bunk beds, each bolted to a wall, and no other furniture. At the back were three toilets with barrier walls between them and swinging doors without locks. New monsters had to sleep in the bunks closest to the toilets.

Monster women and kids were all put in Barracks 1, though sometimes Barracks 2 ran out of space and some of the male monsters were sent over. Both barracks had a lot of cameras and intercoms installed, along with loud horns and strobe lights and even gas if the monsters were bad enough. That had only happened once in Toby's experience. Becca had pushed him to the floor and against a wall, pulled his shirt over his mouth, and told him not to move or open his eyes. It had still tasted awful and made him cough and his eyes burn for weeks afterward every night. Sometimes he thought he could still smell the gas.

Most nights, though, the monsters were quiet. Only when a group of new monsters arrived did it tend to get noisy.

Becca had told Tobias that it was okay for him to come to her bunk after the lights shut off, because that was the last check the guards made to make sure they were all in their beds for the night.

Tobias counted to sixty, then slipped out of his bunk and made his way soundlessly to Becca's, climbing in with her. She pulled her blanket up to let him in, then tucked him close between her and the wall, smoothing his hair back with her arm that ended in a stump.

In a hush, breathing into the space between the canvas mat and her chin, he whispered, "The real boy told me to call him Jake. He asked me what I can read, and I told him about our library, but he said he wouldn't take our books away."

Becca laid a finger over his lips, then asked in her very serious voice, "Did you make him upset? What did he tell you to do?"

"He didn't ask me to do anything. We just sat down and he asked me my name and what kind of monster I was. He said it was okay that I didn't know. And he said he would come back!"

"Shh, shh." Becca touched his mouth again. "Did he say why he was here? How old was he?"

"He was a kid. Maybe Nala's age. How old's she?"

"Nala?"

Tobias tried to remember what name the guards used. "Ragdoll?"

"Jake was just a child? Did you hear a last name, Toby? Did anyone mention his last name, like reals have?"

Tobias started to shake his head, then remembered. "After Jake's dad called—*oh,* Jake has a *dad*—one of the guards said, 'That Hawthorne squirt's got balls like his dad.'"

Becca's hand tensed on his shoulder. She didn't say anything for several moments, then she said quietly, "He won't come back, Toby. Try not to think about it. Don't talk about it. Okay?"

"But he said he would!"

"Tobias. Do what I say."

He shut his mouth and rested his head next to hers.

He knew Becca wasn't his mom. She had told him so. She was a witch, and that was why she only had one hand. But she told him when to stay quiet and when not to look, and he always did what she said. Bad things happened when he didn't listen to her, but he didn't think he could stop thinking about Jake.

REBECCA MARLOW HAD ONCE WANTED a child of her own more than anything in the world.

That dream had died with the impact of her boyfriend's fists. She'd been young and naive, believing that she could trust who a man was when he was sober instead of when he was drunk. Her sister held her as Rebecca bled and shook with sobs so hard she thought she would die on the bathroom floor before morning. But she survived. She got to her feet a different woman, one who would not need to be taught the same lesson twice.

That wasn't all she learned. She returned to her job in the Oklahoma City library, ready to open books that had long caught her eye. She would never again be so helpless, and her former lover would know exactly what her pain felt like.

She soon lost her appetite for vengeance, but she learned she had a knack for witchcraft. In her teens, she had dabbled with the incantations and rituals—just long enough to be frightened and intrigued by what a few words and herbs could offer a person willing to go the distance.

With more knowledge came contacts, and she learned there was a living to be made if you were willing and able to cast basic hexes. She discovered an endless demand from the bitter and desperate looking to inflict their own pain on whoever they thought deserved it. People were willing to pay—and pay well—to make others hurt. Rebecca dealt in jealousy and vengeance, and she cared less and less what she was casting. She was just a well-paid medium for other people's malice.

She quit after the Liberty Wolf Massacre and burned all her illicit materials, but it wasn't so easy to give up for good. She'd gotten used to the extra income, and so had her family. She had the steadiest job among them, and they'd made a habit of going to her with money problems. It was hard for her to say no when it came to her nieces and nephews, whom she loved more than anything in the world, each a precious glimpse of the child she'd never had.

Months after Liberty Wolf the first hysteria over werewolves and vampires died down, and people seemed less inclined to turn on their neighbors because of a funny smell in their backyard. Rebecca built her business back up cautiously, using false names and PO boxes out of town. She only worked spells in motel rooms, never at home.

The ASC still caught her. She'd just begun calling on the

usual names, reaching for the knife with one hand and the flame with the other, when the motel door had burst in. She'd found herself lying on her stomach, handcuffs snapped over her wrists, men shouting about exactly how few rights she had.

Later, replaying all the jobs to see what she had done wrong, she realized that there had been no warning signs, no details that were off. She had just taken one too many jobs, and someone had put the pieces together.

The judicial process went with the usual speed for an accused witch: a closed hearing to consider the evidence, no jury. That same night she found herself trundled into a van headed to Freak Camp.

Most of the blind terror that had suffocated her since her arrest—and through the long, sleepless hours of trial and transportation—bled out after they sawed off her right hand.

Two months later, a new shipment of monsters arrived, including a little boy, maybe five years old—one of the youngest she had seen behind these walls. His look of wide-eyed innocence and tousled sandy hair jarred horribly with the new leather collar bound around his neck. He was still crying and tugging at it when she found him curled in a bunk, face pressed into a torn, stained blanket. He already sported a blackened eye, though whether it was from the trip or the unloading process, she didn't know.

Tobias was a gift, though a bittersweet one. A child his age should have been anywhere but Freak Camp, and she felt sick when she thought of the cruelty in store for him. At least she had knowingly broken the law, taken the risks; Tobias and the other children who were born with strange abilities or had been victims of attacks hadn't done anything to deserve this nightmare of a life sentence.

But now she had a focus, a reason to be thankful she had been stupid and gotten caught. This was what she had wanted so badly, and though Tobias had not been born to her, she had paid for him in pain and blood, and in turn she was the only one looking out for him now. He would never see his real, human family again. And if he were going to live to see his next birthday, he needed her.

Everything she had once dreamed of doing for a child of her own was impossible here. No shopping for clothes as he grew, no enrolling him in swimming lessons and soccer leagues. She couldn't even plan on helping him through adolescence. Monsters—especially one-handed witches, weaker than even the average human on the outside—didn't last long in Freak Camp, and she couldn't count on being there long for Tobias, to do everything she could to ensure he lasted longer than she would.

But even while she bargained and fought for the best food she could get for Tobias, watched him scarf it down and turn to her with wide eyes to ask for more, she couldn't escape the thought that if she really cared for him, she would be negotiating for a lethal dose of morphine instead. One quick injection would be Tobias's ticket out of the camp, the only possible escape besides Special Research and the incinerator. She would be saving him years of pain and abuse, of growing up to be the guards' plaything, punching bag, and worse.

But every time she thought of ending it, even gently pushing her folded blanket down over his face while he slept, holding it hard until he moved no more, she knew that she couldn't do it. It might have been the most selfish choice she had ever made, but she could not kill this child, could not take the one bright piece of joy and love out of her life. Unable to make the truly merciful choice, she went for the second-best option: equipping Tobias to survive.

She taught Tobias to keep quiet, to obey quickly and without questions, to avoid attracting attention. She taught him not to run to her or hug her in public, not to show what he wanted, not to want. He was a monster, she told him, and this was how monsters were treated and must behave. There was nothing he or anyone else could do to change it.

She could tell he was a smart child. He listened, and though he didn't understand at first, the lessons sank in. He did what she taught him, and it made life a little easier for them. That was all Rebecca had to console herself that now, finally, she mattered. She didn't feel the need to atone for what she'd done, all the curses she'd cast, but she was glad that at last in her life, she was doing real good.

She tried to protect Tobias in every way she could, which was usually about preparing for the worst. When he had food, she warned him there might not be much more. When the guards ignored him for a few days, she reminded him that he might get a beating tomorrow for nothing more than looking at them wrong. When the weather was bearable, she reminded him that in the night it would be too cold, that the next day it could be too hot.

She tried to train him not to have expectations, because then he wouldn't be broken when they were stripped away. She taught him to fear everything, to accept fear as an everyday condition, and how, when the things he feared came to pass, to make them not matter.

Somehow she kept him alive and as healthy as it was possible to be in Freak Camp, even when there wasn't enough food to go around, even when that hunter's kid started talking to Tobias.

Of all the threats facing them every day, that one terrified her the most. Attention from hunters—whether they were grown sadists like Victor or baby hunters like Hawthorne's son—meant nothing good for her or Tobias.

Tobias believed it all, that the world could always get worse, but she never quite managed to get him to fear the other boy, who could have had him whipped or killed at a word. She just hoped that the first human child he'd met wouldn't be the thing that broke him.

"So, Jake. What did you learn today?"

Jake straightened, dropping his Game Boy onto the motel bedspread. Dad sat at the small table, writing in his leather notebook. Jake always hated that question when it came from a teacher, but when Dad asked, it was different. Mrs. Morales only asked because she wanted Jake to say he'd learned some dumb lesson about playing nice with the other kids, but when Dad asked, it was important.

"Freak Camp's got top-notch security for all kinds of supernaturals. They organize all their buildings based on what kind of monster is allowed inside. They've never had a runaway." *And I learned baby monsters exist.*

"What'd you notice about the guards?"

"They seemed pretty cool. Like they knew what they were doing. None of the monsters could scare them."

"Yeah? Did you notice any of them slacking off, any weaknesses?"

Jake paused. "The one who walked us around, Officer Todd. Sometimes he wasn't as careful as the others. He'd stare at one thing for a while instead of always looking around."

Dad nodded.

Jake hesitated. It was on the tip of his tongue to ask Dad what *he'd* learned in Freak Camp, but he knew that would go nowhere. Instead he asked, "Where to next? Are we picking up the trail of that weird-ass pixie with a thing for Taco Bell?"

Dad snorted. "Back to Albuquerque with you. You've got a week or two of school to catch up on."

"Aww, Dad! I thought we were going to Vegas. Just one night? It's on the way."

Dad didn't give an inch. He never did. "Nope. This time you're finishing the whole school year in one place. And you'll keep a lower profile than you did in Kentucky. No more wise-ass ghost stories that get the teachers asking questions."

Jake fell back on the bed. "Can't I just, like, be home-schooled? That way no one would notice me."

Dad huffed out a laugh. "You think I can pull that off while tracking down freaks? Or like you'd actually do your homework without anyone checking it? I don't think so. What kind of hunter do you think you'd be if you don't finish fifth grade?"

"Loads of good hunters probably didn't. Like the ones in the Middle Ages."

"And they dropped dead after their first flesh wound because they had no idea how to wash or sterilize anything. Or how to calculate fractions when you're running out of ammo and need to make every ounce of salt count."

Jake sighed loudly. "Can we at least go see Roger in T or C?"

Dad paused. "Yeah, why the hell not? Bastard's always got a new book or something no one's seen yet. Wouldn't hurt to swing by."

In Truth or Consequences, New Mexico, it wasn't unusual for heat waves to shimmer over the land. In Roger Harper's scrapyard of gutted-out cars, the heat could radiate into something like a furnace on the worst summer days.

This September evening wasn't so bad as Roger sat on his porch and kept a cold can for company, sorting through his basket of black-market amulets, until he looked up at the rumble of a black Eldorado turning into his drive.

The Hawthornes never did call in advance.

Roger stood and stepped to the top of the porch steps as the Eldorado came to a stop and the driver's door swung open, followed a moment later by the passenger door. Leon's tread was slow and deliberate, but Jake raced ahead of him, backpack bouncing, taking the porch steps two at a time.

"Hey, Rog!"

"Hey, kid." Roger ruffled his hair, even as Jake tried to duck.

The screen door slapped shut behind Jake as Leon reached the first step, brow furrowed as he looked up at Roger. "Harper."

"Hawthorne. To what do I owe the pleasure?"

Leon shrugged one shoulder and made his way up the steps, a duffel bag slung over his shoulder. "Intel swap. Like always."

Roger rolled his eyes as Leon moved past him, then turned to follow him into the house. "Right."

Jake had grabbed a Mexican Coke from the fridge and was already settled before the TV, lounging on the floor with his back against the couch as he flipped through the channels. Leon and Roger moved into the kitchen, where Roger withdrew two beers and passed one over.

"Just got back from Nevada," Leon said.

Roger's eyebrows quirked. "How'd Vegas treat you?"

Leon shook his head, then swigged his beer. "Winnemucca."

Roger paused. "You mean Freak Camp? You?"

"Yeah, me." Leon set his beer on the kitchen table and crossed his arms, still staring into the living room. "Knew I had to sooner or later."

Roger took that in. "So you got a lead?"

Leon didn't answer.

Roger checked his pantry, scanning for snacks fitting for a ten-year-old. He pulled out a half-empty box of Fruit Gushers that Jake had left behind on his last visit. "Who'd you find to babysit Jake? Tell me you didn't leave him in the car." He tried to sound offhand, not suspicious.

"Nah. Took him in with me."

Roger didn't think he could still be surprised by Leon, but goddamn. "Jesus, Hawthorne, you took the kid inside?"

Leon looked hard at him. "You got something to say, Harper?"

Roger scowled, eyeing Jake, who looked to be in one piece. "Well. Did you get anything?"

After a pause, Leon said, "Maybe." Roger figured that was all he was going to get.

Ever since Leon's wife, Sally, died in the Liberty Wolf Massacre in 1984, he had had a single obsession: hunting the monsters behind the werewolves' assassination attempt of the president. Those werewolves took down a dozen Secret Service agents, bit the First Lady, and killed Sally Hawthorne as she threw herself before the president. She had been there with her father, Elijah Dixon, who survived the attack. He used the national shock and spotlight to expose the existence of supernatural creatures in the shadows throughout the country. He told the world how he was one of a few dozen professional hunters in America who risked their lives to stop these inhuman creatures bent on slaughter.

Roger had been one of those hunters operating before the Liberty Wolf Massacre. He'd known Elijah Dixon, though not on a personal level. The Dixons were unique in how they passed down monster hunting like a family heirloom, allegedly all the way back to the American colonies before the Revolutionary War. They certainly had the most power and money of all the ragtag hunters who usually operated solo.

Roger learned later that Elijah had already been using his government contacts to lobby for federal funding to create an official, though secret, monster-hunting agency. Something like CIA: Supernatural Division. But the tragedy of the Liberty Wolf Massacre gifted Elijah the opportunity to go public with national support on a level he'd never dreamed of.

It was a perfect storm for achieving his lifelong ambition. The national shock and horror gave him the stage to face the cameras and tell the country that he knew exactly what "unknown" menace had tried to kill their president, and he knew how to wipe them out.

Congress handed him a blank check within a month, and Elijah Dixon used it to create the Agency of Supernatural Control and to build the first facility to hold supernaturals: Freak Camp. The facility opened January 2nd, 1985, and First Lady Dorothy Peterson became inmate 85WW0001. She was never seen in public or on camera again.

Elijah's son-in-law Leon Hawthorne did not join his mission. Before all the funerals had finished, he took his four-year-old son, Jake, and disappeared onto the back roads of America, far away from the national spotlight and cameras focused on the tragedy and its heroes, including the slain young mother.

Roger had met Leon a couple of years later at a hunter's bar. Leon was traveling under an alias, as he always did, and Roger joined him to take out a couple of mountain trolls before learning who Leon and his son actually were.

Even aside from the aggressive secrecy with which Hawthorne guarded his life and his son, he wasn't an easy man to get along with or to keep in touch. Hawthorne tended to discourage those who tried, intentionally and unintentionally. Roger had only managed it for as long as he did because Leon knew that Roger could keep a secret, and that they could fall back on Roger's homestead in New Mexico if they needed a pit stop or to bone up for a hunt. For better or for worse, when it came to knowing Hawthorne, Roger was a steady, even-tempered man who'd survived as many hunts as he had by never losing his head, so he could tolerate Leon's dark, broody moods well enough.

Plus, there was the kid. When Roger first met him, Jake had been a tiny terror who'd learned well his father's distrust and paranoia of the whole damn world. It had taken a few visits for Jake to decide that Roger wasn't a threat who needed a pocketknife waved in his direction whenever he entered the room. A few more years had smoothed out Jake's jumpiness, replacing it with bravado that was at least half-earned. Not even the Dixon kids knew more than Jake about the supernatural or could load a shotgun faster, even if the recoil would still knock him off his feet.

Roger had never had kids of his own or even wanted to go the fatherhood route, but he couldn't shrug off the knowledge that he was one of maybe a handful of people in the country who had the privilege of knowing who Sally Dixon's son really was. Nor did it miss his attention that he was one of few familiar, reliable faces in Jake's world. The kid needed some role models who were no more than half the asshole his father was.

The Hawthornes stayed for dinner, which was sloppy joes, one of Jake's favorites. The canned corn was less of a favorite, but it went over better than the green beans Roger had tried before.

Afterward Leon asked to borrow a couple of books on vampiric subspecies and settled down in the living room to read and take notes. Roger took Jake onto his back porch, where he had some walkie-talkies that needed fixing. Jake had quick fingers with anything mechanical, and he loved to brag that his dad already taught him everything there was to know about fixing cars.

"So you got to see the inside of Freak Camp, huh?" Roger asked. "There's probably not a hundred hunters out there who've been inside."

Jake grinned, straightening up. "Yep. Dad knew I could handle it. And it was a breeze, no sweat." Roger raised his eyebrows, and Jake hastily added, "But I never let my guard down. I know how dangerous freaks are."

"You bet your butt they are. And remember that just 'cause something felt easy the first time don't mean it won't put a Jake-sized hole in the wall the second time. Plenty of hunters get taken out by your standard-issue vengeful spirit when they get cocky."

Jake nodded. "Dad always tells me that too." Then he hesitated, and Roger looked up. "Did you know there's kid freaks in Freak Camp?"

Roger didn't answer immediately. He had only visited the facility twice since it had opened in 1985. The whole place and the people who ran it left a bad taste in his mouth. He didn't remember seeing monsters there that weren't adult-sized, but he couldn't say he was surprised that the ASC had built a policy to hold younger ones too. "What kind of kid freaks?"

Jake shrugged. "All kinds. I mean, they only look like kids. I get that vampires and shifters can be any age. But they got some weird ones too. Stuff they don't know how to label."

Roger watched Jake's face. Something was bothering the boy, even if he didn't know how to talk about it. "Y'know," he said at last, "you're twice as old as the whole darn ASC and their Freak Camp. By rights, they should be in kindergarten."

Jake grinned, and Roger set down his tools and stretched. His back still ached from a recent tussle with a mountain troll. They were his specialty, as he lived so close to the Black Range Mountains. Jake was forever asking when he could come along for a mountain troll hunt, and Roger always told him they didn't make kid-size harnesses for hunting trips, so he had some growing to do.

"Let's go kick your dad out of the living room and see what's on TV."

Jake scoffed, his grin broadening. "I'd like to see you try."

"Kid, I eat mountain trolls for breakfast." Roger tilted his head in pretend consideration. "So all right, I'd say I got a fifty-fifty chance against Leon Hawthorne."

True to his word, Dad took Jake back to Albuquerque, where they'd rented a mobile home back in August. Jake had started fifth grade there at César Chávez Elementary, but just a month later Dad had pulled him out for a hunting road trip through Colorado, Utah, and finally Nevada. Dad had told Jake's teacher there was a family emergency, which was his usual excuse. Not many people wanted to argue with him or ask questions.

Now Jake had to go back to the boring old routine of riding the school bus, sitting through classes, and waiting for recess like all the boring kids around him. None of them knew a fraction of what he did, and Jake knew that whatever Dad said, the two of them would probably be somewhere else by Christmas, so there wasn't much point to making buddies. At his last school he used to get into fights, until Dad told him that it wasn't fair to the other kids to fight someone who was more than half a hunter already.

Sometimes Jake thought about the monster boy he'd met inside Freak Camp. He knew Tobias didn't have anything like normal school for humans, but it sounded like he learned plenty in that library. It was hard for Jake to picture him while Jake sat in his brightly colored classroom with all the kids' drawings on the wall and dumb posters telling them how great it was to learn math. Nothing had been colorful in Freak Camp. Out here in Albuquerque, it didn't feel real.

When school let out, Jake was free to roam the neighborhood, making friends and enemies with older boys, figuring out ways to sneak into the movie theaters or snitch stuff from the convenience stores. The key was to run fast and not show up around the same place again.

Dad had returned to his part-time job at an auto shop. When he couldn't get enough hours, he spent evenings at the pool halls around town. Dad could run a hell of a game with either pool or poker, and Jake knew how to heat up the frozen dinners by himself.

Sometimes Dad did other stuff that wasn't pool or poker, and Jake wasn't supposed to know about it. But he knew enough not to be surprised when they had to leave town in a hurry. That always happened sooner or later.

The weekend before Halloween, Dad told Jake to pack his bag, but they'd be coming back to the trailer. They hit the road at dawn Saturday morning, driving down to the border and into Mexico.

LEON SETTLED back with his bottle of tequila in a broken-down folding chair outside their rental in Chihuahua, Mexico. Twilight was fading into night, and Jake had disappeared an hour ago onto the streets, chasing some boys and exchanging taunts in Spanglish.

This week was the sixth anniversary of his wife's death, which was also the national day of mourning of the Liberty Wolf Massacre. Leon preferred to spend it as far away from Washington, Dixons, and TV sets as possible.

He and Sally had met in one of those old-fashioned romantic tales: he'd been pinned to the hood of his car by a vampire, and she had leaped out of nowhere and nailed it with a stake. That had been Leon's introduction to the monsters of the night, the creatures he'd never dreamed were real.

But Sally wanted out of the hunting business, and after Leon's stint in Vietnam, he also saw the appeal of a quieter life, the kind with picket fences. Running away to elope in Vegas had been her idea, and he'd been just as eager to stick it to her asshole of a father who never saw Leon as anything but West Virginia trash. The Dixons were a blue-blooded Pennsylvania pedigree, like they individually had the Declaration of Independence tattooed on their ass cheeks. In their view, Sally had been slumming it the minute she'd crossed the state border, even if she was chasing a vampire.

Leon wasn't the one who got her killed, though. That was her sonuvabitch father who had cajoled her back into one more mission, a firefight she had no business being anywhere near. The way the bastard told it, she'd wanted a getaway from home, like it was some fucking marital problems that drove her to it. Like he'd known anything about their marriage or what Leon and Sally had argued about.

Dixon blamed his daughter's death on Leon because he couldn't face the truth. It was his idea to go to Liberty, his idea to bring his daughter along even though she hadn't been on a hunt in years. And when all hell broke loose, Sally ended up on a pyre while her father walked away unscathed.

Then it just so happened that the aftermath of the slaughter lined things up perfectly for Dixon to achieve his lifelong dream of government power, with Congress falling over themselves to hand him the keys to the US Treasury. The murder of his only child was a small price to pay for that legacy.

So Dixon had turned a blind eye to what had actually gone down the night of the Liberty Wolf Massacre, what everyone had wanted to forget, just like it was easier to believe the First Lady had died that night. People had said that, even insisted on it, wouldn't hear otherwise. The truth was that no one outside the ASC had any idea of when Dorothy Peterson actually died in the FREACS facility, or even if she might still be alive.

Leon didn't care much about her fate. He wanted to know who had really killed his wife, his son's mother, because it sure as hell wasn't just the werewolves who were brought down that night.

No fucking way had it been a random attack. Dixon knew it too, even if he wouldn't admit it. Leon would find the truth if he had to dig up every grave in the country.

TWO WEEKS after they got back from Mexico, Jake heard his name called over the school's PA system during lunch. He braced himself for an interrogation about Carla's backpack (he'd had nothing to do with all the cheat sheets packed inside, whatever Noah said), but when he got to the front office, Dad was waiting for him. Jake knew in an instant that they were leaving.

A weird kind of numbness settled over him. He didn't hear what Dad said to the receptionist, didn't remember where he picked up his backpack, and he wasn't aware of getting in the car. Dad had already packed their other bags into the back seat, and the next thing Jake noticed, they were driving north on Highway 550.

Outside the city limits, Leon turned off the radio and glanced at Jake. "You okay, son?"

Jake shrugged.

After a pause, Leon said, "You want to know what went down?" His tone made it an offer, a fun story to entertain him like the cop chases on TV, but in reverse. Jake used to love hearing Dad's narrow escapes, how he hoodwinked the bartender and truckers and local sheriff.

Today he found that he didn't want to know why they were leaving behind the kinda-nice Mrs. Capizzo and those boys he hung out with after school, Enrique and Alberto, who maybe weren't as dumb as all the other kids in his class. He wouldn't get to see any of them ever again. That was the ironclad rule of his and Dad's life: when the heat turns on, they're miles away before the oven gets warm. Like they were never there at all.

Jake didn't want to think about who they were leaving behind, the promise he'd made (and now couldn't keep) to repay Enrique for the comic books in his bag. So he answered the way Dad expected. "What went down, sir?"

Leon told him, and it was the usual cast of dumb assholes that Dad had played like the easiest game of cards, like he could've done it all blindfolded. Jake nodded and smiled and even laughed when he was supposed to.

But as the sun set, after they stopped for McDonald's and then turned back onto the highway, still heading north, Jake rested his head on his arm against the passenger window. He pretended to sleep, and Leon turned the radio back on.

Through half-closed eyes, Jake watched the mile markers and car lights flash by. It wasn't like he could remember the faces and names of the places they'd lived before Albuquerque. Soon enough Mrs. Capizzo and Enrique would fade away. He wondered how long it would take before they forgot him too.

CHAPTER TWO

NOVEMBER 1990

THEIR NEXT VISIT to Freak Camp came when Dad found a lead after catching a llorona. All Jake knew was getting woken up in the middle of the night and being told they had to get out of there, pronto. Leon hustled Jake out of the motel while he was still half asleep, bundled him in the back seat before tossing his notebooks, papers, and weapons into the front, then hooked a trailer to the hitch on the back.

Jake could have sworn he heard clinking and whimpering noises from the trailer all the way to Winnemucca.

This time Jake didn't have to walk with Dad through the front door and lobby because Leon drove the Eldorado and the trailer around through the big loading gates.

He must have made a call while I was out, Jake thought, rubbing his eyes. He'd pulled on a pair of jeans and a T-shirt when they stopped for a bathroom break and gas station breakfast sandwiches, so at least he wasn't still in his pajamas.

Five or six adults stood around the trailer, peering at the thing inside, arguing with Dad about where it should go and who had "a first shot at answers." Jake grabbed a jacket against the chilly morning air and a deck of cards and waited impatiently for them to return to the door that led into the camp.

Walking behind the well-wrapped stretcher the group had extracted from the trailer, Dad looked back at him. "Jake, I don't know when this will be done, or what I might be able to figure out, or even if these assholes are going to let me be present for the interrogation that I damn well let them have." He shook his head. "Don't offer me a fucking bounty and then say I can't ask a few damn questions. They can keep their fucking money for all I care."

"I can hang out, Dad. No problem."

"I'll be in Special Research. I'll try not to be long. You get into trouble, you give 'em hell, understand, Jake?"

Jake wasn't exactly sure who he was supposed to give hell to—there were a lot of possibilities, ranging from reckless monsters to fucking Dixons, and various hunters and support personnel in between—but he nodded anyway. He assumed it would be clear at the time. "Yes, sir!"

"Good boy," Dad said, and then he was gone in the rush. He hadn't even closed up the Eldorado properly.

Jake took the keys out of the ignition and slammed the door shut, eyed the trailer—he wondered where Dad had found it at such short notice, if he had stolen it, bought it, or if it had belonged to the monster Dad brought down—and then went in search of Tobias.

He was briefly deterred by a guard wanting to know his business, but Jake scoffed and bullshitted his way into the yard. He'd learned that from Dad too, how most of it came down to flaunting the right blend of confidence and impatience. And while they never used it anywhere else, he could throw his name around—*yeah, I'm Jake Hawthorne, my dad's already inside and he's wondering what the holdup is, you wanna talk to him?*—and the guard backed down, radioing in that he was letting in the Hawthorne kid. Open sesame.

Dawn was breaking over the edge of the distant mountains, and when Jake rounded the corner into the central yard of FREACS, he came to a sudden stop. All the monsters were out of their barracks, shivering in the early morning light. Some stood straight as rods, others hunched on themselves from various deformities.

While Jake watched, a guard standing in front of the monsters called out numbers from his clipboard. Monster after monster called, "Present." Other heavily armed guards patrolled and occasionally struck a monster that wasn't fast enough to respond.

Finding Tobias turned out to be easy. He was standing in the second row between a witch and a shapeshifter and stared straight ahead, stiller than any kid Jake had ever seen.

The guard holding the clipboard snapped it down. "That's it, then. All these stupid fucks are still here. Good thing too, or we'd have to whip the skin off your monster asses again, and that would take all fucking day. There's no assembly, so go find your assigned work station."

The neat rows of monsters broke up, dispersing toward the barracks, mess hall, and Workhouse. Tobias stayed where he was. Jake wondered if Tobias had an "assigned work station" or if this would be a decent time to say hi. He really hadn't planned this out. He had just assumed that he could hang out with Tobias when he came back. It never occurred to Jake that maybe Tobias would have chores to do. Though maybe it should have occurred to him. Jake shouldn't fool himself into thinking Tobias's world revolved around him.

Tobias looked up, face expressionless, until he saw Jake. Then his lips parted in amazement, and he rocked back on his heels before moving forward—not running, but walking with a bounce in his step and a look in his eyes like he couldn't quite believe what he was seeing.

He looked so happy that Jake felt the little knot of worry in his stomach uncoil, replaced by a warm feeling. If Tobias was excited too, that meant it was okay for Jake to be glad to see him again. Even if he was a monster.

"Hey, Toby." Jake leaned against a wall, fiddling with his deck of cards. "Told you I'd come back."

Tobias beamed at him with the biggest smile in the world, like Jake had just given him a million dollars. Jake couldn't remember anyone looking at him like that before.

"Hi—hi, Jake," Tobias said, soft and breathlessly, almost like he'd forgotten how to say his name.

Jake smiled back and reached out to ruffle his hair the way Roger did to him. Tobias ducked his head to the side, but not like he was really trying to get away. "C'mon, let's find somewhere out of the wind." Again he saw that delighted flash of a smile.

They headed around the corner of a building, close to the wall, where they were out of sight of most of the guards and monsters, though Jake saw a security camera pointed in their direction. He didn't care about that, though. It made sense that they would want to keep track of their monsters when there weren't enough guards to keep an eye on all of them.

Tobias crouched down, arms wrapped around his knees.

Jake slid down the wall to sit next to him. It was cold against the concrete. He wondered if Tobias felt it like he did. "How've you been?"

Tobias blinked at him, then shrugged. "Good, I guess. H-how have you been?" He stumbled over the words.

Yeah, it was a stupid question, Jake decided. What was he going to do, tell Tobias about Albuquerque and the people he'd met there when there wasn't any point remembering them?

"Yeah, fine." He shuffled the cards and then thought of something. "I checked out the big library in downtown Albuquerque. It's a whole city block, dude."

Toby's brow furrowed. "What's a city block?"

"It's—" Jake gestured and looked around. "Maybe half the size of Freak Camp. Or like, from here to the Workhouse over there."

Toby's eyes went round. "And the whole thing's a library?"

"Yep. Aisles and aisles of books, you could probably spend your whole life trying to read them all." He and Alberto had met up once in the reference section after their latest heist at the corner store, their jackets filled with soda bottles and snacks. They'd spent a triumphant (though quiet) afternoon celebrating how slick they were.

"Jake?"

Jake blinked and looked back at Toby, whose smile had faded a little. "Yeah, sorry. You wanna play cards?"

Toby turned his head, confused. "I d-d-don't know, Jake. If you want to, of course I'll . . . how do you play?"

Jake stopped moving the cards between his hands and stared. "I mean, it's cards. Like, war or slap or seven-up or poker. I'm not that good at poker yet, but Dad's started to teach me and . . ." He trailed away when Tobias still looked lost. If anything he looked nervous, shifting back and forth on his heels. "You've never played cards before?"

Tobias shook his head and hunched farther over his knees, looking down at his toes like maybe they would teach him the mysteries of a straight flush.

"Hey, don't worry, that's cool. I mean, lots of kids don't play card games." Okay, so in Jake's experience everyone knew at least one card game, at least war, *something*, but he supposed that Tobias couldn't really hang out with other kids. He was technically a monster, after all.

"I'm sorry, Jake," Tobias said. "I'm really stupid sometimes."

"Hey, that's not true!" Sure, it was still hard to imagine that Tobias wouldn't have ever handled cards before, but to say that he was *stupid* was just ridiculous. No little kid who read as much as Tobias did could be stupid. He hadn't even been anywhere interesting in his life, but he knew a hell of a lot more about books and history than Jake did. "Come on, it'll be easy. You know numbers, right?"

Tobias nodded quickly. "Of course. Becca taught me."

"Cool. And for war, that's all you need." Jake dealt out the cards—just splitting the deck would have been faster, but it felt important to make sure that they each had an even number. Especially since this was Tobias's first time playing with cards. "We each get the same number of cards. Then we each turn over one card, and whoever has the highest number gets both cards. If we get the same number, we have a war, where you lay down three cards, and then turn over the fourth, and whoever has the highest number then gets *all* those cards. And whoever ends up with all the cards in the deck wins. Got that, Toby?"

Tobias swallowed nervously, eyes on the pile of cards in front of him. "Sure, Jake."

They started slowly, Jake adding explanations when their first queen, jack, or king appeared.

On their second war, Tobias turned over an ace as his final card. He smiled and started to push all the cards toward Jake. He almost looked relieved, which was weird.

"No, you keep those," Jake said. "You won that war."

Tobias froze. "But it's a one."

"It's an ace," Jake corrected. "And it's higher than anything else."

"It's a *one*," Tobias said. "That's too many cards, Jake. I don't need . . ." He waved his hand, which was already considerably thicker than Jake's.

Jake snorted. "I mean, we don't *need* the cards. It's a game, Tobias. I won't be mad if you win, I swear. After all, somebody always wins."

Tobias looked down at his thick stack of cards, and he looked a little sick. "Yes, Jake."

They played, the sizes of their decks varying wildly. Jake had forgotten how *long* a game war was.

But when Tobias took the last card, Jake lifted his empty hands and grinned at him. "Look, you cleaned me out. You can't be that bad at cards." Then he took in Tobias's face, which was both blank and made him think Tobias might puke. "Hey, what's wrong?"

"I won," Tobias said. "That means you . . . didn't win. I'm sorry. I didn't mean to. I couldn't . . ." He waved at the ground between them, face pinched.

"Dude, I'm not gonna get bent out of shape because you beat me." Jake scoffed. "I mean, that's what happens in card games. Especially war. It's all chance. Now, poker . . ." He smirked, but when Tobias looked even more worried, he dropped the smile. "Come on, that's a joke. I wouldn't care even if you beat me at poker. Or anything."

"But I'm a monster."

Jake blinked, and he had to stop himself from automatically saying, *So what?*

Because it *did* matter. Monsters were dangerous, and letting your guard down around one got you dead, just like Mom.

He could hear Dad's voice in his head, telling him he was a damn fool for relaxing even for a second around a freak. *They find your weak points and they rip you up. You can't trust those sonuvabitches for a second.*

Jake reached slowly for the cards and Tobias shoved them into his hands a little too quickly. Like Tobias didn't want to hold on to them any longer than Jake wanted him to.

Jake shuffled the cards slowly, thinking hard about monsters, Tobias, and what Dad would say.

When he looked up, he saw Tobias staring in fascination at the cards flying together.

Tobias caught Jake's eyes, and a smile flickered across his face. He looked again like just an amazed little kid. "That's really awesome," he said. "That . . . thing." He gestured at the cards and mimed shuffling them. "What . . . how do you . . . is it a *real* thing?"

Jake frowned. "A real thing?"

"You know, a thing real humans can do that a monster couldn't? I mean, like me. Could I do that?"

"Sure, give it a try."

Jake watched Tobias fumble with the deck. He gave him a few pointers at shuffling until Tobias could almost do it, though nowhere near as fast as Jake could. Jake liked teaching him, and he almost broke a rib holding back a laugh while he watched Tobias painstakingly handle the deck, the tip of his tongue sticking out of one corner of his mouth while his small hands managed the big, worn cards.

Once Tobias had gotten the basics down, smiling proudly and eyes gleaming as he glanced up at Jake, Jake grinned back. He felt like he'd just come to a decision, an important one, though he couldn't put it into words yet.

"Wanna learn go fish?" he asked. "It's real easy."

Tobias still looked worried. "You're sure you won't mind if I . . . don't lose? I mean, you said you wouldn't, but if I'm new at a game, I won't be able to figure out how to . . ."

"Toby, there's one thing I want you to never do," Jake said.

Tobias sat up straighter. "What?"

"Let me win." Jake shuffled the cards, twice as fast as Tobias had. "Because if you get good enough to make sure I win, then that'd mean I'm super bad at the game *and* too stupid to see you cheating. And that would just be embarrassing. Got that?"

"Yes, Jake." Tobias grinned, a bigger smile than Jake had seen since Tobias had first seen him in the yard. "You're the best."

By the time a guard came around the corner to tell Jake that Leon was waiting, he had successfully taught Tobias the games war, go fish, and what he knew about poker. He had a feeling he'd gone wrong somewhere with poker, but the result was still fun for both of them. Next time he saw Tobias, Jake promised himself that he would be able to teach him the real version. He'd make sure that Dad taught him the rest of the rules.

"Sorry, Jake," Dad said, rubbing a hand over his face. He looked exhausted. That made sense. Jake had slept in the car on the drive over here, but that meant that Dad had been up for twenty-four hours or so. Jake couldn't wait until he could help Dad with the driving. "You do okay without me?"

"Yes, sir. Me and . . ." He almost mentioned Tobias, but stopped himself. Dad had dealt with a lot of monsters today. He didn't need to think about another one. And Jake had the whole thing with Tobias under control. He wasn't at all like other monsters. "I took care of myself. No problem."

Leon nodded. "Good. Let's get the fuck out of here."

Jake followed him out. Right before he left the yard, he glanced back.

Tobias was smiling at him. Jake just barely stopped himself from waving.

WHATEVER THE LLORONA had told Dad meant that they had more business at Freak Camp. He and Jake coasted around Utah, taking care of a few rogue spirits and poking into the occasional hokey Sasquatch sighting, but every couple of weeks they turned back for northern Nevada. Jake didn't know what the deal was, and he knew better than to think Dad would give him the details, but from what Dad muttered under his breath during the long drives, he didn't trust the Dixons to handle it alone or to share everything they found.

That made sense, of course. Jake didn't mind their frequent trips back to Freak Camp. The guards knew Jake now and would let him into the yard where he could find Tobias. They'd head to some out-of-sight corner where Jake would pull out his card deck or some other miniature road trip game Dad had gotten him. He once found a half-finished candy bar in his pocket and offered it to Tobias, whose astonishment at the taste made Jake laugh. He couldn't believe the kid had *never* had candy before, so he started bringing different kinds for Tobias to try, whatever he could slip into his pockets.

He didn't talk much about Tobias to Dad. He knew exactly what Dad would say, and it wasn't anything that Jake didn't already know. Sure, Tobias might be a monster, but he was already secure in Freak Camp, and he didn't have extra-sharp teeth or claws or any other way of hurting him.

Jake was pretty sure Tobias wouldn't have tried to hurt him even if he had the chance, anyway. Tobias always looked like Jake's arrival was the cherry on his sundae, the best thing that could have happened to him that week. Jake liked feeling important, like he mattered that much to someone, even if it was just to a monster kid. But he found it harder and harder to think of Tobias as a monster—at least, not like the ones Dad killed. Tobias was different. He was just *Tobias*, and that was enough for Jake. He didn't think he'd be able to explain that to Dad, though.

That was also why he liked to take Tobias somewhere without guards watching everything they did. It didn't matter if Jake and Tobias were playing cards or eating Snickers bars, it wasn't any of the adults' business—Jake was a hunter, so they should trust him and leave him alone.

One unusually warm November day, they sat against a wall of the barracks, as far as they could get from the guards' curious eyes, and passed a bag of chocolate-coated peanuts back and forth.

"So, this Becca chick, she's like your mom, right?" Jake said, dumping four or five peanuts into his mouth and then holding the bag out to Tobias.

Tobias never took the bag or grabbed more than a couple of

peanuts at a time, but at least he wasn't wincing and looking out for the guards every time Jake pushed the bag in his face. "Yeah. She takes care of me, she . . ." Tobias shrugged and put the candies in his mouth. "You must have a mom. What's she like?"

Jake looked away and tried to act casual. "She's perfect."

Tobias just looked at him, his big brown eyes expectant. He didn't seem to care what details Jake chose to share about his life, he just loved that Jake talked to him. Jake stared at his left knee, where the jeans were wearing through, and braced himself for the next question. But Tobias waited for the story, patient in a way that few people were in Jake's life.

Jake could make up anything he wanted, and Tobias would smile that same way, with the expression that lit up his whole body and seemed to only be for him.

Jake had used to wish he had a little brother, someone who would look up to him, who he could teach about hunting like Dad taught him. Someone who would trust him the way he trusted Dad, even when Dad was drunk, or angry, or left him with other adults for weeks at a time. He was almost a grown-up now, and he knew he didn't really need friends and that playing was stupid, but it would still be nice to have someone. Of course, Tobias was a monster and shouldn't be his friend, but Jake still felt warm when they sat together and Tobias looked at him like Jake was made of all the pie in the world. Tobias would believe anything Jake said, not because he was stupid, but because he trusted Jake.

And Jake couldn't lie to him. Even about Mom.

"She's dead," he said, not looking up from his knee. "She was Sally. Dixon. Hawthorne." He always said her name that way, because every part was important. The name that was her, the name that was a hunter, and the name that made her theirs, his and Dad's, and no one else's. For some reason people tended to forget that last part of her name. He said her name like it was a chant that, said enough times in the right way, would bring her back.

He knew it wouldn't, of course. He wasn't a stupid little kid anymore.

He waited for the reaction. Everyone had a reaction. Sometimes amazement ("Oh, you're *those* Hawthornes?") or disappointment ("*He's* Sally's son?"), or an expression that said they had expected more from the son of a national hero, that he should be better than he was. But he wasn't, and she would never be there to teach him how.

But Tobias didn't react. When the silence stretched out, Jake glanced up at Tobias. The boy was staring at his knees too.

"I didn't mean to ask about something that . . ." Tobias fingered the hem of his baggy gray pants. He took a deep breath, still without looking at Jake. "My mom's gonna be dead soon too," he offered. "She says that's how we leave camp. It's a good thing. So maybe Becca and your mom . . . maybe they'll be together?"

Jake's head snapped up. "What do you mean, your mom's gonna be dead soon?"

Tobias hunched over and wouldn't look at him. "She's going to Special Research. For being a witch. Monsters don't come out of Special Research."

"Tobias." Jake stared at him. He couldn't wrap his head around it—knowing that his mother was about to die and not doing something about it, not kicking and screaming and fighting every second of every moment to stop that horrible, horrible thing. "Tobias, I didn't know."

Tobias glanced at him, and then away. "I mean, it's not a big deal, she's a monster. All monsters go there. Oh." He seemed to realize what he'd said, eyes going wide, staring back at Jake. "I'm . . . stupid. Becca and your mom wouldn't be in the same place. I'm sorry I said that. I mean, I'm sure your mom was awesome."

Jake took a deep breath and scooted closer to Tobias. He

offered him the peanuts, and after hesitating, Tobias took one. "She was awesome," he said. "She was a hero, and she—" *killed monsters.* "She loved me, and she made the best waffles, and when she was around"—*Dad smiled, unless they were shouting at each other*—"we were a family."

"That sounds awesome," Tobias said, reaching for the bag and helping himself to another few candies. "What's a waffle?"

Jake was delighted that Tobias actually *reached* for the food—he'd felt the same thrill once when he'd gotten some birds at one of their apartments to come to the windowsill after he left crumbs there, marveling at the idea that something so skittish and wild would trust him. He could shove memories of Mom back where they belonged, far enough away that they didn't make him feel so much like punching someone. Anyway, it was way more important to fix Tobias's horrifying lack of knowledge about breakfast foods.

Jake launched into a fifteen-minute monologue in praise and description of waffles, complete with gestures, eating sounds, and recommendations for toppings from the best to worst. The whole time, Tobias watched him like he was the only thing he wanted in the world. Which was ridiculous, because any sane person should also want waffles.

"That's it, dude," Jake said at the end, when Tobias seemed no closer to understanding what a waffle was. "Even monsters should know what a waffle is. Next time I come, I'll bring you one."

Tobias crunched the last candy. "No such thing," he said, with a glow in his eyes another child might have at being told that Santa was just as real as all the bad monsters out there. "Not here."

"Hey!" Jake grabbed Tobias's hand. "If I say I'm bringing you waffles, I'm bringing you waffles. That's a promise."

Then he caught sight of Dad walking across the yard toward them, and he quickly let go as he stood up. Time to go before one of those guard jerks came over. But he turned back to Tobias for a second, sliding the crumpled peanuts bag into his jacket pocket. "Hey, Tobias. It would be cool if our moms were together. Just like it's cool when we're together. You know?"

Tobias nodded, really fast and smiling up at him like the friend Jake had never really had, someone who trusted him and liked him and listened.

Jake couldn't stop smiling, even when Dad glared at him, until they were out of the camp and back in the Eldorado.

THE NEXT TIME Jake went to Freak Camp, he tried to bring a waffle.

It was technically more of a pie, because waffles weren't really any good if you tried to bring them anywhere. Jake had seen in a gas station a plastic-wrapped dessert labeled as a cherry pie with a waffle base, and he figured that was as close as he was gonna get. Plus, it was small enough that he could wedge it into his pants by the small of his back—where Dad kept his gun—and walk without anyone noticing the bulge.

It didn't occur to him that the waffle-pie tin would show up in a metal detector until the alarm went off. Weapons were allowed in the camp, but unless you were going in the back entrance with a freak delivery, you had to take them all out and send them through the X-ray machine.

His cousin Lucas Dixon made a big deal of patting him down, then pulled out the dessert. Laughing, he tore open the wrapper, sniffled it, and raised the tin up high like a trophy. "Check it out! Jake Hawthorne is bringing a little cherry into Freak Camp!"

The other guards in the room chuckled.

Lucas smirked at Jake. "Does your father know?"

"Shut up, Lucas," Dad said tiredly.

Jake glared, his face hot, aware that he was being made fun of, but more focused on the half waffle that he somehow had to get to Tobias. "I get hungry," he said, ignoring the snickers across the room. He turned to Dad and stuck out his jaw. "You're gone so long, and I get hungry, and there's nothing decent to eat in the camp, so yeah, I brought a snack. Sue me."

"He can't bring the tin in, Hawthorne," Lucas said. "I mean, we do a lot to these freaks, but giving them a pie in the face? Inhumane, man."

Dad yanked the tin out of Lucas's hands hard enough that Lucas nearly stumbled. He continued glaring at the other man while extending the waffle-pie to Jake. "Take what you want. Dump the rest."

"Yes, sir." Jake hastily scooped up the waffle base, folding it around the cherry filling, and shoved it into his pocket. He threw the rest of the tin in the industrial-sized trashcan by the metal detector.

Later, sharing the smushed waffle-pie with Tobias, Jake told him the story. He waved his cherry-stained hands in ways that made Tobias grin and lamented the unfairness of life. "Sorry it's all squished," he said. "I had to think fast. Who knew they'd be waffle-hating dickwads?"

Tobias nodded, his mouth full of cherry filling. "You were right, Jake," he mumbled. "This is the best thing ever." He stopped and bunched his forehead in a way that Jake had come to recognize as him thinking very hard. "Well, second best."

Jake was outraged. "*Second best*. What the hell's better than *waffles?*"

Tobias swallowed and closed his eyes in bliss. "You bringing me a waffle."

It took Jake a long, unusually silent minute process that answer. In that time, Tobias started to look worried, chewing more slowly. But Jake eventually pulled him close and ruffled his short hair.

LATER, in the Eldorado with Dad driving east, trailing a lead that he had picked up in Special Research, Jake wiggled his fingers in the cherry residue in his pockets and couldn't stop grinning. Tobias had gotten to eat something that was at least part waffle, and Jake had actually managed to get it into the camp. Granted, it had almost gone wrong, but that was okay. Sometimes trial and error was necessary. That was why Dad always stuck around a few days after a ghost burning to make sure that they had gotten the right corpse, just in case.

"Why pie?" Dad asked eventually, when they were a good half hour out of Freak Camp. He had been staring into the approaching mountains with the tense, focused expression that Jake associated with a long day in Special Research.

"It looked really good," Jake said. "And it said it was a waffle." *I promised Tobias,* he didn't say.

Dad's hair was damp and slicked back. He must have showered before he left Special Research, but there was red under his nails where he held the wheel. He had been there for over two hours this time, and while Jake didn't mind having that much more time to spend with Tobias—the guards didn't make Tobias go do things that monsters usually had to do, as long as Jake was with him—he still didn't like to think about what that meant. Tobias had said that monsters died in Special Research, and that his *mom* was going there. Jake knew that Dad killed monsters, and it had never bothered Jake before, but suddenly the monsters he pictured in Special Research looked more like Tobias and his mom than the vampire that had almost killed Dad a month ago.

Dad looked over as though Jake thinking about Tobias and Dad in the same moment had pinged him, and his brow furrowed, mouth twisting down in distaste. "You shared with that monster, didn't you?"

Dad could find out if he really wanted to know. A couple of questions to the guards who had passed by Jake and Tobias on their rounds, and he would know pretty much everything they had done. There really wasn't much of a point in trying to hide anything from Dad. Everyone knew that, even the monsters. "Yes, sir."

"I don't like you hanging around with that monster boy," Leon said. "Have the guards checked to make sure that he's not some kind of siren or anything like that?"

Jake didn't know, but he assumed that they wouldn't be so chill if Tobias was dangerous in a mind-control sort of way. "I think so, sir. I mean, he hasn't got a T brand or anything, and you know I know how to look for the other signs. I'm pretty sure they've checked everything."

"Damn stupid of them if they haven't," he muttered. "I don't know, Jake. It could be dangerous. That boy in Tulsa thought he was inviting a friend over for homework, you saw what happened. Evil, real evil, it finds a way."

"Come on, Dad!" Jake said, immediately nervous about where the conversation was going. It had been a good day. Tobias's expression when he had seen the waffle-pie had been *perfect*. Now all the good feelings were sliding away from him. Why did Dad have to treat this like a hunt? Yeah, Tobias was a monster, but it wasn't like that was a mystery. That was the whole reason why he was in Freak Camp, and Jake wasn't dumb enough to miss that. So why did Dad have to keep *harping* on it all the time?

Because he cares, said a voice in the back of Jake's head. *Because he doesn't want you to end up like Mom.*

Jake told the voice to shut up. Dad did dangerous things all the time, and he never seemed to think about how he could also die at any time, and where would that leave Jake?

Like usual, Jake's brain froze up at the idea of Dad dying. It was impossible. Dad couldn't die. Nothing bad, not really bad, could ever happen to Dad. Sure, he could get hurt, he could be bleeding or in the hospital, but that wasn't something *really* bad. That was just what happened to hunters.

For the first time since leaving camp—Dad was always distracted after a long session—Leon turned to look directly at his son. "You need to be careful, Jake. Do you understand me?"

"Yes, sir."

For a second, both Hawthornes waited. There were many things they didn't talk about—feelings, the past, Sally Hawthorne's death—and one of those taboos hovered on the edge of the conversation. When it failed to manifest, they both relaxed. They had lived side by side in this car for six years, and silence, or rock music played too loud on the radio, was usually better than talk.

"Hungry?" Dad asked at last, when they crossed the state line into Utah.

Jake was starving. The one piece of squished dessert had been *ages* ago, and he had really tried to give Tobias as much as he could, because it was his treat after all. But before he let it slip, he remembered that he'd said the waffle was his snack. So he modified. "A little, sir," he said casually.

Only after the words left his mouth did he realize that it was the first time he had lied to Dad. Really lied. About a monster, no less.

But if Dad noticed, he didn't comment on it. Jake worked very hard to keep his eyes on Dad so that he wouldn't suspect. If he didn't break eye contact, often civilians thought he was telling the truth.

Either it worked, or Dad just wasn't thinking about it, or what Jake was saying was close enough to the truth that Dad didn't notice, because he didn't call him on it.

"We'll stop at the next exit," Dad said. "Drive-thru. I want to keep going. McDonald's good?"

"Yes, sir," Jake said, leaning back and looking out the

window, but all the time thinking about Tobias. Jake was far too proud of the successful start of his career as Jake Hawthorne, waffle smuggler to worry about much of anything else.

———

WHEN THE GUARDS called for her, Rebecca could usually brace herself for whatever would come by the time she finished standing up. Her only fear was the final call when she would disappear into Special Research.

But when they called for Tobias—using that new nickname, Baby Freak, which put her heart in her throat every time—Becca thought for a moment she would lose it right there, over the bullet-packing table on the second floor of the Workhouse.

Toby, however, had already jumped down from the thin bench and was moving toward the exit behind the guard, no dawdling. He knew better than to trust them, than to expect anything good to happen, but he still had no idea how bad it could be, what could be about to happen to him. What if Toby was going to Special Research now? And Rebecca was shaking, unable to control it, and hating herself because she was just making herself and Toby more vulnerable by it, should either of them live another day.

What could they want with Toby? What could they want with her innocent boy who shouldn't be here at all, who certainly couldn't know anything or provide any useful information in an interrogation? She couldn't keep herself on the bench, filling bullets one-handed, not when the only thing worth living for in her life was walking out with a guard. She moved to the window, pretending that she just had to catch her breath for a second, but really watching the yard through the narrow opening in the bars. She had to see where he went, if he made the turn to Special Research. After a minute or so, she saw

Toby leave the building in the guard's shadow. She watched as they walked up to another boy waiting in the yard.

The real boy. Jake.

Jake Hawthorne.

Maybe it was partly because she hadn't gotten enough food lately (hard not to give everything to Toby), but Rebecca had to grip tight the edge of the window frame to keep herself up. She couldn't look away now.

The guard had walked away, and Toby and Jake were just standing there, looking at each other. Dear God, Toby was looking him in the *face*. Had he forgotten everything she told him?

But nothing else was happening. From the way Jake moved his head, she figured he was talking. And there Toby was, nodding. Then Jake looked over toward Reception, glanced back at Toby, who nodded again, and they both walked that way.

Jake even walked like a hunter, though he probably wasn't more than ten or eleven. It made her physically ill watching her small boy, both so resilient and delicate, walking next to him. *Next to,* not even falling a step behind. She could barely believe what she was seeing—Toby was so good about remembering everything. How could meeting another boy—a real child—have made him forget everything that was vital to keeping him alive?

Nothing good could come of this.

They disappeared around the corner. After a moment more, prodded by the speculative eyes of the guard, Rebecca forced herself away, forced her shaking hand back to measuring salt and iron into the bullet casings. She couldn't do anything for Toby now but hope he came back to her.

He did, slipping early into the barracks before most of the monsters returned for curfew. When he saw her, his face lit up with the biggest smile that had probably ever been seen in Freak Camp.

"Jake gave me a waffle, Becca!" Despite his excitement, he kept his voice in a breathy whisper. "A cherry waffle, from the real world!"

Rebecca's heart missed a few beats, and the horror that must have shown on her face dimmed Toby's smile. She swallowed hard, pulling him forward into her lap, grasping at him with her hand and stump, like she could feel his face between her palms. His skin was the same temperature as before, just slightly warm —all the same, she was nearly shaking again, this time with rage. Child or not, she wanted to kill that boy. She could choke him with one hand, given the opportunity.

"What—what kind of food, Toby? What did it look like?" Like he would have any fucking clue what a waffle or cherry was, like he should have ever believed—but there she couldn't berate him. No matter if Toby had known from looking at it, if a hunter said *Eat it,* he would have had to.

The smile had entirely vanished, replaced with a puzzled frown. "A waffle. It was good, Becca. Well, Jake said it was half waffle, half cherry pie. It was red and gooey and kinda squished, since he took it out of his pocket."

"His pocket," she echoed.

"Yeah. See, Becca, Jake promised me last time he would bring me a waffle, because he said even monsters should know, and then he *did*." Toby bounced on his knees, and she stilled him automatically with a hand on his shoulder. What would have been sweet and cute on the outside was, in Freak Camp, just a clear invitation for the guards to come over and see what was getting the monsters worked up. And maybe shut them up. "He even let me eat most of it!"

That stopped her in her tracks. "He—he ate it too, Toby? The same stuff he gave you out of his pocket?"

"Yeah." Toby looked a little exasperated. "I told you, Becca. Jake's not like the other hunters. He's different."

He's a Hawthorne. That was all that mattered. That boy was

Leon Hawthorne's son, and anything that brought them closer to catching that man's attention . . . Still, the constant knot of anxiety in Rebecca's chest had eased, even if she remained confused and suspicious. Could it just have been a dessert? But why? Why would a hunter's kid, clearly already raised in that life—why would he do something like that?

Toby had fallen forward now to lean contentedly against her side, and she could feel his steady heartbeat. Looking down, she thought she saw a spot of red at the corner of Toby's mouth. She wiped it off with her thumb and brought it to her own lips almost without thinking.

Sweet. Real sweetness.

CHAPTER THREE

WINTER 1990–1991

TWO WEEKS BEFORE CHRISTMAS, Leon and Jake turned the Eldorado again toward Freak Camp. Jake couldn't tell if Dad was on to a bigger clue than before or if something about Freak Camp kept drawing them back, but either way, getting to see Tobias again was fine with him.

As Dad signed in, Jake caught sight of an argument between his distant cousins (like Dad and Jake, Mom had been an only child).

Tina Dixon, who was about fifteen, threw up her hands in frustration, and Matthew Dixon glanced over with a tight, angry, but satisfied smile. He met Jake's eyes. After the first startled second, Matthew stopped looking surprised and held his gaze. Jake wondered if this was how it felt to be caught by the eyes of a basilisk.

Matthew was a couple of years older than Tina and already a hunter and a sometimes-guard at Freak Camp. Jake was pretty sure that Matthew was on the fast track to be a regional hunt leader someday.

If Jake had been raised differently, if he hadn't already wanted to be Dad, Matthew might have been everything that he wanted to be. But Jake knew that Dad was a thousand times better than any Dixon anywhere (except Mom, and she didn't really count as a Dixon), and they could all screw each other for all he cared.

Jake looked away first, and Matthew moved to join Dad as he opened the security door into the yard, offering to join him in Special Research while Dad scowled at him. Tina approached Jake, her friendly smile obviously fake. "Hey, Jake."

Jake eyed her warily. He wondered where Matthew was really taking Dad. They wouldn't try to grab him again, would they? Last time . . . well, Jake had been a lot younger, and he hadn't really known what was going on, and he hadn't fought back nearly enough.

But there were other hunters around that time, he thought. *You wouldn't have gotten away if not for them, and they're not here now.*

A few years ago, the Dixons had tried to take him away from Dad at the Crossroads Inn. Jake had been just a little kid, but he had known that these strangers, the cold-eyed hunters that *claimed* to be family, were just trying to steal him away from Dad. Jake had reacted instinctively by pulling out his knife, assuming that they were some kind of monster trying to separate him from Dad to make them easier prey. Hawthornes were always stronger together.

That was the first time he'd met Roger, who had stepped in before Jake could do more than take a swipe at the Dixons. That night Jake had realized what Dad meant when he told Jake to be careful and not trust anyone. *Especially* Dixons.

He gave her a curt nod. "Tina."

She held the smile for another second—it looked uncomfortable—and then dropped it. "Elijah wants to see you."

Jake stared at her, and she scowled. "You know who Elijah is, don't you?" Her tone said that she had always suspected that he was an idiot, but it was still irritating to deal with.

"Elijah Dixon," he snapped back. "He's the Director of Freak

Camp and the ASC." He didn't think he had to mention some of the other things Dad said about Elijah Dixon. *Scary son of a bitch* and *bootlicking government asshole* were some of the milder descriptions.

"Yeah." Tina drawled out the word. "You could say that. You could also say he's your grandfather."

Jake froze. He knew that. It was a fact. But he had never let himself think of the Director of the ASC as . . . family. Not even in the same thought as Mom. Elijah had always been his and Dad's enemy—especially since he and the other Dixons had tried to take him away.

"Yeah," he said. "I guess."

"Yeah, well . . ." Tina's tone indicated that she didn't really give a shit about Jake being family, but talking to him was a duty she would fulfill. He wondered what Matthew had said to get her to start the conversation. "Anyway, he wants you. So are you gonna come, or are you gonna be a pissy bastard like your dad?"

"Keep your mouth off my dad." Jake wasn't used to his voice coming out like that, a hard and sharp growl. He hadn't often felt this smooth, easy, adrenaline-producing rage either, but he thought that maybe he could get used to it. The room felt brighter, and he felt sharper with that anger humming under his skin.

Tina looked interested. "Or you'll what?"

"I'll gut you," Jake said. He didn't even sound angry. This was how Dad sounded when he talked about the monsters that had killed Mom. When he told some jerk he'd just met that he could stuff it, that Hawthornes needed nothing from nobody.

Tina blinked, as though that wasn't the response she had expected. Looking a little impressed, she nodded thoughtfully. "You might even have it in you. Maybe there's more of Auntie Sally in you than I thought."

She could think whatever she liked. She hadn't actually

known Jake's mom. That was just the usual Dixon bluff and arrogance.

"So," she said, putting a hand on her hip. "You gonna see him? He really does want to see you. And he's not . . . well, he's old, you know?" She shrugged. In that moment, she almost looked like a normal teenage girl, not a Dixon.

"My dad will know if you grab me. He'll burn this place down around your ears." Dad would too. Dad would do anything to get Jake back.

Tina rolled her eyes. "We're not gonna nab you. I don't know why we'd want you. Elijah just wants to talk. At least, that's what Matthew told me." Jake could hear the irritation in her voice: *And he could have told you himself, if it really mattered.*

"Why'd he make you do it?" he asked.

Tina scowled. "My feminine charm."

Jake snorted, and Tina's mouth quirked. Their eyes met, and for that moment, Jake felt like they might be on the same side. They both understood how stupid that idea was. Tina Dixon, like all Dixons and Hawthornes, fought and killed freaks and witches and monsters, and while charm was useful, charm wasn't everything. When charm failed, as it so often did, you fell back to silver blades, shotguns, and gasoline.

That felt disturbingly like *family*.

"Yeah, I'll come," Jake said.

Tina nodded. "Good. That'll get Matthew off my back. And, you know, make Elijah happy."

Jake didn't know if he wanted to do anything to make Elijah Dixon happy, but when Tina turned to lead him into Administration, Jake followed.

TINA LED him into a sterile stairwell where their footsteps echoed, up to the second floor of Administration. She used her hip to bang open the door into the hallway, and he followed her down the carpeted hall, past dark brown doors without names or markings, to a large pair of doors set at the end. She rapped on it twice and didn't wait for an answer before twisting the doorknob and leaning inside.

"I found him!" she announced, and Jake glanced back toward the stairs. He had one last chance to make a run for it. "It's the real Jake Hawthorne, or so he says," Tina said, and pushed open the door wide.

Jake Hawthorne did not run unless he knew damn well he ought to, and that wasn't the first impression he wanted to make with Elijah Dixon.

He stepped into the large office with a worn wooden desk that looked more like a tool bench set in the back. It looked a little funny in the glossy, imposing office.

Elijah Dixon sat behind the desk. To Jake's surprise, he looked old and kinda shrunken. He'd seen Elijah's picture in books and newspapers over the years, and he always looked as tough and untouchable as Dad.

But Elijah stood with a quickness that suggested he wasn't too slow to be caught off guard yet. Jake tensed, but Elijah didn't move from behind the desk. He smiled and waved at the high-backed chair before the desk. "Jake, come in. Please."

Jake slowly walked forward as Tina closed the door, leaving them both alone. Elijah nodded at a soda can at the end of the desk. "Care to have a can of pop with an old man?"

Jake moved to the desk and inspected the lid of the soda can. It didn't look like it'd been tampered with, but you never could tell.

Elijah gave a harsh laugh that ended in a cough, and he offered his own can toward Jake. "Wanna trade?"

Feeling defensive and a little silly, Jake picked up his can and popped it open, sitting down. "No thanks."

Elijah smiled and sat back, opening his own can. "Jake. It's . . . good to see you again."

Jake eyed him. When had they last seen each other? It might've been around the time Mom died, but he didn't remember. Still, he knew enough manners to use them when it counted. "Good to meet you too, sir."

Elijah's smile became more like a grimace, but he said with approval, "I hear you're already a hunter. And looking to be a damn fine one."

Jake straightened, his chest puffing out even as he tried not to give away how cool it was that Elijah Dixon already knew about him as a hunter. "Only some salt-and-burns. I do my best."

"And you're still here, so your best must be good enough. Ghosts have gotten the better of lots of hunters."

Jake snorted. "A crack in the sidewalk can get a hunter who lets his guard down."

Elijah's mouth quirked. "Your mom used to say the same thing. Never had to tell her twice to do her research before going into the field."

"You knew my mom?" Jake blurted out, and then immediately realized he was an idiot. "I mean, duh."

Elijah had drawn back, the grimace back on his face, but he smoothed it away. "Yeah, you could say I knew her pretty darn well for the first twenty years of her life. Or nearly twenty. She tore off with your dad not long after she turned eighteen." An awkward silence fell, and Elijah cleared his throat. "One thing I do know about her: she loved your dad a hell of a lot. I shouldn't have argued with her about that."

Jake didn't know what to say. That was obvious, of course, but he understood that Elijah said it as a peace offering. Jake didn't care so much about the peace offering as he did about the new hoard of information he'd just realized the man across from him held.

"So, uh." He took a swallow of soda, unsure how to ask. "What was . . . she like . . . learning to be a hunter?"

Elijah's face softened. "My Sally gave me as much grief as she did her share of goblins and poltergeists. She was a hell of a hunter in high school. Only problem was, she didn't want to be." He caught Jake's look. "No, she hated monsters as much as you and me. She wanted them blown into dust, but she didn't much care for the Dixon family tradition falling on her shoulders. We found ourselves at loggerheads more than a few times. When she left, your grandma told me it was my own damn fault, and I'm afraid she was right."

Jake had a million questions, but he paused. "My grandma?"

"Ruth." Elijah sighed. "Sally kept in touch with her when she wouldn't take my calls, so she got to hold you when you were a baby. She was staying with you when Sally and I went to Liberty."

Jake's mouth nearly fell open. His grandmother had been with him when his mom died? He didn't remember much of that time, but no one—well, Dad had never mentioned it. "So—where is she now? My grandma, I mean? Back in Pennsylvania?"

Elijah slowly shook his head. "She moved back to Maine, where her family's from. I haven't seen her in a long time now. We separated a couple of years after I opened this place. We had some . . . disagreements . . . about tactics after Liberty Wolf. After my right-hand man was killed by a witch's curse and I imposed the rule to remove their dominant hand—she couldn't take it." He cleared his throat. "We all gotta make sacrifices in this war. I don't care what names they call me for disabling any witch we catch. I've never been sorry for it. Frank was the best man I've ever known."

"But my mom, was she—what'd she like to do? You know, when she wasn't hunting?"

Elijah leaned back, smiling. "Sally, well. She had a hell of a record collection. We'd take her to concerts in Boston and New

York, until high school when she just wanted to go with friends, of course. Never got enough of the Eagles or Fleetwood Mac. Ruth wanted her to learn piano, but Sally wheedled her way into a guitar instead."

They were interrupted by a knock, quickly followed by the door opening. Jake turned to see Lucas Dixon in the doorway, chewing gum as he nodded at Elijah. "Yo, boss, ready for the pissing contest with those Pentagon dickheads?"

Elijah sighed. "I'll be in the conference room in a minute." Lucas shut the door, and Elijah caught Jake's eye with a rueful look. "My grandnephew Jonah's always harping about how I need to instill more discipline, but I don't got enough days left to teach this family of stubborn hunters new tricks."

Jake jumped off the chair, setting his empty can down on the desk. "It was, uh—nice talking to you."

"Maybe we can do it again next time you find yourself 'round these parts?"

Jake hesitated. He knew what his dad would say if he found out. "Maybe."

Elijah gave him another crooked smile, then nodded. "Keep making your mama proud."

Jake found Tobias standing in the shadow of the Administration building. He had expected to have to search for him, like he had a couple of times before, but this time it seemed like Tobias had been waiting for him.

When Tobias saw Jake walking toward him, relief filled his face. Jake was always glad Tobias was happy to see him, but it wasn't quite that kind of expression.

"Hey, Tobias," Jake said, ignoring the looks that the guards were giving them. Jake didn't know if it was because he was talking to a monster or because he had just been talking to the Dir—to *Elijah,* but he wished they would all butt out.

"Jake." Tobias still looked anxious. He glanced toward Administration, at the guards, and then at his own feet. "Are you okay?" he whispered.

Jake stopped farther away from Tobias than he usually did. Something was off about the question, something he didn't understand. He didn't want to deal with any more weird shit right now. Meeting his grandfather had been weird enough.

"Yeah, I'm fine, Toby," he said. "Why wouldn't I be?"

Tobias hunched his shoulders and looked anywhere but at Jake. No, that wasn't completely true. He glanced at Jake with quick, furtive movements that took in every part of him, reminding Jake of a hunter's evaluation, but he didn't raise his eyes to meet Jake's. "I saw your da—Hunter Hawthorne come in, and I figured you weren't . . . I'm not . . ." He shrugged, seeming to think that finished his sentence, even though Jake was still confused. "But *then* . . ." Tobias stopped again and swallowed, and Jake felt his heart jump. "Then the guards said you were seeing the D-Director, and that the D-D-Dixons sent you to Administration, and I j-just want to know if you're all right."

Tobias looked so worried. Jake wasn't quite sure why—sure, Dixons had tried to nab him before, but that had only been once and he hadn't even told Tobias about that—but he could see that Tobias had *really* been upset. Which must mean that he cared.

And in so many ways, that was much less complicated than whatever had just happened between him and Elijah.

"Not a scratch on me, see." Jake stepped forward and nudged Tobias's arm with his knuckles. He wanted to say something, but he wasn't used to talking about feelings and stuff like that.

Tobias jumped like Jake had just given him a static shock. He stared up at him, straight in the eyes for the first time that visit. He looked terrified for a split second. Then whatever he saw in Jake's face made him break into a huge smile.

"Good," Tobias said. "That's really good."

They moved away from the guards, and Jake crouched by one of the walls, where the wind whipping through Freak Camp couldn't cut quite so easily through the seams in his jacket.

"Wanna play cards?" Jake asked, holding up the deck. It was chilly out, and he could see his breath, but cards were always helpful to fall back on. "And . . ." He dug in his pockets. The new coat Dad had gotten him was awesome. It had tons of pockets; he could always find something interesting in them that he had forgotten. Like today. "And I have M&Ms!"

Tobias brightened and knelt down with Jake as he shuffled the cards and started dealing out seven. After the deal, Jake swept up his pile and frowned at the fives in his hand, but Tobias fumbled picking up his cards, fingertips working to catch the edge under the dirt. He got a few of them up, but half of them slid out of his hand.

"You got it, Toby?"

Tobias hunched one shoulder up, frowning as he tried to keep hold of the cards. "Y-yeah." He didn't look okay, though. His small hands were red, and his blue jacket barely covered his wrists.

Jake put down his cards and held out his hands. It had been a weird day, but there was no way in hell he was just going to let Tobias shiver like that. Tobias had waited for him. He'd been worried that Jake had been with Elijah. Dad might never know, and the other hunters didn't give a crap, but Tobias . . . "C'mere."

Tobias looked up in surprise, glancing at Jake's hands, and hesitantly put out his own. Jake trapped Tobias's hands between his to rub them vigorously, like Dad did when Jake had forgotten his gloves. Tobias looked astonished, but he didn't move until Jake let go.

"That better?"

He tentatively curled and wiggled his fingers, then smiled. "Yeah. Thanks."

Jake would do a lot for one of those smiles. He suspected he might've had a doofus grin of his own on his face. He picked his cards back up and held them close to his chest.

Four games later, Jake was feeling better. Toby always made him feel better. Maybe that was his monster power.

"Come on, let's walk around." Jake got to his feet and shoved the cards into his pocket.

Tobias jumped up after him, and they started around the edges of the yard, passing the bag of M&Ms back and forth as they went.

It was too cold to walk around in the open for long. Jake didn't know how Tobias managed it in his thin coat. He felt a little bad about his nice warm jacket, but he didn't think that the guards would let him bring Toby a coat, even assuming that he could find or snatch one without Dad noticing. Tobias didn't complain, though, and Jake hoped that he was the kind of monster who didn't feel the cold, even if his hands had been stiff earlier.

They ended up on one of the external air conditioning units attached to the back of Administration, munching through the rest of the M&Ms. Tobias was small enough to sit on the air conditioner with a boost up, but Jake opted to lean against it, arms crossed. He decided that he looked very cool in his new jacket. And Tobias was cool because he was with Jake.

They were scraping the bottom of the bag, arguing about who should eat the last M&M—Jake always made Tobias eat it if he remembered, but Tobias would never take the last one if he could help it—when Jake heard a sharp "Tobias!" and snapped his head up. If this was some guard, Jake was going to give them the *glare*, because the last thing he wanted right now was to have to deal with another stupid adult.

Instead of a guard coming to check on the Hawthorne kid and his monster, a woman in a thin blue jacket and baggy gray pants had rounded the corner and stopped short at the sight of them sitting together.

Jake's hand went to his knife, but Tobias brightened, straightening up on his perch. "Hey, Becca!"

Jake blinked. This was Toby's mom? He looked her over dubiously. He didn't pay a lot of attention to girls—while girls could be hunters, of course, like Mom or Tina, they weren't inherently *interesting*—but he could tell that she wasn't nearly as pretty as Jake's mom had been. Becca was bony-thin, with a haggard, pinched face and matted blond hair tied back. Like every monster Jake had seen in the camp, after a first startled, nervous glance, she kept her eyes on the ground. She stayed a good six feet back from them, even though she had seemed before in a rush to talk to Toby.

If Tobias noticed her hesitance, he gave no sign. He swung his legs back and forth, as openly happy and lively as Jake had ever seen him, but he didn't move to get off the air conditioner. "Becca, look, this is Jake, the real boy I told you about." He grabbed Jake's jacket sleeve, as though afraid that Becca wouldn't believe him unless he had the physical evidence in his hands.

"Hey," Jake said, awkward. It was cool that Tobias had just grabbed him like that—hell, it counted as a major win, as it had been a struggle at first for Tobias to get close to him at all—but Tobias was the only monster he had ever talked to, and he felt uneasy all over again facing another one, even if she was Tobias's mom.

Becca took a couple of steps closer, keeping her eyes on Tobias. They flickered to Toby's hand on his sleeve and then up over Jake, just for a second before dropping again. "Hello," she said, voice soft.

Tobias held up the empty bag of M&Ms between them. "Look, Becca, he brought me candy."

The ghost of a smile tugged her lips. "That's very kind of him. Did you say thank you?"

She sounded more like a mom now, Jake thought.

"Yep." Tobias bounced on the air conditioner.

"I brought you something too." She extended her hand, showing a small apple peeking out from beneath her sleeve. When Tobias reached out with both hands to take it, she added, "Be sure to offer some to Jake."

"No thanks," Jake said, holding up his hands to ward off the fruit. "Apples aren't my thing." He could see that the fruit was just as much of a treat to Tobias as the candy, which was weird, but he guessed monsters really liked fruit, and anything that was a treat for Tobias should be all his.

As Tobias took an enormous bite into the little green apple, Becca knelt to adjust his shoe, which was threatening to slip off his heel. Smiling to himself, Jake guessed that Tobias had been too busy swinging his feet against the air conditioner to notice it getting loose.

Then Jake saw, with a jolt, that Becca's right hand ended in a stump.

Witch. Toby's mom was a witch. Jake felt a surge of fear and adrenaline. He had known Becca was a monster, but had never thought to ask what type. A witch in Aberdeen had gotten Dad so bad they had actually gone to the hospital, and Jake had had to wait alone while they pumped Dad's stomach for the poison she had given him, hoping that Dad would walk out alive, that he wouldn't still be coughing up blood.

For a moment, Jake's breath stopped, his vision went a little gray around the edges, and he had the crazy image of the witch in Snow White handing out poisoned apples to the good, sweet children she wanted to kill.

Jake wasn't worried about himself. He could call a guard who would shoot her in the head the second he raised an alarm, and even the fastest curses couldn't do too much damage in that time, not with the ASC's resources. And something about the way they removed a witch's hand made it harder for their spells to work. Though maybe that was just because it was harder to do *anything* with only one hand.

No, Jake was afraid at the thought that Toby trusted this witch every day, let her give him food without checking it for spells or poison or dirt, and that he *loved* her when she was a witch and she had probably killed people, and maybe she had slipped them pretty little apples too. Monsters were liars, after all, and she could be . . .

But then Jake stopped and told himself that was stupid. Witches wouldn't have access to poison in the camp, and Tobias wasn't falling over snoring or choking or anything. Even Elijah had told him that he should do his research, and he didn't have nearly enough information about this Becca witch yet.

Besides, even witches wouldn't poison their own kids. Not usually, anyway. The evil queen stepmother in Snow White didn't count, because she had never really cared about Snow White. Becca clearly cared about Tobias. Jake could tell. Mom used to smile that same way when she helped him pull on his coat. Sometimes he had pulled it off again just so he could see her face as she buttoned it up.

Finished with Tobias's shoe, Becca straightened and lifted her remaining hand to rest her knuckles against his forehead. That was all, the barest touch, before she dropped her hand to her side and turned away, walking out of sight around the corner without another word to him. Tobias didn't say anything either, still eating his apple in large quick bites—it was already nearly gone—but his eyes followed her.

Jake was abruptly homesick, homesick and lonely, and what he wanted more than anything in that second was *Mom.*

He tipped his head down, away from Tobias, and pinched his mouth together. He would *not* cry, because he was grown up and Mom wasn't ever coming back and crying wouldn't do a damn thing about it, and it wasn't Tobias's fault that he missed Mom so damn much.

They'd been talking fine before, but now he didn't know what to say to Tobias. Missing Mom was a familiar ache, but this new part was weird. He'd never thought about witches being good moms, taking care of their kids the way his mom had taken care of him. That didn't seem possible, what with them being witches and hurting people. Maybe Becca had learned her lesson when they cut off her hand.

If she had learned her lesson . . . Jake wondered suddenly if monsters were ever released from Freak Camp, even though everything he knew told him they weren't. None of them ever left, because they were always dangerous. But for those who had started as people, maybe they did learn their lesson after a while in the camp, the same way other criminals did . . .

Then Jake knew he wanted Becca and Toby to be able to leave Freak Camp, to have a normal life again. Tobias especially couldn't have hurt anyone. Jake had been convinced of that for a while, even if he couldn't exactly admit it to anyone. He didn't know how Tobias had ended up here, but he was positive Tobias wouldn't try to hurt anyone if he were out.

He wanted that a lot, he realized. He wanted Toby out of this bare, cold, dangerous place almost more than anything else in his life, anything he could actually have, anything but Mom. He wanted Tobias and his mom to be out of Freak Camp, to have a second chance. After all, Tobias still had his mom. Maybe the ASC could watch them to make sure they didn't hurt anyone or do anything wrong.

But monsters didn't leave Freak Camp.

Tobias was absorbed by the apple until he had eaten the whole thing, even the core. He only had a handful of little black seeds left in his palm, looking them over as though he might have missed something. Then he looked up at Jake and frowned. "What's the matter?"

"Nothing."

Tobias held out the apple seeds. "Are you sure you didn't want some? I would've shared."

"No, man, it's cool." Toby still looked worried, so Jake lied impulsively. "I had a couple this morning."

"Oh," Tobias said, eyes going wide and round. "*Two*?"

Jake tried not to smile. "Do you want me to bring you fruit next time, or another Three Musketeers? I've seen apples twice as big as that one."

Tobias's mouth dropped open, and he clasped his hands in his lap as he rocked back and forth, overwhelmed.

Jake couldn't help laughing, and he reached out to tussle Tobias's hair and pull him over into a one-armed hug. "How about I bring both? Will that work?" He was rewarded by the most dazzling smile Tobias had. He only got a glimpse of it before Tobias buried his face in Jake's shoulder.

"You're the best, Jake."

If he couldn't have Mom, and he didn't know what to do with a grandfather, being the best in Tobias's world was pretty damn good.

"IT WAS MY BIRTHDAY LAST WEEK," Jake told Tobias. "I'm eleven now."

Tobias didn't say "happy birthday." He tilted his head, examining Jake like he might have undergone some critical change. "What's a birthday?"

Jake's jaw dropped. Surely even *monsters* knew . . . But Toby was just a little kid. "You know. *Birthdays*. It's the day you're born, and everyone in school sings you that stupid song and sometimes the teacher has cupcakes or something, if she's nice. People give you stuff and are extra nice to you. Dad took me out for an ice cream sundae, and later we went shooting and he let me try out his new shotgun." Jake grinned, even though his shoulder was still sore from the recoil. It had been an awesome birthday.

"Oh." Tobias shrugged dismissively, a gesture Jake recognized as meaning Tobias found the information so alien as to be completely useless. "Monsters don't have birthdays."

Jake looked at him, dumbfounded. "Yes, you do. You gotta have a birthday. I mean"—he waved a hand in the air, grasping for the right word—"it's the day that you're *born*. What, do you think you just . . . *appeared* someday? Popped out of an egg? Even then, it'd still be a birthday."

Tobias shook his head again. "Monsters don't have 'em. Not like reals."

Jake sat back. Not often did he run into a stubborn belief contradicting what he knew to be true, but he'd been learning how to do research to prove he was right. It could be really boring, but sometimes totally worth it. "Okay, Toby. I'm gonna find out your birthday for you. Just you wait."

Tobias looked at him like he was crazy, a look that Jake got at least once a visit, usually when Jake told him about his latest showdown with a teacher, principal, or mall cop. "How are you gonna do that?"

"You'll see." Jake stood up. "I'll be back in a minute."

Tobias bit his lip, nodding as he dropped his gaze.

"Really," Jake insisted, because he didn't like Tobias looking the same way he did when Jake had to leave. "I'll be back in a flash." He turned and headed for Reception, quick and determined.

The guards let him through with a basic silver-cut test, just to make sure he wasn't a shifter trying to sneak out. The lobby was empty, except for the receptionist, Mrs. O'Donnell, so Jake went straight up to the desk, folding his arms on it, and smiled brightly through the Plexiglas. "Hi."

Mrs. O'Donnell looked like she might smile for a moment, but instead she said, "Where's your father?"

"Special Research. Don't worry, he can take care of himself."

Now she did smile a little, before turning stern again. "You should stay here to wait for him."

"Nah. He likes me to have firsthand experience with monsters. Actually, he sent me here for a bit of research. I need some information on one of them."

Mrs. O'Donnell raised her eyebrows, even as her fingers moved to the computer keyboard. "What supernatural would that be?"

"Eighty-nine U I six seven zero three." He had been sure to get a good look at Tobias's collar before he left.

She typed it in, frowning a little. "What does he need to know?"

"How old is he? Dad wants to know exactly, down to the birthdate." When she hesitated, Jake put on his best *I'm a very trustworthy young man* face. "Dad's very interested in 89UI6703."

Mrs. O'Donnell shook her head. "We don't always have that information, particularly for those brought in for bounties."

Jake's stomach dropped. He didn't know how else he'd find out, unless he found out Tobias's hometown and persuaded Dad somehow to visit there. He *had* to find out after promising Tobias—it seemed really important to prove that he was right about Tobias having a birthday.

"Most of the information on 89UI is locked—I suppose because he's unidentified. But I do have his birthday here: April 11, 1984."

Jake repeated it, once aloud and again in his head so he wouldn't forget. "Cool. Thanks, Mrs. O'Donnell, my dad'll appreciate that." He flashed his best smile again—*never let your guard down, Jake, whether it's a monster or a con*—and he darted back out before she could stop him.

Tobias was still in the same spot, and he looked up as Jake approached, eyes wide.

"Guess what I found out!"

"What?"

"You," Jake informed him, "have a birthday." Tobias didn't look blown away, so Jake went on. "It's April 11th, 1984"—*same year Mom died,* he realized, but pushed the thought aside at once—"and that means you'll be seven in a few months."

Toby looked like he didn't know what to do with this information. He blinked at Jake, then glanced at the ground.

Jake's glow of triumph slowly slipped away. He looked around at the packed dirt yard, fences, and patrolling guards, and realized that Tobias had been right. Monsters might have a birthday, a day they were born, but it wasn't the same kind of birthday everyone else had. It couldn't be—not here.

It made him kind of mad, after all that hard work he did, after he'd promised to prove to Tobias he had a birthday.

"It's okay, Jake," Tobias said. "I have lots of birthdays. It's my birthday whenever you come see me."

Jake laughed, and though Tobias smiled too, it didn't look like he was kidding.

He was still going to bring Tobias something awesome when April rolled around. But maybe he wouldn't remind Tobias that it was his birthday. This was an idea that Jake would keep safe for Tobias until he could enjoy it himself. Though he didn't know how that could ever happen.

THEIR NEXT VISIT, a couple months later, started off with Dad storming angry. Jake left him in Reception shouting at the new receptionist—Ms. Hart didn't look nearly as nice as Mrs. O'Donnell—while he went to find Tobias. In his pockets Jake had crammed a foot-long submarine sandwich and chips, plus a jumbo bag of M&Ms, ready to share along with the story of what had pissed Dad off *this* time (Dixons, it always boiled down to Dixons).

But he couldn't find Toby.

Jake scouted the yard, looking in all their usual spots, but there was no sign of Tobias. He was starting to get frustrated and a little worried, when he saw a guard making a round of the yard.

"Hey!" Jake jogged up to him. "Do you know where Tobias is?"

The guard raised his eyebrows. "Who?"

Jake clenched his teeth, feeling stupid and annoyed. "Monster, uh, 89UI6703."

"Oh." The guard glanced around. "You might look around the barracks. He's been hanging there for the past couple of days."

Jake found Tobias in the dark alley between two barracks, sitting with his knees pulled to his chest, his hands pressed into his armpits. He didn't look up even when Jake said hi and crouched down next to him.

"Hey." Jake leaned forward, trying to get a glimpse of his face. "What's wrong, Toby?"

Tobias said nothing. Jake was about to ask if Tobias was pissed off and ignoring him for some reason—shit, why did this happen when Dad was angry too, and Jake just wanted to talk to someone who wasn't throwing off sparks?—when Tobias whispered, so low he almost didn't catch it, "Becca's gone."

A horrible pit opened in Jake's stomach, and he dropped forward to his knees. He had forgotten Tobias's mom would be dying. Tobias hadn't mentioned it after that first time. "Shit," he whispered.

Tobias pulled out his hands and rubbed the heels of his palms into his eyes. "She told me not to cry, but I already did twice."

Jake wanted to get up and break things, to take Dad's shotgun and shoot stuff up, which was how he felt whenever he thought about Mom dying. But he already knew there was no chance of bringing a gun to Tobias. He stared at his empty hands. "I'm sorry, Toby." He hated it when people said that to him; it always made him want to hit them. He saw now that they did it because there was nothing else to say.

"Why?" said Tobias expressionlessly, and Jake realized he wasn't crying. "She was a monster. That's what happens to monsters."

Jake grabbed his shoulder hard, angry for a reason he didn't fully understand. "She was your mom, Toby. Doesn't matter that she's a monster, she was your mom. I'm sorry she's dead."

Tobias shuddered. He didn't raise his head, but a moment later he slowly leaned his head against Jake's arm. He still wasn't crying, but his breathing was ragged.

Jake swallowed and nudged Tobias gently, not to push him off. "Hey, remember what we talked about? Maybe our moms are together now."

Tobias looked up, blinking in confusion. "How? Your mom's a hero. Mine's a monster. They wouldn't be in the same place."

Jake shook his head. "Becca was a good mom too, even if she was a witch. I saw that. I think my mom could see that too and wouldn't mind hanging around her. They could be friends." He looked down at Tobias. "Like we're friends."

Tobias's mouth opened. He stared at Jake with his widest look of astonishment yet, bigger even than when Jake told him about waffles. "Friends," he repeated. Like he couldn't quite believe it. Jake watched as his breathing went uneven again, and his eyes filled up.

He pulled Tobias against his chest, resting his head on top of Tobias's as the little kid buried his face into Jake's shoulder and his shoulders shook. Jake held him until he heard the guards start calling for him. He left both halves of the sandwich in Tobias's hands.

He wasn't sure what made him feel worse: how close Toby had been to crying, or the fact that he never really had.

HALF AN HOUR away from Freak Camp, Dad noticed that Jake was only halfheartedly responding to his diatribe about fucking ASC bureaucracy. He stopped himself in the middle of another explicit description of Matthew Dixon's character to glance at Jake. Dad half coughed, like he had to clear his throat to get the anger out. "You're awfully quiet."

Jake shrugged, not looking at him, still staring out the window. He'd been thinking, and something had occurred to him about Tobias's mom. Something horrible that he couldn't get out of his head. He didn't really want to ask, but he had to know. "Dad—what happens to monsters in Special Research?"

Dad looked surprised, then his expression closed down. "Why do you want to know?"

I think Tobias's mom went there. Jake shrugged. "Just wondering. It's where you always go."

Dad didn't answer for a long moment, until Jake thought he wouldn't. "It's not pretty," he said at last. "It's where hunters find out what they need to know."

Jake stared at him. "You mean—torture?"

Dad sighed, resettling his hands on the steering wheel. "No, not torture. It always has a point. And they're monsters, Jake, like the ones that killed your mom." His voice hardened. "Don't forget that. Don't go feeling sorry for them."

Jake would never forget, he couldn't believe Dad would think that, but—Toby's mom hadn't killed Mom. But then again, she *had* been a witch. She had hurt people.

But Tobias hadn't. He couldn't even remember what made him a monster. Jake couldn't imagine Tobias hurting anyone.

He scuffed his shoes on the floor mat, trying to ignore the sick, twisted feeling in his stomach. He didn't want to think about how Tobias would feel if he knew his mom was tortured before they killed her. "Do all monsters go to Special Research?" he asked, a little desperately.

"I don't know, Jake."

He swallowed. He had never been carsick before—having the flu or shaking off the nausea of a near-miss curse wasn't the same thing—but he was starting to think it might happen soon. "Not all monsters are the same, though. Some of them get caught when they're babies, before they do anything. Why should they—"

"Jake." Dad's voice held a warning. "I know you've been talking to that freak kid, and I would never have brought you to Freak Camp if I hadn't thought you'd learned what I taught you and got your head straight. Monsters are monsters."

Tobias is a monster. Jake slumped back. He would not cry or puke. He would not think of Toby going to Special Research. Monster or not, he would never let Toby go there. He had no idea how he could stop it. But he *would.*

"Yes, sir."

CHAPTER FOUR

SUMMER 1993

July 5, 1993, Tobias wrote neatly in the top right-hand corner of the page. He paused before opening the crumbling, leather-bound book to where he had left off yesterday, combing through the later sections of the sixteenth-century grimoire for any mention of djinn and their relation to aconite, also known as monkshood or wolfsbane.

Six months ago today had been Jake's thirteenth birthday, and he had last come to see Tobias sixteen days ago.

This was the worst part of summer. Tobias knew deep down that wasn't true, that August was still ahead, but Becca had taught him this years ago. Each morning he thought, *Today will be the worst day*—whether that meant the hottest, the hungriest, or the unluckiest, where he'd be in the wrong spot at the wrong time when the guards were looking for some fun, or the full-grown monsters decided he was an easy target. That way, he was ready. He never let his hopes rise for tomorrow either. When winter came, he would wish for this heat, heat that suffocated him or made the world spin when he was required to stand outside. In each season of Freak Camp, something was always the worst.

Except for one thing. One thing that didn't count because it wasn't part of Freak Camp; it came from the outside, and it was always just for Tobias. He kept it close and hidden deep inside himself all the time, knowing better than to even think about it around certain guards or when certain things were happening around him. That was another of Becca's lessons: the more you cared about something, the more important it was to never, ever let anyone else find out. She hadn't even let Tobias tell her what mattered to him. And this secret was far, far too important to risk.

So Tobias didn't let himself think about it, didn't let himself consider the possibility that today might not be the *worst* day, but the *best* day if Jake strolled in to see him.

He knew Jake would be back to see him, because Jake always came back, and each time he promised to return again. It was better, though, for Tobias to hold off that promise, to think that maybe next week Jake would show up again, so he had to get through the next days. He could manage knowing that today was the worst, and if he made it through, he would be rewarded, because Jake would come to see him again, but only if he made it through.

Some days he knew better than to let Jake cross his mind. Other days, he thought it was okay to pretend that Jake was there with him, as long as he didn't ever forget it wasn't true. It helped the time go by to think of Jake, especially during roll call, punishment assemblies, or rock salt grinding: Jake sauntering around fearless of the guards, or complaining about how bored he was and pulling out his cards or maybe a new bag of candy to wave at Tobias until he took some. He could remember exactly how they had spent every moment of the last visit, mostly because he replayed it in his head during every morning roll call, every free moment in his day, though he made sure not to miss the guards calling his number.

Of course, the guards weren't the only ones he had to watch

out for. The other monsters, though often stupid, could be even more dangerous.

Becca had told him repeatedly not to trust—not to even talk to, if he could help it—any of the other monsters. Tobias remembered all of her lessons, but this one she had been especially fierce about. *Don't believe them, Tobias, no matter how nice they pretend to be. They'll just take your food or blanket or anything else they can get from you. Blood or energy or worse. Don't let them get close to you, and always watch your back.*

That wasn't hard to remember. None of the other monsters were like Becca, and Tobias could tell from watching them that they would hurt him in the blink of an eye if they thought it would get them an extra bite of food. Or just for the fun of it.

Tobias had gotten good at keeping out of sight and not getting cornered. And they never expected a nine-year-old to fight so well. He was faster than they expected (looking so much like a real had its advantages), and he didn't hesitate to use his nails, teeth, or elbows to strike fast and hard to get out of a tight spot. At least most monsters wouldn't start anything when the guards were watching. Tobias also wasn't stupid like most of them; he never drew the guards' attention. He never talked back.

He had a system, and it worked. It kept him as safe as you could be in Freak Camp. He'd never been hurt too badly, hadn't even lost a single finger or toe, and they still hadn't taken him to Special Research or even any interrogations with hunters. But the thing about Freak Camp was that just when you thought you had figured out how to make it not so bad, something changed. A new shipment of monsters or a different set of guards could upend everything. And it was never for the better. Because Becca's most important, unspoken lesson, one that Tobias had only figured out after she was gone, was that life in Freak Camp always got worse.

THE NEW GUARD, Elmer Sloan, didn't look like much. He was muscular, but not the way some of the monsters were built, like they could break their own bones just by moving too fast. He had big hands and a flat face that didn't show much emotion while Matthew Dixon and Victor Todd showed him around the camp. But a certain blank focus in his eyes made Tobias nervous, made him keep as much distance as possible.

After the second tour around the yard, through the Workhouse and the barracks, Victor turned to Elmer with a grin. He liked messing with the new guards, especially if they were a little shocked by their first real look at FREACS. He liked it more when they got as much of a kick out of the place as he did. "So what do you think, Elmer my man?"

The new guard barely glanced at him. "Don't call me that."

Victor raised his hands defensively. "Hey, strictly an expression. It's not like I swing that way."

Elmer shook his head, eyes flickering over the yard, somehow locking on Tobias, where he was trying very hard to blend into the gray of the building. Elmer's eyes barely blinked as he answered Victor. "No. Elmer. I don't like that name. Don't use it."

Matthew and Victor exchanged a look behind his back. FREACS often attracted hunters that had gone a little wacky, one too many close calls in the dark, but this was different from the usual paranoia and itchy trigger finger.

"Sure, Elm—Sloan," Matthew said. "Whatever you want."

"Don't much like that one either," he said. "So we can do anything to them, right?"

"Within reason," Matthew answered, cautiously. "There's a handbook."

Victor coughed. "So what the fuck you want us to call you, then?"

Elmer shrugged. "Don't know. Never quite found a name that I liked."

"Gotcha," Victor said. "Well, I guess we'll just keep looking for something that fits."

Matthew glared, but if Elmer Sloan noticed that he was being mocked, he didn't give a fuck. Instead his wide, colorless eyes followed Tobias out of the yard.

FROM THE SCREAMS and sobs last night, Tobias had figured a new shipment of monsters had come in while he was working in the library. That was confirmed when he saw unfamiliar figures limping through the yard after roll call. The new ones always stood out from the way they held themselves, whether frozen in fear or still clutching some remnants of bravery or pride—which was so, so stupid. The guards could smell defiance a hundred yards away and enjoyed breaking anyone who held on to it. The new ones were always tugging at their collars too, wincing at how the leather chafed their skin. Tobias didn't even notice his anymore, nor could he imagine what it would be like not to wear it.

He stayed out of the monsters' way, and none of the new monsters came near him, either—until the next night in the mess hall, when a shadow moved over his plate.

Tobias looked up to see that the shadow belonged to a sturdy, dark-haired boy with a fresh bruise livid over his cheekbone and silver werewolf tags on his collar.

He's about Jake's age, Tobias thought, and felt a moment of uncertainty. Generally he could treat other monsters with the wariness and contempt they deserved, but he had an impulse to trust anything that reminded him of Jake. He squashed the feeling down. This was just another monster who would love to exploit any weakness in Tobias.

So he wasn't surprised when he got the demand.

"Give me your bread," the boy said, pointing at the roll on Tobias's plate.

Tobias looked down at it. It was good bread for once, no maggots or weevils, just a little dry. He'd been saving it for after he swallowed the rest of the slop-stew on the off chance it would get the odd bitter taste out of his mouth. He hoped that they weren't doing a toxins experiment again. Becca would—

Tobias shut down that train of thought. It was just him now, taking care of himself. He couldn't trust anyone or anything (*except Jake*) to watch out for him.

Certainly no one else was going to deal with the werewolf in front of him.

"No," Tobias said.

"What do you mean, no?" The other boy glowered and tried to loom threateningly over Tobias. If his shiny new leather collar and well-fed build hadn't given him away, that response right there would have marked him as painfully new to Freak Camp. Anyone in the camp longer than a week knew that someone who said no to a threat wasn't going to cave to a little glowering and looming.

"No, you may not have my bread." Tobias wondered what else he would mean by *no*.

Tobias knew how a lot of monsters would have reacted to that. None of them had ever looked that baffled before. "Oh," the boy said.

The guards were noticing. Shit, the guards were looking at the werewolf and exchanging those looks and elbow nudges that meant they were deciding who would go beat some sense into the monsters who didn't know their place.

"Sit down," Tobias snapped. "They're looking at you."

Startled, the boy sat, even though he was older and a werewolf. Even when they weren't in their wolf form, werewolves were usually stronger than a normal human and always stronger than Tobias.

"I'm Marco," the boy blurted out. While Tobias tried to figure out exactly what he was supposed to do with this information, Marco looked over his shoulder at the guards who had decided that they weren't interesting enough to be worth ending their own conversation.

After a moment, Tobias grudgingly shared his own name. "Tobias."

If a few monsters ate together every day or seemed to talk too much, sometimes the guards would break it up or separate them. A mostly naked vampire was chained right then out in the sun with her skin peeling off because she hadn't stopped talking to a couple of other vamps when the guards told her not to. But the guards didn't care as much when the monsters were younger. They had barely given him and Becca any—

Tobias cut off the thought by focusing on the boy in front of him, who reminded him in the briefest, least significant ways of Jake. "How long have you been here?"

Marco shrugged. "A few days? Maybe a week. I don't know, it all runs together, and they . . ." He glanced at the guards again and swallowed. "I can't ask them how long I've been here."

It would never have occurred to Tobias to ask the guards anything like that. But maybe that was what came of thinking that you were a real person for your whole life. It gave you unrealistic expectations when you finally ended up in Freak Camp with the other monsters.

Tobias was grateful that he had never had ideas like that, that he'd never had anything to unlearn. That's what made it all the more incredible and wonderful that Jake ever gave him a second of his time.

"You haven't been here for a full moon yet," Tobias said.

Marco looked nervous, and then his expression shifted into something like defiance. Tobias's hands clenched. He hardly ever saw defiance unless a monster was about to try to steal his meal—and he'd eaten the bread as soon as Marco sat down—or someone was about to do something stupid in front of a guard.

"Yeah," Marco said. "Just wait. I'll show them." He glanced down at Tobias's plate that held nothing but the disgusting slop, and stood again when the guards looked distracted. "Well, if you're out of bread, I'm outta here."

Tobias watched him walk away while spooning the last of his food into his mouth. He wondered what exactly Marco thought that he would be showing the guards at the full moon. Tobias had never been in Intensive Containment, where the more dangerous freaks were caged and where the werewolves went for a few days every month, but thinking about the possibilities distracted him from the taste in his mouth. It made him sick, but at least it helped him choke down the food.

EVERY GUARD HAD his own little quirks, and smart monsters got to know them as individual tormentors. Sometimes it kept you safer, and sometimes it didn't do a damn thing to know that Karl smoked like a chimney and Victor liked to crack jokes that no one else cared about. Sometimes you could hear them coming, or smell the smoke on their clothes, and do *something*—stand a certain way, hide, put on the expression that they liked—and avoid or at least minimize the pain. Sometimes it just meant that you knew what to expect when one got a nasty look on his face.

Elmer liked his billy club. He liked handling it and hitting monsters with it. The other guards made jokes about that—when he was out of earshot.

Hank Allendale was the first one to slip up.

"Hey, Clubby," he called, walking up to Elmer. "Boss wants to see you. He has some concerns about—"

Elmer let Hank get within arm's distance before he grabbed him by the collar and slammed him against the barracks wall, billy club pressed against his throat. Right in the middle of the barracks, in front of a bunch of monsters that Elmer had been inspecting before curfew.

Victor, who had been on inspection duty with Elmer—he was the only guard who seemed to like the new, crazy-eyed stranger—threw himself on his partner's shoulder. "Fuck, man. Cool the fuck down, Sloan."

Elmer leaned a little harder on his club, and Hank choked, eyes bulging. "Don't call me that," he snarled. "I'm not a fucking freak."

"And we're currently *in front* of a bunch of fucking freaks," Victor hissed. "He didn't mean it, didn't mean anything by it. Come on, cool the *fuck down.*"

Elmer put his hand on the other guard's head, almost a caress. "I could crush your skull with my hands," he said. "Remember that."

When Elmer let Hank go, the other man bolted. Elmer turned and continued the inspection. The monsters pretended that they hadn't seen anything. Elmer was one that, even if you knew what he liked, knew what he sounded like approaching, you couldn't always predict what he would do when he had that look in his eyes.

They all expected pain, expected him to take his anger out on one of the monsters in their bunks. Instead, under Victor's sharp eyes, Elmer was almost gentle, making sure that every monster was safe in their cot, a pleased, distracted look in his eyes.

"Night night, darlings," he said, before the security cameras turned to their active, watching position. He and Victor stepped outside, locking the door behind them.

Tobias didn't see Marco again until next week, when the werewolf was assigned to help him with research. Not many young monsters got to work with the old books or were trusted not to sabotage the information, but since Tobias had been there longer than most, never made any trouble, and always presented his work clearly and error-free, he got the fairly light —and air-conditioned—library duty most of the time. Still, he never took it for granted. Especially when stupid new monsters were assigned to help him.

Marco was more subdued than he had been in the mess hall, and his eyes darted around the room. Tobias explained what they were doing—it wasn't hard, just making a comprehensive list of all the different ways certain monsters and weapons were used in different lore—but the boy was fidgeting, and Tobias didn't know if he had fully understood. That irritated him, because if Marco missed something, Tobias would get in trouble too and might lose his place in the library. He made sure to check all of Marco's work.

A guard had been stationed by the door, but he disappeared around noon. Tobias kept working. Monsters never knew when the guards would come back, and Tobias knew it was worth a beating if the guard didn't find them still working.

Then Marco blurted out, "Aren't you starving?"

Tobias looked up slowly. "I got breakfast this morning. Didn't you?"

Marco snorted. "If you can call that breakfast. No, I mean—lunch! Don't you *ever* get lunch?" He sounded desperate.

Tobias sighed and reminded himself that new monsters couldn't help being so stupid. "Lunch is for reals. Not monsters. We're lucky we get meals twice a day."

Marco studied him closely in a way Tobias didn't like, but all he said was, "How long have you been here?"

Tobias tugged down his shirt to reveal his ID number. "Since '89."

"How'd you get caught?"

Tobias shrugged, turning back to his book. "Don't remember."

"Nothing? Nothing at all? But what *are* you?"

"Not a werewolf," Tobias said shortly. "Nothing you've seen before, so don't mess with me." That was his newest line to keep monsters off his back. Sometimes it worked, and sometimes it just made them want to test him more.

Marco made a derisive noise. "But you're just a kid. How'd you last here this long?"

Tobias had had enough. "By not asking stupid questions," he snapped, and he picked up his pen.

Marco didn't try to talk to him again for a few days. Friday, Tobias was sent back to the Workhouse to help pack salt rounds for a special hunter shipment. Marco was only a couple of spots down the table from him, but apart from a flicker of his eyes every time Marco wiped sweat off his forehead, Tobias didn't look at him.

They'd only been at it for an hour or so—silence in the workroom, apart from the guards' boots pacing down the wooden floors, the sifting salt and the click of metal casings—when Victor appeared in the doorway. "Hey, Baby Freak! You got a visitor in the yard."

Tobias stopped, catching all of his thoughts and instincts that screamed *Jake*, refusing to let them take off. He focused instead on the one task of not letting the casing slip from between his fingers. Deliberately he set it on the table, and just as deliberately he stood up, keeping his chin tucked to his chest so no one could see his face. This was the most dangerous part.

He walked stiffly around the table, until Victor yelled, "Pick up your feet, freak, you don't want to keep Hawthorne waiting," and then Tobias broke into a run. It was an order, wasn't it? Everyone had heard it, of course you had better do what the guards said.

Slowing down just enough at the door so he wouldn't bump into Victor, he skidded to the stairs, jumping down two or three at a time to the next landing, then bursting out the door into the staggering July heat.

The brightness overwhelmed him, and he had to stop, squinting hard.

"Hey, Toby!"

There he was. Tobias turned toward Jake, grinning even though he couldn't see yet, because this was the *best day, best day,* and nothing else that happened before or after could possibly matter. He was safe, safer than he ever was in Freak Camp, and light as a feather. Even the heat didn't matter.

Jake came toward him, taller than Tobias had remembered, strong and confident, and Tobias looked down at the ground because right then he couldn't handle it; it was as overpowering as the sun. The simple knowledge of Jake being *here,* here to see him, was enough.

"Dude, it's freakin' *hot,*" Jake said, as though he'd personally discovered this fact. "Don't any of these buildings have AC? C'mon, let's find some shade or something."

His hand landed on Tobias's shoulder, and Tobias couldn't keep from jumping—not from fear, but surprise and delight that Jake had touched him again, and Jake never touched him to hurt him.

But if Jake noticed, he didn't take his hand away. Instead he bent close until Tobias could feel Jake's breath against his ear. "I got a couple popsicles snuck through, and if we're quick there'll still be some left. I can feel it dripping down my *leg.*"

Tobias snorted out a laugh—a strange sound, weird to him, but he didn't mind around Jake—and followed Jake to the far side of Reception. He caught sight of the new guard watching them, but it only made his heart jump for a moment. Then he skipped closer to Jake, close as he could get without actually touching, and reminded himself he was with Jake, with a hunter. They couldn't touch him now.

THE DAY ELMER GOT A NAME, Tobias was standing quietly in roll call when one of the shapeshifters—a too-thin, brown-haired man with livid burn scars over his arms from hot silver applied during interrogations—cracked.

Victor called 92SS448 to no response, and when Hank went in to "hit him awake," the shifter went for his throat with teeth that were not designed for a human mouth. Elmer and Lucas—working "Dixon" shift, as the other guards called it when a high-and-mighty Dixon tried to do their job for a day—moved at the same time, but Elmer was closer. He aimed a vicious blow at the shifter's head.

Shapeshifters, especially desperate ones, had reflexes that put normal humans to shame. The shifter knocked Elmer's club out of his hand and reached for him with hands showing long claws of bone through the sloughing, pink flesh.

The guards went for their guns, not sure they would be able to fill the freak with bullets before Elmer got his heart ripped out. The monsters watched, not sure if they should jump in or run.

Then Elmer Sloan caught the shifter's hand, a fierce grin on his face. Before the shifter could scream, Elmer had caught his other hand and twisted until it looked more like a dead spider than a hand.

The shifter dropped when Elmer kicked out his right kneecap. Slowly and deliberately, the guard stepped on the shifter's shoulder and ground his sharp, iron boot heel down. The grin on his face never wavered. With more pressure, the shifter screamed and writhed. Everyone in the yard could hear the shoulder bones breaking. Then Elmer kicked him in the head until the shifter's jaw broke, and he moved to the other side and broke the other shoulder.

When Elmer moved to the shifter's hipbone, Hank stepped forward. "Easy, Crusher," he said. "I think he's fucking down."

Elmer looked up at him—pupils blown and breathing uneven—and Hank, realizing what he'd said, stepped back. "Sloan . . . I'm sorry, man, slip of the tongue, I didn't mean—"

"No, I like it," Elmer said. "*Crusher.*"

The silence after that stretched like a gagged witch on a rack.

Lucas Dixon finally broke it. "You should get that freak out of the yard," he said. "He's getting the dirt all bloody."

A couple of guards laughed nervously, and Hank moved toward the unconscious body.

"Can I?" Crusher asked, stepping forward. Hank flinched away from him, then clearly regretted it. He glanced at Lucas.

Lucas sighed. "Who put me in fucking charge? Yeah, sure, go for it, Slo—Crusher. Special Research."

Crusher smiled and leaned down to pick up the freak. The movement was almost gentle.

No one watched where he went—if the monster never actually ended up in Special Research, no one would ask questions, as long as the monster finally ended up in the incinerators. Whatever happened to him after Crusher took him out of the yard, that shifter never came back. Hank turned in his resignation, someone put Lucas in charge of a monster retrieval team, but Elmer "Crusher" Sloan stayed, made friends, and enjoyed his work more and more every day.

FULL MOON WAS a bad time for everyone, not just for the werewolves and other lunar-centric monsters who were moved to Intensive Containment for their dangerous periods. The guards had lists of who to round up, but sometimes they forgot, and sometimes they made deliberate mistakes. Mistakes such as taking monsters that had nothing to do with the moon, either because they wanted to, or because those monsters were "necessary for transformation-based experiments." And sometimes the mistake went the other way, so none of the monsters could feel safe after the barracks doors were locked for the night.

Once, when Tobias had still been small enough to curl up with Becca in one bunk, the guards had forgotten a name, or maybe a paper-pusher somewhere had filled out the forms wrong, and a wolf cut its way through half the barracks and ripped the heart out of a guard before she was taken down.

And even if the guards did everything right, if the werewolves ended up in Intensive Containment and all the other monsters remained in their beds, it felt no safer. The camp wasn't that big, and whoever had designed Intensive Containment hadn't bothered to add sound insulation. No matter what kind of gags they used, anyone with ears in Freak Camp could hear the screaming and snarling, no matter how they tried to drown it out.

Some monsters speculated that werewolves didn't have to make noises while they were transforming, and the screams were caused by the *things* that the guards did in Intensive Containment to try to stop them from changing forms. The werewolves wouldn't talk about what happened to them. Other monsters weren't sure if it was so terrible that no one dared speak, or if the werewolves couldn't remember anything but three days of pain.

Every full moon, the population of Freak Camp decreased.

Tobias didn't know what happened in Intensive Containment. He hoped never to know. Nothing in Freak Camp drained new monsters so fast of their hope, their defiance, than three or four days there and the knowledge that this would happen the next month, every month, until the end of their lives.

He watched, four days after the full moon, to see if Marco would come back. It wasn't that he cared. He couldn't care, and Marco hadn't been nice, and there was no reason that he should care. So he didn't.

They were all standing in roll call, and this was when the surviving werewolves would limp back through the gates, eyes bruised and sunken from sleep deprivation, sometimes bleeding through their clothes from silver lacerations. They showed unnervingly little damage other than the exhaustion and the occasional cut. The werewolf transformation sped up healing and prevented anything other than silver from leaving injuries.

Marco was there, limping to a place in the new line, mouth tight and eyes vacant. He didn't look at Tobias. He didn't look at anything, really. But when Crusher moved toward him, he cringed.

Crusher saw the response and grinned his brightest, scariest smile. He cupped himself through his pants and stared at Marco, and when the boy didn't respond, he laughed and turned to the rest of the line of silent, broken monsters.

Tobias felt queasy in a way that had nothing to do with hunger cramps before breakfast. He might not know what happened in Intensive Containment, but he thought he knew now what Crusher had done to Marco. Something the guards did to monsters, usually to the female ones. Sometimes it happened in the showers, but Becca had always made sure he didn't watch. He knew, though, that it involved close body contact, a great deal of pain, and it broke monsters very fast.

Marco looked the same as other monsters who had been hurt that way: hollowed out, like he had been cut into so many times that the bits of him that made him strong and defiant had been scooped out.

He was weak and he was a monster. But beneath that broken look that was so familiar, Tobias could still see the early cockiness and youth and well-fedness that had first reminded him of Jake.

He hoped he never saw Jake looking the way Marco did now. But in spite of telling himself he didn't care, he was glad to see Marco back.

"You survived," Tobias whispered, while roll call continued. He didn't look at Marco. He tried very hard not to move his mouth at all and didn't raise his eyes from his toes, didn't even glance up from the earth.

Marco didn't look at him. "Don't talk."

Tobias smiled briefly, then emptied his mind and focused on the roll call again. But at least no one whose name he knew had died today.

THE TWENTY-SECOND DAY after Jake's last visit was definitely the worst day.

Breakfast was the decent kind of bread (only stale) and gruel (tasteless and filling), but Tobias had slipped up and not watched his bowl closely enough, so it got swiped by a skin-walker and was empty before Tobias could even think about snatching it back.

Then he'd been assigned away from the library, on cleaning duty in the barracks, Reception, and Administration—back-breaking work not made easier by the stuffy, airless confines everywhere except Administration. But Tobias hated going in there more than anywhere else, because it was the Dixons' headquarters, and while monsters didn't disappear there like they did in Special Research . . . no monster wanted to be called inside.

He was relieved to escape at dusk, hurrying across the deserted yard to the mess hall, praying dinner would be something digestible, at least—

"Hey, Pretty Freak!"

Tobias jerked to a stop, catching his breath. That wasn't his name—that most definitely was *not* his name—but he was the only monster in the yard, and Crusher had called it. He stayed perfectly still.

"C'mere, freak."

Tobias turned and walked mechanically, but not slowly, over to where Crusher and Victor stood smoking outside the break room (*bitch room,* monsters called it). He kept his eyes on the packed ground and the guards' steel-tipped boots.

"Stand there," Crusher said, and Tobias's eyes flickered up enough to see him waving toward the wall, directly under the floodlight. Tobias put his back to it, trying to keep his hands still and chest moving normally, wondering if he'd missed something in one of the bathrooms. He hadn't done anything like that shifter, though—

Crusher's boots moved in front of him, less than a foot between them, and Tobias focused on breathing in and out at exactly the same pace, two seconds for each.

A hand settled on the back of his head, gripping his hair painfully and without an inch of slack, then jerked his head back and chin up. The fierce white light pierced his eyelids, and Tobias lost control over the pace of his breathing.

"So you're Pretty Freak, huh?"

Victor barked out a laugh. "No, man, that's Baby Freak. Where'd you get that—no, you know what, I don't want to know."

"Baby Freak, fine," Crusher said. "That's what they call you, ain't it?"

Tobias tried to swallow and failed.

"Still got your tongue, don't you?"

"Yes, sir," he gasped out.

"Good," Crusher said, and twisted Tobias's head to the side. "That's good. Don't use it much, though, do you? You're a quiet freak. Think we can't see you?" Something hard and blunt pressed into Tobias's cheek—Crusher's club, he realized, and he couldn't make his mouth work to answer. "I see you," Crusher said softly, and jabbed the club harder into his cheek.

"Hey," Victor said. "Just so you know—Pretty, Baby, whatever you want to call him, but that's Hawthorne's freak."

"I don't see his name anywhere." Crusher jerked Tobias's head back and forth, as though looking for a mark somewhere that said *Hawthorne*, but at least the club dropped away.

"Yeah, well, that's why his kid's always bringing him out. Guess they're keeping an eye on him for some long-term project, maybe waiting for him to get big enough to swing on a hook. Maybe Hawthorne's hook." He chuckled nervously.

Tobias didn't listen. He didn't care what they said, and they knew nothing about Jake. They couldn't begin to understand, because Jake was nothing like them.

"Well," Crusher said, twisting Tobias's head to the side, "if he wants him, he better hurry up and get him. Freak Camp is a dangerous place for freaks." He leaned close. "And I like this one —look, he's so fucking *easy*." He shook Tobias's head back and forth again. "Like a fucking doll. Look at that face . . ."

Victor waved his cigarette. "Yeah, yeah, I see freak faces every fucking day, Elmer-my-man."

Crusher turned. "What the fuck did you call me?"

"What? Crusher, of course." Victor raised his eyebrows innocently, smoke from the burning cigarette curling up from his nose. "Dude, seriously, that's Hawthorne's monster. You don't fuck with Hawthorne. Even the old man knew that."

"The Director?" Crusher snorted, letting go of Tobias's hair, letting it fall through his fingers, and moving away with a last caress across Tobias's face with the backs of his knuckles. "What do I care that that old idiot was afraid of his son-in-law? New blood now, better that way. Anyway, it's a fucking crime that Hawthorne can just reserve a monster, you know, a young one, and everyone just bows before him like he's a fucking god. It's not right, you know, special treatment like that."

Tobias moved away slowly, not so fast that he would attract attention, not even so far that they would be sure that he had moved. But even the smallest distance between himself and Crusher helped him remember how to breathe. If he could just get far enough away . . .

"Yeah," Victor agreed. "And the fact that you've laid claim to that puppy and we all keep our hands off while you're having your fun don't mean a thing." He took a drag. "Completely different situation, right?"

"Fuck yourself, Todd," Crusher said.

Victor laughed. "Why should I? I've got freaks to do that for me."

They chuckled, but Tobias didn't stick around to see if they would turn back to him. He had made it to the corner, and from there he bolted, feet quiet on the dirt of the compound, listening hard for signs they were following him. If they came around the corner, he would have to stop. Monsters didn't run in front of guards unless they had a good reason to be going somewhere fast. And monsters definitely didn't run *from* guards if they wanted to survive and remain intact.

When he reached the door of the mess hall, he could still hear them distantly. He stopped and panted at the door, straining his ears for a clue of the kind of trouble he had brought on himself for that move.

"Fuck, where'd he go?" That was Crusher, voice husky with a hint of anger.

"Leave it, man, he's Hawthorne's. And hell, the puppy should keep you occupied for a week or so at least."

Tobias ducked into the mess hall and grabbed a seat as fast and as quietly as possible. The guard patrolling saw him enter and came over, slapping his club into his hand. "Where the fuck you been, freak?"

Tobias wet his lips. "Crusher, sir." It was true. But if the guard didn't believe him . . .

The guard stared at him and then shook his head. "Goddamn pervert," he said, almost to himself. And then, sneering down at Tobias: "You don't fucking get up to eat. You stay right there or maybe I let Crusher play with you after dinner too. You got that?"

Tobias kept his eyes locked on the table. "Yes, sir."

"Good." The guard walked away.

Tobias let out a sigh of relief and glanced around.

Moldy bread and green porridge. No big loss. There'd been plenty of days he hadn't gotten anything to eat, and a number of times he'd gone without for two days. So that wasn't a good reason for why his whole body was shaking, as much as he tried to hide it by huddling over the table.

His name had always been Baby Freak. Except to Becca, long ago, and on those best days when Jake visited. *Then* he was Toby. But all the guards and other freaks knew him as Baby Freak, and he hadn't realized until now how much armor that name was.

The guards weren't that creative, so nicknames got recycled as freaks came through the loading gate and eventually left through the incinerator. Marco wasn't the first Puppy, and every witch was usually some version of Handy.

Pretty Freaks were different. Bad things happened to them. Things Becca had told him not to watch. Those freaks never lasted long.

That wasn't him, though. Victor had told Crusher—he was *Baby,* Baby Freak. And Hawthorne's. That was even more important.

Hawthorne's, Tobias thought, over and over, making it one with his breath (*Haw* when inhaling, *thorne* when exhaling), until the monsters were permitted to put away their spotlessly cleaned plates and return to the barracks. *Hawthorne's.*

He would never know it himself, but he was glad there was another world outside Freak Camp for Jake. There had to be more than fear, pain, hunger, and nicknames that predicted how long a freak's pathetic life would last.

Suddenly—shivering with hunger and fear in his bunk—he needed to know that the rest existed. Even if he would never see it because he was a monster, even if he didn't deserve anything better than these walls in his life, he knew that that other world had to exist because sometimes he had Jake. He needed to know that it was out there, or he didn't know that he would be able to keep sitting down to the same nothingness and still believe that this was any better than Special Research and the incinerator.

There had to be more to the world than pain and fear and monsters screaming on the full moon and disappearing in the night. Maybe Jake would tell him about it if he asked.

JAKE BROUGHT a half-crushed bag of potato chips the next time he came. They made Tobias's mouth intensely thirsty in the hot summer day, but he still savored them as he chewed, because he'd never had anything quite so overpoweringly . . . salty.

Waving a dismissive hand—so casual, like it was *nothing*, that was how amazing Jake was—Jake had set the bag in front of Tobias, saying he had some earlier. Tobias had gotten his meals lately, but he still took each chip with the same slow reverence with which he always treated Jake's food. Even when he was hungry, he tried not to show it or do anything gross like a monster would. It was amazing enough that Jake wanted to see him at all, and Tobias wasn't going to do anything to make him reconsider. Sometimes Jake asked what he liked more, or what he wanted Jake to bring next time, but Tobias usually shrugged or told him to bring whatever he wanted. It was *always* good, and Tobias was both amazed and glad that Jake had access to good food like that, all the time. Surely if he brought some to Tobias, that meant he ate plenty for himself too.

Tobias knew he could count on Jake to bring him something wonderful, and he didn't care much past that.

He really didn't want to ask for anything, like he expected Jake to go out of his way for a monster's requests. He remembered the last time he had complained to Becca about being hungry. *"We're all hungry, Tobias," she snapped. "Monsters always are. It's nothing special or different from anyone around you, and it's not going to change anytime soon. No one wants to hear about it."* But later that day, she had brought him a hunk of bread half as big as his head, all for him to eat.

As Tobias ate the potato chips, Jake went on full-speed about their drive up the California coast after a rumored pair of djinn. Tobias liked to hear him talk, and Jake knew that Tobias didn't have much news to tell him or anything cool to share, so he usually did all the talking.

But now, as Jake's story wound down, Tobias took the opportunity to ask what he'd been hoping to for a while. "What's it like—out there in the real world?"

Jake stopped completely, looking at him in surprise, but Tobias didn't look away. He knew it was okay, safe, because Jake wanted Tobias to look him in the eye. He reminded Tobias every visit.

"It's . . ." Jake trailed off, unusually lost for words. "What do you mean, Toby? What do you want to know?"

Tobias shrugged.

"I don't know, it's just—really big." Jake waved his hands apart. "And people are mostly the same everywhere you go. They believe the same stories, anyway, even if they talk a little different place to place. But it's mostly the same . . ."

Tobias waited patiently, but Jake looked more uncomfortable than he'd ever seen him. He fidgeted with the peeling rubber on the edge of his tennis shoe, and Tobias's confidence faded. He was about to tell Jake not to worry about it, about to apologize for asking stupid questions, when Jake started talking.

JAKE HAD SEEN MORE of the country than just about any kid his age, but now he had trouble fitting it into words. It was hard to remember that Toby had seen nothing Jake had, had no frame of reference for comparison, didn't know any of the TV or movie jokes. No matter how hard Jake tried to describe the small towns he and Dad dropped into for a few days or weeks, or a Little League baseball game, or some idiots faking a haunting in an abandoned house—Tobias's eyes never showed comprehension. He gazed unwaveringly at Jake, listening to every word, but they weren't getting anywhere.

It frustrated Jake more than he could say, made him almost want to punch something. Bringing Toby presents made him feel good, useful and important, more than anything else in his life did, and this was the first big thing Toby had asked him. It killed Jake that he couldn't give it to him.

He bit off his words, realizing what he had been about to say: *just wait, Toby, someday I'll show you myself, I'll take you there.* He couldn't promise Tobias that. Tobias was a monster in Freak Camp, and monsters didn't leave. Not until they died.

Jake looked away, rubbing his palms on his knees as he tried to ignore the tight pressure building in his chest. It hurt the same way it did when he thought too much about Mom.

"Jake?" Tobias huddled closer, almost leaning against Jake's side. "What's the matter?"

Jake swallowed, throwing his arm around Toby's shoulders. He couldn't have said why it eased the pain inside, though he did notice how Tobias relaxed a fraction, leaning back into the touch.

"Nothing, Toby," he said, though he wanted to say, *This frig-*

gin' sucks. I hate this. "I'll bring you some pictures next time, okay?"

WHEN THEY GOT BACK from their next trip to Mexico, Jake and Dad stopped at a motel outside El Paso and split up piles of newspapers. Dad was hot on the trail of another monster, one that tended toward cattle mutilation but wasn't above the occasional mysterious murder, and he wanted to check everything.

Jake had ended up with the older state papers. Even though they weren't likely to have anything about their case, research was important. Dad had told him that, and even his gr—Elijah Dixon had told him that, which was *almost* like Mom telling him too. So Jake read—okay, he skimmed, looking for any unusual deaths or mysterious disappearances.

He was about to skip all of *The Oklahoman* because it was a couple of weeks old and he was fairly sure Dad had gone through it already, when a smaller article on the front page caught his eye.

DIXONS, ASC LOOK AHEAD AFTER PATRIARCH'S DEATH

The nation mourns a hero this week with the death of Elijah Dixon, father of Sally Dixon-Hawthorne and longtime director of the Agency for Supernatural Control (ASC) and the Facility for Research, Elimination, and Containment of Supernaturals (FREACS). He passed away at the age of 64 from heart failure. Those closest to Dixon admitted that he had been having health trouble for some time, but he had been unwilling to let down the country or weaken the ASC by stepping down from his extensive duties.

"While we are all grieved by this loss, we will move forward," said Jonah Dixon, nephew of the deceased and presumed successor for the

directorship of the ASC and FREACS. "The ASC will not stop because Elijah has left us, and we would disgrace his memory by faltering in our mission now. You may expect the ASC to strengthen, grow more vigilant, and take new measures to protect our country from the supernatural menace."

"HEY, DAD." Jake slid the paper onto Leon's pile. "Did you see this?"

Leon glanced at the newspaper. "Yeah, I saw it."

"Did they . . . invite us to the funeral or anything? I mean, you didn't like each other, but . . ." *He was my grandfather.*

Leon shrugged. "Haven't heard anything. Not like we would go anyway."

Jake nodded. "Course."

"Find any incidents in your papers?"

"Yeah, but only a few." He told Dad about the handful of mutilations he'd found in the national papers, and they agreed those probably weren't significant.

Leon turned back to his papers, and Jake was left with the Oklahoma paper. After checking to make sure Dad was absorbed in his research, he read the article again. It was short and said almost nothing about the life of the man he really hadn't known.

Jake put the paper down, unsatisfied. He wasn't sure how he was supposed to react. On the one hand, Elijah Dixon had been his grandfather. On the other, Jake had only met him once, and even that meeting seemed blurry and uncertain in his head. Dad hated him, and the nation loved him, and Jake wondered if there was something wrong with him that he felt very little at all.

Elijah Dixon was just a stranger he'd had a conversation with once, and that didn't mean much at all.

———

Tobias didn't look for Marco, knowing it was better for both of them if they kept apart, but he took note whenever he saw him. Despite himself—maybe because Marco had made him think of Jake, however briefly—Tobias found himself hoping Marco would learn to adapt and adjust even to whatever happened during the full moon.

Tobias knew there was no actual point in learning to survive—there wasn't any reward for it—except even with one worst day after another (so many before he could be granted a *best day* with Jake), he still knew this was infinitely better than Special Research. No price was too high to avoid that, which was what he reminded himself when he was scrubbing out the monsters' toilets, enduring assemblies, or being punished for just being a monster. He was a monster, so he couldn't hope to be anywhere other than Freak Camp, but if he remembered everything Becca taught him and stuck to the system, they wouldn't take him to Special Research.

Even though Marco was a jerk at times, Tobias didn't want him to go there either. That was why when Tobias had a chance—when he knew no one would overhear them or notice, like when they were sent together to collect the laundry from the Workhouse—he would give Marco a small piece of advice, like how to always think that this would be the worst day, or how to avoid the guards' attention in the showers. Marco didn't respond much, but he usually did what Tobias said.

A few days before the lunar monsters were taken away again for the full moon, Marco and Tobias were together in the library again. Marco was distracted, shuffling his papers around without reading, twitching at any sound from the door where the guards would come through, occasionally burying his face in his hands.

At last, he turned to Tobias. "How'd you last this long?"

Tobias shrugged. *Becca taught me.*

Marco watched him. "They say it's because you're

Hawthorne's pet. They've got dibs on you. That right? That why Hawthorne's kid always comes to see you?"

Tobias bent his head over his books and didn't answer.

Marco grabbed him by the shoulder. Tobias jerked away, but Marco's grip tightened, pulled him closer so that Tobias could see his bloodshot eyes and feel how his hand was shaking. "Tobias, how did you get him? You gotta tell me. I'll do anything, but I won't—come on, Tobias, I'm begging . . ."

Tobias jumped up from the table, wrenching out of his grip, and Marco didn't follow. "I don't know. I don't know why. It just . . ."

Jake was the inexplicable light in his life, the one good thing that had ever happened to him, the paradox within Freak Camp. Tobias didn't deserve him, and he didn't understand why he'd gotten Jake, but it was what kept him going: the hope that Jake would return, and for a few minutes, maybe an hour, Tobias wouldn't have to be afraid.

"I can't. I'm sorry."

Marco turned back to his books, but his hands still shook. "Yeah, whatever. Shouldn't have expected a lucky bastard like you to give a shit."

Tobias watched him for a second. It wasn't that. If Jake were a skill, or a piece of information, he would share it with Marco, even if it wouldn't work as well for the older boy. But he *couldn't* because he didn't understand it himself, and he didn't want to think about it too hard.

They worked in silence for the rest of the day, and after Marco left, Tobias checked all his work and fixed the errors. He didn't want Marco to get into more trouble than he was already.

When the werewolves returned at the end of the next full moon, Marco was not among them.

CHAPTER FIVE

FALL 1993–SUMMER 1994

IT WASN'T easy to convince Dad that Jake was serious about picking up a photography hobby. Jake ultimately won twenty bucks playing cards with some of the dumb kids at the next junior high—no one his age could beat him in poker—and bought a disposable camera himself. Taking pictures as they traveled through Arizona and New Mexico was a lot more fun than he expected, and Dad finally caved and helped him pay to have the photos developed. They looked pretty good, Jake thought, as he stored the packet of photos at the bottom of his duffel bag until they turned, inevitably, north again for Nevada.

Of all the things he'd smuggled into Freak Camp, the photographs were among the easiest. He tucked the envelope into the back of his jeans, under his jacket, with a bag of candy in each pocket. He smirked at the guard as he strolled through the metal detectors, heading out the exit to the yard while Dad continued on to Special Research.

One of the guards—a newer one, Jake might have seen him once before but didn't know his name—was pacing aimlessly, swinging his club in an arc. Jake stopped him. "Hey, I'm looking for 89UI6703."

The guard gave him a skeptical look, but lifted his radio. "Karl, send Baby Freak out. Hawthorne's kid is here to see him." An affirmative crackled through the air, and the guard jerked his head toward the building behind Jake. "He'll be out in a minute."

Jake nodded curtly before turning away.

Sure enough, Tobias trotted out the side door a minute later. Jake, who had hung back to watch all the doors, jumped forward to meet him. "Hey, Toby, just wait until you see what I —dude, what's up? Are my shoes more interesting than my face?"

They always went through this—Toby refusing to look him in the eye for the first few minutes of a visit—but normally Jake got a peek of his face and a smile at the start. This time, though, Tobias had his chin tucked close to his chest until Jake's words snapped his head up.

Jake sucked in a breath, grabbing Toby's chin and barely noticing when Toby flinched. "What the hell happened?" He leaned in close to examine Toby's black eye and split, swollen lip.

Tobias swiped his tongue over his cut, fidgeting without pulling away. "Monster fight. It's not so bad."

"Shit." Jake touched his thumb to Toby's lip, drawing away when Toby winced. "You need some ice."

Toby tilted his head, confused. "What for?"

"Just . . ." Jake sighed. "Never mind, probably too late now."

Toby blinked at him with his one good eye. "Doesn't hurt anymore."

"Well, that's good." Jake smiled crookedly, then reached around Tobias's shoulders as they walked around the building to one of their secluded spots. "Did they get their ass kicked? The monster who did that to you?"

He felt Toby's shoulders shrug. "He got hurt too. We all got in trouble."

Jake blew out his breath. "Yeah, well, that's bullshit, going after a kid your size. There are plenty of bigger monsters here to pick on."

Toby's mouth tugged in a smile. "Monsters don't care, Jake."

"Yeah, of course they don't." Jake squatted down against the wall, only then remembering the bulge tucked into his back pocket. "Oh, yeah—got something for you." He twisted to reach back behind him.

Toby brightened, sitting up. "Chips?"

"Nah, M&Ms this time." He stopped to dig into his pocket and toss a bag to Toby, who quickly tore into it and tossed a big handful into his mouth. Jake grinned. "You like those, huh?" Toby nodded, chewing happily, and Jake pulled around the photo packet. "This is the other thing I brought you, what I promised last time—pictures I took over the last month, when we were down south."

Toby's left eye went very round. "*You* took these?"

"Yep," Jake said. "Wasn't that hard." He spread them out and launched into explaining what was taken where. Here was one of the stuffed jackalopes he saw in the gas station where he bought the camera. One later, outside that same stop, of Dad scowling at him while leaning against the Eldorado. The next six were of different angles of the Eldorado—Jake hadn't been able to decide what was the best to really show off its glory to Toby.

Next was one of Independence Rock—from pretty far away, Dad hadn't wanted to stop. And then a view of the Rocky Mountains, the Eldorado again in the foreground. Jake hadn't realized how many pictures he'd taken until they were all laid out in front of them and Toby was staring down at them, fingers cautiously reaching for their edges.

"What the fuck you doing, freak?"

Tobias jumped, and Jake reached automatically for his knife —a bit awkward, because he and Tobias had pressed together to look at the pictures, and Jake's knife was wedged between his hip and Toby's—but none of the guards were looking at them. The same guard that Jake had talked to earlier was heading toward a shapeshifter, who looked terrified.

"I'm talking to you, freak, you think you can just ignore me?" The guard snagged a hook in the shapeshifter's collar, jerking him off his feet, and then he saw Tobias and Jake. He smiled nastily. "Look at that," he said to the shifter, but kept his eyes on Jake. "You're bothering Hawthorne's kid. I think we ought to have a chat. Sorry about that, boy." He pushed the shifter around, and they moved out of sight, the shifter stumbling along.

"My name's Jake!" Jake called after him, angry and unsettled. The guard made no reply, but Toby's hand clenched on his jacket.

When Jake turned to him, Toby had shrunk down to where he'd been at the start of the visit, head hanging and shoulders tense. He had dropped the last photo to fold one hand—the one that didn't have a death grip on Jake's jacket—tightly over his front ankle.

Jake studied him, and both the adrenaline from the guard's shout and the happy rush he had felt just a second ago ebbed away, impossible to catch and pull back. It would take a while—maybe longer than he had before Dad was done—to coax Toby to lower his guard again.

He scowled in the guard's direction, reaching across to touch Toby's opposite shoulder. Toby glanced up, surprise across his face. Jake didn't drop his hand, still frowning after the guard. "They're assholes, aren't they?"

Tobias made a soft sound, almost like a sneeze. Startled, Jake lowered his head to get a glimpse of Toby's face, but if it had been a laugh, there was no trace of it now.

JAKE OPENED the door expecting pizza and got Child Protective Services.

He saw the cop first and grinned at him automatically. Some kids smiled at their grandmothers for a little extra cash, others knew when to drop a compliment, but Jake knew that around cops it was best to look cheerful, easy. *Nothing to hide here, officer.*

"Can I help you?" he asked, trying to remember if the guns were visible from the door or if he had moved them into the bedroom to clean them.

The cop smiled back. "Hello. I'm Officer Elden, this is Miss Donatelli. Is your father home?"

Dad was working a nasty case one town over. He'd been gone three days. Two more to go before Jake had permission to worry. "Sorry, no, he just stepped out."

"Your mother?"

He'd stopped telling the truth after he realized that it got a stronger reaction than any lie he could invent. "Divorced," he said.

"What's your name, son?"

"Jake." He racked his brain for the last name Dad had on the credit card. It had started with an H, of course. Holly? Harold?

"Your father is Larry Hayes? This man?" The cop flashed a picture too fast for Jake to see, but it was probably Dad.

"Yeah."

The cop stepped closer. "Can we come in, son?"

"What division does she work for?" Jake asked, nodding at the thin, dark-haired woman, Miss Donatelli, behind Officer Elden.

"Protective Services," she said.

Jake knew what that meant. He looked old for thirteen, but that still barely put him at driving age. "No," he said, and slammed the door hard enough to push the cop's foot back over the threshold. He locked, bolted, and put the stupid little chain on the door.

"Jake! Jake, open the door! We just want to talk."

Jake ran to the single battered telephone in the room and stumbled over the number for Dad's new mobile phone. It rang, a counterpoint to his racing heart and the pounding on the door. "Pick up, pick up, pick up," he muttered under his breath.

The second he heard the click of the phone answering, he started talking. "Dad, it's CPS, they're—"

"Jake, you know fucking better than this," Dad's voice snapped over him. Jake could hear screaming in the background, the sound of a shotgun being reloaded.

"I know, but they're at the door, and I—"

Something crashed in the background, something snarled. "They're just fucking human, Jake. Run, I don't know, I don't have time for this right now. Deal with it!"

Then the phone went dead.

"Okay," Jake said. "I'll deal with it."

He pushed the rickety table against the front door, threw into his duffel his sawed-off shotgun and Dad's box of fake IDs and credit cards, and climbed out through the bathroom window before the super could arrive to unlock the door.

WHEN ROGER HARPER picked up the phone and heard Leon's voice, he checked his pulse to make sure he was still alive. He was fairly sure that the last time they had talked, the conversation had ended with Leon promising to see him next when he spat on his grave, and with Roger kicking his ass out of the house with a shotgun pointed at Leon's head.

"Roger," Leon said, hoarse enough that Roger had to strain to hear. "I can't find him."

Roger froze. There were only two *hims* in Leon Hawthorne's

life. One was the nebulous enemy that Leon blamed for Sally's death, the epitome of all monsters—a damn crack dream, Roger had told him more than once, not that he expected Hawthorne to *listen*—and the other was Jake.

"Something got Jake? Fuck, what grabbed him and *how*? Your boy is damned careful."

Leon made a sound through the phone that sounded like he was choking on blood, half rasp, half wet. Roger paused. "Leon, it got you too?"

"Dammit, Roger, nothing got him. I came home, and he wasn't here. He ran . . ."

Roger could not imagine Jake Hawthorne running away from his father. Sure, they were messed up in all the usual ways, and in a few that were purely Hawthorne, but he had seen how the kid always looked up to his father, followed his lead, did what he was told because he had that much trust in Leon.

The last time Roger and Leon had "talked," when the guns came out, Jake had looked ready to pull his knife on Roger if he could only get a good angle. More than once, Roger had wondered if he would shoot Leon some day or if Jake would always be there to remind him that it wasn't worth it because the obsessed jackass actually mattered to someone. He had never met Sally, but he assumed that she either had had the placidity and patience of a saint or had been woman enough to kick Leon's ass every day and have him thank her for it. He could not imagine anyone else living with Leon for longer than a weekend.

" . . . he ran because I told him to, I told him to deal with it, and now *I can't find him.*"

"Slow down, Hawthorne." Roger had a hard time believing that Jake had run, but if Leon had told him to, if Jake hadn't gotten grabbed by something nasty, then there was a good chance that Jake would just show up again, one of those wicked grins on his face, like when he had been a kindergartner and ended up under the hood of one of Roger's old beater trucks. Roger had found the kid chewing on a sucker, covered in old engine grease. Roger had tried to give him a tongue-lashing, but it had been damned hard with Jake so happy to see him. The kid had charm that made people like him and convinced them that they could trust him. "Tell me what happened. Are you hurt?"

Leon was struggling to breathe, and Roger could hear every inhale and exhale as a gasp, full of pain. "My son is gone," he snapped. "I told him to leave and he left and now I can't fucking find him, what do you think?"

Slowly it dawned on Roger that it might be tears in Hawthorne's voice. *Holy hell,* he thought, *I never thought I'd hear Leon cry. Didn't think he could.*

"Leon, take a deep breath. Jake's smart, resourceful. He knows how to take care of himself." He bit back more scathing words about how losing Jake was maybe what Leon deserved for the way he had raised the boy. *You taught him better than anyone how to disappear.* "How long's he been gone?"

"Two weeks."

"Fuck, Hawthorne." Roger was expecting a few days, a week at most. "Where . . . what happened?" Not that he really wanted to know. He didn't think that one antisocial hunter could solve the Hawthornes' problems. He didn't know if God could solve the Hawthornes' problems.

"I was on a hunt, and he called in the middle, said that CPS was there, and I couldn't . . . Dammit, Roger, he's my son and I told him to deal with that. He's thirteen and . . ."

"What happened after that?" Roger didn't want to address Leon's choices, and more importantly right then he had a kid to save.

"I . . . I came home, back to the apartment we'd been staying at, and . . . nothing was there, it was empty, the locks were changed. I asked around, but there was some . . . trouble. I tried following the trail, but it was cold, so damned cold, Roger . . ."

"How long between the phone call and when you got back to the apartment?"

The silence made Roger nervous.

"Leon? Leon, I can hear you breathing. You don't remember, or . . ."

"It took me three days to get back," Leon said bleakly. "I figured . . . Jake's never been in a situation that he couldn't handle, and I thought . . ."

You thought that you could take your time because you're so damned used to Jake being his own damn parent. Roger didn't say it. He had said it in the past, and he had a couple of broken knuckles to prove it. He didn't need to say it now. His silence said enough.

He was surprised when Leon broke the silence first, and not by hanging up. "Help me, Roger. You have to help me. I can't . . . I can't go to them and say that . . . I can't tell them I lost my son. I'll lose him forever. They've been trying . . . I can't lose Jake too."

It took Roger a long minute to realize that Leon was asking him to use his hunter contacts, to quietly ask people to be on the lookout for Jake. Maybe even to talk to ASC, in case they had the resources to find the kid.

Roger wondered now if maybe Leon had disappeared so thoroughly off the grid because he had been afraid that the Dixons would take Jake away and make him one of their own, make him "Sally's son" and not Leon's at all. Roger had always thought that Leon was a little crazy, the way he disappeared, trusted no one, rarely used his own name, rarely told anyone the truth. He was a conspiracy theory nut even amid the crackpot group that Roger knew as hunters. But maybe only half of that had been because of the way Sally had died. The other half might have come from trying to keep a four-year-old and a vintage Eldorado off the radar of what had become the most powerful government agency in the country.

Roger would have liked to think that the Dixons wouldn't have tried to take Jake away, but if *he* had thought about stealing the kid just so Leon would stop fucking him up with his own particular brand of crazy, there wasn't much doubt that the Dixons would have gone after anything or anyone that they considered one of theirs. Roger had only met Elijah Dixon once or twice before he died, but Roger had always considered the man to be disciplined, intelligent, unshakable in a fight—but not nice, not an easy man to live with, not a man who would let any outsider come between him and family. And to the Dixons, Leon Hawthorne would never be family. No matter how many vamps he staked or werewolves he gave a bullet to, he would always be *that damn civilian Sally married.*

"Yeah," Roger said heavily. "I'll help you. Don't worry, Leon. I'm here, and we'll get him back." He just hoped that he wasn't lying as much as Leon lied to everyone else.

LEON FINALLY FOUND Jake through law enforcement gossip. In towns, he drank slowly, and nothing but beer; he was there for information, not because he wanted a goddamned blackout. Cops around him started talking about a wild kid that had turned up a state away in Jefferson, half crazy, stronger and meaner than he should have been. Kid wouldn't say where he'd come from, how he'd been surviving on his own, but he might have been the son of some outlaw, might have been just a poor abandoned shit, or even some kind of monster. No one knew what kind—horrifying to think that monsters could look like kids too, all innocent and helpless—but anything was possible. *And you should have seen what the little bastard did to one of the arresting officers!* They weren't sure how the officer's nose would set.

It wasn't that far a drive, but it felt like forever. It felt longer than that first night when he had carried Jake into the Eldorado after Sally's funeral, wrapping him in a coat in the front seat even though it wasn't as safe as the back—Leon had been a careful man in those days, and Jake had been his baby, the only thing he still cared about—and driving, driving until he didn't know the name of a single goddamned road. He figured that if he didn't know where he was, then the Dixons wouldn't be able to follow. If he didn't have a plan, they couldn't show up at his front door with that polite, insincere smile on their face, asking after Jake, asking if Leon was dealing okay, if maybe he would find it easier to deal with his grief without sole responsibility for an also-grieving four-year-old.

"He's a child," Elijah said. "Of course you can't expect him to really understand what's going on. We'd be happy to take him for a few days if you need a moment to yourself . . ."

"You can get off my goddamned porch," Leon replied.

The smile dropped off Elijah's face, and he was the same bastard Leon remembered from the days when he had been courting Sally, when Elijah had looked at him like the blue-blooded Pennsylvania gentry he thought he was and like Leon was just trash, born and raised in West Virginia. "Watch your mouth, Hawthorne. That boy is ours as much as yours."

Leon cocked the shotgun. Elijah looked unarmed, but he didn't believe that for a second. "Leave and don't come back."

Elijah stepped back. "You can't cut us out of Jake's life. We'll talk later." He turned and walked away.

Arriving at the police station was worse, because only then did Leon realize that he didn't have a plan.

Hunting was easy. Hunting made sense. *Find a monster, then shoot it. If it's not human, if it's hurting people, then it's a monster, and you put it down.* He'd seen how any kind of power, any kind of extra ability could turn bad, could twist a person up inside until they weren't really human any more.

Hell, he knew he had some black spots, and those he blamed

on monsters too. Even the spots that he sometimes had to admit had been there before Sally died. It was easier.

If he walked into that station and said he was there to pick up the kid, they would check his ID, and if Jake had been giving them as hard a time as he expected—*that's my boy, give 'em hell*—they would be thorough enough to see through the fakes that usually worked on civilians. The civilians would accept anything he said, but these cops . . . They would want to know, especially given all the rumors about where Jake had come from.

Rumors that made going in and admitting that Jake was his son—*he was Leon's goddamned son, give him back right now*—more impossible. He would be in for neglect at least—*how could you leave a thirteen-year-old alone for a week? Jesus, Leon, when did you become such a bastard?*—perhaps abuse; maybe they'd even have the balls to nail him for some of the things he'd done to keep them alive, back when he would have rather spit in his own eye than accept any aid from the fucking government that employed the Dixons. Now he took the stipend, collecting through so many channels that they'd never been able to trace it, but over the years he'd done everything from small-time scams and credit card fraud to shoplifting and bash-and-grabs. Yeah, he'd done things that he wasn't proud of, but he didn't think about them much, and no one gave a damn when he was saving their asses from the latest poltergeist.

He'd never had to think about any of that until now, when he knew any mention of his name could land him in a jail cell across from Jake. At the very least it would send up a red flag, and a Dixon would be there within a day, maybe a few hours, and then they would take Jake away from him. He knew they could. He had seen the Dixons put away enough monsters, had seen them convince enough senators and civilians that their torture camp was not only a good idea (though he had to admit, it was useful sometimes) but also a humane one, that he knew taking one thirteen-year-old away from a drunk, obsessed, criminal hunter wouldn't be a problem for them.

But there was one way he could get Jake out with no one asking questions. Yeah, the Dixons would see, and they might suspect, and it would give them more damned ammunition to use against him if they could ever really catch him, but he and Jake would be in and out before anyone could show up here. They would hit the ground, head to Truth or Consequences, and lay low at Roger's for a few days. Leon hated taking charity, hated bringing anyone else into their problems, but it would be good to have another head, another pair of eyes watching Jake, making sure that someone was around to protect him when Leon was being a fucking idiot.

He wouldn't even have to say that Jake was a monster. He could just flash the ID, and no one would ask any questions, because that was how the ASC worked. They would just look in his eyes, and they would know there was a monster in their building.

Shame that they would always guess the wrong one.

Two states, ten days, two stolen cars, and three close misses—two authority figures and one pervert who hadn't expected him to know how to break his fingers from that position—after running from the apartment, Jake got caught and was dragged kicking and screaming into the local precinct office.

After the first broken nose, they stopped treating him like a scared, misguided teen and took off the kid gloves. Jake was good, but they were full-grown adults, and there were a lot of them, forcing him into cuffs and dragging him deeper into the police station.

In the middle of trying to fight them off in an interrogation room, kicking kneecaps and calling them every dirty name he knew—and a few he made up on the spot—Jake realized that this prison, this confinement, was Tobias's life every day. Trapped in a little box, held down, beat up just because he was considered less.

Like a shoulder popping into place, a lot of things that Jake had been feeling for a long time, maybe for years, snapped together, and he knew what he was going to do if he ever got out of there, if he ever got to walk out in the sun, burn ghosts, or just get out of the damned cell.

Right then he decided he was going to get Toby out, no matter what. No one should have to live like this, and especially not Toby.

It wasn't a new idea. It had been brewing in his head for a while. But it crystallized the moment when his teeth sank into some asshole's hand and an elbow slammed into his diaphragm. After that it was just Jake fighting them, fighting them with his eyes when his arms and legs were tied down, and waiting for Dad to spring him. He knew he would. Dad always came for him. He just didn't know if it would be gunplay, or a bomb, or a kind of one-man extraction heist like in the movies.

When Dad finally came for him, it was terrifyingly easy.

Leon walked in and held up his hunter ID. The Agency for Supernatural Control ID that he never used, barely touched, wouldn't talk about.

"You have the boy," he said.

The cop swallowed. He looked into the man's face and saw death. Cold, merciless, unflinching death.

"Yeah. I mean, yes, sir." He nodded at the ID. "Makes sense for him to be a monster. He put up quite a fight for a, what, fifteen-year-old? Couple of our people had to get medical attention. Guess we were lucky."

"About what I expected," Leon Hawthorne said, tucking the stiff, pristine, silver-edged ID back in his suit. "I need you to burn everything you have on him. Every photo, every file you put together. In fact, you should forget you ever saw him. It's better that way. Where do you have him?"

The officer had never turned a monster over to ASC before, but he knew how it was supposed to work. No questions, no paper trail. "First door on the left, Mr. Hawthorne."

When Jake saw his father at the door, when the cop released him from the cell—but didn't take off the cuffs—he got up without a word and let himself be pushed through the halls with a rough hand between his shoulders. All the way to the door, he noticed how eyes skittered away from him, afraid to catch the monster's attention.

In the car, Leon's face was even more emotionless and cold than usual. He didn't look at his son, even as he handed over a small key. Jake twisted off the cuffs and threw them in the back seat. "Sorry," he said, rubbing his arms and staring at the dash. "I fucked up."

Leon didn't look at him. "At least you're not dead."

The Hawthornes didn't talk again for the next three days.

Tobias hunched over his food, keeping an eye on the new shapeshifter. The newcomer, nicknamed Hulk, was over six feet tall with muscles bulging against the thin fabric of his camp clothes. The shape had probably seemed like a good idea while hunters were after him, but in camp it meant that he had more of a body to feed. Food and kindness were both hard to come by in Freak Camp.

Everyone here understood the need for food. But that didn't mean they appreciated it when someone, like this asshole, decided to go after other monsters' rations. Tobias watched the shifter's progress through the mess hall, accompanied by the occasional fist to the face, little stifled cries of pain as those accustomed to abuse gave up their meager portions to Hulk.

Those who still had enough self-preservation to notice approaching threats shoved their food into their faces, chewing furiously.

Usually, Tobias would have been among those stuffing his mouth with the dry bread and mush, but today he ate slowly, watching the shifter's progress.

The guards, who usually would have stopped the shifter or made him be more subtle about his thievery—and whose presence would have limited Tobias's options—were absent. Tina Dixon had been in and out of Special Research all week, and some of the newer guards had been snickering behind her back from the first moment that she stepped inside the yard. The male Dixons broke a few heads, but eventually Dave Donovan dropped a comment about her trying to make up for her lack of balls by borrowing the monsters'.

"Tina would do better to find a real man to put some steel in her spine," he'd laughed as she walked past him.

She'd turned—the cheerful, angry look in her eyes the same one that had earned her the nickname Crazy-GDB Dixon—and smiled. "How about I break your spine and see if you've got any steel to spare?"

Now all the mess hall guards were outside, cheering on their favorites, betting mostly on Dixon to wipe the dirt with Donovan's ass.

No one was watching the mess hall to make sure the monsters didn't kill each other.

Hulk worked his way down the tables, stopping next to Tobias. Tobias kept his eyes on his plate as he carefully scraped up the last of his mush with the last of his bread. He knew he looked like an easy target, younger and smaller than most of the monsters in the camp. As far as this shapeshifter was concerned —so new that the chartreuse tag on his arm still oozed effluvium where it pierced the skin and ran between his arm bones —Tobias didn't seem like a threat.

Hulk placed one hammy fist on Tobias's shoulder and pulled him back from the table.

"Hey, Baby Freak," he said, slurring his words, grinning down at Tobias in a mediocre impression of Crusher drunk on some poor bastard's screams. "Hand over that plate. You don't wanna get on my bad side, do you?"

The hand on Tobias's shoulder tightened. Tobias glanced around the room, meeting eyes frightened or as eager as the guards to see pain.

Tobias jabbed backward with his elbow, digging right into the sensitive point of Hulk's thigh. Gasping, the shifter loosened his grip. Tobias seized his hand, twisting it over and in front of him, forcing Hulk headfirst into the table, just as Tobias stood up to slam all his weight down through his forearm on Hulk's elbow. The shifter screamed as his bone broke, and Tobias rolled him over on the table—he was stronger than he looked—and brought the edge of his cheap plastic plate to the bastard's throat, just under the stiff new collar.

"You're not a real," Tobias said, staring down into the monster's eyes. "You're just a freak, same as me, and you don't fuck with other freaks. We fuck back. And don't call me Baby Freak, muscle boy. Understand?"

Snarling, the monster tried to reach for Tobias with his good arm.

Tobias crushed his windpipe with the plate and heaved the shifter's considerable bulk off the table.

He was sitting at another table, calmly licking his plate clean, when the guards arrived in belated response to the scuffle. They caught the shapeshifter just as he was staggering to his feet, the throat wound already sloughing. He bellowed and charged at Tobias, and then the guards brought him down. *They* had silver.

Tobias glanced over, and then back to his plate, satisfied that the situation was resolved. Maybe later he and Hulk would have another round behind the barracks. But the shifter wasn't a real, a hunter, or a guard.

Very few things could hurt Tobias, and Hulk wasn't one of them. It was about time Hulk learned that before Freak Camp got him killed.

JAKE CLEANED his shotgun in the living room while Roger sat in his study and pored over an ancient scroll. Then Jake cleaned the rest of the weapons Dad had left him—machete, knife, jury-rigged flamethrower—and gave Roger's coffee table an extra shine to get the cleaner off.

Finished, he wandered into the study. "Can I help?"

Roger didn't look up. "Can you read medieval Japanese?"

Jake shifted. "No."

"Then no."

Jake sighed and turned for the front door. He needed some air. "Back in twenty," he called, and got a casual hand wave in reply.

The run around the junkyard brought out a light sweat that cooled beneath his shirt. It always took a while for Truth or Consequences to cool off after summer, but he could almost feel that autumn was in the air.

He ran the perimeter first, checking that all the trip lines and traps that Roger had shown him were still in place and unsprung, and then worked his way back and forth between the cars. Roger had some sweet old beasts, many gutted and nonfunctional. Jake noted a few cars he wanted to take for a spin, if Roger would lend him the parts to get them running again. Dad was teaching him his backup job as a mechanic just so they could have the same cover.

He made the run in twenty-six minutes—no urgent need to

get anywhere, not like he had anything else to do—and Roger was still behind his desk, a new book under his nose.

Jake leaned against the study doorway and panted. He'd pushed the last mile or so, just so he could feel something.

"Glad you're back," Roger said, still without looking up. "I was just about to go looking for you."

Jake checked the clock on the wall. "Six minutes over."

"Can't be too careful."

"God!" Jake hit the wall behind him. "Is he gonna hold that against me forever? I did the best—"

Now Roger glanced up. "I know, kiddo. Don't sweat it. Just for a while, Leon prefers—"

"He wants me babysat. I'm fourteen, Roger, and I'm useless." Jake hit the wall again, hard. The wood left his knuckles aching, but nothing else changed. "Are you sure I can't help? Can you" —he waved a hand at the books— "teach me the frickin' Japanese or something?"

Roger raised his eyebrows. "In an afternoon? No."

"Dammit." Jake returned to the living room, back to his weapons and the duffel that held everything Dad had left him.

"You know what, Jake? I think I've gotten about as far as I can get with this." Roger stood, closing the book. "I've gotta talk to someone at Freak Camp."

In two steps Jake was back in Roger's office. "Freak Camp? Can I come?" When Roger gave him a suspicious look, he held his hands out. "Hey! Please, don't leave me here, there's *nothing* to do. Please, Rog. You don't want to just leave me here alone, do you?"

Roger sighed. "What the hell. Yeah, I don't want to come back to find the place reduced to rubble. Grab your gear, we're gonna be gone a few nights."

Jake laughed, smacking the doorframe with his open palm in victory this time. "You know, I've never turned even a corner of this place to rubble before, but I got a suspicion I just might this time if I'm left alone. Maybe I'll invite all the kids in T or C over for a kegger and orgy. I dunno if I can help myself. Since I am an irresponsible teenager, after all."

"And you tell me you don't need a babysitter." Passing Jake on his way out of the office, Roger aimed a smack at the back of Jake's head, which Jake easily deflected.

The drive was long. Longer because Roger insisted on stopping for naps on the way. Jake had offered to spell him driving ("Come on, it's *four in the morning*. I'll drive the speed limit and the cops won't give a crap") but had been turned down. But it was all worth it when Roger's Camaro pulled into the familiar gravel parking lot.

Jake tried to look chill. He had seen hunters all worked up when they went into Freak Camp, but Dad never was, and in all things Jake took his clues for how to behave from Dad, as a hunter and a Hawthorne. Dad had never looked anything but stoic walking through the camp's gates. When Roger hauled from the trunk his bag full of ancient Japanese books, he also looked grim, like he wanted the staff checking them in to understand that he didn't really want to be there.

It was hard to look sober and professional, but Jake did his best to put his stony game face on. He knew that the guards would notice any excitement—he had been here often enough to know that no matter how sloppy the guards seemed, they really did notice everything—but he hoped that Roger wouldn't mind Jake's eagerness. He wasn't sure why Dad and Roger didn't like Freak Camp when so many other hunters seemed to get a kick out of it, but Jake knew that he should at least try to imitate their attitude. He didn't want to be seen as just another hunter after monsters for the bounties. He was a Hawthorne. He had a mission. They weren't in it for the money—it was about saving lives so no one would lose someone the way he and Dad had lost Mom.

The guards' attention was one reason he always took Toby

to whatever hidden corner he could find, as much out of sight as possible—though the guards tended to walk around so they could check on them. They were probably just as sure as his dad was that Jake couldn't handle himself alone. He always brought Toby out of the guards' earshot at least, and Toby seemed no more eager to have their conversations snooped on than Jake. It wasn't like they were planning to lead a monster uprising or to firebomb the camp or anything.

Jake brought in his own pack, much like Roger's, but his didn't have anything really useful for hunting—just a sandwich and a jumbo bag of M&Ms that he'd grabbed at the last gas station.

When they were alone in the camp, Jake always made sure that he was between Tobias and the guards, made sure that he was blocking any possible view the adults might have of Toby's face, because those smiles . . . those smiles were Jake's, and he didn't want anyone else to know about them. That was probably crazy and obsessive of him, but obsession was okay. He'd heard his dad called an *obsessed bastard* more than once, and anything that Dad was was good enough for Jake.

The prefabricated metal buildings looked the same, maybe bearing a few more dents, another layer of grime. Jake knew that the monsters had to clean the buildings every month, but the heat and dust still built up. Every time he visited, Toby seemed to have another layer of dust too, a layer of dullness that burned away the more minutes he spent with Jake.

Jake loved that too. It warmed his insides like the shot of whiskey that Dad offered him on Christmas, but so much better because he'd never forgotten a second of the buzz he got from being with Toby.

He was so distracted with anticipation that he forgot to hide how impatient he was, until he saw Roger watching him.

Jake was suddenly self-conscious. Any second now, he would see Toby. A guard would spot him and bring Tobias out from wherever he was, or a monster would notice him and go tell Tobias, or Tobias would just be there. But usually by this point, Dad's long stride had eaten up the distance to Special Research, while Jake stayed in the yard because *his* goal, his monster, was right here. But Roger was still here, watching him, and Jake felt his momentum stuttering to a halt.

He didn't know what he saw in Roger's eyes, but he knew what he would have seen in Dad's. They'd had the argument often enough that Jake didn't push back when Dad brought it up. He just nodded and let it go and stopped talking about Tobias for a while—as long as he could help himself, before he forgot again. Then Dad would say something about how Jake had to stop thinking so much about a monster, that monsters were always dangerous no matter how innocent they seemed.

Jake was grateful that Dad couldn't sustain an argument by himself. With someone else to fight, he could lock horns forever, and usually it ended with them getting kicked out of wherever they were, or losing another friend, another contact. More than once Jake had thought that Dad would never talk with Roger again, and he barely remembered a handful of other hunters who had seemed decent but Dad hadn't spoken to in years. But when Jake just shut up, Dad didn't seem able to sustain the anger or the interest. There was only one thing that Dad could lock his rage onto, and it had never been Jake.

"You looking for that monster?" Roger asked.

That was how the arguments with Dad started too. Jake met his eyes. Roger wasn't Dad. Jake didn't know how he would handle the argument with someone other than Dad. No one else —other than the guards who Jake didn't give a shit about—had ever noticed.

"His name's Tobias," Jake said.

Roger ran a hand over his head. "Kid . . ."

Out of the corner of his eye, Jake saw Toby come around the corner at a trot. He tried not to look. He had never fought with

Dad at Freak Camp—they kept an absolutely united front against other hunters and ASC personnel—but he had long ago decided that there was no way in hell that he would get Toby involved in that fight.

But Roger saw Tobias at the same time, and Jake had to look over. He couldn't just let Roger look at Toby without acknowledging him too.

He put himself between other hunters, other guards, and Toby, and he knew that he would step between Toby and Dad too. And if he would do that to family, he knew without a doubt that he would get between Toby and Roger. Turning, he stepped away from Roger, toward Toby.

Toby didn't stop, didn't seem to see Roger. Jake couldn't hold back his smile, had to fist his hand around his bag strap to stop himself from reaching out.

His heart jumped when a bright smile lit up Toby's face, wider than Jake could remember seeing it, so big he could actually see a flash of teeth. In that moment, Toby looked *happy*, just like any other kid. Then Toby's eyes moved to Roger, and in a second the smile and all his emotion vanished, wiped clean from his face. Jake knew that they hadn't gone away, that the feelings were still inside of Tobias somewhere, but looking at his blank face, skin peeling a little from the eternal sunburn, it was hard to imagine ever finding that smile again.

Tobias had stopped, suddenly hesitant and unwilling to come any closer. He looked down at his feet and then to the side, as though trying to convince anyone watching that his eagerness had been an illusion.

Jake glanced around. A couple of guards were watching and smirking. In that second he hated them and almost hated Roger too.

ROGER LOOKED at the monster called Tobias. Damn, the kid looked maybe ten and thin enough that Roger could fold him in the bag with his rifles.

Roger didn't like monsters, didn't like Freak Camp, didn't like the new hunters who were in it for bounties. Hell, he sometimes hated monsters with a passion that he didn't like to look at too closely—but that kid didn't look like he could threaten a fly.

And the way he had smiled at Jake, for just a second before it vanished from his face, squeezed Roger's heart in a way he hadn't felt in a long time.

"That's Tobias?" Roger hadn't missed the way that Jake had stepped away from him, toward the boy. He wondered if Jake and Leon argued about this often, if the kid ever put up any kind of fight with his father. Roger argued with Leon often enough that he found it hard to believe that anyone could live with the man and not want to knock his skull open so that some sense might creep in. But even at his angriest, Jake worshiped the ground Leon walked on.

Jake nodded. He couldn't seem to decide where to fix his gaze—on Tobias, on the guards watching them, or on Roger. "Yeah." He straightened his shoulders and finally met Roger's eyes. "He's Tobias."

Out of the corner of his eye, Roger saw the tension in the monster's shoulders. He thought Jake could too. Roger sighed and turned to the kid.

The monster wouldn't look him in the eye. Fuck—the *boy* wouldn't look at him.

Roger raised a hand, beckoning him. "C'mere, kid."

Tobias came forward immediately, his eyes locked on the ground. He didn't look at Jake, while Jake didn't take his eyes off of Tobias's face for a second.

"Look at me," Roger said.

Tobias looked up, but not in Roger's eyes. His gaze settled

somewhere in the area of Roger's left ear and stayed there.

Roger moved to touch Tobias's face, to try to make the kid look him in the eye, but lowered his hand even as Jake started between them, anger and guilt mixed on his face. Roger couldn't touch the kid because of the way his eyes had changed from emptiness to—Roger couldn't describe it. He'd seen a shifter's eyes flash on video footage, he had watched more than one demon's eyes change into depthless black or red, but what happened on Tobias's face was worse than all of that because the response looked completely human. No longer empty and hopeless, but prepared. He hadn't flinched, hadn't moved at all, but those eyes said, *I know your type. Go on, hit me.*

There were creatures that had been in Special Research for years that didn't have eyes like that.

"Rog," Jake said. "Don't . . ." He bit his lip, then glared. Roger saw more than a little of his dad in him, which half made Roger proud and half made him want to smack the kid.

Roger wished that he could see Jake excited again. Since all the shit had gone down when Leon had pulled Jake out of jail using his hunter ID, Jake had been angry, subdued in a way that he couldn't express except by running or setting up a homemade range for target practice or drifting around the house like a restless spirit. Even though his excitement had been about a monster, a kid that could grow up to be one of the dangerous things Roger put down without hesitation, it would have been good for Jake to be out of his funk for a little longer.

"I'm not gonna do anything to him." Roger glanced at Tobias. "You. Stand back there for a second."

Tobias retreated, though he didn't turn his back. Roger got the feeling that he was watching their every move and trying not to be seen doing it.

Roger pulled Jake aside. "He looks all right, and he's never tried to hurt you, right?"

Jake swelled in outrage. "Dammit, Roger, he's never even come close. Why can't you just understand—"

Roger held up a hand, cutting Jake off. If only that worked as well with Leon. "They're monsters, kid. You know that every single freak in this camp did something or was a threat in some way. That's why they're here."

"Tobias didn't do anything!" Jake's voice rose, but he caught it, glancing at the guards, and then glaring back at Roger. "He didn't do anything," he hissed. "He got dropped here before fucking kindergarten and he doesn't remember anything. How can he be a monster?"

"He says he doesn't remember anything," Roger said. "That doesn't mean nothing happened. Werewolves—"

"Tobias's not a werewolf, not a vamp, not a psychic or a witch or any damn thing that they can pin a label on. He's just Tobias, and sure, he's here, but that doesn't mean—"

"Jake." Roger was surprised that just saying the kid's name shut him up. Maybe he was channeling Leon. Chilling thought. "He's *here*."

Jake looked away. "That doesn't mean everything. Papers get fucked up all the time, otherwise I wouldn't have spent weeks as Jackie, getting detention for not showing up in Home Ec the whole time we were in Buffalo."

Roger eyed the sullen teenager in front of him and the silent hopeless boy standing just out of earshot. He could almost believe that Jake knew what he was talking about. Then again, he was barely fourteen.

But hell, Leon had abandoned his son to CPS, and Roger had made his share of mistakes. They were well over Jake's age. Roger just hoped that this wouldn't be another one of his.

"Hell," he said at last. "I'm going to Special Research. Do you want to come with me?" Not that Roger wanted Jake anywhere near that place. The longer Jake went without being exposed to that part of hunter life, the better. He felt relieved when Jake shook his head, even though Roger could feel the bitterness rolling off of him.

"Jake." The boy looked up. Damn, that kid was as stubborn as his father, but Roger was pretty sure that his heart was in a healthier place. "I know that you're going to hang around with that kid, probably give him the candy in your bag, right?"

Jake's face closed down, stubborn and angry. "Maybe, sir."

No maybe about it, Roger didn't say out loud. The kid didn't need to know that Roger could read him like a book, and he was no frickin' medieval Japanese either. "Watch yourself, Jake. Be careful."

Jake relaxed slightly. Roger wondered if that was something that Leon said before he left, before he showed Jake that he trusted him. "I always am, sir." He sounded confident, but a touch resentful. Recent experience had taught him that being careful wasn't always enough.

Roger wished he could explain to Jake that Leon wasn't angry at him, but at himself, and that Hawthorne had never been good at channeling his personal self-loathing and rage onto the people and objects that deserved it, but he didn't think that Jake could understand. Jake had never been responsible for anyone but himself—and maybe sometimes for his father. He'd never known the furious, deep-rooted love that Leon had for him even when Leon was doing a piss-poor job of showing it.

Instead Roger said, "You do good, kid." With one more glance at Tobias, he walked away.

JAKE BREATHED a sigh of relief when Roger moved away. He had felt the argument growing, had known that he wouldn't be able to stop himself from defending Toby, and Roger might've been forced to grab him by the scruff of the neck and drag his ass out of camp—which wouldn't have helped

Toby—and then they would have fought. Jake thought sometimes that it would be nice to fight with someone about Toby. He still hadn't been able to get to that point with Dad. He couldn't shake his certainty that his dad knew best, his dad knew how to keep him alive, and Jake should never question him.

Of course, there was the fact that Dad wasn't talking to him, was so fucking ashamed of how Jake had behaved with the whole CPS thing that he had left and probably wouldn't be back for a long time.

But now Roger was heading toward Special Research, and there was nothing to stop Jake from turning to Toby.

Tobias watched the hunter leaving, expression tense, his gaze darting to Jake and the guards around the yard.

The nervous energy between them reminded Jake of when he and Dad weren't talking. Except at least he and Toby were in the conspiracy together.

They both waited until Roger had disappeared around a corner, and then they simultaneously breathed a sigh of relief. Tobias started, but Jake laughed. It was good, damn good, to be around someone else who wasn't an adult, someone who also eased up when he was finally left alone.

"Hey, Toby."

Tobias gave him a nervous smile, and Jake couldn't hold back his own. He wished that Toby would look as happy as he did when he had first seen Jake, but he figured that was too much to hope for. He rarely got to see Toby excited. There was only so much emotion that someone could have in a prison, Jake knew that now. No surprise that Tobias had been there so long that he couldn't manage anger anymore. Well, Jake might be able to stay angry for both of them.

"C'mere." Jake jerked his head, and Toby followed him to the side of a building. Jake turned his back to block the guards' view of Toby, and no one could even see their lips moving. He didn't know if any of the guards were lip readers, but he would take no chances.

"I got something to tell you."

Tobias blinked rapidly and ducked his head. "What—what is it? Your dad . . ."

Jake waved him off. "No, this isn't about Dad. This is . . ." *This is me realizing that you shouldn't be here, that no one as good as you should ever get locked up like I was.* "Something completely different."

"Okay," Tobias whispered. He wasn't looking up. His hands were folded tightly together as though bracing himself for the blow.

Jake wanted Toby to look at him. He wanted Toby to believe him. No one else did, but of all the people in his life, Toby was the one that Jake most wanted to trust him.

He cupped Toby's hands between his own like they were a fragile bird, stroking the back of his knuckles, until Toby looked up at him. "I'm gonna get you out of here. I'm gonna get you out of Freak Camp if it's the last thing I do."

Tobias stared. He blinked a couple of times, and then shook his head, hard, like he had water in his ears.

"J-J-Jake, don't joke about . . ." Jake saw Toby's chest rising and falling rapidly, and were those tears? "Please don't say things—"

"I'm gonna get you out." Toby had to believe him. Suddenly, in Jake's fourteen years, this was the most important goal he'd ever had. He had let down a lot of people lately, but Toby had to believe that Jake would never let him down as long as there was one more breath in his body. "That's not me fucking with you. That's a promise."

Tobias stared. "Jake . . . you can't. I mean, I know you'll try, but you can't take a monster out. And I'm just . . ."

"I'm gonna do it, Toby. Just you watch. I gave you my word, didn't I?" *And you don't deserve to be here.*

"You did. I just don't . . ." Tobias shook his head again, then took a deep breath. When he looked up, he had tears in his eyes, but Jake could see no trace of doubt or the panic that had been there before. "It's hard to believe," he whispered. "It's hard . . ."

"You don't have to believe," Jake told him. "Because I'm gonna make it happen, and then it won't be a fucking fairy tale, it'll be real."

Once Toby was out, Jake would make sure he was safe forever. He would make damn sure no one would ever be able to make Toby afraid again.

And everyone else could go to hell, as long as he had Toby.

CHAPTER SIX

1995–1996

Occasionally, when Jake and Dad visited Freak Camp, they passed other hunters on their way in or out.

Sometimes they chatted, and sometimes Dad made it clear that he hated their guts.

This time the other hunter was Henry Miller, and he was sitting on one of the metal and plastic chairs in the Reception lobby. The sharp-faced, dark-haired receptionist (Deborah, Jake thought her name was) sat across from him, handing him paperwork. A shapeshifter—clearly a Freak Camp inmate by the gray clothes and the bright green tag through her arm—sat in the chair next to the hunter. She wore the shape of a young, bony blond woman and couldn't seem to keep her head upright. Her eyes seemed unable to focus on anything, and it was so unnerving that Jake reached for his knife involuntarily.

"What excuse for a hunt dragged you up here, Miller?" Dad snapped. It had been a rough drive; he'd gotten his leg cut up a few weeks ago, and even though Jake had offered, he hadn't wanted to let Jake drive.

If Miller gave a damn that Leon was in a bad mood, he didn't show it. He grinned up at the Hawthornes, pausing over his paperwork. "Well, if it ain't the father-and-son dream team. Rumor had it you were retired in Florida by now, drinking those martinis with little umbrellas."

"Aw, Miller, we wouldn't dream of a beach trip without you," Jake said, mock hurt.

The shifter in the chair next to Miller moved weakly, twisting in her seat. Miller turned and hit her hard between the ribs, making her cringe and cough, pulling her knees to her chest. That was when Jake noticed the sturdy silver chain binding the monster's collar both to the table and to Miller's belt.

Dad's eyes had narrowed on the same chain. "What the fuck is going on there?"

"Just checking out a monster," Miller said. "I'm hunting a nest of Bray Road Beasts up near Elkhorn, and those things are like sharks: you throw a little blood on the ground, and they'll come straight for you. Sure beats trudging up and down rural Wisconsin trying to dig up the little fuckers' nest."

Dad's mouth twisted. "That's sick, Miller."

Miller slapped the shifter on the shoulder, more affectionately this time. "Not like I'm using a civvie, Hawthorne, so don't get your panties in a twist. Shifter blood and human blood smells about the same to those little Roadies. And this shiftie will probably keep me warm and entertained up in those crap backwoods motels. Can you believe that they don't have cable in some of those shitholes?"

Jake stared. This was a hunter, taking a monster out of FREACS. Granted, it didn't look like the guy was getting the shifter out for anything close to the reasons that Jake wanted to get Tobias out—it made Jake a little sick to think that anyone would get a monster out just to screw and kill them. But seeing firsthand evidence that it really was possible, what he had promised Toby, untwisted something inside him, lifted his hopes, even as Dad got more pissed.

Dad's face was stony. "And you think that's gonna convince me you're *not* a sick bastard?"

Miller shrugged. "We can't all be hunting demigods, Hawthorne. Besides, Bray Roads bring in a decent bounty. I don't need your approval when I've got Dixon cash."

Dad jerked his chin at the drugged shifter. "You're basically *working* with a monster, Miller."

Miller laughed and pushed his stack of papers to Deborah. "Don't worry, Hawthorne, the freak will end up dead eventually. Just might take a bit more time than you, or she, would like."

The shapeshifter slid down in her chair and gave a low, pained moan. Miller scowled at her and looked over at the guard standing by the wall. "Can I get a little more tranquilizer in my freak here? I don't want her putting up a fight when I pack her into my trunk."

"Come on, Jake," Dad said, moving toward the door. "I'm sure Miller and his freak will be very happy together."

"Fuck yourself, Hawthorne," the other hunter called.

Dad ignored him—if he got angry at all the people who told him to fuck himself, he wouldn't have time to be angry at people who questioned his judgment or had different opinions—and Jake barely glanced back, though he really wanted to crane his head over the paperwork that Miller had signed.

Probably Jake would have to be a licensed hunter to get Tobias out, and his eighteenth birthday was still three years off. Maybe he could convince Dad to sign for some of the paperwork, if he asked the right way.

But as they walked through the Reception, Jake had to admit that convincing Dad to get Toby out wasn't very likely—but a kid could dream, couldn't he?

At least Dad was trusting him again, letting him help on hunts. Really help, not just leaving Jake in the Eldorado as a lookout and getaway driver. Dad had put his faith in Jake, had let him use his own shotgun and brought him along to watch his back. He didn't leave him alone in crappy motel rooms as often either. Jake knew this was at least partly because of the CPS shitstorm, but it felt good, like he and Dad were partners. More than once, Jake had kept Dad from getting seriously injured, saving him while together they saved the civvies. They were a good team, and Jake tried not to mess that up by talking about Tobias too much.

At least as much as he could help.

"You seeing that monster?" Dad asked as they stepped out into the chilly fall air.

Jake shoved his hands in his pockets and shrugged. He had brought apples today, the biggest ones he could find in the gas station. He'd been bringing Toby chocolate the last few times, and even though he couldn't imagine getting tired of chocolate, Toby loved fruit. Jake also had a bag of chips that he'd found in the back seat when he was looking for the knife he always brought with him into FREACS.

"Yeah," he said. "Probably."

Dad scowled. "I don't get the fascination. You like Miller back there?"

Jake gaped at him. "Dad, gross, no!" He wasn't sure if Dad meant staking Tobias out as monster bait, or Miller's other sick comments, but either way, *hell no*.

"Because at least I'd understand that." Dad glanced at Jake out of the corner of his eye. He didn't have to look *down* quite as far anymore. These last few months, Jake had shot up nearly as fast as a shifter trying to join a basketball team. "I told you I don't have a problem with you swinging both ways, but at least make sure they're human."

"Dad!" Jake could not believe that they were having this talk, and in *Freak Camp* of all places. It had only been a couple of months since Dad had returned earlier than he was supposed to and caught Jake in the motel room with a half-naked visitor. Dylan had been the only redeeming part of that hick town with his soft sandy hair, sweet lips, and mind-blowingly talented hands. At least Dad had stepped aside as Dylan bolted down the street. It had been another twenty-four hours, and Dad bringing home a six-pack to split between them, before he and Jake managed to have as brief a conversation as seemed necessary. Until *now*.

Jake fidgeted, checking that none of the guards were nearby. Hell, Dad *asking* that was awkward enough without any of the sick fucks guarding the monsters listening. "That is not what bisexual *means*. We've been over this. And it wouldn't mean—come *on*, Dad, you seriously think I'd do that?"

"Not unless something's gotten into you that'd take an exorcism to get out. Hawthornes don't fuck freaks." He shook his head, brushing off the conversation. "I'm in Intensive Containment today. Won't be long. Try not to get too distracted with . . . whatever you do."

"You know I'm not possessed, we just crossed the goddamn pentagram!" Jake called after him, but Dad was already across the yard.

It took Jake several minutes to find Tobias. True, he wasn't as focused as usual; typically if he couldn't spot Toby, he got a nearby guard to radio for him. Today he walked slowly around the yard, watching a few passing monsters turn their heads sharply away from him. He looked at the row of posts, spaced apart in the yard with cuffs dangling from the tops. How many times had he walked past them without ever wondering why they were there?

Sometime since he was ten, this had become one of the places he most looked forward to returning to—because it meant he would see Toby again. He loved Dad and he loved hunting (they *saved* people), but sometimes it felt like their life, his life, was nothing more than an endless series of rundown motels, abandoned shacks, waste-of-time schools, and con stories fooling everyone into thinking they were someone they weren't. Didn't much matter if they were in Maine or Texas—hunts and monsters were found everywhere. Even the hunts blurred together. A violent spirit wasn't much different from a wendigo in the end.

Only Toby was different from all of them. Toby was special, because Toby was always the same person. Jake could mention a hunt he and Dad had done in Las Vegas (that turned out, awkwardly, to be not a shapeshifter, but a businessman with a particular fetish), and Toby would laugh because he remembered. Jake loved talking to Toby, but more than that, they had stories and a history together. Jake supposed that he and Dad had history in Morgantown, West Virginia, where they had lived before Mom died, but that history was old and dead, like Mom, and they had never been back. Toby, along with Roger, was the only thing in Jake's life that he looked forward to seeing again. He guessed that was why his heart jumped anytime he heard someone say *Freak Camp,* and why he always hoped his father would find another reason to go back soon.

But now, standing in the middle of its yard, he realized he hated the place. It made his skin crawl, and he felt dirty and gross just being there, like when that tentacle monster in Florida had tried to fight him off using its own saliva.

"J-Jake!"

Turning quickly, he saw Tobias standing against the wall of the mess hall, arms folded over his chest and hands clutching his thin blue jacket. He was looking up at Jake—more like peeking up through his hair—but there was no trace of the usual smile he had when first seeing Jake. He looked worried, even frightened.

"Toby." Jake started toward him, then checked himself, glancing around for any guards or monsters watching. Abruptly he was pissed off at everything, including himself. When the hell had he ever cared before? He didn't have a single fucking thing to be ashamed of. Scowling, he joined Toby against the wall. "Hey, Toby."

Tobias seemed to be attempting to disappear into the metal wall behind him, tucking his chin in, though still peeking up at Jake every few seconds. He didn't say anything else.

Jake sighed, shaking his head once, then reached in his pocket for the crumpled bag of chips. "Brought these for you." He couldn't summon his usual enthusiasm. *Fuck Miller*. Before they'd walked into Reception, he'd been looking forward to seeing Toby just as much as ever.

"Th-thanks." Tobias held the bag but didn't open it. Then he blurted out, without looking up, "Are—are you okay?"

Jake blew out his breath and slid down the wall to sit on the ground. "Yeah, Toby." He patted the earth next to him. "It's okay, I promise—I've just got some shit on my mind. Nothing to do with you. Go ahead and eat."

Tobias dropped to his knees next to him, but he only fingered the top of the bag until Jake began telling him about this monster that he and Dad had dealt with in Northern California that, *kid you not,* had possessed a deadly fart attack. At least three cops had ended up in the hospital, mauled and knocked out, because of the thing. No way of knowing how many people had just been eaten. He and Dad had taken the thing out, but only after a week and a half of tromping through the woods to find its nest.

"We wore *nose plugs* the whole trip, Toby. Dad's nose looked, like, twice the size. It was ridiculous."

Tobias relaxed gradually, eating each chip with care and relish, laughing at the funny parts and fixing his eyes more confidently on Jake's face. As he did, Jake felt better too, more sure that whatever the hell Miller or Dad thought, it wasn't true and didn't matter when he was here with Toby, laughing about monsters and hunts, sharing a bag of chips and an apple.

All the same, Jake stopped himself from leaning over to

bump his shoulder against Toby's. With Dad's words echoing in his ears, it just didn't seem right. Though he couldn't pin down what would be wrong about it.

True to his warning, Dad was out of Intensive Containment in less than an hour. Jake was glad that a guard found him and told him that his father was looking for him. Jake didn't want Leon to see them together, not now.

The thought made him feel horrible, and he didn't know why he felt *that* either.

Jake stood up and shoved the empty chip bag into his pocket. "I'll see you later, Toby."

Toby whispered something, and Jake turned to look at him. Toby still crouched on the ground, looking at his hands.

"What'd you say, Toby?" Jake grinned, but he couldn't put a lot of heart in it. "Maybe I got one of those nose plugs stuck in my ears."

Tobias looked up. "I hope you come back soon. I just . . . yeah."

That didn't sound like what he'd said the first time. It had sounded like Toby didn't expect him to come back at all.

Jake didn't think he could stay away. He'd *walk* back to Freak Camp if he had to. "I'll always be back, Toby. It's a promise." Jake smiled and almost reached out to ruffle Toby's hair but thought he heard Dad approaching. He turned away.

Jake felt Toby's eyes on him as he crossed the yard, but when he glanced back, Toby's head was bowed.

IN ADDITION to not much liking the entire FREACS institution, Roger wasn't fond of the Dixons.

Before the ASC, hunting had traditionally been a violent, unpaid, loner occupation that made a man paranoid about small sounds, shadows, electrical failures, and small inconsistencies in human behavior. It was a recipe for crackpots and excellent liars, but rarely a respectable, mild-mannered, nine-to-five family man. Roger's theory was that hunters were generally arrogant assholes with some level of death wish—himself included—and it worked down from there. On an individual basis, he probably would rather kill things with fellow hunters than make small talk.

The Dixons had always been an exception for how they professionalized monster hunting generations before Elijah Dixon created the ASC. This meant that for decades before the Liberty Wolf Massacre, they already regarded themselves as hunting paragons and were generally unbearable to be around for more than a few hours at a time. And that was before they received the official blessing of the United States government in 1984.

Fifteen years later, the Dixons were a perfect case study of what happened when you combined the mania of hunting, an unshakable conviction in the righteousness and patriotism of their cause, a possessive family dynamic, and a tendency to conflate their own identity with the national one: you had a gang of gun-wielding, pathological liars who tended to shoot first and ask questions later—if at all.

But even if he disliked them for how they snubbed any hunter outside their pack and how proud they were of tiny Dixon kids handling shotguns and salt packages almost as soon as they could walk, he wouldn't sit out when they needed him.

"We could use your help, Harper," the caller said. "Rougarou, Silver City. Available?"

Roger recognized the voice as a Dixon more by subject matter and the use of *we* than anything else. "Rougarous, huh? It's been a while." Rarer than werewolves, rougarous were more ravenous. They were also more dangerous if they figured out what they were, because unlike werewolves, they had a chance in the first hundred and one days to shake the rougarou curse and regain their humanity, but only if they bit someone else.

"We've got a team here, but some of them are green. Looking to balance it out with a gray beard."

"I ain't got a beard, gray or any other color. All right, give me . . ." He did a quick calculation in his head. "Two hours?"

"Yeah, good. We'll wait for you. You can reach me at this number. Ready?" The Dixon rattled off a number, and Roger took it down.

When he arrived at Silver City, it was the early afternoon. He pulled into the bar with a crowded parking lot, too many for a usual crowd of noon-drinkers.

Walking in, he nearly got shot by some hot-headed young hunter—a sandy-haired kid, not a Dixon himself, but a trainee from ASC Hunter Academy, judging by how he had both jumped in surprise and responded automatically with the shotgun. The kid was new. If Roger *had* been a monster, he would have been able to rip the kid's throat out before he got to the weapon.

Lucas Dixon snaked out a hand and jerked the kid's elbow before he could send a shot into Roger's chest, but the kid still pulled the trigger. Two other hunters dove for cover behind the pool table. The gun clicked empty—the idiot had gone for a gun that wasn't even *loaded?*—but Roger still had to work to stop his heart from beating out of his chest. If the gun *had* been loaded, it would have blown a rock-salt hole through the bottles on the back of the bar, if not the gaping bartender's head.

Lucas just sighed and pushed the mortified kid away while the two older hunters—both clearly Dixons from their similar facial structure and the easy way they stood with their weapons—looked disgusted.

"That's Harper," Lucas said. "Better not shoot him." Recognizing his voice from the call, Roger felt old. Lucas had been a snot-nosed brat the first time they'd met in 1985, when the

Dixons had gone around to all the other known hunters, asking them to join up. Roger had told them he wasn't the club-joining sort, but a year later he had to cave and apply for his own ASC license. He might be stubborn, but he wasn't stupid enough to pass up a sizable paycheck for what he used to do for free, not to mention a shit ton of resources and excellent healthcare.

The bartender cleared his throat. "Hey, fellas—I support the troops as much as anyone, and I can give you a free beer if you come back tonight, but while you're handling firearms—"

"Yeah, yeah." Lucas straightened up off the bar and waved them toward the door. "We'll take it outside."

"How'd he find us?" asked one of the other trainees, a girl with two long brown braids. Roger decided he wasn't going to ask their names. Probably they'd be dead in a couple of years once they came off the Dixon training leash, if not before. That question just hadn't been that bright.

"He's a hunter," one of the Dixons laughed. "What do you think?" He had crooked teeth that glinted in the dim light.

"Voodoo," the other, taller Dixon suggested in a mock-spooky voice, but he just sounded like a brainless moron and not like he was making a threat Roger would have to challenge him on.

Lucas was playing Good Leader and keeping his mouth shut —usually a smart-ass, Roger remembered—but he was smiling.

"There's a lot of cars in the lot for this time of day," Roger pointed out. "And hunters tend to meet at bars and not, say, beauty parlors."

"Not me, Harper," Lucas said. "I was all for Chic Cuts but got outvoted."

Roger ignored him. "This is an awful lot of people for one rougarou."

Crooked-Teeth grinned again. "You wouldn't even be here if it wasn't for the squirts, old man."

Lucas shrugged. "Don't worry, Harper, you'll get your share

of the bounty." Roger started to say that wasn't what he'd been concerned about, but Lucas went on. "I called you in because we think it has help. No reported deaths yet, which is weird given how this freak's bloodwork came back from the lab. Bastard thought he had some kind of stomach infection, got it checked out, and we got the intel. But since then, there's been *nothing.* We don't know if this freak's been eating homeless guys or if he's still looking human, and we don't know why there isn't more info coming in."

"I've never heard of a rougarou running in packs or communities," Roger said.

"Yeah, but doesn't hearing start to go around your age?" Lucas asked with mock concern. Roger gave him an *I can still kick your ass* look, and he raised his hands jokingly. "So if you're up for it, Gramps, we could use the backup. Serious, professional backup." He grinned. "After all, you may not be family, Harper, but you're damn good."

Roger rolled his eyes. "I was throwing trolls down mountains when you needed your diapers changed. Now tell me what you got."

Lucas laid out the information and the plan with typical Dixon efficiency and professionalism. Four hunters in through the back, three through the front, spreading out as they went until they got the monster.

"We think the wife may be involved," Lucas added. "Helping the freak."

"Like a Renfield, just for a rougarou and not a vamp," said Crooked-Teeth. "Christ, what a thought."

"Yeah, I don't want to believe it either, but there's freak lovers out there." Lucas's lip curled. "Remember, if something attacks, you shoot it on sight. If it keeps coming, torch it. I want the freak alive for the bounty, preferably—rougarous are rare, and we could use any new info—but I don't want anybody doing something stupid to get a live capture. It's just money, info, and glory, folks. Not worth losing hunters."

Everyone nodded—the Dixons with boredom, the newbies with eagerness. If one of them didn't do something stupid to get the bounty, Roger would buy himself a drink.

At first the attack went down without a hitch. The kids followed the Dixons' lead quietly, efficiently, and the all-too-human-looking rougarou barely had a chance to take one swing at its attackers—Lucas, who dodged the blow easily—before the other hunters filled it with tranquilizer darts.

Rougarou research was minimal, so Lucas had them use a combination of twine, iron, silk, copper, silver, catgut and little plastic zip ties. They were just tying the last knots when the wife came home with groceries.

She stepped through her front door, saw what they were doing to her husband, and dropped the bag full of neat packages of freshly butchered meat.

Roger was in the kitchen, discovering stacks of raw steaks wrapped in the refrigerator and freezer, when he heard the screaming and two shotgun blasts. He ran, expecting to hear the flamethrower at any second, but in the living room, the monster was still safely down with the tranquilizers. Instead one of the newbie hunters was splayed across the couch, gasping in agony at a hole in his chest big enough to fit a cantaloupe. The wife, wispy brown hair flying around her enraged face, had a smoking shotgun.

"What are you doing to him?" she cried. "Get your hands off my husband! Let him go!" She swung the shotgun around.

Lucas, who had been securing the second floor, was suddenly *there*, snatching the gun out of her hands, breaking the arm she swung at him and kicking in one of her knees. She went down, keening with pain and rage, but still tried to go for Lucas's eyes with her good hand. Crooked-Teeth Dixon emptied his clip of tranquilizers into her back.

Lucas stood, pushing back his hair with his free hand. "Fucking freak lover. They're worse than freaks." He spat on the floor.

The taller Dixon—who had been examining the young, dead hunter—looked up. "So, what do we do with the bitch?" He wrinkled his nose in distaste at the woman lying motionless on the floor. "I suppose we can't just shoot her and drop her body at the dump? Let her feed all the other nasties, since she wanted to so bad." He smirked at Crooked-Teeth, who chuckled. Roger, not for the first time, had the urge to slug a Dixon in the face.

Lucas shot his cousins a look and turned to the two young hunter trainees, horrified and shell-shocked, staring from the monster to the unconscious woman to the lifeless body of their comrade-in-arms, whose blood was now soaking into the couch. Roger wished he could say something comforting to them, but he didn't know what he could say that wouldn't be either a lie or useless. This was part of hunting life. Even if you were lucky, people you knew died. If you were unlucky, it was the people who mattered the most.

"Two stretchers," Lucas told them.

The kids, grateful for a direction, ran for the door.

When they were out of earshot, Lucas turned back to his cousin. "We'll dump her in with the roogy. If the tranqs don't kill her and he doesn't kill her, we'll let Freak Camp deal with her."

Sweat chilled on Roger's skin. He knew what happened at Freak Camp. Usually he tried not to think about it. "She's human," he said. "We know she's human."

Lucas shrugged. "Can't be *sure* 'til we get her inside, can we?" He didn't say it like he expected Roger to believe it. He was just sharing the line they used for civilians so that everyone could keep their stories straight.

"You son of a bitch," Roger said. Lucas raised an eyebrow, and the other two Dixons paused in their cleanup activities, turning to keep their eyes on him, ready for trouble. Roger would have been an idiot to ignore the way their hands drifted to their guns. "She's *human*."

Lucas threw up his hands. "What do you want me to do, Harper? You want me to just dump her with local police, have her tell them some bullshit story about how armed strangers came in, beat her, and stole her husband? Legislation against freak lovers ain't what it should be. They might take the bitch's word, and then ASC's gonna have to get into it with local law enforcement, and somewhere along the way we're gonna have to drag her through the legal system for shooting that kid over a *freak*. I mean, she's guilty as hell of sheltering a freak, killing an officer of the law, and pissing off the Dixons. Faster, easier, less of a hassle for everyone just to dump her in with the freaks she loves. See if she still loves them when she finds out what they really are."

Roger took a breath, ignoring the ringing in his ears. "You do this a lot, Lucas?"

Lucas shrugged. "They're all monsters, Harper. Don't care if they're freaks or fucking them. World's a safer place with less of this shit on the street. You gonna be a problem?"

Roger didn't answer. He knew the fight was already lost. Dixons got their way, whether it was on a public stage or in private scenes like this. No witnesses, just silent and complicit accomplices and assholes like Roger himself, who told themselves that kicking up a fuss would do no one any good. Even if it also felt like the truth.

Hunting had never used to make him this kind of ill before the Liberty Wolf Massacre. Back then a hunter could hold to his own code that let him sleep the best he could at night. Now it was the Dixons' way or getting arrested for interference with ASC operations. Roger didn't kid himself that if you were already on their bad side, you'd end up in a black van headed to Nevada.

"Don't call me again, Lucas," Roger said finally. "Not when you're storming a civilian's home."

"Freak lover," Lucas corrected, "not civilian. But I'll pass the word along. Thanks for the time. Considering your moral objections, I'm guessing you don't want your share of the cash, huh? And you probably won't help load the bitch in the van, either." He grinned.

There was the sense of humor that Roger remembered wanting to smack out of the snot-nosed kid. "Fuck yourself, Dixon."

The Dixons laughed, just as the two surviving kids came back in, each one pulling a stretcher awkwardly through the door. They looked confused but didn't ask about the joke.

"Not today, Roger," Lucas said. "There's folks that do that for me. Enjoy your sanctimonious life!" He waved as Roger walked out the door, feeling sick. He didn't look at the Dixons, the rougarou, the woman, the kids, or the darkening stain where one of their team had bled out his life.

Maybe the tranqs will stop her heart before she gets to FREACS, he thought. That would be a mercy.

After all, the tranquilizers had been designed to bring down a full rougarou. No one knew what they would do to a real, non-supernatural human.

He buried the thought that there was no way in hell that that should be any measure of comfort.

SPEEDING ALMOST a hundred miles an hour down a deserted Alabama highway, Jake found his eyes blurring, crushing the mile markers and the sharp bright stars into intermittent flashes of light that sketched out his world.

Or maybe it was the blood loss.

But probably not. The whatever-the-fuck warthog monster

had barely touched him, and he had tied the injury off right away. More likely it was the concentration required to keep the Eldorado steady on the road with one hand, keep pressure on Dad's gut wound with the other, and, above all, to *not panic.* Panicking never helped. He just had to get to the nearest hospital before his hand went numb or Dad's guts started oozing through his fingers.

The clock in the dash of the Eldorado clicked over to 12:02 a.m., and Jake realized that it was January 5th, and he was sixteen.

The laughter that bubbled up through his lips tasted a bit like blood and shook him until the road vibrated in his vision. The sound was semi-hysterical enough to bring Dad out of his half-shock, half-drug-induced slump between the bench seat and his son's hand.

"Jake?"

"It's okay, Dad."

"Did we—"

"Yeah, we got it."

Dad frowned. "You were . . . crying, or—"

Jake glanced over at him, wondering if he could hold his own wound closed, or at least help Jake wrap it better. But would he really want to put his right hand, covered in Leon's blood, back on the wheel? It wasn't like Hawthorne blood hadn't soaked into the Eldorado before, but this was the first time that Jake could watch it dripping and do nothing to stop it —nothing to make it better—but drive.

"I just realized," he said, when he saw Dad's eyes sliding out of focus again, "that I'm sixteen today." He took his one hand off the wheel. "Look, Dad! I can drive!"

Dad tried to smile, but it didn't look good.

What would Jake do if Dad died right there? His mind reached for the next step and then stopped, pulled back. Jake couldn't, *refused*, to imagine a world without his dad. Without his mom, the world had shattered, and Dad had reassembled something that worked, that held them together. Without Dad, Jake couldn't imagine building his own world. There wouldn't be enough pieces to sew together. Fuck, he didn't even know that he would be able to stop the Eldorado when he found a destination. With the signs moving past too fast, with his foot weighing on the gas, he could have already passed the exit.

Jake started talking. He tried to catch the edge of his father's attention, tried to keep him from slipping away. Dad's head slumped down again, but Jake kept talking. He told Dad how sick he was of going to school, what he'd seen on TV last week, the latest weird sound he'd noticed in the Eldorado's engine, and somehow he landed on talking about Tobias. Toby talking to him, Toby smiling at him, Jake reading books just so that he could share them with Toby and actually know what he was talking about the next time he walked into Freak Camp.

He talked until his throat went dry, then kept talking. He stopped forming sentences and moved into impressions, moments, dark corners, pretty boys and girls, but everything always spun back to Toby.

"Sure, he's a monster, I know that," he said to the darkness and his father. "But I don't get what he could have done. I mean, he's younger than me and I've never seen him hurt fucking anything, won't even bite M&M's really hard, you know? But he's there and everyone says he must deserve it, but I can't fucking see it. I mean, what could make a kid like Tobias a monster? He's just . . . *Toby.*"

Jake had no idea how much his father heard, and after a while he didn't want to know. The words weren't important, and maybe he shouldn't have said any of them. But he had to talk, because with each hand gripping one of the two things he loved most in the world, he needed to hear a voice to convince himself that the Eldorado and Dad and Toby weren't just an illusion, something that he had made up in the dark to hold his sanity together.

The Eldorado purred under his feet, and Leon Hawthorne bled through Jake's fingers, and Jake kept driving, kept talking about Toby, who was so far away.

LATE SPRING in Freak Camp was almost tolerable, especially when compared to the imminent scorching summer, but it was still hot enough to burn the skin off a vampire and leave everyone else heat sick and sunburned.

Jake always made sure that they at least had a piece of shade, whether because he didn't like the heat or because he cared—Tobias wrestled sometimes with which it could be, Becca's voice and his own instincts warring with each other. Sometimes, being Sally Dixon's son, he could even talk their way into one of the air-conditioned buildings.

This visit, Jake had convinced the people in Administration to let them through, and he and Tobias sat in an out-of-the-way corner under a stairwell, against the cool plaster of the wall, and shared what Tobias was sure was the biggest meal he had eaten in his entire life.

"Dad'll be busy for hours," Jake said. "No need to rush, Toby. We've got lots of time today."

He hadn't believed it when Jake kept pulling food out of his bag. Two sub sandwiches, three apples, a huge bag of chips and two small, squashed cupcakes in plastic wrapping. Tobias nearly shook from the effort not to snatch some of that food and shove it into his mouth before someone—monster or guard—took it away.

Only the fact that he was with *Jake*—and Jake looked happy and relaxed, which he hadn't always the last few visits—kept Tobias from acting like a filthy, grabby monster. Tobias knew that Jake would give him some of that bounty, because Jake had never been cruel enough to show him food and not allow him to eat it.

Jake beamed at him as he shook out the bag. "Dig in. I'm just glad they give me less shit about bringing in food these days."

Cautiously, still not quite believing the feast before him, Tobias reached for a sandwich.

By the time Jake had finished his sandwich and opened up the bag of chips, Tobias's anxiety had ebbed. He still tried to eat slowly—too much food at once, *good* food, could come back up if he scarfed it, and Tobias didn't want to lose *any* of the wonderful food that Jake had brought him—but he was smiling and able to laugh at the stories Jake told around his mouthful of chips.

He had been afraid, sometimes, on Jake's recent visits. Not because he was afraid that Jake would hurt him—nothing Jake did could possibly hurt—but because Jake was sometimes tense, distracted, and unhappy. Tobias assumed it had something to do with his father, or maybe the real world, but Tobias always had a nagging fear that it was his fault and that someday Jake would stop coming because of something Tobias had done without ever knowing what it was.

But not today. Today Jake smiled and pushed chips in his face and grinned when he made jokes so that Tobias could be sure that he should laugh.

"Sub taste all right?" Jake asked. "I wasn't sure what kind to get, so I went with everything."

Tobias nodded. "It tastes great. B-b-but . . ." He stuttered to a halt, not sure how to ask. "Why so much . . . I mean, I love it, this is amazing, but . . ." God, Jake's food was so good. He felt full for the first time in months, he was sure he wouldn't have to eat for the next week if he had to, but he couldn't even pretend to understand why Jake had done all this. "It's just so much."

Jake colored a little. Tobias blinked, not sure he could believe that Jake was blushing for him.

"Well," Jake said. "It's April. You know."

Tobias stared. He had no idea what Jake was talking about, unless . . . "My . . . birthday?"

"Yeah." Jake cleared his throat and looked away. "I mean, I know it doesn't make much difference here. It's not really a big deal like it is outside, but I like to do something special. Just between us, so I know I'm doing something, you know? And you only turn twelve once."

Tobias stared as the idea sank in. Jake cared so much that he would remember something as pointless as the day Tobias had been born and make it special.

Tobias thought about last year. Usually he tried to forget the day-to-day of Freak Camp. Why would he want to remember pain—his own and others'? Why should he keep track of bad food, miserable hungry nights, and punishments doled out to monsters who disappeared before he could ever know their real names?

But he remembered every one of Jake's visits. He stored them up like some monsters hid food, because it got him through the bad times. Like some of the rare stories he found in the library, every one of Jake's visits was a moment when he could, at least for a little while, escape everything that could hurt him.

If he thought back, he could clearly remember this time last year when the weather had been warmer. Jake had brought a small cake in a slightly crumpled box. It had been an even better day in all the best days when Jake had visited.

For a second it was hard to breathe, but not because he was in pain or because he felt faint from hunger. It was because of Jake, who looked so embarrassed but happy. Because Jake was good to him all the time and didn't expect anything from Tobias. He just did it because he cared. Tobias knew this was true because Jake never pointed out when he was doing kind things, things Tobias would never be able to repay. He just did them and didn't ask for anything in return.

Tobias clenched his hand in his shirt to keep from reaching for Jake. His fingers were coated in salt from the chips, plus a little sauce from the roast beef sandwich, and he didn't want to repay Jake by dirtying his jacket.

No chance he could ever find the right words, but he swallowed and said, "You're the best," as authoritatively as he could, sure of this one fact. Jake was not only the best person in his life, but probably in the whole world. Tobias wasn't sure if anyone else knew it the way he did, though, and that was a strange thought. A freak shouldn't be the only one who knows how awesome Jake was. Surely there were lots of other reals outside who did too and treated Jake like he deserved, the same way he treated Tobias.

As they finished the food, Jake told him about his and his dad's last hunt for a ghoul that had crossed four state lines and evaded three Dixon hunting squads.

"So get this, the news reports made it sound like a pack of rabid bobcats, and all the stupid ASC intel said it looked like it had four legs. I told Dad that none of them would know a ghoul if it ate their entire ass, they've never made tracks like that before—"

"Unless it's a ghoul-type hyena," Tobias said, then caught himself—why was he such a stupid, insolent freak that he interrupted and corrected *Jake*—but then Jake gave him a dazzling grin and snapped his fingers.

"Dude, that's it! You could've wrapped up the whole hunt the first day. But no one remembered that! Not me, not Dad, not all the goddamn Dixons in the country. Shit, I should have you on speed dial—" Jake stopped short and looked away, color rising in his cheeks again.

Abruptly Tobias felt sick. He was such a stupid little freak ruining one of his best days, his few precious hours with Jake. "I'm sorry, Jake. I shouldn't have said—"

Jake met his eyes again with a crooked smile that still looked real. "Nah, it's not you, Toby. You're a badass genius. I just wish I really could—you know."

Tobias wasn't sure he did know, but he didn't dare say anything else, hoping if he kept his mouth shut, they could recapture the light mood of just a minute ago.

To his relief, when Jake smiled at him again, it was as genuine as it had been when he first saw Tobias. "So, there we were sitting like jackasses, waiting for the next attack..."

Once or twice, a guard or staffer passing by would stop and stare at them, but Jake glared, and then they went away. Tobias didn't know if Jake had this power because he was a hunter, or a Hawthorne, or just because he was Jake. With him Tobias felt safe, and it felt like some of that protection stayed with Tobias even when Jake was gone.

An hour later, feeling unnaturally, pleasantly full, as well as a buzzing kind of lightness through his whole body that he could only guess was *happiness*, the way reals felt it—Tobias sensed someone staring at him. He looked up from their card game expecting a guard, and instead he saw Leon Hawthorne.

Tobias forgot all his lessons in survival and stared, terrified. Maybe this was how the fresh meat felt with the regular guards. He trembled from that stare alone, and he could feel the cards slipping from his hands. He forced his eyes down and swore at himself. Freaks didn't look at guards or hunters. Above all, freaks didn't invite attention by showing fear. Especially now, when it could cost him so much more than a beating. He tried to think of a way to warn Jake that right behind him stood the only person in the whole camp, maybe in the whole world, who could hurt Jake.

If Jake was punished because Tobias had contaminated him just by sitting next to him, dealing him cards, and reaching into the same bag of chips, Tobias didn't know how he would ever be able to look at Jake again.

Maybe that was why Jake had been tense and unhappy before. Tobias hadn't seen any welts, scars, burns, cuts, bruises, or even the stiffness that he got sometimes after a beating or other punishment, but that didn't mean it hadn't happened.

Maybe if Jake hit Tobias now, treating him like a monster deserved, he would be safe, and Leon Hawthorne wouldn't take his disgust out on his son.

"Tobias, what's wrong?" Jake reached for his shoulder.

Tobias pulled away, afraid of Jake's father seeing the way Jake touched him—gently, kindly, without pain. Only then did it occur to him that he should have flinched.

"Your father," Tobias whispered, keeping his eyes locked on his hands and the fallen cards. The jack of clubs looked up at him with one eye. "You can hit me if you—"

Jake swung around. "Dad! What are you doing here?"

Leon Hawthorne's eyes shifted between his son and Tobias, the scowl never altering. "ASC's full of assholes."

"Yeah." Jake dragged out the word, like it was a basic fact that didn't require acknowledging. "But I thought you were in Special Research all day."

"The interrogation protocols are biased in favor of the fucking Dixons, and they're trying to tell me I have to come back another fucking time to finish my . . . research. I'm here to find someone whose ass I can shove those protocols in and see if they get as pissed as I am. What are you doing?"

Jake shrugged and gestured between him and Tobias. "Just talking." He straightened defensively. "It's research of my own. Can't I research while you do? It's the same thing, isn't it, you talking to monsters, me talking to Tob—other monsters?"

Tobias didn't look up, but he could feel Leon Hawthorne's eyes boring into his head. He hoped that maybe if he didn't move or speak, Leon would forget he had been there, contaminating his son.

Leon jerked his head. "Come on, pack your stuff."

Jake jumped up and scrambled to sweep up the deck of cards. His hands brushed Tobias's, and Tobias jumped. "We're leaving? New hunt?"

"No, we're not leaving, but you're not staying here."

Jake paused in the act of shoving cards and wrappers into his duffel. "Dad, if we're not leaving . . ."

"You should learn how this shit Dixon administration works." When Jake didn't move, Leon took a step closer. "Jake, you're coming with me *now.*"

Jake straightened like he'd been slapped, but his expression was still sullen, angry. "Yes, sir."

He continued packing up, but more slowly. Tobias was glad that anger had never been directed at him, and he marveled at Jake's bravery, that he could be angry toward a hunter like his father. Maybe it was something that came with being a real person, or maybe it was just Jake.

"*Now*, Jake," Leon said.

"I'm coming already." Jake zipped the duffel closed and swung it over his shoulder. "See you later, Toby."

"No, you won't," Leon said, and Tobias felt his lungs seize up for the second time that day.

But Jake didn't even flinch. "Well, maybe not today." He glanced at Tobias, but the next words were still directed at Leon. "But I'll be back sometime."

If anything, Leon's scowl deepened. "Come on."

"Toby needs to—" Jake began, but his father cut him off.

"The freak can find his own way back to the yard. *Go*, Jake."

Jake was sullen and pissed off, but to Tobias's surprise he didn't look afraid. "Yes, sir," he muttered, and walked past his father deeper into Administration.

Tobias expected Leon to follow, but he stood there looking at Tobias, long enough to stop his breath in his chest.

Just when Tobias had resigned himself to being whipped—at least beaten or kicked a couple of times—Leon Hawthorne turned and strode off after Jake.

Tobias breathed a sigh of relief and stole out of Administration, careful not to let anyone else see him.

ON ANY GIVEN OCTOBER 30TH, if the Hawthornes weren't on a hunt or in the hospital, they found themselves in a bar.

This year it was the Crossroads Inn, and Leon was halfway to drunk on the hardest whiskey he could buy.

Leon was an old-school hunter, an ex-Marine who had entered the great fight against inhuman threats after his wife died at the turning point of the war, when the things crawling in the dark suddenly came into the light. He was a hard man to get to know—he had few friends, and those he had he tended to piss off—but everyone knew that with a weapon in his hand, Leon Hawthorne was one of the most frightening things the monsters would ever see.

Jerry Bentham took a seat next to the hero and bought him a few rounds of drinks. It was an honor. And, drunk enough, perhaps Leon might let slip some secrets, some insights that—beside his ruthless obsession—had made him the best.

"Where's your boy?" Bentham asked, gesturing for another pair of whiskeys. "He's, what, fourteen, fifteen now?"

Leon gave a bark of laughter. "Almost seventeen and growing like a goddamn beanstalk. He was here, you saw him. Left with a girl."

Bentham blinked. He'd noticed the kid who had a couple of drinks with Hawthorne and then left with the hot blonde on his arm. He hadn't looked twenty-one, but he sure as hell hadn't looked sixteen. Sixteen was the age of high school drama and pimples, not that cold-eyed assessment of the room and the brazen confidence in his smile at the girl.

"Damn, Hawthorne, you've got a good kid there. Lucky all the way around. I've even heard you've reserved yourself a damn fine piece of monster ass. Good stuff."

Leon's eyes were no longer muzzy, but startled and dangerous. "Monster ass? What the fuck are you talking about?"

Bentham tensed. He didn't know what Hawthorne was reacting to—he'd heard the guy could get damn right sanctimonious if rubbed the wrong way—so he proceeded carefully. "There's a kid at the freak facility. They call him . . ." *Baby Freak,* yeah, not going there. "89UI . . . something like that. I've heard that you've . . . you know, shown an interest."

Hawthorne snorted. "Oh, *Tobias.*"

That surprised Bentham. Most hunters, if they called the freaks anything, used the guards' nicknames. "You know his name?"

"Jake talks about him." Hawthorne scowled. "Don't know what he sees in the freak, no matter how human it looks. If I had my way, I'd put a bullet, stake, or a fucking axe through every one and leave 'em for the turkey vultures."

"So," Bentham said slowly, "you don't care about the kid? You don't have . . . a plan for him?"

"What the hell would I do with a monster? All these fucks who want to study them, want to get close to them, make my skin crawl. Right up there with perverts who get off on little kids." Hawthorne threw back the latest shot. "I see a freak, I kill it. End of story."

Bentham was relieved he hadn't talked more about the freak. If Hawthorne hadn't gutted him for implying he was fucking a monster . . . well, the guy clearly didn't share any of the private interests Bentham held in common with some of the camp guards.

But this opened up opportunities for guys like his friend Victor. And maybe for himself, if he played his cards right.

"So you don't have any interest in that damn monster," Bentham repeated, just to be safe. "It's just your kid, Jake?"

Hawthorne nodded. "And he'd better fucking grow out of his stupid obsession before he gets himself killed. I keep telling him."

Bentham ordered another shot and somberly clinked glasses with the hero. "Here's hoping."

TOBIAS HAD ONLY BEEN in the library for half an hour that morning, researching accounts of international crop circle activity and their relative connection to recorded demon activity outside the North American continent, when Victor appeared in the doorway.

"This is a special day for you, Baby Freak." He twirled in his hand an ugly, heavy lead line—the kind they used to drag big, defiant monsters around.

Tobias went very still before he tucked his paper into the book and closed it, so carefully it made no noise. He pushed the book to the center of the table with both hands, then stood up and kept his eyes on the floor as he walked over to the guard.

"Hands out."

Tobias extended his wrists, keeping them limp as Victor slid the zip tie cuffs over them and yanked them tight.

But when Victor clipped the stiff lead line onto his collar, Tobias's well-honed composure broke. The floor tilted underneath him, his vision swam until he closed his eyes, and an audible keen—that he knew was a mistake, he could have told any other monster that—rose through his throat. When Victor gave the line its first jerk, his legs almost gave way.

"Aw, what's wrong?" He tugged again, and Tobias nearly

stumbled against him, just catching himself in time. "Not used to being on a leash? You've been pretty privileged until now, haven't you? Our little spoiled monster. Those days are over, freak. No more special treatment."

Tobias could barely walk out of the room. The lead provided no slack, just a few links between the snap hook and stiff metal rod, enough for it to rotate in the guard's grip. He couldn't remember the last time he was put on a leash. It might have been when he first arrived, but that was so long ago, he barely remembered anything of those days. Even Becca's face was dim.

Now, with Victor ruthlessly yanking him along, shoving him ahead an extra step or hauling him back, all of Tobias's coordination was off. He stumbled repeatedly into doorways and walls, despite all the times he'd watched monsters on leashes and thought how they should just cooperate to make things easier. There wasn't any way to make it easier. He'd never been so conscious of his collar—not since he'd been fitted for a new one a few years ago—but now it seemed to shrink around his neck. He would be strangled before they got to wherever Victor was taking him.

And where else could they be headed but Special Research?

Tobias had last seen Jake two weeks ago. Jake, who had given him a sandwich and then found him a bottle of good, cold water from inside Reception. Who had smiled at him so openly, gently, looking fully relaxed again, and hadn't hesitated to brush Tobias's hair out of his eyes and rest his hand on his shoulder. Jake hadn't known that would be the last time. Would he be upset when he next came and they told him 89UI6703 had expired? How long would it be before Jake forgot about him, about that pathetic little freak he used to visit?

Tobias's shoulder cracked hard into the next doorway, and he couldn't hold back a wretched moan that wasn't about the pain.

"Come on, freak, I ain't got all day," Victor snapped, hauling him forward. Tobias lost his footing, slamming to the floor. Though the leash jerked in Victor's grip, Tobias's weight still caught on his collar before he struck the floor with his forearms, and he choked, struggling to breathe, before Victor hauled him up again.

Tobias's legs nearly gave out again when they reached the stairs at the end of the corridor, but Victor made him go first, holding him steady enough with the lead line that even when Tobias would have lost his balance, he couldn't fall forward.

At the first-floor landing, instead of turning for the door to outside and across the yard to Special Research, Victor dragged him deeper into Administration. Tobias couldn't make sense of it, but his feet kept stumbling along.

Then Victor stopped, jerking him to a halt, and swung open one of the steel doors—solid but for a small window set at the height of a man's face—before pushing him inside, where Crusher and a hunter were waiting.

This was Tobias's first time in an interrogation room.

"Took you long enough," Crusher said. Tobias's eyes had dropped to the floor, fixing on the hunter's steel-tipped boots the moment he crossed the threshold, but he didn't need to look up to know how Crusher was staring at him.

"Yeah, the freak isn't too used to being on a leash." Victor unclipped him, and Tobias didn't move.

Crusher barked a laugh. "Well, he's gonna get used to it now."

The hunter moved closer, walking around Tobias. "This is Baby Freak?"

"Yep," Victor said. "He's been here a long time, he's very well-trained. Ain't ya, freak? Have a seat."

Tobias moved stiffly, but without pause, sitting on the rusty metal folding chair. His mind wasn't quite blank enough not to notice the brown stains on the seat nor recognize they weren't rust.

Victor propped his ass on the corner of the table, leaning over Tobias. "Hands up on the table."

They felt like someone else's hands, not his at all, but he had no choice but to obey. He told them to move, and the numb, foreign hands came to rest on the table.

"No." Crusher thumped his club down in the middle of the table, next to a set of metal cuffs bolted there. "Here."

Tobias swallowed, then stretched his arms farther out, placing his wrists in the cuffs. Crusher snapped the bolts into place, then leaned over, setting his club under Tobias's chin to tilt his face up. "My, my," he whispered. "I thought I'd never see this day."

Victor rolled out a set of knives—all different types, including silver, iron, bronze, and something that looked like black glass—tucked neatly into a cloth, onto the table. He plucked one out, twirling it once before setting it to Tobias's cheek, just under his eye, and trailed it down across his lips, to under his chin.

"So, Baby Freak. Exactly what kind of monster are you?"

Tobias's heart rate jumped to a thunderous pace, but he fought to have no reaction, fought to give Victor nothing that he could latch onto, no reaction that would guide the knife. He fought to think of everything—his eyes, his nose, his lips—as unimportant, so that maybe Victor would pass them over, would just . . . stop.

Tobias focused hard enough that the room went gray, that his heart seemed distant and unimportant, that even the guard's words and questions became distant and unimportant. *This is a good place,* he thought. *I might save something for Jake if I can just. Stay. Here.*

It was a good place, the safest place he could be. And when the screaming started, he barely recognized it as his own.

[illegible] on the corner of the [illegible] Tobias. [illegible] the table.

[illegible] hands [illegible] money. He told [illegible] to move, and [illegible] to the right.

[illegible] dumped [illegible] down in the middle of the table [illegible]

Tobias swallowed, [illegible] placing his [illegible] in the cuffs [illegible] the hole into [illegible]

[illegible]

PART II

CHAPTER SEVEN

WINTER 1997–1998

ONE YEAR *later*

When the gate between Special Research and Intensive Containment swung open and a new shipment of monsters stumbled into the yard, dazed and blinking, Tobias was blindingly, selfishly grateful. Fresh meat, unmarked by the abuse and hardships of Freak Camp, always pulled the guards' attention away from their favorite targets, at least for a while.

Winter was a bad time for fresh meat to learn the rules of Freak Camp. The excruciating summer heat dropped even the hardier monsters when forced to stand outside for hours in the middle of the day. But the winters, in Tobias's view, were far worse.

In November, most monsters got an extra pair of clothes—heavy canvas pants and ragged jackets—to wear over their usual grays. They were supposed to get a second blanket when temperatures dropped below freezing, and a third when it went below zero, but that didn't always happen, especially if a monster wasn't as cooperative as the guards liked. Some of them knew how to pay for one in the alley between the barracks if a guard was interested.

Until last winter, Tobias had always gotten his extra blankets without any issues. He was quiet, he made no trouble, never snarled or tried to get away when the guards grabbed him. Plus, with the Hawthornes visiting the camp as regularly as they did and Jake always making a point of seeking him out, Tobias understood he had a thin shield about him, an invisible Keep Off sign.

A year ago, something had changed. That was when he'd been taken in for his first interrogation. He couldn't figure out why, despite all the sleepless nights, but the Keep Off sign had vanished. The guards had decided it was open season on Tobias, and not just for interrogations.

There were downsides to new monster arrivals. It got tiresome watching them make the same mistakes, learn the same painful lessons, that every new batch of monsters suffered. Tobias thought he could give an instructive half-hour—no, even ten-minute—orientation that would have saved them a significant amount of blood and skin. But the guards would never have allowed it, because they enjoyed the breaking-in process. New monsters screamed in ways no one else did because they still carried those notes of outrage and shock.

After Becca and then Marco disappeared, Tobias had learned not to get close to any other monster, not when they would be heading to Special Research tomorrow or the next day, and in the meantime they would likely slit his throat to get the last bite of his bread. Tobias didn't trust any of them, no matter how nice they tried to play. If he ignored them long enough, one day he'd look around and they wouldn't be anywhere. Sometimes they lasted a few years, but no one was there who had been around the same time as Becca. Most of the guards came and went the same way, with just a handful sticking around year after year. Those veterans and Tobias were the constants of Freak Camp. All the other monsters flashed through like the desert rains that faded into the air above the parched earth, the grimy concrete, and bloodstained dirt of Freak Camp: fleeting, faceless, and forgotten.

Tobias had had years of practice detaching himself from the new monsters' screams and sobs. He only felt irritation because they didn't even know how bad it was going to get. They were just so *stupid* and weak, and he often wished the guards would hit them harder to get the point across, or that they'd just hurry up and die already.

But he hadn't had much experience getting used to the sounds of a small girl sobbing.

She had been one of the last to appear in the yard, tiny wrists bound with thick rope threaded with silver. Her brown eyes had been enormous in her pale face, streaked with tear tracks and dirt, and her brown hair still looked shiny and soft, like it had been well-cared for. She was smaller and younger than Tobias could remember any other monster here, and he heard someone nearby—he didn't know or care who—swear softly.

"What is she, seven?"

Tobias didn't know. He didn't have much experience guessing ages—there wasn't any point to it. Jake had told him when his birthday was, occasionally reminded him how old he was now, and Tobias listened and remembered because it was important to Jake. So he knew that he was thirteen now (and Jake would turn eighteen in just a couple of months). According to his entry date in his ID number, he'd been in Freak Camp since he was five. If the other monster was right and this new monster girl was seven, that wasn't so bad. If he'd made it, she had a chance . . . for what? To last longer for Crusher to have his fun? Tobias's mouth twisted, and he turned away, tried to forget he had ever seen her.

It was just his luck, of course, that she ended up in the barracks near him, just a few bunk beds away, in one that had been vacated a week or so ago. Since she was a shapeshifter, she had the shiny new green bracelet shot between the bones of her forearm.

Maybe she was still crying from the shock of that pain, but Tobias thought the cold was more likely. Karl had announced there was a blanket shortage and decided that since the new monster girl (the guards hadn't decided on a nickname yet) was so small, she could double hers up as two. Like two helped when the water in the pipes had frozen.

Tobias's blanket was coarse but thick. He couldn't remember when he'd learned how to wrap whatever fabric he was given around himself as tight as possible with no holes, with his nose and mouth inside to keep the warm breath trapped, and to rub his hands, arms, and legs together as long as he could to generate warmth. This would be one of the lessons of his orientation, if they'd let him have one. He didn't think the girl would be able to listen and understand, though. Not tonight.

So he burrowed deeper, tried to wipe out everything he was hearing—but it wasn't just the girl's steady, predictable tears. Other monsters were muttering and hissing, angry, like they had a right to peace and quiet and a good night's sleep. *Ha.*

Then there was a wet shredding sound, followed by the smack of something hitting the concrete floor. Louder groans filled the barracks, and it didn't take long before Tobias could smell the discarded skin, tissue, and fluids coming from the girl's bunk. She was shifting her skin, using her one power as though it could take away the pain or get her out.

Tobias closed his eyes and breathed out. If everyone would just shut up, he'd be able to block everything out and get to sleep.

But clearly that wasn't going to happen, especially as a second wet *plop* sounded and the pitch of the girl's sobs changed again. The older inmates' snarls grew more threatening, with mutters like *I'll get up and take care of this myself,* and the newer ones complained in loud, querulous protests that illustrated how little they understood: *Fucking ridiculous, why doesn't someone stop her or do something?*

Tobias gritted his teeth, rolling over. He knew exactly how this would go: someone would get up to "take care" of this, someone else would rise to argue about what form of violence to take, and within seconds, the lights would be glaring and the guards would be filling the room with their clubs to smack around all the monsters, both standing and prone, and no one would get any sleep that night. Maybe the guards would come in anyway to see who was crying, what shifter was violating the rules about keeping a single form, and give her something to really cry about.

There were only a few ways to avoid that outcome, and fewer still were in his power. Trying to talk or yell at other monsters only made himself a target—why would they trust *him*, even when he had the earliest ID number of anyone in the camp—and he'd probably end up attracting the guards' attention first when they showed up. The monster girl was not likely to stop crying soon, even with all the threats coming her way—unless she was given a reason.

Tobias swore again silently, then rolled off his bunk, jumping to the floor and clutching his blanket around him. He walked down the row of bunk beds, ignoring the taunts thrown his way. He stopped before the girl's cot, ignoring the piles of stinking shifter skin at his feet. A slightly bigger frame now huddled beneath the thin blanket, and he could barely make out the glint of watery blue eyes peeking out at him.

Pulling the blanket from his shoulders, he dropped it on top of her and said, "Stop crying."

The barracks fell silent.

She had stopped midbreath, staring at him in astonishment. Tobias waited to see if she would start bawling again. He wasn't sure what he'd do if she did, but he didn't think hitting her would make her stop. But she didn't make another sound, and neither did any of the other monsters who had been snarling and grumbling seconds before.

Now the only problem left was the cold numbing his fingers and toes.

Tobias turned away from the girl, his own bunk, and all the monsters' eyes on him, to walk to the door.

He knew someone was watching the camera set in the upper corner of the barracks. If a guard wasn't already on his way because of the girl, they'd be there fast enough since he'd tripped the motion sensor that activated at curfew. No one cared, though, as long as the monsters stayed in Head Alley.

A moment later, the door buzzed under his hand, and he pushed it open. Victor stood outside, bundled in his padded jacket and gloves. "Well, well. What does Pretty Freak want?"

Tobias said, "I need more blankets." He tried to hold still, not to shiver too visibly. At least the wind wasn't cutting between the barracks.

Victor sighed loudly. "But we gave you yours. What happened? Didn't you take care of it?"

Tobias didn't budge. "I'll pay."

Victor threw his head back and laughed. "Ain't you greedy?"

Sure, Tobias thought. *Whatever.* He didn't expect Victor to turn him down. But the guard wouldn't make it easy for him either.

Victor sauntered farther into the alley, into the shadows between the buildings and the one blind spot between cameras. He leaned against the aluminum siding behind him, his feet in a wide stance, and he unbuckled his belt. "Get on with it."

Tobias dropped to his knees.

Afterward Victor sighed. "Wait there, freak. I'll see what we've got."

Tobias didn't react, not even to the suggestion he would get nothing for his trouble. He knew better than to even think of any threats if Victor never came back with anything. There wasn't anything he could do—except hope that if he stayed where he was without moving, soon he wouldn't feel the cold or anything at all.

Victor did come back, though. He tossed down two ratty blankets, showing holes big enough for Tobias to put his head through.

Tobias didn't feel anything at the loss of the blanket quality he'd had before. He wasn't surprised. This was how it went in Freak Camp.

Lesson number one of orientation: no matter how bad you thought it was, life always got worse. The longer you stayed alive, the worse it would get.

Jake had made him a promise more than three years ago now, and Tobias wouldn't lose faith in him—because he was Jake, he would eventually come to get Tobias out—but Tobias didn't expect to make it that long. Even so, he had to keep trying to stay alive. If he gave up, it was like saying he didn't believe or trust Jake, and he did, more than any other truth of Freak Camp that he knew in his bones.

He still had Jake's visits. They weren't as frequent as they used to be, but Jake always looked glad to see him. As Tobias got older, he was more and more at a loss to understand *why* Jake cared about him, why he was different to Jake from any other monster. He couldn't spend time questioning it, though. It was, had always been, the only thing that made Tobias's life remotely worthwhile. You didn't question what you were afraid of losing, what you feared more than anything else that might happen to you. You just had to accept it and hope: *tomorrow, perhaps tomorrow, he will come again.*

Tobias got up slowly, staggering more than once at the pain he finally felt in his knees, and he turned to trudge back inside, blankets in hand.

JAKE DID NOT COME the next day. Instead, during breakfast, Tobias found the shapeshifter girl inching closer to him on the bench. He ignored her until she said, "I'm Kayla."

I don't want to know your name, Tobias nearly said. *You were luckier than you can imagine, but you're going to get hurt soon, and bad. They usually go for the girls before the boys. I don't think you're going to last long, and I don't want to know your name.*

But he didn't say any of that, because it wouldn't have helped anything. He couldn't remember what Becca had told him in the beginning, how she had made him understand. "Tobias," he said at last, because there was no harm in telling her his name. It was better than what everyone else—everyone besides Jake—called him.

She scooted closer, nearly touching his side now, right there in the hall where everyone could see. Tobias moved away. "Don't." Then, because he couldn't help himself, and maybe this was a chance someone would actually listen to him: "You can't let them know what you care about or want."

She stared at him, too shocked and bewildered to even show hurt. Something in her eyes looked raw and naked, and Tobias looked away. He didn't like it. It made him feel things, things he hadn't felt since Becca was around, and they would only get him hurt worse in the end.

He shut down the thought of Becca as he had every time she'd come to mind over the last year, since he'd learned to survive as Pretty Freak.

If this shapeshifter girl could understand even a little how Freak Camp worked, there wouldn't be any more scenes like last night. Maybe she wouldn't be among those broken in—one fewer monster he'd have to hear screaming.

So he leaned forward, elbows on his knees, looking down at the table so no one could tell he was talking to her, and spoke. "I mean it. You can't let any of them know what you want, or they'll take it away and use it against you. Don't trust any of the other monsters, no matter how nice they act—they aren't your friends, they're just using you for whatever they can get, and they don't care what happens to you. You shouldn't trust me either. Monsters don't have friends, especially not in Freak Camp.

"You can't fight any of the guards. Don't try, and don't even think about questioning or arguing. Just do what they say, give them what they want. It'll be worse otherwise." He stopped there, before the wealth of details he could have given her on what to do when they decided they wanted her body. Crusher probably would first. He liked those that seemed most helpless, innocent, most likely to squirm. But Tobias couldn't tell her about that. It wasn't a mercy or kindness, but he wouldn't do it. Hopefully when the time came, she'd remember his advice about not fighting, and they wouldn't bring out the silver nails.

Kayla said nothing. Tobias chanced a sideways glance at her from under his hair.

She had bent her head down, like him, and was picking at her fingernail. "Where'd you get the blankets last night?"

Tobias shifted, but he made it look like he was just moving as he ate. Never a good idea for the guards to get interested in the conversation of a couple of monsters. "I paid for them."

She kept staring, though not as directly as before. "With what? Do you have money?"

Tobias resisted the urge to bury his face in his hands, to block out her eyes and the mess hall. What could he tell her? Should he tell this frightened girl about blowing Crusher when it looked like what he really wanted to do was cut his name into your back with a silver knife? Should he tell her what Victor liked him to do with his tongue or what to say to Karl to get him hard?

He risked a glance at her, into her clear, pretty eyes—*not even her eyes, she's a shifter, remember*—and knew he couldn't. Becca hadn't told him, though looking back, he knew now where all those extra meals and blankets had come from.

But he wouldn't lie to Kayla either. Pretending it would get better would just kill her faster.

"We don't have money here," he said. "I . . . do things for the guards."

She hesitated. "Like . . . chores, or . . ."

Tobias shook his head. "No, no, I do things . . . the others call me whore."

The other monsters always filled the word with enough venom that he'd twitch in response, but not just because of the word. It was because of the threat and loathing in their voices. He wasn't sure if they were simply jealous of the skills that earned him his extra blanket and food, or if what he did really was that bad. If in the real world it was really that horrifying and shameful to say yes to the guards—when it was that or getting forced to do it anyway, with a lot more pain—or to ask for it when he could feel himself starving after a day without food.

Head Alley was just a dark corner where they pushed Tobias down and unzipped their pants. By the time he got there the negotiations were over, the bargaining was done, and he no longer had the option of talking his way out of putting out. He just had to hope they kept up their end of the deal.

Most did. It meant the freaks worked harder for what they wanted.

All the monsters got fucked one way or another, but the others hated him for how easily he complied. A real wouldn't do that. The other monsters still often thought they were reals, or better than reals.

How different it must be to have the luxury to think you deserved more than pain, and death, and shame. He hated them sometimes, that they could think themselves worthy of being human. Then again, he had seen that belief break them over and over, and he was still alive.

"Does it hurt?" she asked.

Not always, Tobias thought. *Not now that I know what to do.* "Yes, it hurts," he said. "But it hurts more if you fight. They hurt you more," *and enjoy it more,* "if you fight."

Tobias saw the vampire coming out of the corner of his eye and braced himself, but Kayla jumped when the vampire shoved Tobias into the table.

It hurt, the unyielding metal grinding against his ribs, but it didn't do damage. Celler knew better than to injure Tobias seriously while Crusher and Lonny Fitzpatrick (who didn't like getting sucked, but liked to watch) were guarding the mess hall. Celler's jaw had been permanently wired together after the second time he'd managed to get out of his muzzle. He'd gotten his longer nickname Cellulitis from the raw, red way his skin looked from frying in the sun. (The guard who had named him had transferred to Special Research soon after. Victor scoffed that "the young punk was too smart to be stuck herding the general freaks.")

"Found yourself a pet, whore?" Celler mumbled. Because of the way they'd wired his vampire fangs to his human teeth, and then to his lower jaw, every word had to fight its way through two layers of clenched teeth. He got his ration of blood intravenously when the werewolves came back from Intensive Containment—if he'd been "good." The borderline starvation made him even nastier than vamps usually were because of the sun char. "She pay you back yet for last night?"

Tobias wished Kayla would stop flinching. Movements like that drew more attention from the nasties, whether that was monsters like Celler or humans like the guards. He kept his focus split between the vamp and Crusher, who watched from his position leaning against the wall.

"Maybe you just like to put out. Is that it, Pretty Freak?"

Celler slid a hand over Tobias's shoulders. "If you're so hot to hit your knees, why don't you buy us all feather quilts? I could hold you down."

Tobias suspected that Celler was just envious. Vamps couldn't bargain with their mouths, and unless they could offer a particularly competitive handjob, the other kind of fucking always hurt worse.

Tobias waited until the hand reached his collarbone—no way was he letting a vamp get a grip on his throat; he'd seen shifters with their throats ripped out while a vampire held their mouth under the wound so the lifeblood would seep through the muzzle. Then Tobias slammed his head and body backwards as hard as he could, unbalancing Celler and loosening his grip. Tobias knocked him to the floor with a quick thrust of his elbow.

Celler was up almost instantly, hiss-whining through his teeth—what would have been a scream of rage for any other monster—but by that time, the guards had decided to notice. When Celler went for Tobias's throat, Crusher was there.

The first blow of Crusher's club against the back of Celler's head echoed with a wet crack through the mess hall and slammed the vamp's head into Tobias's shoulder. Celler collapsed bonelessly to the floor, where he whimpered through his wired jaw and twitched his limbs. The next three unnecessary blows silenced the moans.

"You fucking with my freak, sucker?" Crusher panted. "He's too pretty for you. You know what might fuck you? I think I once saw a bulldog ugly enough to fuck your ugly face."

Celler scrabbled against the floor, arms and legs not quite working right, and Crusher kicked him. "Fucking get up, Celler. You're in the walkway. Or do you want me to get you up?"

The vampire dragged himself beneath a bench, tucking his arms and legs beneath the table. It seemed to be enough.

Tobias was expecting it, but Crusher's punch still slammed

his face into the table. "You wanna fuck a bloodsucker, Pretty Freak? You rolling that slut tongue at him?"

"No, sir," Tobias said to the table.

Crusher clenched his fingers in Tobias's hair and jerked his head up, arcing his neck back. "What you say, freak?"

"No, sir. I'm not going to let them fuck me, sir." *Not going to let anyone, anyone . . .*

Crushed pulled his face close. "You're waiting for me, aren't you? I'm gonna be the first cock in your ass." He shrugged. "Maybe second. Don't care if Hawthorne goes first. Long as you scream for me. And you will scream for me, won't you?"

"Yes, sir," Tobias said.

"Think Hawthorne will want to watch while I make you scream, Pretty Freak?"

Tobias kept his breathing even. It wasn't like Crusher hadn't said it before. "I don't know, sir."

"You think I should ask—"

"Crusher!"

Tobias didn't relax as the guard turned away. If Crusher noticed, he would take it as a challenge.

"What?" Crusher snapped at Lonny.

Lonny jerked his head around the room, where some monsters were taking advantage of Crusher's distraction to huddle and mutter together. "Focus!"

Crusher snorted and muttered under his breath about fucking spoilsports, but he let go of Tobias's hair after one more slam down into the table. "Don't let it happen again, freak."

Tobias looked for Kayla after Crusher was far enough away that he couldn't interpret it as some kind of disrespect. She had slunk away in the confusion so quietly that neither he nor Crusher had noticed. Tobias found her two tables away, eyes down.

Smart girl, Tobias thought, even though he didn't want to. He didn't want to give a damn about anyone in Freak Camp but himself. *Maybe you'll learn fast enough to survive.*

He wasn't sure if that was a good thing.

THAT NIGHT, after evening roll call, Tobias got back into the barracks just in time to see Celler filching his blanket.

For a second, a small, weak, irrational part of him thought, *it's not fucking fair*—stupid, useless thought; he was a monster, and life wasn't supposed to be fair to him. That was quickly swallowed by rage.

Hell no, I paid *for that.*

"Put it back!" He picked up his stride. Celler wasn't going to give it back, Tobias knew that.

The vamp laughed through his wiry smile. "Buy another one, whore."

Tobias hit him with all his weight, putting a little extra speed into the battering ram motion while the bastard was distracted. Tobias clawed for his eyes, and the vampire flinched back. Of course he did—Tobias could never hope to match the reflexes of an identified supernatural, but he had been fighting other freaks his entire life, maybe even before Celler had become a vamp. Tobias didn't catch the eyes, but instead caught his fingers in the wire around both sets of Celler's teeth. He jerked the vampire's head sideways and down and heard his neck crack—snapping bones Crusher had missed earlier. He forced Celler's head down, his other hand wrenching at the blanket in the vamp's grip.

Celler snarled, twisted, and managed to kick Tobias's feet out from under him, but Tobias jerked hard on the vampire's shoulder and arm as he fell, throwing him over his own body and headfirst into another bunk bed before he hit the concrete floor.

The spectators screamed, snarled, and swore. Someone was wailing about the guards coming at any moment ("*Oh, stop, please stop!*"), but all Tobias really cared about was that Celler still had his blanket.

A smart freak would have let it go, but the thing was, he really couldn't buy another one. Sure, Victor liked Tobias's mouth, but he liked variety too, and Tobias had a good instinct for when Victor wanted him on his knees and when he wanted him on a cutting table. If Tobias tried to get *another* blanket, Victor would get his blow, and Tobias would get another interrogation, if he got anything at all.

So he ignored the way his back ached from hitting the concrete and launched himself at Celler. They tumbled together into another row of monsters, and soon enough everyone was doing their best to rip each other's throats out.

In the chaos, Celler and a couple of other vamps—vampires stuck together, even when they hated each other; it was some kind of nest-bonding instinct and tended to get them in trouble—managed to pin Tobias to the floor, the very blanket he had been fighting for pinning his arms down. Celler knelt on him, knees digging under Tobias's ribs.

"We're gonna *bleed* you," he growled, sinking his fingers into Tobias's throat under his collar. "Then I'm going to bleed *into* you, you little cocksucker. Wanna be a vamp like me? Wanna burn like me? Let's see how much shit you get when they wire that pretty mouth shut."

Tobias bucked beneath the vampires, almost blanking out from panic. Celler couldn't, he couldn't take away Tobias's only bargaining skill, couldn't make Tobias one of them. *They'll kill you*, he thought frantically. *You can't, they'll kill you if you bleed me.*

As a vampire, Tobias would have nothing, less than nothing. In Freak Camp, vamps were in constant pain from the sun, never had enough blood to fill them, and could survive incredible amounts of damage without dying, without *ever* dying. Tobias remembered one vampire woman, how the guards had—

Tobias's mind shied away (*that could be you, under Crusher*). He could imagine very few things worse than being stripped of the surety of death.

There was only one thing worse.

Jake couldn't ever take a vampire out of Freak Camp. Not even Jake could do that, even if he's stupid enough to want to.

Tobias struggled and fought harder than he ever could or would against the guards, he snarled every curse and threat he'd ever heard, he jerked his arms and legs in their grips until his sockets ached, but the vamps had the numbers and the advantage.

Then Kayla jumped on Celler's back and sank her teeth into his shoulder.

Celler jerked back, knocking off another vampire, and suddenly Tobias had leverage to claw and kick the other vampires aside.

Then the vents slapped shut—the last warning before gas came hissing into the barracks to knock them out.

The monsters noticed. In the ensuing panic, Tobias wheeled to Kayla and grabbed her by the shoulders.

She almost punched him in the face, but hesitated when she realized it was him.

Don't hesitate, Tobias thought. *Don't trust that just because it's me, I won't hurt you. Don't trust that just because it's my face, it's me.*

"Hide," he snapped. "Now. Don't come out."

She stared. "But you're—"

"Don't let them see you, do what I say, hide *now.*" Tobias shoved her roughly toward a bunk bed and spun just in time to catch a clawed hand before it ripped open his face. He hoped she had listened to him. Becca had always had him hide under a bunk in the corner during brawls.

The guards burst in, clubbing down anything that moved

hard enough to break bone, and Tobias stopped fighting the second a guard appeared in front of him. Silas Dixon slammed his club into Tobias's diaphragm and dropped him to the floor, gasping. The other monsters—those that needed an extra blow to be incapacitated—had more than the breath knocked out of them.

The guards dragged them out to the yard. Tobias pushed aside his moment of relief that he didn't see Kayla among them.

When Tobias was chained to a whipping post, back-to-back with another monster so that all the brawlers could be strung up, he saw that Celler had both legs twisted at unnatural angles.

After stringing them up, the guards did a little more work on the instigators. Tobias got punched repeatedly in the stomach and across the face, and he could hear Celler making harsh, choking noises a few posts over.

The guards left them eventually. The icy wind cut through Tobias's thin clothes, and the only warmth came from the shifter chained at his back. Even the floodlights and stars Tobias could barely pick out in the dark night made it seem colder.

I hope dawn comes quickly, Tobias thought, hands numb. But he knew it wouldn't.

THE NEXT MORNING after roll call, all the combatants were whipped. Silas pushed Tobias's shirt up over his head (*"Can't scar that pretty mouth, can we?"*) without unchaining him.

After assembly and breakfast, the troublemakers were left on the whipping posts and the rest of the monsters from their barracks were herded back into lockdown and chained to their bunks, the same way they had spent the night after the fight. Tobias hoped the guards hadn't been taking their anger out on the other monsters. It would only make life that much harder if they wanted revenge.

Kayla found him days later, when he had finally gotten back the full use of his hands, though any kind of movement still set his back aflame in pain. She had a slightly different face, less pretty and innocent than her original one. Nothing the guards would notice and cut her open for, but Tobias saw and approved.

She sat next to him and didn't look at him—not directly, at least. Tobias caught quick, furtive glances his direction. That was okay. If anyone noticed, they'd think she was afraid, and fear was acceptable. Much safer, for both of them, if people thought that their relationship was based on fear and not on . . . whatever else it might be based on.

It was stupid to care about other monsters. He wasn't strong enough to be Becca, and he had no faith that this shifter girl would survive him. She was still fresh meat.

"I hid," she whispered.

"Good."

She shifted her plate slightly. She hadn't licked it clean. She should learn to do that soon. "You didn't say what I owe you. For the blanket."

"I didn't do it because I care," Tobias said harshly. He couldn't afford to care. And he didn't. He wouldn't. "The guards come in whenever someone's being noisy or shifting. Sometimes they just beat the shit out of the instigator, sometimes they chain everybody to the bed and—"

"Like lockdown," she said.

Tobias nodded.

"Still, you could have just hit me," she whispered.

Don't think about it. "Might not have worked."

"You told me to hide. You saved me again. What do I owe you? I know I do."

Tobias thought. He wanted to say it didn't matter—it disgusted him to think of taking anything from her, even her food—but it *did* matter. If she hadn't asked this, he would have just walked away and it would have been that much easier, later, to listen to her screaming under the guards. Easier when she started calling him *freak bitch* and *whore.*

Now he had to care, if only the same way he cared about anything that could keep him alive or kill him.

"We helped each other," he said at last. "I protected myself by giving you a blanket so you'd stop crying. You jumped Celler because of the blanket. I told you to hide because you jumped Celler."

Kayla looked like she knew he was giving her an easy deal. "I still owe you."

If not for you, I'd be a vamp right now. "We're not friends," Tobias told himself as much as her. "It's a mutually beneficial relationship." The big words helped him distance himself.

"What's that mean?"

"I help you, you help me. We keep owing each other favors."

"So . . . we keep helping, and it'll even out in the end?" Kayla asked, and he nodded. "I'll save you some day."

Tobias flinched. No one was saving anyone in Freak Camp. The only person who would ever save him—*maybe, possibly, please*—was Jake. "Whatever."

Tobias stared at his empty plate—the guards were taking their time kicking the monsters out of the mess hall today—until he came to a decision. If they were (*not friends*) combining resources to survive, he might as well tell her now. At least he might not have to hear her scream.

"When Crusher comes for you," he said, "don't fight, don't struggle, don't cry, don't make a sound. Sometimes if you're silent," *blank, absent,* "they get tired and they finish faster, they come back less often."

She stared. "Silent."

"It's best if you can blank out . . . separate . . . like you're not even there. So you don't have to think about it."

He couldn't read the expression in her shapeshifter eyes. She looked away, down, and nodded.

He hoped the things that kept him alive would help her as well. Only because she still owed him and it would be nice, however briefly, to have a monster willing to take his advice.

And maybe—*don't get your hopes up, Tobias, the fight was a one-time thing, she owed you*—to watch his back.

CHAPTER EIGHT

JANUARY–APRIL 1998

JAKE WOKE up the morning of his eighteenth birthday buzzing from the twin highs of monster asses kicked and pain medication. Yesterday had been his first truly independent hunt. Dad had been away on a job—one of the jobs that he wouldn't tell Jake about, muttering that it was something he had to do himself—so Jake handled it. Using public transport to get to the big, downtown library for research had been embarrassing, but it was all worth it for the adrenaline of the successful hunt.

Jake had called Dad before he went after the ogres, leaving a voicemail. If he didn't survive, Dad would know where he had gone and be able to take care of the problem after him.

He hadn't expected Dad to show up at the last minute to drag him away from the wreckage of the quaint little waterwheel—Jake was still appalled that of all the dark places the ogres could have settled, they chose a minigolf course—but it was okay that Dad had been there in the end, because Jake hadn't really needed him. Though he had to admit, it had been nice to ride away covered in a blanket in the front seat of the Eldorado rather than trying to wheedle his way onto a bus without getting an ambulance called on him.

Jake stretched experimentally to see what hurt, yawned, and blinked open his eyes, not sure he could trust them. Leon was sitting on the other bed, watching him with a thoughtful, almost soft look on his face.

"Hey, Dad," Jake croaked. He pulled himself up to lean against the headboard.

"Hey, Jake. Feeling okay?"

His head hurt, and his shoulder ached—not broken, thankfully—where he'd gotten smacked by a hamlike fist, and he had bruises everywhere (fucking golf-ball-throwing sons of bitches), but he felt good. Really good, on a level that had nothing to do with bruises and broken bones.

"Awesome," he said.

Leon looked down at his hands, and then back up. "You did good out there, son."

Jake blinked and grinned, a new kind of high burning through him. He knew he'd rocked that hunt—two dead monsters, no civilian casualties, and minimal collateral damage in the form of a minigolf course that looked like a tornado had ripped through it—but there was a world of difference between the satisfaction of a job well done and one of Dad's rare compliments.

"Thank you, sir."

Leon nodded. "Eighteen today."

Jake blinked. "Sir?" He had only killed the two monsters last night. Unless Dad was counting the ghosts he'd helped burn, in which case it was a hell of a lot more than eighteen.

Leon smiled at him, and Jake basked in the pride on his face, even if he still didn't understand. "You're eighteen. An adult."

"Oh. Yeah, I forgot, you know, with the hunt? But whatever. I can smoke, fuck, vote, and . . ." Jake smirked. "Dad, I'm already doing all of those that I want."

Leon laughed. "Yeah. Yeah, I know." He sighed. "Jake, I know

I've missed a lot of them, but happy birthday." He held out a thick letter and a hard-cover sunglass case.

Jake took both warily. He especially didn't like the look of that letter. It could have anything in it, from a new set of lock picks to a letter from Mom. Under Leon's eyes, he slit it open with his knife.

He read the papers, and then looked up, eyes wide. "You got me an ASC license?"

"Yeah." Leon's face broke into a broad smile. It looked strange on his usually tense, focused face. "I put in the paperwork for you months ago, way before this hunt. And then you just went out and *did* the job . . . I'm damn proud of you, Jake."

Jake looked down at the paper. Hawthornes, especially eighteen-year-old ones, did not tear up. "Thank you, sir."

"Go on, open the next one. I figured now that you're official, you might like some wheels."

Jake popped open the sunglass case. Yeah, a car would be damn nice sometimes, if only so he didn't have to ride the bus like a loser or try to walk home if he broke a bone or something on a hunt, but . . . he didn't really want a new car. Nothing would be as sweet as the Eldorado, and being in the Eldorado meant he was home, that Dad was back, and they would be okay. Even without Mom, even without food, even with Dad working his way through a bottle, it was home. Hard to give that up forever by opening a sunglass case with peeling faux leather.

And then his jaw dropped. He looked up and gaped, his mouth working, while Leon grinned at him.

"These are for the Eldorado!"

"You love that car," Leon said, then winked. "I know you'll keep the rust spots off her."

"Holy shit." Jake jumped off the bed and gave Leon a crushing hug. He couldn't remember the last time they had hugged, but it felt right when his dad had just given him the best gift possible.

When they broke away, Leon was still smiling and kept his hand on Jake's shoulder. "Knew I had to hand it over to you sooner or later, the way you love that car. I'd tell you to take good care of her, but I'm pretty sure you'll get her cleaned up before yourself."

Only later, after Jake had rushed out and turned the key in the Eldorado—which was *his,* all his—did it occur to him to wonder what Dad would be driving if Jake had the Eldorado.

A few months later, Jake found himself chasing ghosts in Massachusetts. Literally chasing ghosts, because there was some kind of stupid haunted livestock truck, and it was just so stupid.

And so far from Nevada.

He hated the truck too. Dad's big black truck. The truck that he used to disappear on Jake more often, getting farther and farther away. Sometimes he left a note, sometimes just a phone message a couple of days later. If Jake had known when Dad gave him the keys to the Eldorado that Dad would be gone *more,* that he would have such faith in Jake that he wouldn't even give him a heads-up before disappearing . . . Well, Jake didn't know that he would have thrown the keys back in Dad's face—damn, he loved this car—but he might have started researching ways to sabotage Silverados, Tundras, F-150s, and worked his way down the list. As it was . . . Fuck. Just fuck.

Black was fine, and Jake supposed that a truck was practical at least, and it had special iron/silver spiked bumpers and reinforced-steel sides and a fancy, mechanized artillery trunk—*how long were you planning this, Dad?*—but the Eldorado could take it in a knife fight any day.

Sometimes when he saw the hulking monster truck—for hunting monsters, haha, not funny—in the parking lot next to his, his damn Eldorado, he still had a half-smothered urge to slash the tires.

He knew he wasn't exactly being mature about this, but Jake was pissed, and when Dad wasn't there to be pissed *at,* it all just built up until Jake wanted to smash something. Preferably a certain fancy-ass piece of slag steel.

It wasn't until Dad was gone *again,* leaving Jake in another ass-backwards town without a single hot chick or dude, that Jake realized he didn't have to just sit where Dad had left him and mope and drink and fuck. He had the fucking Eldorado, and where there were roads he could drive them, and where there were bridges he could cross them. Leon fucking Hawthorne—who clearly didn't give a damn, who had his truck to keep him company—could find him if he wanted to. Dad could find anything.

Jake could drive anywhere. He could drive to Freak Camp and see Toby if he wanted to.

Like a silver bullet finding a werewolf's heart, that thought hit home. Jake grabbed the Eldorado's keys, paid the hotel bill—fake credit card again, Dad had taken most of the cash—and hit the road humming at the thought. *I can see Toby any time I want.*

Tobias was scrubbing fresh stains off the floor of the barrack showers—on his knees with a brush, the astringent cleaning solution stinging his hands, searing like acid in his fresh burns and cuts—when a guard walked in behind him. Tobias glanced back through his bangs, saw it was Crusher, and then focused on his job.

It was a bad place to be. Maybe Crusher would cut a deal, go for the blowjob, and Tobias wouldn't have to risk fighting him off. A handful of other guards were getting too close for comfort, but Crusher always had that edge of crazy that scared him in ways no one else did.

"Get up, Pretty Freak. Hawthorne wants you."

Tobias kept the first sharp rush of relief off his face. Relief so intense that his hands shook and he felt lightheaded. Crusher would see the shaking and think it was fear. Might even get off thinking about it later, with some other poor bastard mouthing his dick.

That image reminded Tobias of what he had done. Of all the times—

He didn't have to fake the sick look on his face when he stood up. How could he face Jake, look him in the eye (and Jake would tell him to look him in the eye, he always did, he'd always tilt Tobias's face up, so gently, the calluses on his fingers brushing down Tobias's jaw) when he had been about to blow Crusher to get out of a beating?

Tobias didn't want to go. For a breathless, insane second, he considered saying, "No, I won't see him," punching Crusher, running until they caught him and he fell beneath their clubs. Letting the pain and blood wash away the scalding shame that burned his insides worse than anything he'd swallowed. Better that than being in the same room with Jake, looking at Jake, contaminating the only good thing in his world with the filth he did every day and didn't even feel any more.

He couldn't do it. He couldn't walk into that room.

But running was suicide. Of all the ways Tobias could kill himself, saying no to a hunter was not the one he wanted to pick. They would probably just drag him to Jake anyway, dump him bleeding on the floor. They might apologize that Tobias couldn't suck Jake off with his jaw shattered like that, but at least he still had an ass, right?

That's all you need, Tobias, to make him happy.

Crusher pushed him out of the showers, and Tobias wiped his hands on his pants, wishing he could stop to wash the cleaner off before Jake—

Before Jake touched him. Every visit Jake touched him, whether on his arm, his face, or his shoulder, totally unlike the way anyone else here touched him. Soft, slow, not to hurt or hurry or because Tobias was looking at him wrong, but . . . Tobias didn't know why Jake touched him like that, but it was one of the things he couldn't stop thinking about. Couldn't stop craving.

Maybe Tobias wouldn't have to talk, wouldn't have to say anything. Maybe today was the day Jake would turn him over the table and take him—no preliminaries, no gentle questions, no smiles, no jokes that Tobias didn't quite understand but laughed at anyway. Maybe today Jake would grind his face into the table and pull his pants down, and Tobias's meager, pathetic dreams would die in the feel of Jake forcing his way inside him.

Shit, he should believe that. He should remember what he was—a worthless monster, a freak with only one use for his mouth—and he should not believe that nothing with Jake could hurt that badly. That Jake would never hurt him.

Of course, it would hurt. Tobias had been in the room enough times when the guards bent over some guy unwilling or unable to wheedle out of it, and he knew that it would hurt like hell, that he would bleed, probably scream, maybe not get up afterward if Jake was too rough. But he still wanted that. He wanted it to be *Jake* because Jake would be touching him then, holding his shoulders while he forced his way in, maybe holding Tobias there after he was done instead of dropping him or telling him to pull his damn pants up and get out of his sight. Nothing Jake did to him could be that bad if Jake really wanted it.

Better Jake than any guard, any other hunter. Better that Jake got the last part of Tobias that hadn't gone through a dozen hands before someone else took it. Otherwise Tobias would have nothing left to offer. Jake could have anything—why would he want what everyone else had used and cast aside?

By the time Tobias crossed the yard, he was calm, almost hopeful. Of everyone in Tobias's world, Jake was the only one who could rattle him, could send him from horror, to despair, to . . . something like contentment in the time it took to walk from one end of FREACS to the other. He wanted Jake. He wanted Jake to do anything he wanted to him. Hunter or no, real or no, Jake was the best thing in his world. Any day he saw Jake was a good day in Tobias's book. That would be true no matter how it ended.

Then Victor smiled at him when he got to Reception, and his stomach dropped again.

"Here to see Hawthorne, Pretty Freak?" He made a mark on his clipboard. "Good boy. Jake's looking good, you know, full-grown hunter. He's got special plans for you today—requested a private interrogation in Room Three." If anything, Victor's expression got nastier. "Real shame. No cameras."

Tobias's mind shut off. Sure, a hunter would ask for no cameras if he wanted to fuck a monster in private, but he might also ask for no cameras if he wanted to cut a monster up without bothering with questions, without bothering with the forms and pretense of an interrogation.

Suddenly, Tobias couldn't think of Jake, a hunter, without thinking of all the other hunters, the other guards who had tied him down and laughed while they hurt him, even as the cameras ran. He could imagine Jake smiling at him while he—

Tobias shut down the thought, clamped down hard, and retreated until he felt nothing, until he couldn't feel the cold air around him. Jake could do whatever he wanted with him, of course. Tobias was just a monster. That was what he told himself. But he knew, deep down where he hid all the things he could never admit even to himself, that if Jake tied him down and started cutting, Tobias wouldn't be able not to care. And without that shell that had kept him alive for nine years, he didn't think there would be anything left of him. Or anything Jake would find worth saving.

What are you doing, Jake Hawthorne?

The hardest part had been rattling off the ID number and not saying that he wanted to see *Toby*. They'd shown him into an interrogation room: stainless steel walls, table, and two chairs.

After what felt like an hour but couldn't have actually been more than fifteen minutes, the doorknob turned, and Tobias stepped in.

He looked tired, thinner than he was the last time Jake saw him (and he hadn't thought the short, skinny kid could get thinner), his eyes sunken and dark. He didn't look healthy, but what stopped Jake's breath was Toby's blank, hollow expression. He could have been a sleepwalker or a ghost. A little panicked, Jake looked for some kind of recognition, and he thought he caught a flicker of some half-sick, half-longing expression, but then Toby's face shut back down.

He sat without a word and put his hands on the table, palms up, fingers slightly curled. He didn't blink.

Jake shifted in his seat. Something was wrong. Something was really fucking wrong. "Hey, Toby." He had no idea what the words would do. Maybe Toby would actually look at him. Maybe he would shatter. Jake couldn't fucking tell.

Thank God the hollow-eyed stranger in front of him relaxed slightly and became *Toby*. He didn't change his position at all, but Jake could see the sharp, brittle edge of fear draining out of him. Toby tilted his head and met Jake's eyes. He tried to smile and failed. "Hey, Jake."

Relieved, Jake reached across to rest his fingers inside Toby's palms. Toby jumped at the contact, but that didn't worry Jake. Toby always twitched at first contact in every visit. Jake rubbed gently, careful not to push too hard on the reddened skin, smelling ammonia. Toby must have been on some kind of cleaning duty again.

"Hope you don't mind the change." Jake lifted one shoulder to indicate the room. "I was getting tired of people eying us everywhere we went." Toby's eyes flickered to the camera mounted in the upper corner. "I told them to turn it off."

Another layer of blankness thawed from Toby's face. "Just so we could . . ." He swallowed, and a smile and some deeper, softer emotion flickered stronger in his eyes, a spark that could almost light.

Jake grinned. He never failed to get a nice buzz from producing that reaction in Toby. "I'm a Hawthorne. What are they going to do, tell me no?"

Tobias ducked his head, but Jake saw the flash of a grin before it disappeared.

Jake squeezed his fingers. "Sorry it's been so long. I was chasing a bunch of ghouls down the East Coast, then got stuck hunting down a swamp monster in Florida. And then I was in *Massachusetts*."

"That's okay," Toby said, as he always did. He was looking at Jake's hands over his, the faintest smile still on his face. "So you got them all?"

Jake launched into his stories about the hunts, from the start of the drive down from Ohio and the weird-ass family he'd met on the way, along with all the other quirky details he'd filed away as Things to Tell Toby. He probably talked more about that stuff than he did about the actual hunts. He'd worried once about whether it was rude to recount his adventures killing monsters to Tobias, but Toby insisted he didn't mind. "They're doing bad things," he'd said. "It's good to kill them."

Still, Jake knew monsters weren't the interesting part of his stories to Toby. He focused more on the interviews, the lies he'd spun and how the poor saps fell for them every time, because he was just that good. Toby smiled nearly the whole time he talked, and Toby looked him in the face too, if only because Jake's voice insisted *look at me, look at me, Toby*. Jake was an awesome storyteller, if he did say so himself.

Toby had even been entranced by Jake's description of the mysterious series of camouflage billboards without any text that he'd seen on the side of the road in Ohio. "What're they normally for, though? The billboards?"

"They're just trying to get people to pull off the highway and buy their shit. Souvenirs and burgers and antiques." Toby had still looked perplexed, and Jake moved on—easily, by now, with so much practice—to telling him about the weird-ass family he'd encountered at a truck stop down south, who were on a four-state tour of art museums. "Like libraries but for paintings and shit," Jake had explained, and Toby's eyes had gone round with wonder, and Jake had found himself telling Toby about the time he and Dad had had to break into an art gallery to torch a haunted painting—that wasn't exactly the same, but Jake didn't think he'd ever actually been to an art museum.

Now he was finally getting around to the climax of the hunt, which had been pretty badass, the way he'd tracked the vampiric giant gila monster through the marshes and staked out its lair for hours from a vantage point high in a tree.

"Then, right as it started crawling down to its pit, I *jumped* its ass—" He grabbed Toby's forearms in emphasis, and Toby gasped sharply, yanking his right arm back.

Jake stopped. He was used to Toby's small twitches, but this had been nothing like that. "Toby?"

"S-sorry," he said, but his face had gone gray, and he blinked fast as he stared at a low point past Jake.

Jake let go of his arm slowly. Toby's sleeves were long enough to cover his knuckles, but they were bunched around his wrists. Jake covered Toby's right hand with his own before turning it over and pushing his sleeve up to his elbow.

Toby gasped again, now from shock, and his body jerked

back, though he didn't try to wrench his arm away again. Jake didn't notice. His eyes were fixed on a series of small, circular burns on the inside of Toby's forearms, two of them still shiny and pink, the others darker and scabbed over. Turning his head, Jake saw they formed a smiley face.

Only after Jake had stood up, and Tobias had twisted his body as far away as he could with Jake's hand locked around his arm, was Jake aware of moving at all. His breath came slow and steady, and his voice only sounded a little tight as he asked, "Who did that to you?"

Toby was trembling, his head bent so close to the table that nothing of his face was visible. He didn't answer.

Jake felt his tenuous control slipping. He seized Tobias's shoulder with his free hand, shaking him and shouting, "Who did it, Tobias?"

Even as his head rocked back, Tobias kept his eyes tightly shut. "K-K-Karl," he choked out.

Jake released him, pushing back from the table hard enough to knock over his chair as he left the room.

Karl was assisting another interrogation in Room Four. He had just slid a hot, blessed knife into the vampire's stomach when Jake Hawthorne kicked in the door.

"What the fuck—" He backed away from the vampire alongside the other interrogator, a hunter.

Jake grabbed a red-hot iron poker—also blessed—from the burner and advanced, a blank and wild look in his eyes.

When the hunter tried to charge him, Jake punched him hard in the jaw and sent him smashing into the burner, scattering coals and ash over the floor. Then Jake grabbed Karl by the collar.

"Why the fuck did you do it?" he snarled. "You get your jollies marking up kids like Toby? What the fuck did he do? Can you tell me one fucking thing he did, you sadistic son of a bitch?"

Karl clawed at Jake's hand, his eyes widening when he couldn't break the grip. "Let me go, you crazy bastard! Put that fucking poker down!"

Jake pushed him away and Karl dropped, going for the knife he'd left in the vampire. Jake swung the poker around, tip glowing, and cracked it into Karl's chest and shoulder. He heard bones crack, probably the collarbone, maybe a rib, but he could still see the red wounds on Toby's arm—not just those fucking burns, but welts and cuts and old scars that had faded into his skin—and then it wasn't fucking enough to break a few bones. He stepped, hard, on Karl's broken shoulder.

"I'm gonna mark you up, you son of a bitch," he said. He pressed the glowing end of the poker to the guard's face.

Karl screamed, and other guards burst into the interrogation room, ready to subdue the threat.

It took three men to pull Jake off.

They were better than the cops he'd fought off when he was thirteen, but they still had to punch the air out of his lungs before they could manhandle him to a room in the nearest administration office.

Makes sense, Jake thought. *You have more experience beating up children.*

After throwing him into the room, they closed and locked the door behind him. The deep blue carpeting, hardwood desk and bookshelves, and leather chairs were a striking contrast from the bare gray room and steel table and chairs where he had been talking with Toby. The doors were just as solid as the rest of the furniture. The only thing in common between the interrogation room and this one was that they were both designed so nothing could get out. Jake straightened slowly, feeling the new bruises on his jaw and trying to catch his breath.

The door burst open under the force of his cousin Matthew Dixon, who slammed the door behind him. The fury in his face stiffened Jake's back.

"What the hell is wrong with you, Jake?" Matthew searched for words to describe his outrage and couldn't come up with anything. "What the *hell* is wrong with you?"

Jake glared back. Who the fuck did Matthew think he was, his father?

"Let me get this clear. You met with your particular freak, 89UI-whatever, in Room Three. Then you charged into Room Four, knocked out a hunter—also legally interrogating a monster, by the way—beat a guard, and then burned him with a poker. Have I left anything out?"

Jake folded his arms and stared stonily back. He had no obligation to explain himself to these Dixons.

"Look, you might have gotten away with that when Uncle Elijah was Director, but Jonah's not going to put up with shit like this. You have problems with the staff, you take it up outside of FREACS. You have problems with the monsters, you file the fucking paperwork." Matthew studied Jake's hardened expression, and he shook his head. "You really do think you're something, don't you? You and your old man both."

"What're you trying to say?" Jake snapped.

Matthew lifted his hands, palms out. "Nothing! Jesus, kid, you need to get into anger management."

"*I* need to? I'm not the one who's fucking *torturing* kids!"

Matthew's eyes narrowed. "Monster kids, Hawthorne. Did you forget that?"

Jake hissed, fingers still itching to smash, break *something*. He was still so angry, could still feel the fury pounding in his blood. He didn't give a fuck what Matthew was saying, what arguments they had—he couldn't stand the thought that these bastards had been hurting Toby while Jake had been away shooting stuff and getting laid. "You have no fucking right."

Matthew started to laugh, then cut himself off. "We have every fucking right, Hawthorne. Then again, you and your old man never did get on the family boat, did you?" With his forefinger he mimed shooting a gun between Jake's eyes. "Uncle Sam wants *you*." He laughed again, and then paused with a thoughtful, intent look. "What're you saying? You want to lay some kind of . . . claim to this particular monster?"

"Yes," Jake said. "Yes, I do."

Matthew's eyebrows shot up, his mouth forming a thoughtful little O. "Well then. You should've filed the fucking paperwork, asshole. Or *said* something. I mean, we'd noticed how you always went after him, but Hawthorne Senior said—"

"This has nothing to do with my dad," Jake interrupted. "Tobias is mine. Got that? He's *mine*. Gimme whatever shit papers you need to get that through your skulls. I don't want any of you sons of bitches touching him."

Matthew smirked. "Touching him? My, my, I had no idea, Hawthorne. How does Dad feel about that?"

"Shut your mouth, Dixon. Did you hear me? Tobias is *mine*." Every time Jake said it, he felt better, more certain that this was the way the world should work, Toby being *his*.

"Yeah, yeah." Matthew moved to his desk. "We'll put a note on his file. But this doesn't get you off the hook, Jake. We respect hunters' . . . interests when we can, but legally, all the monsters belong to us, and we treat them according to our discretion. You have zero right to assault an employee who's only doing his job, and you don't get special treatment just because you're Sally's son." He ignored how Jake tightened his fists. "You're just lucky the Director isn't here today. He'd chew up your ass and spit out your tailbone. I'm making a report suspending you from FREACS for the next eight weeks, and as soon as you leave this office, you'll be escorted out of the facility. Next time you come, don't fucking shove pokers in the faces of my staff."

"What? No." Jake took half a step forward. "I need to see Tobias again before—"

Matthew cut him off. "With the shit you pulled today, you're lucky we're letting you back in at all. Trust me, this is light, because you're young, stupid, and family, but don't expect to slide like this again." He considered. "I could cut your suspension down to four weeks from eight weeks, maybe, if you apologized to Karl—"

"When your tits freeze in hell," Jake snapped.

"Yeah, didn't think so." Matthew shrugged. "Get out of my sight, Hawthorne. Take some time to cool off. You've got the license, you're a real hunter now, so be professional and cut out the tantrums. Try not to mutilate anyone on the way out."

Jake glowered at Matthew, contemplating the satisfaction of punching him into his fancy wooden bookshelves versus leaving with dignity.

Eventually, more for Toby's sake, so everyone would take Jake seriously—*I'll be back, Toby, sorry I fucked up today*—he left quietly, albeit with a few snarls for the guards to keep their hands off of him, and didn't look back.

AFTER JAKE HAD GONE, slamming the solid iron-reinforced door on his way out, Tobias collapsed into his chair and shook.

What had he done? How had he made Jake so angry? It was just cigarette burns. He shouldn't have flinched, that was clear, but he hadn't expected Jake to squeeze right where the pink burns were still raw and tender. Karl had given eyes to the smile barely a day ago when Tobias's performance had disappointed. The worst part, the absolute worst, was that he had only jumped because he had let his guard down—shit, being with Jake was the only time he allowed himself to relax, and yet when he had the most to lose—and then when it *hurt*, he hadn't been able to stop the reaction.

He wanted to hear the end of the story. He wanted to keep watching Jake smile. He wanted to tell him about the last book he had been allowed to read that wasn't about monsters. It had been about vehicles, and there had been a section about altering motorcycle engines to get the maximum speed out of the vehicle. Maybe Jake knew how the information could be applied to the Eldorado. And even if he didn't, he would have *cared.*

But instead Tobias was alone in Interrogation Room Three with nothing to do but think. He had been in here when they asked him if he ever had visions, psychic projections, nightmares that became real. There had been a specialized rack, and they had pinned his arms—

Tobias jerked his mind away—interrogations weren't that often and best forgotten as fast as possible—and focused hard on the chair Jake had knocked over on his way out. He'd been so angry, terrifyingly angry. Tobias's neck felt strained from Jake's shaking, and the wounds on his arm and shoulder hurt where Jake had gripped him.

Tobias didn't dare think that was all Jake was going to do to him. He didn't know why Jake had been angry, but there had been so much rage on his face that Tobias felt nauseated just thinking about it. Maybe he'd come back with a rod or a whip to punish Tobias for whatever it was. That would be the kind of beating that he could get any day from any guard. It wouldn't be so bad.

But the longer Jake stayed away, the more Tobias just wanted him to come back. *Bring the hot irons, the flaying knives, the boiling holy water. Bring the clamps, the flails, the tasers. Just please, don't leave and never come back.*

Maybe he had *known* just by looking at the smiley face what Tobias had done. Karl had said the first time, when he began the shape of the mouth, that it could either be a smiley face or a frowny face, that Tobias could either be a good boy or a bad boy. So Tobias had been good to Karl and Lonny and Dave and that hunter who had asked the questions, and Karl had kept his word.

Maybe Jake knew all that just from looking at the little smile *("You were a good boy, Pretty Freak. Just gonna mark down my smile to remind you to* keep *being a good boy"),* and he was so disgusted he would never come back.

Tobias sat alone in the room, in the silence. He did his best not to move, not to twitch, not to show his panic or his fear. It was all he could do not to scratch at the healing burns as though if he could rip them off his arm, like a shifter, Jake would come back.

It had been at least two hours—Tobias had started counting once it was clear that Jake wasn't coming back *soon*—when the door opened. Tobias had been analyzing the floor, tracing out pictures in the faded bloodstains the way Jake had taught him to do with clouds, and he looked up hopefully, but it was Victor.

Tobias swallowed and let his mind blank.

"Get up, freak."

Tobias stood and walked to the guard. Victor snapped a flimsy leash onto his collar.

"The hunter's gone?" Tobias asked. He'd wrestled with the risks of asking at all, but he had to know. He wasn't stupid enough to use Jake's name.

Victor scowled and slapped him, but not hard, not even hard enough to rattle his teeth. Weird. "Hawthorne Junior's gone, freak. Must have decided he didn't want your ass today."

Tobias's mouth went dry. *Jake's gone, Jake's gone.* He seized onto the only word that gave him even a shadow of hope. "Today, sir?"

Victor raised his club, and Tobias braced himself—Victor always hit where it would reopen his knife wounds—but after a moment's hesitation, he lowered it.

"Fucking Hawthorne," he muttered with venom. He tugged on Tobias's collar with the lead line, and Tobias followed him from the room. "You better keep doing whatever the fuck you do to keep Hawthorne obsessed with your ass, freak. Because the second he's gone, we're going to feed you to Karl, and he's going to take every inch of his pain out of your hide."

Tobias knew that should probably frighten him. He didn't know what he did that kept Jake happy, or why Karl was in pain, and uncertainties like that could get you killed in Freak Camp.

All he understood was that Jake had left, but he would be back.

It wasn't a great day. It would have been better to be able to spend more time with Jake, but he wasn't gone forever, so it wasn't bad at all.

When he walked back into the yard, all the guards were acting jumpy around him, didn't look at him long, and not one touched him. They seemed to go out of their way to avoid any contact.

And that made it a good day too.

CHAPTER NINE

SUMMER 1998

"Hey, Pretty Freak!"

Tobias closed his eyes before standing.

It had been nice to be invisible for a while. In Freak Camp, being invisible was the best a monster could ask for. But he'd known it wouldn't last. It figured that Victor would be the first to break it. In a group of sadists, thugs, and Dixons—the last of whom didn't like to get their hands dirty outside of Special Research—Victor was the smartest.

Victor grinned at him, watching him approach. Tobias kept his eyes lowered, shoulders down. "Sir."

"How was dinner?"

Tobias swallowed reflexively. The mealworms had gotten into the bread again. He could tell himself all he wanted that it was extra protein, but a slice of vaguely moving bread and a cup of tepid, flavorless liquid hadn't done anything to make him feel less like he was consuming himself instead of the food. He had hated touching the guards, but he hadn't realized how much of his food came as a reward for what he did on his knees until it was gone. He didn't answer.

Victor brought his billy club under Tobias's chin, nudging

his head up. Tobias kept his eyes almost shut. "I asked you a question. Still hungry?" He tapped the club against Tobias's jaw, and Tobias flinched away. He clenched his fists, angry at his body's betrayal at so light a move.

"Yes, sir," he muttered, because whatever was going to happen now, it could only be worse if he lied.

The billy club fell away. "I got a nice fat sandwich back in my office. You want it?"

Tobias's face didn't twitch.

"Come on," Victor wheedled. "Don't you even want to know what I'm asking for it?"

Tobias inhaled and exhaled deeply through his nose. Might as well ask. "What's the price, sir?"

"You on your knees in Head Alley. One-time payment."

Not much work, usually over quickly. Yeah, it was worth it. He just had to hope Victor really did have a sandwich in his office. Tobias jerked his head in a nod.

"Did I read that right? Let's be absolutely clear." Victor held up his hands, open and mock-innocent. "I'm not forcing you into anything. You are voluntarily offering to blow me in exchange for something extra that monsters shouldn't get. So don't go running to Hawthorne with any stories when I'm doing you a favor. Got it?"

"Yes, sir."

"If you don't want it, you can walk away right now. If you want it, you gotta tell me."

Tobias sucked in his breath. "No, sir. I want it."

"Good." Turning, Victor strode away to the break room, not looking back to see if Tobias followed.

THEY STARTED up again after Victor, but it was different. They didn't just force him to his knees or wrap his hand around their cocks and hurt him until he jerked them off. There was always something—a sandwich, an apple, a blanket—after, and they always made it very clear that he had to want it. There were no interrogations at all.

Tobias figured that it was all because of Jake—he'd seen what Karl's face looked like now, and it wasn't pretty—and he was both grateful for the space and terrified, every day, that Jake would come back and learn what he had done, what he was doing. Jake wanted him untouched, and Tobias was anything but that.

He shared with Kayla when he had more than what he desperately needed, building up credit for when he needed something and couldn't get it himself. They weren't friends, but she watched his back, and it was good to have at least one monster who wouldn't try to cut his throat for his blankets or just because he was the whore. He occasionally gave her advice, which she took. The guards called her Dream now, because after the first time Crusher fucked her, she never made a sound when they touched her.

"Carpenter's dream," Crusher had said, pushing her into the showers with the other monsters. "Lies still as a board, waiting to get nailed."

Victor looked up. "Not your taste, then?"

"Boring as hell," Crusher said.

A vamp might be Toothy because he couldn't retract his second set of teeth, and witches were named Handy if they put out, the name traveling from one witch to the next as they died or moved on to their executions. But Tobias called the shapeshifter girl Kayla, and she called him nothing because she hadn't spoken since the first time Crusher got her alone.

Then one day, after an assembly demonstration—one naked werewolf, caught trying to lunge through the door to Reception, now tied between the whipping posts—Tobias and Kayla found a place where they couldn't see the bloodstained dirt. Tobias leaned against the wall, trying to think only about how it was a good temperature today (bound to get worse, but good right then), while Kayla looked at her hands.

Then he heard her voice: rough and emotionless, like the words were put together by someone with a perfect understanding of the meaning but no comprehension of the emotions involved. "I want to rip off their dicks and stuff them down their throats."

Tobias looked at her in surprise. After a second, he licked his lips and answered the only way he could. "We don't get to want things."

She turned her head to look up at him, face flat and inscrutable, until she spoke with the same lack of inflection or feeling. "You want that hunter boy to come see you."

Tobias jerked hard, twisting his head sharply away. He had reacted far less during his last beating. No wonder the guards all used that against him, if he was so transparent.

Kayla was still watching him. "Why? What does he do to you?"

He drew his arms tight around his knees, setting his chin between them. How could he possibly talk about Jake's visits—how Jake *talked* to him so differently from anyone he'd ever met, how he touched him so lightly and never to hurt, how he never asked anything from him? There weren't any words for it, none Kayla would understand nor believe. Tobias didn't have any words for it himself.

It was beyond comprehension, the brief flashes of light that were Jake's visits, the fact Tobias had ever been in his presence. It just *was,* and while he couldn't have begun to say why Jake always returned to see him and smiled the way he did when he saw Tobias, the truth that Jake would come back (*please come back, I'll be good for you*) was the only reason some days that Tobias didn't rush the guards, hoping to get a bullet before a club.

Kayla's gaze was still on him. After a long pause, she asked, "Does he fuck you?"

Tobias took a sharp inhale through his nose. "No."

She leaned closer to get a better glimpse of his face. "But he's going to, right? That's why no one else's fucked you. That's what they all say."

Jake had never said anything about it, not one comment or suggestive smirk. He'd never reached past Tobias's hands, shoulder—occasionally his cheek, but never his lips. He'd never hurt Tobias, even that time he was so angry.

"I guess so." He didn't know why else Jake would be so interested in him.

"What's he waiting for?" At last Kayla's flat tone changed, rising on a note of incredulity.

Tobias shrugged and turned away. He wished he could answer, but he didn't know. She had been silent long enough to understand his silence now.

NOT FAR INTO Jake's eight-week suspension, it fully sank in just how much he had fucked up.

Four years ago, Jake had promised to get Toby out. He'd never forgotten that promise, and he'd always known it would be fucking hard and take a lot of work, but it wasn't like there was any amount of work that would stop him or make him give up. Not when it came to the most important task in his whole damn life.

But somehow it had never occurred to him that this wasn't like any other hunt that would take research, legwork, night watches, and willingness to go mano a mano with something not yet documented, including how many limbs it had or if it might spit poison or acid. Fuck, he wished it was all those things, night after night for endless days. That, he could handle.

He had to admit he hadn't done much research for getting Toby out yet. Maybe he'd assumed some kind of instruction manual would be handed to him when he turned eighteen and got his official license. But to snatch Toby out of Freak Camp—that would require something way worse than the dirtiest, smelliest hunt ever did.

Jake was going to have to *suck up* to the fucking *Dixons*.

In retrospect, assaulting and branding the face of a Freak Camp guard and refusing to apologize was not how one went about sucking up, even in Jake's very limited experience. But every time he remembered those smiley-face burns on Toby's arm, he knew he was a cowardly piece of shit. Of course he'd kiss any body part of every Dixon he could find, a thousand times over, if he could just get Toby safe.

After some research and consideration, he called his cousin Leah Dixon who worked in the D.C. office. The few times he'd needed something straightened out, she'd been a total boss at getting it done faster than a wendigo jumping a sleeping camper.

The call felt awkward and unnatural as hell, but Jake did his best to make a good impression and asked about procedures and protocols for getting a monster out of Freak Camp—and *not* with a short-use bait permit.

She was silent a long while on the phone, which was not a good sign. "Tell you the truth, Jake, I'm not sure. I don't know if anyone's ever gotten that kind of request through. I'll ask around and let you know if I hear anything."

Jake swallowed, resisting the urge to thud his head against the window of the Eldorado, which was where he was making the call. "Thanks, Leah. I'll owe you everything, down to my fucking ass."

She laughed shortly. "Don't say that, now. You don't know how much that could be worth here in the Beltway, let alone the paparazzi. But I'm not about to sell out family."

Jake had never been so thankful for a Dixon to call him family.

WHEN JAKE finally got back into Freak Camp—eight fucking weeks had never felt so much like forever—he thought at first they were hassling him because of what he'd done to Karl (*sonuvabitch deserved a lot worse*). They took the blood tests a hell of a lot more seriously, dumped a cup of holy water over his head, *and* read an exorcism. They did an honest-to-God pat down when he was going through security, and for once they didn't allow him to keep his gun or his knife when he went through. The standard-issue bayonet they gave him—loaded with a mix of blessed silver and iron buckshot, topped with a silver blade—felt like cheap shit in his hand.

They tried to give him shit about the sandwich too, but they let him pass eventually. Jake kept his opinion of their asswipery behind his teeth and did his best to smile. If it looked a little like he was baring his teeth, well, that was okay too.

Only when he stepped out into the yard—no private rooms were being issued without prior appointments, according to the new cold-eyed Dixon secretary sitting in Madison's chair—did he realize that maybe it was about more than just him. The guards were all heavily armed and sweating under the extra weight of flak jackets. A lot fewer monsters were in the yard, and any that seemed too close to a guard got a cuff to the head or a club against the ribs. Jake saw two monsters get knocked down in the short walk from Reception to the barracks area.

When he asked where to find Toby—89UI6703, the sandy-haired guard with a scrape along his scalp told him to "find the freak yourself."

Jake felt something in him relax, a fear that had been growing in his chest. He hadn't seen Tobias anywhere, and there were so few monsters in the yard, and clearly, some kind of shit had gone down.

He found him eventually. Toby was huddled with a group of monsters in a narrow strip of shade between the barracks, but the second he saw Jake, his eyes widened and he scrambled up toward him, into the light.

First Jake saw Toby's expression: massive relief washing over with happiness. Then Jake saw the damage.

The sunlight, so bright that Jake was squinting even through his sunglasses, brought into sharp relief the blue-and-purple bruise along Toby's cheek. He was limping too. Not obviously, but Jake could tell from watching Dad—and practicing it himself often enough—that Toby was placing every step carefully to avoid showing weakness.

Jake hissed, stepping forward. "What the hell happened, Toby?" Not getting enough information last time had landed him in that eight-week shithole. This time he wasn't going to fucking abandon Toby in some interrogation room. This time he would be calm, collected. He would gather information and be polite while filling out whatever *forms* it took to beat the fuck's face in. Or at least he would *wait* until the guy was off work to jump him.

See, Jake Hawthorne could be rational and professional. *Suck that, Matthew.*

Toby stopped, and Jake got a glimpse of the smile vanishing under pure fright before Toby dropped his gaze to the ground. Immediately Jake felt like the complete ass he was. Sure, eight weeks had sucked for him. But that had been plenty of time to think of how Toby hadn't known what the hell was going on, and Jake had just *left* him.

Jake was trying to put together an apology when Toby answered. "There was a . . . raid. About two weeks ago. Monsters tried to . . . I don't know, we've been in lockdown and high security since they tried to breach the loading gate, and . . .

I'm sorry I don't know more, Jake. I'm sorry." Toby's gaze was fixed on the ground.

Aw, fuck. Jake stepped closer and brushed Toby lightly on the arm. "That's not what I meant." Toby's head snapped up, his eyes wide, but Jake squeezed his shoulder. Part of him was just relieved that Toby wasn't flinching from the touch. Maybe there were no more *goddamn fucking smiley faces* burned into his skin. "No, it's okay. I guess that's why you look a little knocked around."

"I'm sorry." Tobias's eyes fell as sure as gravity to somewhere around Jake's middle.

There was something else going on here, something that Jake didn't like at all. But he was afraid that pushing for it would only hurt Toby more. Like a goddamn burn. "Toby, don't be. I just meant your face and . . ." Jake gestured to the leg that Toby had been favoring. Guards and monsters were watching—not staring directly, but Jake could tell. He knew from long experience when someone or something was watching him.

Toby looked relieved. He raised a hand to his face, as though making sure that nothing else had happened to his cheek. "Yeah. It's just because of the raid. Everyone's been . . . upset."

"Hey, Toby. Look at me." Jake waited until he did. "I'm sorry I was gone so long. I lost my temper and . . . Fuck, I'm sorry. I was so pissed off that they'd been hurting you, and I didn't know—I kinda lost it. They haven't . . . you're okay, right? Now, I mean."

Toby stared at him, stared at him like Jake had spoken only gibberish, and then smiled. It was the smile that put the sunlight to shame. "No, don't worry, I'm fine. They haven't . . . they stopped after . . . last time."

Jake nodded. "Good. They hassle you, Toby, you tell me, okay? I'm sure there's some paperwork I can fill out to let me smash their faces in."

Tobias smiled and ducked his head. "Yeah, probably. I'm

really okay, Jake. They've done nothing I haven't . . . they've done nothing."

"Good. And it better stay that way." Jake stretched and wiped his forehead. It was already September, but it was still fucking hot. "Hey, wanna play cards?"

They found a spot in the shade—Jake felt a little bad at how the other monsters scattered out of the cooler spot next to Reception, but when he glanced at the doors to Administration and saw the guards posted there in heavy armor, he figured he probably wouldn't be able to get himself and Toby inside.

Jake dug in his jacket pockets while Toby shuffled the cards almost as fast as a Vegas dealer.

"Crazy eights?" Toby asked, already dealing five.

"Yeah. Aha!" Jake pulled the squashed sandwich from his pocket and ceremoniously presented it to Toby. "For you."

Toby froze at the sight of the sandwich, cards fluttering from his hands.

Jake frowned. "Hey, are you okay? I know it's fish patty, but you never said you had a shellfish allergy . . . Toby?"

Tobias shook himself. "Sorry." His voice was a little hoarse. "I've been . . . eating better lately, and I just . . ."

Jake looked down at the sandwich. He loved bringing Toby food, and he really was happy that Toby had actually been getting enough to eat for a change—but something about Toby's response felt weird. "Well . . . you still want it, maybe save it for later?"

"Yes, I want it, s—" Tobias said the words by rote, without emotion, until he cut himself off by jerking his head to the side. He curled in on himself, shrinking his shoulders down with his chin to his chest, and clenched his hands over his knee. He didn't seem to notice his grip crushing the queen of hearts, despite how appalled he'd been the last time he thought he'd bent the corner of one of Jake's cards.

This whole visit was weirding Jake out. Something had

happened, and he had no fucking clue what it was. He didn't know how to ask, and he wasn't sure what he could do even if Toby gave him an answer.

So he settled for what he knew how to do. He shoved the sandwich into Toby's lap and shifted a little closer to him. "It has tartar sauce on it. I hope that's cool. I was going to stop at a burger joint like usual, but I was coming from the other direction and there was this fish shack and I figured, 'Hey, never got Toby a sandwich from here before,' so I pulled over, and this chick at the counter asks why I never called her back last week, and I tell her I've never even been here before, and she says yeah I was and I ordered, like, twenty double-fish sandwiches, which I didn't, and why would anybody need twenty of 'em, and she . . ."

Jake talked, and Toby slowly opened the sandwich, took a bite, and smiled. Jake talked until Toby had eaten, until he had dealt out the cards—not poker, Jake didn't feel up to poker, and he didn't want to bluff to Toby right now—and they played war until the sun had moved a couple of hours in the sky. Toby was smiling at him, laughing a little with him, and telling him about books he had read and work he had done around the camp. One book about altering engines sounded like it would make the Eldorado purr, and Jake thought, once again, how amazing it was that Toby could stay here, never leaving, and still be the smartest kid Jake knew.

I'm getting you out of here, Toby. He just didn't know when. It was time to give Leah another follow-up call.

Tobias watched Jake leave, one hand tracing his arm where Jake had touched him, over and over again, the taste of tartar sauce on his tongue. Only when he couldn't see Jake any more, when the guards started to notice a monster standing suspiciously out alone—monsters had been killed for that during the raids —did he return to the shade.

Kayla was waiting for him. She shoved a werewolf out of the shade and bared her teeth at him when he made a move back to the place that Tobias had taken. Few knew that Kayla could talk, but everyone knew that she could bite.

When Tobias slid down next to her, the cool of the shade compensating for the heat of too many bodies close together, she turned her head slightly, eyes watching everything. Her lips moved—her lips often moved soundlessly, Tobias had heard some of the guards say they thought she was brain damaged, probably from being under Crusher—but he heard the word.

"Unfucked," she said.

He gave a short nod, a jerk of his head downward.

Eight weeks, and Jake had still come back to him. Tobias had lived through the raid and the new interrogations of all monsters—after the scare with the outside attack, the Director suspected that someone on the inside could be feeding information out—and Jake had come back, just to play cards, to give him a sandwich Tobias had paid nothing for. To smile at him.

It never made any sense, but Tobias was still the luckiest son of a bitch in Freak Camp.

CHAPTER TEN

FALL 1999

FREAK CAMP MADE Roger's skin crawl. He only went when he absolutely couldn't avoid it—like now, when a captured demon might have intel on a case he'd been working for the last six months.

He tried never to linger. He'd walk in, see what he could get, and leave without glancing in the observation windows to see what was drawing out *that* particular human-sounding scream.

He finished working over the demon—straightforward enough with a hefty supply of salt, holy water, and a crucifix—and though there was minimal damage to the host, the smell of burning skin was never a happy one. He thought only of the shower he would take back in the motel. He didn't like using the showers that the facility provided; they might wash off the blood and sweat from interrogation, but he'd just have to shower again later to get the smell of Freak Camp off his skin. He had just stepped out of the room when he heard his name.

"Harper! Well, look who's slumming in the freak playground." Dennis Beam was walking down the hall, holding some black rods under his arm.

Roger took his hand in a quick shake. He'd only run across

the man on a couple of hunts, but Beam had been full of admiration for Roger's knowledge. "Only got here this morning, and I'm heading back home tonight."

"What's got your tail on fire? Guerrero, Sanders, and me are getting together at Hunters' Deck for a round. Sanders owes us after we had to save his ass from a bunch of pixies."

Roger shook his head. "Another time."

"Well, before you go, let me show you something I just picked up from Sloan. A neat trick for taking down the freaks with softer nervous systems. And it don't even leave any marks." He held up one of the thin, gleaming black prods and nodded to the room behind him. "Come check it out." He pushed open the door, and Roger reluctantly stepped inside.

His stomach turned over at the sight inside. Tobias—he could still recognize Jake's monster in the painfully thin teenager—lay on the floor, his hair and shirt soaked with sweat, wrists bound in front of his chest with plastic zip ties, and two chains stretching from either side of his collar to hooks set low in opposite walls. There was barely enough slack in the chains for him to rise up on his elbows, though he wouldn't be able to do even that with the handcuffs. His glassy eyes didn't move from the ceiling as Roger entered.

"Look how good this works." Beam stabbed the prod toward Tobias's chest, stopping several inches short of it making contact, but Tobias's body spasmed violently in anticipation. Beam and the guard—Sloan, by the name on his uniform—roared with laughter. Panting, Tobias turned his face toward the wall, though his face showed no emotion.

"You sick fucks," Roger muttered. "What'd he do?"

Beam looked at him, surprised. "C'mon, Harper, it's a freak."

Out of the kid's line of sight, Sloan nudged Tobias's thigh with his own prod. A guttural cry ripped from Tobias's throat as his body seized, jerking for several moments before falling still again, facing the opposite direction. He choked and gasped for breath, and Roger realized his collar had half strangled him. Tobias's chest rose and fell so rapidly he looked ready to have a heart attack. But most disconcerting of all was how—even as his limbs still twitched—Tobias's face had smoothed over again to utter blankness.

"You're a sadistic bastard." Roger couldn't keep his eyes off the kid on the floor, didn't know when his right hand had crept to where his gun usually was. He forced himself to move his hand away. "What the hell did he do? You can't pass this off as an interrogation."

"I don't know." Beam glanced at Sloan. "What did he do?"

Sloan shrugged and stepped between the monster's legs. "Getting careless with his teeth."

A shudder worked down Tobias's shoulders, but he made no attempt to close his legs, even as Sloan lifted his boot and slowly pressed down on his groin. Tobias keened, the sound slipping high and agonized from between his clenched teeth.

"Aww, what are you whining about?" Sloan cooed. "Monsters don't need these, do they, Pre—"

"I'm having a hard time telling who the monster is!" Roger snapped.

Tobias's eyes snapped open, and he looked at Roger—the first thing he had focused on in the room. Roger saw in his eyes no gratitude, pleading, or hatred—just a curious intentness as he looked at him. Roger swallowed, unable to break eye contact.

"What'd you say?" Beam said, face twisting ugly.

Roger scowled, raising his eyes. "You heard me. Bunch of tough guys, going after a malnourished freak kid with his hands tied. That how you get your rocks off?"

"Well," Beam said, much cooler, "if you're not enjoying yourself, Harper, you don't have to stay."

Roger glanced back at Tobias, but the kid's gaze had moved to the ceiling again, lost and flat. Roger swallowed, fists clenching, bile sliding up his throat, then glared at Beam. "Lose my number. I don't want to hear from you again, I don't care what you need." He slammed the door behind him.

Roger swore viciously under his breath with every step out of the complex, barely pausing to sign out and nod at the ever-so-sweet receptionist girl who bade him goodbye by name. As the security door swung shut behind him, he was dialing his cell phone.

"Hey, Rog, what's up?" Jake sounded cheerful, oblivious, and it only increased the sick roiling in Roger's stomach.

"Jake," he growled. "You still interested in getting that Tobias kid out of the camp?"

"Wh—yeah, of course I am."

"Well, you better start filing the paperwork. I don't think he'll make it another year."

"What?" Jake sounded like he had just been punched in the gut. "What do you mean?"

"Just what I said." Roger hung up, seething too much to trust himself to keep talking. It was stupid on every level, he knew, to get emotional over a monster in Freak Camp. Couldn't end well.

But he wasn't able to just walk out on two sadists torturing a kid and not do a damn thing about it.

JAKE STARED down at the phone. That was . . . not what he had expected when he had seen that the call was from Roger.

The mobile phone was new. It still felt like a reward when someone called him, even though Dad mostly didn't—unless they had to get together—and not many other people had his number. When Roger called, it was usually to point them in the direction of a new hunt, or sometimes just to say hi. Jake thought of it as *checking up on him,* but that didn't mean it didn't feel good to get the call.

He turned to see Dad watching him with a frown. It was one of their rare weeks together, when both of their respective hunts were over—or a different hunt had brought them back together—and Dad sat on the second bed in the hotel room cleaning his guns, getting polish all over the cheap, ratty bedspread.

"That was short. Harper in trouble?" His tone implied that Roger could go fuck himself, but his hands, hesitating over the weapon he was cleaning, said that if Jake said the word, they would be on their way.

Jake liked that, how Dad trusted him sometimes, how he'd pay attention when Jake brought him new information. Not that Jake ever really knew anything that Dad didn't. Dad was still the best, and Jake loved working with him, not just because they were family, but because if Leon and Jake Hawthorne went after something, that sucker was going down. It was just a fact of life. Together the Hawthornes could stop anything.

Usually he liked that more. But then again, usually Roger had not just told him that he had to get Tobias out, *get Tobias out now,* in a tone that Jake had only ever heard before when he was telling some civilian to *get the fuck down, it's going for your heart.*

Jake took a shaky breath, and then reached for his own guns. "Roger's fine. You know how to get a monster out of Freak Camp?"

Leon Hawthorne froze and looked up from his gun. "Why would I know a fucking thing like that?"

Because you're my dad and you know everything. "I'm getting Tobias out," Jake said. "Figured I would ask you first because you usually know these things. I already called Leah Dixon in D.C., she hasn't had any luck, so maybe I can try a different ASC resource hotline, and they can . . ."

With a scowl, Leon tossed a greasy rag to the floor, next to the trashcan. "Jake, I thought you were over this."

Jake's mind had been spinning, trying to find a starting place for how to get Toby out. Research always had a starting point, after which the monster's profile and vulnerabilities would fall into place. Even if this was a hell of a lot bigger than confirming a werewolf attack from a list of fatal animal attacks, or pinning a string of strange deaths on a shapeshifter. *At last, at last, you're going to do it, you're going to keep your promise and stop putting it off like a coward*—but he came back to the here and now at his dad's tone.

"Sir?"

"I thought you had stopped obsessing over that monster."

Jake blinked and considered. He still thought about Toby. He still thought about him all the time. He still . . . but no, he hadn't talked about him in a while, not to Dad. Not since the fight at Freak Camp and the eight-week suspension.

He and Dad had had an hour's shouting match about appropriate behavior with other hunters and ASC personnel. Somehow the point Dad had landed on was that everyone ass-kissing the ASC really deserved a brand in their faces anyway, just for being Big Brother assholes, but Jake was still stupid and impulsive to do it. Dad hadn't connected that fight with Tobias, and since then Jake had stopped mentioning Toby, because Toby was his, and talking about him just made Dad angry.

Actually, he hadn't talked about Toby much since he turned sixteen. Everything he'd wanted to say about him to Dad, he had said then, even though the man hadn't heard a word.

"Sir, I wouldn't say obsessed." *Unless you mean I think about him every day. And I smile when I see M&M's because he loves those, and I think about reading all these books just so I can share them with him. And my heart jumps every time I see boys who look like him.*

"Yeah, what would you call it then?" Dad glanced at him for a second before turning his head away. "I can barely hold my head up in a hunter bar with sons of bitches cracking jokes about you mooning after that monster kid. Everyone knows, Jake, and you're not ten anymore."

Jake gritted his teeth before answering, "No, sir, I'm not ten. And I think that means that if I say something like this, it means that I know what I'm doing. Or that I've at least thought it through."

Leon snorted. "You let me be the judge of that, Jake."

The worst thing was that Jake would be perfectly happy letting Dad be the judge of things. When they hunted together, Jake let Dad take the lead, ask the questions, form the theories, send him out to do research or to flirt with a pretty girl or boy. Dad always knew the next step they should take. It didn't make Jake angry, didn't rattle him when Dad barked off orders without listening to his input. Jake had a lifetime of knowing that when Dad said to drop he should drop, when Dad said to run he should run.

Jake trusted him about everything but Tobias. Because on nights when Dad was gone, or too drunk to drive, or unconscious and bleeding, Toby had always been in Jake's mind. He had never been able to fully explain, even to himself, even the night he turned sixteen, what Toby meant to him and why Jake knew he wasn't just another monster. They might have only spent a couple of hours together at a time over the years, but Jake was sure about Toby like he was about precious little else in his life. He caught the same look on Toby's face every visit, how Toby smiled at him—whenever Jake managed to coax one out. Nothing else in his life was like it. And while he couldn't put into words what Toby meant to him, Jake knew with absolute certainty what he meant to Toby, and that rescuing Toby from Freak Camp now mattered more than any of the civilians he had managed to save.

Toby was his friend. Toby cared without demanding things from him—even though Jake would be willing to give him anything, anything at all. Toby was not a monster.

"You never ask me what I've thought," Jake said slowly, "so how can you know when I've thought something through?"

Dad paused and looked up at him with something strange in his eyes. "What did you just say to me?"

"I said that you don't listen," Jake said. "I said that I *have* thought this through."

"This being . . .?"

"I'm getting Tobias out," Jake said. The words seemed to echo in the room, as though the space had suddenly expanded. "And you can help me, sir, or you can get the hell out of my way."

Leon stared, and then carefully laid his gun on the bed. "You're getting a monster out of Freak Camp."

"Yes."

"Are you feeling all right? Any dizziness or disorientation, any details not feeling right? Gaps in your memory? Any hesitation at all in making these decisions?"

It made Jake angry that Dad was still convinced that this could be some kind of monster trick. If Toby had the ability to twist Jake's head around—in some supernatural way, and not just with his smile—then he would have done all he could to get out of that shithole earlier, maybe back when they were burning smiley faces into his arm.

"Yes, Dad, I feel fine," he snapped. "It's not like this is a new idea."

"Are you telling me that you have been planning to remove a monster from Freak Camp longer than just tonight?"

Just the last six years, Dad. "Yes."

"What—" Dad's voice broke, but Jake couldn't tell if it was from anger or worry. He cleared his throat and tried again. "What exactly would you do with the freak if you get him out?"

"Do?" *Feed him, for one.* Toby looked thinner every time he visited. *Get him somewhere safe, more than anything.*

"Yes. Do. Do! You can't just want to have a *monster* with you." Leon sounded disgusted, confused, almost desperate, like he wanted the situation to make sense, but no matter how many times he counted there were still not enough guns, too many monsters, one less salt bag than he had expected. "There has to be a purpose. Give me a *reason,* Jake."

"Like, so I can stake him somewhere so other monsters will come and try to eat him? Am I fucking hunting deer now?" *You think I get off on hurting things, on using evil to chase evil?*

"Don't use that language with me, boy. It's a valid question, and if you can't recognize that—"

"He's a *person,* Dad. And he doesn't deserve—"

"Shut your mouth, Jake. Right now, shut your mouth."

Leon stood, breathing hard. He glared at Jake. No longer down, a distant part of Jake's mind noted. They were eye to eye. "There's something that you've got to get through that thick skull of yours, something that you should have known a long time ago, but I guess you're just not that bright, or I've raised you wrong, or something. That boy is not a person. He's a monster. A *monster,* Jake. It doesn't matter what they deserve or what they don't deserve, any more than it matters what a rabid dog deserves. It should be put down. I don't care if it hasn't bitten anyone yet. Frankly, I don't like the shit that goes down in Freak Camp. Some things are basically impossible to kill, but it would be better to put a bullet through everything that *can* be put down."

"Toby is not a freak," Jake said doggedly. "He's just—"

"Jake." Leon closed his eyes. "You can't keep saying that. You can't keep . . . you can't keep being this stupid. You can tell me. You can tell me anything, and we'll deal with it. You want to . . . to sleep with it? I know you've been going home with men and women, and I don't care, but you could do so much better than a fucking monster."

"Dad!" Jake turned away. "It's not about that. This is about what's right, and what I've known I wanted—"

"You can't just tell me that you want to get a freak out of FREACS and it's because you *want* to. That just makes me think you want a pet monster because I never bought you a dog."

"Toby's not a dog!" Jake spun around, anger cracking his voice. "And he's not a fucking freak—"

"Jake, he is."

"—and I'm getting him out of Freak Camp whether or not you approve. Roger said I don't have much time if I want to—"

"I'm going to gut Harper," Leon said abruptly.

"Why do you do that?" Jake asked, moving close enough that he could shove Dad if he wanted to. For the first time, he wanted to. "Why do you blame people for things that aren't their fault?"

"If Harper told you to get a monster out of camp . . ."

"He said that Tobias might not last much longer, not that I should get him out. Jesus, Dad, don't always blame other people for things that you—"

"Are you saying that it's *my fault* my son wants a freak as a pet?" Leon roared.

Jake gritted his teeth and shoved. Not hard, but angry. More of a jerk. Dad's chest against his hands felt the same as any other guy's he'd shoved, maybe a little heavier, maybe a little less give. But there was nothing normal about this. It felt strange, wrong and right all at the same time. "I'm *saying* that maybe you should try listening to me for once."

Leon swayed, put his hand to his chest, and stared like Jake had slugged him. "I don't listen to you," he said softly, almost shaking, "because you come up with fucking stupid ideas like this, ideas that will get us both killed."

"Well, thanks, Dad." Jake threw his arms out and stepped back before he really did slug the man. "If I'm that much of a screwup, why do you even hunt with me? You gave me the Eldorado even though I'm too much of a fuck-up to find my own hunts? When you went off to drink or torture demons or whatever shit—"

"Watch your tongue, or I'll beat some sense into you."

Like you could, Jake thought. "I'm getting Tobias out, and there's nothing you can do to stop me."

The Hawthornes froze, staring into each other's eyes. It was a breaking point for something they had never thought could break, for something they had never thought about much at all. A man didn't think about his bones until he felt them on the edge of shattering.

"He's a fucking monster, like what killed your mother," Leon said at last. "He'll get you killed."

"No," Jake said. He didn't give a damn what Dad thought he was saying no to. Just . . . no. No to all of it. No to everything Dad had ever told him about Tobias, and a big fucking no to his ideas about what were right for them.

Jake went to his bed and shoved things into his duffel. He didn't think about it; he didn't bother reassembling the shotgun before dumping it in with half-eaten granola bars and his spare set of socks. He was waiting for Dad to say something, anything, and at the same time knew he wouldn't say a fucking thing that Jake wanted to hear.

Jake had thrown his bag over his shoulder and reached for the doorknob when Leon's voice snapped the silence, as sure and irrevocable as a silver round cutting through a shapeshifter's heart.

"You walk out that door for a freak, don't expect to come crawling back. Don't come back at all."

Jake froze, his hand on the doorknob. "You don't mean that," he said, but his voice wasn't sure. Dad had never in his life patched up a relationship unless it was a life-or-death necessity. When the emotional waters got choppy, Leon Hawthorne ran like hell and didn't send postcards.

"I damn well do," Leon said. His voice was rough. Jake could pretend it was tears, but he thought rage was more likely, and the skin on the back of his neck prickled in something dangerously like fear. "You can't be my son and a freak lover at the same time, coddling some fucking monster."

"Toby's not a monster," Jake said automatically. He couldn't focus on the other words, what he had just heard his own father call him. Couldn't admit that this was what it had come to. Maybe he was a freak lover, maybe he was wrong, but he had made a promise and he couldn't, would never, break a promise to Tobias.

In that moment, he realized that this could be the end. Because of Toby, he might walk out on the man who had rocked him when he cried, who had carried him sleeping from the backseat of the Eldorado when he was a child. The man who had given him his first gun, had taught him everything he needed to know about saving people and defending himself. Leon Hawthorne might be a royal pain in the ass, but he had been the rock of Jake's life. The one thing to hold on to when blood, death, and monsters—some of them human—were the only real things in the world, and Mom was nothing but scattered ashes and a cold marble monument.

Jake realized that he could lose it all, but he still had to take this last step. Because losing Toby would hurt just as much. And if he didn't go now, everything he took pride in—who he *was*, his identity as Jake Hawthorne—would be meaningless. A joke.

If Leon Hawthorne noticed the moment, if he could feel the same tension in the air that threatened to suffocate Jake, then he didn't pay any attention to it.

"Damn right I mean it," he said. "I would rather see you dead than welcoming a fucking monster into your life and your bed."

Jake tightened his grip on the door and jerked it open. "I'm sorry to disappoint you then, sir," he said, when there was nothing more between him and the night air than the thin hope that Dad would realize what he had said and take it back. Not that Jake expected that. He was Leon fucking Hawthorne, after all, and he had never not meant anything he said: not when he threatened a monster's life, not when he had cried over Mom, not when he told Jake that the greatest hope in his life was a dirty, perverted, malformed desire. Jake gripped the Eldorado's keys in his pocket. "But I'm going, and you can't stop me."

Leon's face went blank, and he reached for the gun on his bed. "Damned if I can't."

"You gonna shoot me, Dad?" Jake taunted. He mocked him so that he didn't break down right there. Maybe to beg for forgiveness, or just to bawl. He hadn't expected Dad to understand. But he hadn't expected this.

"Jake, just close the door and we'll talk about this." But Leon was still reaching for the holy water and his gun. Jake hadn't hunted with the man for years without recognizing the signs that meant he thought something in front of him was worth killing.

"You never fucking listen to me, Dad," Jake said, and then he turned and ran.

He ran to the Eldorado, fumbled the keys into the lock, and was out of the hotel parking lot and speeding for the highway before he dared to look back.

Leon Hawthorne stood in the parking lot, staring after him, eyes wide, haunted and horrible. That was the face he wore when he remembered the people he couldn't save, or when he talked about his beautiful, spunky Sally, dead on a pyre.

He shouted something as Jake turned the corner, squealing the Eldorado's tires to put distance between him and the knowledge that he was leaving behind everything he had once thought made him *him*.

He didn't know what Leon had said, but he had a pretty good guess.

You're dead to me.

"Well, fuck you too, sir," Jake said to the highway that stretched before him.

He was proud of how his voice didn't shake at all.

When his cell phone lit up an hour later, Dad's name flashing, he didn't pick up.

ROGER WAS HAVING a quiet hot tea moment—with a little brandy stirred in to reward himself after a long but satisfying hunt—when he heard one of his proximity alarms placed around the border of the junkyard. Tea sloshed out of the mug and over the table, and Roger grabbed a shotgun, a silver knife, and a flask of holy water and stepped out onto the porch, trying to look casual while looking everywhere at once.

He had plenty more trip wires and safeguards installed at the back of the property, including a motion sensor. Unless the thing moved too fucking fast to trigger those, he'd get another warning before anything happened.

He expected to have to wait ten, fifteen minutes—anything that could track him down in Truth or Consequences was probably smart enough to know that coming after Roger at his house was going to be a festival of pain for all concerned. But about the time he was thinking that he should have brought his tea out to the porch so that it didn't get cold before shit went down, the last enemy he expected to see walked down the dirt driveway.

Jake Hawthorne looked rumpled and a little wild, like he'd been invited to hell and jumped out of the basket halfway there. His eyes looked a touch crazy, and his hand kept straying toward his pistol on his hip, as though the junker cars and random machinery might jump at him first.

Roger moved to set the shotgun down—this was *Jake,* after all—but his hand wouldn't quite let go. Jake didn't look like Jake at the moment, and Roger knew that the last thing the kid would want if he was out of his head or possessed would be for Roger to get gutted just because the enemy wore Jake's face.

Jake stopped far enough away that Roger wouldn't want to

risk throwing the knife, but close enough that it would be easy work to nail him with the shotgun. He took in Roger's gun and his mock-relaxed posture, and the crazy look in his eyes got worse.

"You gonna shoot me, Roger?" he called. It didn't sound like he was joking. It sounded like he was angry and terrified, and that tone hit Roger hard.

"Hey, Jake. Could you throw your pistol down, kid?"

Jake glanced down, his hand moving to the gun, and then looked back up.

Roger felt like he'd been socked in the stomach. Was Jake Hawthorne *tearing up*?

"Why? Want me to make it fucking easier? The unarmed ones are always the best, right? You can take your time lining up the sights." Jake's voice was mocking, but he unbuckled the gun holster and tossed it sideways. Not somewhere that he couldn't get to with a good dive probably before Roger could shoot him, but far enough away that Roger could feel some of the tension loosen in his back.

"What the hell are you talking about, Jake?" Roger put the shotgun down against his chair and stepped forward. He wasn't sure what was going on, but he didn't think it would get better with an iron-loaded shotgun. Maybe a little holy water would help, but he hoped not. "Come here."

"I figured Dad would have told you by now." Jake didn't look any more reassured, but he was at least coming closer, mounting the stairs like each step led to his gallows. "I just hoped . . . seeing as you practically fucking *told* me to . . ."

Roger felt a lurch in his stomach, like the porch had dropped out from under him or a ghost had just tossed him down the stairs. "What did I tell you to do?"

Jake gave him a look. Roger couldn't have said what was in the look, but it was nothing good. Nothing that a nineteen-year-old should have in his eyes. Then again, this was a nineteen-year-old *hunter*. That spelled seven kinds of fucked up already.

He couldn't quite stop his hand from twitching for his knife when Jake reached for something in his back pocket, but it was only a crumpled piece of paper. It looked like a form for a driver's license or maybe a passport.

Jake put it on the table between them, smoothing it out absently, like he couldn't understand how it had gotten those crease marks. "I'm getting Toby out of Freak Camp."

Roger's breath stopped, realization creeping up on him with the same slow horror as a broken-legged zombie. Jake had acted on his advice, and something had gone wrong. Not that Roger was that surprised, but . . . he'd made that call maybe a week ago. Less than that.

He tried to think exactly when it had been but couldn't piece it together. He'd been at Freak Camp, and then he'd gone to clean up a den of mountain trolls that had dared reenter Roger's territory, and then he'd come home . . .

And now Jake was standing on his front porch looking like something the cat dragged in. Or maybe the werewolf. Usually when shit went down, Jake would stand in the middle of it, swinging baseball bats and cursing and holding his own. Not retreating to Roger's porch looking like one shove would knock him down.

"Jake . . ."

"You gonna cut me off too, Roger?" Jake laughed. "I guess that's what I get for being a damn freak lover, right?"

Roger swallowed. That was a horrible sound Jake had just made, and horrible words to go along with them. "Who said that, Jake? Who cut you off?"

Jake still wouldn't look at him, his hands moving over his jeans where the gun and the paper used to be, as though he had lost something and wasn't sure what to do with his hands now that they were gone. "You gotta tell me first, Rog. What do you think? What do you think now that you know I'm a f-freak lover and I'm getting a monster out of Freak Camp for my own perverted ends, or whatever the fuck you want to say? 'Cause I'm getting Toby out. I'm fucking *getting him out* and you can't fucking stop me." Jake's head snapped up, snarling the last few words into Roger's face.

He resisted the urge to back away from the raw rage and pain on Jake's face. "That's going to be hard," he said at last. "You . . . you got all the paperwork?"

From the look on Jake's face, he hadn't expected that. Good. Roger suspected that if he had said anything that Jake *had* expected, the kid would have gone for his throat, unarmed or not.

Jake took a shuddering breath and collapsed into a chair, the one farthest away from Roger's shotgun. He put his elbows on the table and his head in his hands. The paper crackled under his elbow.

Roger inched closer, like Jake was a wild animal that might bite if startled. He wasn't going to touch him yet. Not until he knew what the hell was going on.

"Who cut you off, kid?" he asked again, easing down into his chair. He needed the answer to that question. And he needed whiskey. As soon as he got the one, he figured he'd get them both the other.

Jake didn't look up, and when he spoke, the rage was gone from his voice. Roger hadn't noticed before how much of what made Jake *Jake* was his humor, anger, and swagger. Now, with Jake's voice void of emotion, Roger had to stop his hand from twitching toward the holy water again.

"Who do you think?"

Damn you to hell, Leon, Roger thought. *Couldn't you have just . . .* The thought ended there, because he had no idea what Leon could have done differently. Leon could have done so much better, but Roger knew that Leon would have only one response.

"Fuck," he said. Now it was his turn not to look at Jake. "But . . . I'm here. I'm not . . ." *going to be an asshole like that bastard who calls himself your father*, ". . . going to say a damn thing. I mean, I practically . . ." He took a deep breath. It was a day for breathing carefully. Too many things were too close to shattering. "It's good to see you, kid. You're welcome here, just as you've always been."

Jake's shoulders shook, and for a second Roger thought he was crying. Then he realized that it was laughter, the closest thing a Hawthorne could get to weeping on someone else's patio.

"Thanks," Jake rasped at last, when he'd stopped shaking and looked up again. His eyes were red-rimmed and puffy, but Roger couldn't see any sign of tears. Jake forced a smile onto his face, and it was one of the most horrible things Roger had seen recently. Not in his lifetime—demons and werewolves and shifters and ghosts had given him some pretty devastating memories—but perhaps in the last week or so.

"So," Jake said. "You're okay with the . . . with Toby. And me. Getting him out, I mean that's . . ." He shook his head. "I'm all fucked up, Roger. And it's not Tobias's fault!"

"Didn't think it was," Roger replied. "Yeah, I'm okay with it." *Would I have called you if I didn't think that kid deserved better?*

"Good." Jake dropped his hands to the paper again, smoothing it over and over. Roger figured that Jake was going to have to print a new form before he turned it in to anyone. "Then, would you be okay with . . . I need another couple signatures to say that I'm . . . sane, and shit like that, and I'm not sure . . . I mean, there are a few other people, but . . ." Jake stopped. "If you don't want to, I'll understand. The ASC and the Dixons can be . . . fucked up. I know that some people don't want to get on their radar."

Like Leon, Roger thought. Yeah, he didn't want to mess with the ASC either. But then again, he also wanted to boot them in the ass, so maybe this could count as both. "Sure. No problem. Hand me a pen." *If I wasn't such a coward, I would have done this myself when I realized how bad it had gotten. And when I realized that that kid wasn't the worst monster in the room. Not even close.*

"Good." Jake nodded, and his expression turned into something closer to an actual smile. "Good."

He still looked messed up, but he had a bit more sanity in his face, and that made Roger feel easier. Last thing they needed was two crazy Hawthornes. One—*fuck you, Leon*—was more than enough. "You can stay here, if you want. And pull the Eldorado up. You've still got her, right?"

Jake's mouth quirked. "Yeah, she and I made a fast getaway." He stood, stretching like he'd been in a cramped position for far too long. "I'll bring her around. Then we can start on the paperwork. Fuck, Roger, you should see the forms I need to fill out. And I can't even forge them, because the ASC is going to background check everything. Fucking bureaucracy."

Roger thought that worrying about a little paperwork was better than Jake thinking about his life crashing down around his ears. And he could remind the kid that he had more people in his life than Leon.

"I'm a big bundle of excitement," he said dryly. "You can crash in the guest room as long as you want, and I'll do my best with the paperwork. And if you need more than just my signature, let's call up Alex Rodriguez. I'm sure she'd . . . understand too."

Jake looked up, frowning. "Who?"

"An old friend over in Tucson. Another old-school hunter who works part-time like me. She runs an old mission."

Now that the whole thing was rolling, he was a little nervous thinking about Jake getting a monster out of the camp, taking charge of another life that had been fucked up that much—and might still be dangerous, after all, the kid had been in *Freak Camp*—but it was too late to retreat now.

He'd do his best to keep everyone sane and off each other's throats. Oh, he could see fun times in his future.

Maybe he'd finally shoot Leon.

That shouldn't have sounded as appealing as it did at the moment.

CRUSHER GROUND TOBIAS'S face into the wall, twisting his arm behind him, and pushed his hips into Tobias's ass.

"You think you can disrespect me, freak? I saw that look on your face."

Tobias felt Crusher's erection, felt the hand that wasn't holding him against the wall sliding down his hip, and he wondered, almost idly, when he would have to take the next step and break the guard's arm. Not that that was a smart idea, or an idea that would let him live past today, or even an idea that would actually stop anything, but Tobias knew that he wouldn't be able to control the freewheeling panic spinning under the surface of his careful, blank calm for much longer. There was no way Tobias would let Crusher be his first. He would, quite literally, rather die.

Crusher's hand found its goal, clamping around his groin, and Tobias ground his own face into the wall, twisting his cheek against the rough plaster to keep his whimpering under control.

"You know how long I've waited for you, Pretty Freak?" Crusher hissed. "For fucking *ever*. Too goddamn long to fuck open your tight ass."

It wasn't like Tobias deserved anything more than this. He simply *could not* let Crusher do what he wanted without trying to stop it.

He was just about to break, to throw away all hope, to throw away his life in favor of breaking Crusher's jaw and running into the guards' bullets, when Karl appeared.

"Crusher!" He smacked his billy club against his palm. The burn scar across his cheek was shiny. "Let the freak go. Save it 'til the rest of us can watch."

Crusher eased his hold a little, and Tobias took a shaky breath, feeling a few drops of blood trickle down his cheek.

"You stay the fuck out of this, Karl," Crusher snarled.

Karl laughed. "You think I want to get between you and that freak's ass?" He pointed the club at Tobias. "Hawthorne wants him."

The relief that surged through Tobias almost made him sick. Forty heartbeats ago he had been ready to die, to take the last miserable step into death. Now Jake had come, not to save him —Jake had promised, but Tobias knew how hard it would be to get a monster out, knew that even if Jake tried it probably wouldn't work—but just for those brief moments of kindness, of gentle touches, of casual conversation that didn't end in pain.

He almost ran to Reception, Jake's name a promise of salvation, if only for an afternoon.

The new guard, Charlie, nodded toward Room Four, and Tobias burst through, smiling involuntarily, knowing that Jake liked to see him smile.

Leon Hawthorne turned to face him.

Tobias's back hit the door hard. The cold metal cut through the blind panic—and the instinct to deny that this was happening, to insist that Jake had to be there—but he was still shaking, trapped, terrified. He closed his eyes, fighting hard to bring back that blank emptiness, prepared to submit to any blow or order without a flicker of reaction. After all, Leon Hawthorne was a hunter. That was what hunters wanted. That was what hunters—*not Jake*—demanded, and he had always been able to give it to them before, like a good little monster.

It took too fucking long, already long enough that it might

cost him his life. But shit, shit, *Leon Hawthorne* was the last person he expected—he had come to see *Jake,* he had run like joy was an emotion he deserved to feel because he knew he was going to see Jake, who wanted to see him smile and look him in the eye. Jake was the only person in the world for whom Tobias would lower his defenses. But for his *father* . . . his legendary hunter of a father . . . no, Tobias dared not think about joy in the presence of a hunter.

But given a choice between being trapped under Crusher or being in a room with Leon Hawthorne, he would always choose the hunter. It wasn't a question of death or pain; there was no doubt that the man hated monsters, but he knew Leon would kill him when he was done, when Tobias stopped being useful. And he would kill him clean. Two things he would never be able to hope for from Crusher. It was better here. Better.

But Tobias still couldn't stop shaking.

"Sit down." Leon snapped the order, but it didn't yet carry the promise of pain.

Tobias's legs obeyed immediately, thank God, carrying him to the table and chair. He placed his hands palms-up before him, swallowed, and closed his eyes as he *wished* his hands would stop trembling. Such obvious fear only made things worse, always.

For a long moment, Leon was silent, though Tobias could feel his eyes on him. At last he said, flatly, "That's not what I came for."

Tobias took a quick, deep breath, opening his eyes and lacing his fingers together to force them to be still. He didn't know what the proper response could be, so he went for the safe route. "I'm sorry, sir."

Leon weighed him with his gaze. Tobias felt it but didn't dare raise his eyes from the table. "I'm here to see what kind of goddamn freak hoodwinked my son. Look at me."

Tobias's breath stopped for a moment, but he didn't hesitate.

He looked up and for the first time met Leon Hawthorne's eyes, gray as the camp's concrete walls but colder still.

His face was nothing like his son's, had nothing in common that Tobias could see. It wasn't about physical resemblance; Jake had never looked at him like he was a monster. Jake's eyes searched his face as though looking for what could make Tobias smile; Leon stared at him with the impassive contempt and loathing that Tobias always expected from reals—all of them except Jake.

But Leon's eyes didn't hold the same malice as in the guards and other hunters. Tobias could see that Leon wouldn't touch any monster unless he absolutely had to. From the way his hand kept moving toward the gun in his holster, Tobias knew the man would rather shoot him right now than touch him in any way, even to administer a punishment.

Tobias's heartbeat slowed until it didn't feel like it was going to pound out of his chest, and he took a deeper, steadying breath. Whatever happened here, he would be okay.

"Well, you look human enough." Leon's voice was flat, his face as empty and hard as the walls of the interrogation room around them. "That always makes it harder, when they look human. A vampire is just as likely to kill whether the fangs are in or out, but it's always harder to take off the head when it's a frightened woman staring back at you, or the face of some poor civilian bastard who doesn't know what happened to their kid and why they're covered in blood. I still manage. So you're *Tobias*."

Tobias cringed at his name, his gaze falling, then lifting again. The hunter had told him to look at him, so he would. "Yes, sir."

"That wasn't a question." Leon's voice remained flat, angry. "I came to see you. To see the monster that's going to get my son killed."

Tobias felt like he'd been knocked in the chest with a club, all the breath punched out of him. His head jerked down to stare at his folded hands, at the dents in the table, anything while his lungs fought to fill again. He couldn't believe it. That couldn't be true. He hadn't done anything to Jake, not one thing, and surely he couldn't be that inherently evil that just by talking to Jake, knowing him, he could hurt him. Jake, who was always strong and good and confident.

But Leon Hawthorne didn't say it like he wanted to make Tobias bleed inside—the guards had taught him to identify that edge, even when he couldn't build defenses against it. Leon sounded like a man stating a fact: a bleak, hopeless, plain fact. "He talks to you like you're human, gets it in his head that some monsters aren't monsters, and one day he's going to come up against something that he trusts, and it's going to walk up behind him and slice his spine."

"I wouldn't—" He couldn't stop himself, couldn't break off the words in time.

"Shut up. You know how his mother died, don't you?" Tobias nodded, hunching over his hands. "She went out there trying to help people, save the world, and what did she get for it? Cut down from the back by some cowardly beast not even willing to show his face. That's going to be Jake: laid out on some coroner's table because he trusted one too many monsters like you."

Tobias's nails bit into his skin. He watched, trying very hard not to react, while blood seeped out around them slowly, like Leon's words were eating their way to his heart.

"When he falls, I'm going to come back here and cut your fucking head off," Leon promised.

Tobias whispered, "I hope so."

Leon Hawthorne kicked his chair, and Tobias snapped up. "What did you say?"

Tobias shook his head violently. "Nothing, sir."

Leon stared at him, hand resting again on his gun. He was a hunter. One of the best. But Tobias didn't fear him as a hunter.

The hunters that made him shake were the ones that came in with big grins and toolboxes from the resource room, the ones that enjoyed tying him down, not because he was a monster, but because they could. Leon Hawthorne hated him, hated all monsters absolutely, but there was nothing gleeful in that hatred. He would kill Tobias the same way he'd put down any monster.

Leon could kill Tobias, yes, but like the electric fence could kill if Tobias got too close; it wouldn't hunt down its prey, wouldn't smile listening to the screams. Tobias could have almost felt safe if not for the words.

"I have to keep him safe from you," Leon said. "You fuck with his head, and I can't lose him. He's all I—" He snapped his mouth shut, and his hand tightened on his gun. "Don't wait for him, freak, he's not coming back. I'm not going to let some damn pretty monster sink his claws into my son's head and drag him down, if it's the last thing I do. I let Sally go. You bastards won't take Jake too."

Leon Hawthorne stood and walked around the table, and Tobias flinched, but the hunter didn't notice as he headed for the door.

Tobias closed his eyes tight. "You going to shoot me?" He prayed for that. Better death than a life without Jake. Maybe he would be with Becca. Maybe he would vanish into nothing. Maybe he would be in hell. Better any of those than in Freak Camp, knowing Jake wasn't coming back.

He heard Leon pause. "What would be the point? I have other monsters to spend my bullets on."

The door slammed shut behind Jake's father.

The guards left Tobias in the interrogation room for a long time. Tobias didn't bother to count the seconds. He stared at his hands and refused to think of anything at all.

CHAPTER ELEVEN

JANUARY 2000

IN THE EVENING, after the guards took their pick of monster ass like usual and the rest of the monsters settled cautiously into their bunks, Victor and Karl came for Tobias. They pulled him off his bunk, and panic made Tobias twist in their arms. Karl jerked his arms higher up behind his back until he stopped squirming, and Victor pushed the hair off his face. It had grown long again.

"Director wants to see you. Better make sure he can see that pretty face of yours. C'mon. Don't make us leave bruises where he'll see them."

The two guards snapped a leash onto his collar—doubling his heart rate and making it impossible not to tense against their hands—but he didn't even have the freedom to walk behind them with the leash. They practically carried him to Administration.

Administration was the second floor above Reception. Tobias had only ever been in one room on that floor, which was the library that he had worked in since his first days with Becca. He knew there were other rooms where reals, including important visitors, gathered to discuss FREACS's progress on neutralizing the supernatural threat.

Karl and Victor carried him straight past anything familiar and through the heavy iron doors that monsters were forbidden to enter.

They pulled him through beautifully carpeted hallways, so elegant and clean that Tobias felt he was dirtying them just with his shoes dragging along the floor, and finally to two huge doors. The plaque next to the doors read Director Jonah Dixon. Karl rapped two quick knocks and pushed the door in.

As they entered, Director Dixon looked up from paperwork on his desk. Karl dumped Tobias to the floor, and he hit his knees hard. The rich, colorful rug under him should have felt softer, easier than the concrete yard or packed earth he knew too well, but it struck the same—or worse—chill of horror through him.

"That is 89UI6703?" The Director stood. His huge desk was built in a glossy dark red wood that reflected the ceiling light. A long matching conference table stretched down one side of the room, and a bookshelf took up most of the opposite wall. "Well, don't just stand there and stare, get him on his feet."

Karl pulled Tobias up by his hair.

The Director moved forward. He was a lean but fit older man with brown eyes in a cold, thoughtful face. With a firm grip, he took hold of Tobias's chin in his hand. Tobias cringed, but Karl's grip on his arms tightened enough to leave bruises, and he forced himself to be still.

"I've heard interesting things about you, 89UI." The Director glanced at Victor, who was shifting uneasily behind Karl. "What do the guards call him?"

Victor hesitated. Through his own panic, Tobias noticed that Victor, too, was nervous. "Pretty Freak, sir. Because he's—"

"An attractive young monster amid a crowd of skin-sloughers and muzzled vamps," the Director said. "Yes, I understand, Mr. Todd. I've always said that the guards lacked creativity."

Karl glared, the livid burn scar across his cheek flushing, but Victor kept his eyes just to the right of the Director's face, the way Tobias looked at guards.

"Is he intelligent?" the Director asked Victor, ignoring Karl's glare.

Victor hesitated. "I'm not . . . sure what you mean, sir."

Tobias kept his eyes on the floor. Victor sounded cautious, wary, and he was always the smartest of the guards. Tobias had already been afraid of the Director on principle—he was in charge of FREACS and the ASC, and a word from him could destroy any monster or guard in the facility—but now he knew that he had another good reason to be afraid.

"I realize we pay you to keep the vermin under control and not to think, but do I really need to rephrase the question, Mr. Todd?"

Victor straightened. "No, sir. He seems . . . bright enough." Tobias could nearly hear him struggling to find a better answer. "Takes direction well."

"Obedient, good. You see, Mr. Todd, Mr. Horwitz, I have a theory that the only monster that shouldn't be slit open on a rack is an obedient monster, a monster that can be used. Intelligence in freaks is only useful as far as it can be shaped and wielded by a human. Otherwise it is nothing but guile that serves to make the freak more dangerous. Would you agree?"

Tobias risked a glance toward Victor. The guard had a pinched, sour look on his face, like he knew he was being dressed down to give someone else a lesson and didn't like it at all.

The Director slapped Tobias, and Tobias's head snapped back.

The man's smile looked almost kind, but there was steel and venom in his eyes. "You do not look at humans while I am talking to them. That is disrespect and will not be tolerated. Do you understand, 89UI?"

"Yes, sir," Tobias said, dropping his eyes. The slap had been far lighter than any strike from the guards, but his heart hammered harder than it had during his last beating.

The Director gripped Tobias's chin again, forcing his head back up. He stared into Tobias's eyes for a long minute, and then he came to a decision.

"You may leave us, gentlemen. Hand that leash to me. You may wait in the hall. Naturally if it sounds like I'm being slaughtered or anything along those lines, feel free to come to my rescue." The Director's mouth quirked, and he gave a sharp tug on Tobias's leash just as Victor and Karl let him go.

Tobias unbalanced, barely catching himself in time.

"Good reflexes." The Director pulled him to the conference table. Solid metal rings were set into the table side at even intervals between the chairs. A monster chained to that table would be close, but not necessarily in the way. The Director tied the leash to a ring so that Tobias was wedged tight against the high back of one of the graceful wooden chairs. He would have had more room if he moved between the chairs, but the Director jerked the leash to make sure that Tobias stayed behind the chair, and then locked the leash in place.

The Director caught his gaze and smiled in slight amusement. "The key is in my desk. You'll get out of here when I tell you you may, and not a moment before. Respond when I talk to you."

"Yes, sir," Tobias said, staring down.

"Wonderful. You can respond to basic commands. Mr. Todd is a bright man, though he's certainly not family, but I'm never quite sure if other people share the same definitions of intelligence and training that I do. Uncle Elijah certainly didn't. Are you obedient otherwise, or are you punished often?"

Tobias swallowed. "Not often, sir."

"Good." The Director rubbed his hands together. "Let's see if you're lying, shall we? Put your hands on the chair in front of you. You let go, you lift your hands up, you resist me in any way, and I'll call Mr. Horwitz in here to start cutting off unnecessary pieces. I believe he still has a grudge against you because of that regrettable incident that led to his disfigurement. Do you understand, or do you have questions?"

Tobias licked his lips and planted his hands on the back of the chair. "Which pieces are unnecessary, sir?"

The Director smiled. "He gets to decide."

Then he touched Tobias on the shoulder.

Tobias bowed his head and gritted his teeth, even though the hand was gentle, thoughtful. From his shoulder, the Director hooked his fingers under the collar and pulled Tobias's head hard, sideways. Tobias choked a little but held on tighter to the chair, and the Director smiled and patted him on the back of his head.

"Smart," he said. "Good boy."

When his other hand slid over Tobias's hip, Tobias straightened and stared straight ahead, squeezing the back of the chair until his fingers were numb, trying to hold on to some control to head off the panic.

The Director didn't fuck monsters. That was the rumor. Tobias had never seen proof either way, but he still expected the hand to slide around to where he was pressed against the chair, to hook into the waistband of his pants.

The Director paused. "I take it that the guards, such as Mr. Todd and Mr. Horwitz, enjoy using your body for their own sexual gratification?" Tobias took a shaky breath, and fingernails dug into his hip. "Answer me, freak."

Tobias exhaled. "Yes, sir."

"What sexual practices have you been taught to perform? Be specific and comprehensive."

No. No, no, no. He'd had guards and hunters ask him that

before, though not in those words. The Director's hand loosened and retightened, grinding long fingers into the bruises. "Blowjobs. Handjobs. I stand still while they h-handle themselves or m-m-me. S-sometimes while they are interrogating me, it also seems to c-cause them s-sexual g-gratification."

"Have you been anally penetrated by any object or body part?"

He couldn't stop a small whimper. Worse, he knew the man behind him would hear, would know. He was terribly aware of the Director's hand. Aware of the slowly growing pain in his hip, terrified those long fingers would relax and slide beneath his pants. "N-n-no, sir."

"Why not? You seem to have been used for everything else."

Tobias couldn't slow down the spike in his breathing or the way his arms shook before him, still clenching the chair. "I-I don't know, sir." *Please please please I don't know but please let whatever keeps them off still be there, please not today.*

"Hmm. Do you touch yourself for the sexual pleasure of yourself or others?"

Tobias shook his head violently and remembered just in time to keep his grip on the back of the chair. He pulled back slightly, and the Director slammed him back into the unyielding wood. "N-n-no," he choked out. "No, sir. Never."

"Good." The hand left Tobias's hip. "Spread your legs."

When Tobias didn't move to obey quickly enough—he wasn't thinking right, couldn't get his brain and his body to work together, or maybe it was that his brain had stopped thinking and all his body could remember was to clutch the chair—the Director shoved him forward, hard, over the curved wood and kicked his feet apart. Tobias gasped, and the Director jerked his head up roughly.

The Director's voice was calm, clear, as though reciting an instruction manual. "When I tell you to do something, you will do it promptly and without question. Hesitations will be punished. Mistakes will be punished. Any sign of disrespect or rebellion will be punished, because a monster without obedience is a plague-carrying vermin, consuming resources it does not deserve and existing only as a threat to humankind. Do you understand, or will you require more explicit instruction?"

"I und-d-derstand, s-sir."

The Director used his grip on Tobias's hair to shove him forward, then let him go. "Good. You will not move your legs, you will not let go of the chair, and please keep your noise to a minimum."

Tobias swallowed, gritted his teeth together, and closed his eyes as both of the Director's hands settled on his waist. This time, there was nothing casual or gradual about the touch. The Director's hands moved over his body like he was inspecting a beast in an auction. He squeezed Tobias's arms, ran a hand up his chest, and then jerked his shirt up. Tobias flinched, but managed to stop himself from making a noise as he felt the cool office air against his bare back, and the even cooler caress of the Director's fingertips.

"Fascinating scar pattern," he said, half to himself. "On any other monster, I'd say you were a piece of shit that ought to be burned. But of course, most monsters don't survive for ten and a half years in our facility. You're quite an anomaly, 89UI. With the exception of certain individuals in Intensive Containment, you are our longest surviving monster. I find that fascinating."

When the Director hooked his thumbs in Tobias's pants and pulled them as far down as they would go with his legs spread apart, Tobias couldn't keep back a choked cry, which he repeated when the Director began touching him below the waist, even though he handled Tobias's hips and ass with the same dispassionate thoroughness with which he had examined Tobias's shoulders and back.

The Director paused behind Tobias, his hand on Tobias's inner thigh. His fingers clenched hard, like they had earlier on his hip, and Tobias sobbed again. "89UI, do you honestly expect me to be aroused by touching you?"

Tobias tried to remember how to breathe. It was hard to force air into his lungs when a hand was *right there*, when there was a real human behind him. The Director didn't fuck monsters.

But maybe the Director just didn't let it get out. Few men were like Crusher, willing to pull their dicks out during a filmed interrogation, with the freaks in the shower, or in the barracks with the lights on. Maybe the Director fucked things, but when he did, they were never seen again. The Director of the ASC would have ways to clean up the mess so that no one asked questions.

The Director's hand closed like a vise and dragged his unexpectedly sharp nails upward, cutting into Tobias's skin. He stifled another sound, barely remembering in time to keep his legs spread, his hands on the chair. His fingers were so tightly clenched that he couldn't feel them anymore.

But the Director's voice was calm, smooth, with a hint of warning. "When I ask you a question, you will answer. Do I need to repeat myself?"

Tobias shook his head. "No, sir. No, sir." He could feel wetness dripping down his leg, but he couldn't tell if the Director had drawn blood or if it was just sweat.

The hand didn't loosen. "Are you responding to my directive about not making me repeat myself, or are you answering my original question? I expect you to be specific and clear in your responses, 89UI."

"I d-d-don't . . . I d-don't expect anything, sir. I don't know . . . I can't . . . I'm sorry, I'm sorry." Tobias shook and dropped his head, trying to control himself, trying not to beg, because he didn't know what he would be begging for.

The hand withdrew. The Director stepped back. "You may remove your hands from the chair." He walked back to his desk.

Tobias released the wood slowly, his fingers aching. The Director withdrew a tissue from a box on his desk and fastidiously cleaned his hand. Tobias didn't look at him directly, but he thought he caught a hint of red.

"Put your clothing back on," the Director said. "I have no sexual interest in monsters. But I do have a deep, practical interest in making them useful for humans, instead of the scourge they naturally are. To that end, you will report to me every Wednesday at 6:30 p.m. so that you may be trained, educated, and conditioned into the kind of monster that deserves the food and air you consume. Mr. Todd will bring you next week so you know where to go, but I expect you to arrive promptly and on your own after that. Is that understood, 89UI?"

Tobias pulled his pants up and tugged his shirt down. "Y-y-yes, sir."

The Director came back, and he was smiling. A real smile that reached his eyes. "Good." He unlocked the padlock holding Tobias to the table and unwound the leash. "You may go now."

Tobias left with his head down, walking past Victor and Karl without pausing to look at them. He kept his eyes on the ground all the way to the barracks. He couldn't stop shaking, even when he was in the safety of the night air.

As he jerked the wheel through the last few turns on the winding road to Freak Camp, Jake had to acknowledge that he was acting more like a drug addict minutes from his next hit than an upstanding member of the hunting community.

But according to Roger (as well as Leon, though Jake didn't think of that anymore), "upstanding member of the hunting community" meant Dixons and Dixon kiss-asses. At any rate, Jake's paperwork looked as good as two crafty bastards and a desperate twenty-year-old could make it. Turned out that Roger could stretch the truth better than even Dad had.

He pulled into the FREACS parking lot, slammed the Eldorado's door shut harder than he usually would, and pushed through the entrance. Sometimes he felt he was losing control, and other times he *knew* he was losing control, but right now he badly needed a reminder of why he was doing this: cutting open his life to display it to the ASC, leaving behind the rock he'd built his life on. If he could get Toby to look him in the eye for a few seconds, if he could break the barriers between them—they seemed both more impenetrable and more brittle every time he came—the shitstorm that had become his life would fall into perspective. If he could get Toby to give him even a half smile, Jake could find solid ground under his feet again.

Yeah, seeing Toby would be some kind of hit.

His anticipation slammed headfirst into a wall at the reception desk.

"I'm sorry, Mr. Hawthorne—*Jake,*" Madison said, smiling at him through her lashes. "But with your withdrawal permit pending, I can't allow you access to the facility."

Jake blinked at her. "What?" He felt dazed and stupid, head ringing like he'd just gotten slammed by a poltergeist.

"Your monster withdrawal permit? For" —she glanced down at the computer— "permanent removal of 89UI6703 from the facility. Until that is either approved or denied, I cannot allow you access."

They hadn't mentioned that at Headquarters. They had just taken his information and told him they would be in contact. Leah Dixon had handled the process, and she hadn't said one damn thing about Jake not being allowed back in fucking Freak Camp.

Jake groped for a response. "Any idea why?"

She shrugged. "It's a security measure. The separation helps the review committee determine if the hunter's desire to remove the monster has been influenced by any supernatural ability, like those possessed by sirens and psychics. It's just safer if the hunter does not have access to *any* monster for the period of review. We're all susceptible."

He hadn't told Toby that he was doing this now. He had wanted it to be a surprise, or maybe he just wanted to be sure it would actually work before he got Toby's hopes up. The idea of disappointing Toby hurt too much to risk. And now that indecision had made it so that Toby wouldn't know that Jake was coming for him, wouldn't know why he had vanished. "Do you know how long this usually takes?"

"For a permanent removal? I honestly have no idea, but my best guess is six to twelve months." She interpreted Jake's strangled noise as criticism and bristled. "We take containment very seriously. The background check alone can take months. Any hunter requesting to remove a monster has to be considered absolutely unimpeachable, with a record of successful hunts and no hint of mental instability or supernatural contamination. As a hunter, I'm sure you understand how hard it is to get an accurate profile. Plus, the monster's history and psychological profile must be examined to make sure that when released, the hunter will be able to keep it under control. The committee has to determine if any additional measures—such as fang removal for a vampire or a bone harness for a shapeshifter—are needed to ensure the safety of both the hunter and the civilian population if a once-contained monster escapes its handler's control. The process is involved and can't be rushed."

And no guarantee that Jake could get him out in the end. The fucking Dixon committee could always say no. Then Jake would do his best to burn Freak Camp to the ground and get Toby the hell out anyway. "Is there any way, any way at all, that I can speed it up?"

"Unless you need a specific monster to complete a time-sensitive hunt, or have a previous bait permit—neither of which

I can influence, you would have to go back to Headquarters—no." She smiled at him. "Don't worry. You're *Jake Hawthorne*. I'm sure the committee is already working to grant your request as soon as possible."

Jake didn't know if that would be good enough.

As he stepped outside, the disappointment hit him hard as a body blow. He leaned against the wall, fighting the urge to run around the perimeter to find a place where he could climb and hurdle the wall. All he needed was a minute with Toby, a minute to look at him, to make sure he was okay, to tell him Jake would get him out of there one way or another soon enough.

Jake would infiltrate the camp any way he had to if those old puckered assholes *dared* reject his application. He had nothing left to lose. If it came down to it, he wouldn't hesitate to grab Toby, shoot his way out of FREACS, and deal with the shitstorm after that. But Toby deserved better than a life on the run with Jake and the Eldorado, crap motels, and credit card fraud, so Jake had to try to do this the legit way, through the fucking bowels of government. And that meant keeping his head on straight. He couldn't do anything to jeopardize his permit, especially since he was damn lucky Matthew hadn't put a black mark on his record the last time he'd lashed out inside the camp.

He felt nauseated, thinking how he could have ended all his chances, all of Toby's hopes for survival, that day. He had to be better. He had to wait it out. And he hoped Toby wouldn't blame him too much for how long it took.

He pushed away from the wall and looked back at Reception. Nothing of the camp interior was visible from the outside, but he couldn't turn himself away. *Hang on, Toby. Hang on. I swear on my mom's pyre I'm coming for you.*

Jake turned back to his car.

THE NEXT DAY, halfway through dinner, Victor came to the mess hall, nodded to Karl and Lonny, and scanned the monster heads.

"I'm here for Pretty Freak. Director wants him, says he's to be released to go to Administration this time every Wednesday for the foreseeable future."

Tobias heard him but didn't register the words. That happened sometimes, when something was too awful even for a worst day. It didn't help how his brain just decided something wasn't true even when it was. That would get him killed someday.

Karl scoffed. "Think the boss man's finally fucking something?"

"Shut the fuck up," Lonny snapped. "You want to get your back whipped like Gomez?"

"Take it easy," Victor said. "He wasn't here that day."

"Yeah, well, I was, and I don't want to see that again. Or have it be me. So watch your mouth, Horwitz."

"Where's the freak?"

Lonny jerked his head to where Tobias sat, head bowed, frozen. "Over there."

Victor turned. "Hey, freak!" he called.

The monsters in the room glanced up, eyes wide. Then they saw where Victor was looking and dropped their gazes.

Slowly, the same dull terror he felt before interrogations lining his throat, Tobias stood up and walked to Victor.

He expected a leash, a blow, a threat, *something,* but Victor just looked at him like he was a piece of shit he'd found on the bottom of his shoe. "Let's go, freak. We don't want to keep the Director waiting."

The walk to the Director's office in Administration was silent, tense. Tobias had a strange feeling, like they were walking toward the same thing together—not guard and monster, but two creatures going somewhere they didn't want to go.

Victor knocked twice on the Director's door and pushed open the door when he heard, "Come in."

This time the Director was leaning against his desk, a watch in hand. He smiled when he met Victor's eyes. "Thank you, Mr. Todd. Right on time."

"Of course, sir," Victor said.

"You're destined for great things, Mr. Todd," the Director said. "You may go now."

Victor nodded once. He paused an instant with his eyes on Tobias, mouth pressed into something difficult to define—not pity, but at least acknowledgment that he did not want to be in Tobias's place. Then he was gone, down the hall.

The Director got up from his perch on the desk and moved to a door Tobias hadn't seen before on the far side of the bookshelves. "89UI, come with me."

Tobias followed the Director into the interrogation room. Bare concrete floor, harsh bright lights, and bolts set into the walls at various heights for securing monsters. There were three or four battered chairs, a small table covered in a white sheet, a water tap and a hose by the wall closest to the door, and a drain in the middle of the floor. Two cameras were fixed in opposite corners, and a hook dangled from the ceiling.

The Director nodded at a chair in the corner. "Strip and put on that pair of underwear. I have no desire to view your genitalia, but skin is a necessity."

Tobias went slowly to the chair, and stripped. He carefully folded everything he had removed, wiggled into the tight white shorts, and then turned around.

"In my opinion," the Director said, "there is only one reason to keep a monster around, and that is if he's dependable and obedient. That is my goal here, what we are going to work on every week—to see if I can make you into a dependable monster. Do you understand?"

"Yes, sir."

The Director smiled. "I don't really think you do. Not yet. Come here."

Tobias walked to where the Director indicated, beneath the hook.

The Director took a pair of wide, leather-padded cuffs off the table and snapped them over Tobias's wrists in front of him. Tobias's breath caught, but before he could react, the Director had stepped on a stool and jerked Tobias's arms up until he could slide the chain between the cuffs around the hook.

When he stepped back, kicking the stool away, Tobias was trapped, stretched to his full height with his arms extended. He had to stay on his toes or his weight would fall on his shoulders.

The Director looked him once over, then moved to pull the small table into Tobias's line of sight. Unlike some of the hunters and guards in Tobias's experience, he added no drama as he removed and folded the sheet, unveiling the interrogation tools. Knives, shafts, whips, crushers—not the widest variety Tobias had ever seen, but every tool gleamed, polished and clean, in the unforgiving light of the interrogation room.

A knock came at the door, and Tobias jerked involuntarily, the motion swinging him slightly and pulling on his arms. He was already feeling the ache.

"Come in!" the Director called.

The door swung open, and Crusher walked in. The first thing he saw was Tobias, and Tobias could see the crazy flickering in his eyes. When the guard licked his lips, Tobias couldn't stop himself from making a small sound.

"Good evening, Mr. Sloan." The Director stepped closer to Tobias and rested a hand on his shoulder. "Mr. Sloan has so kindly volunteered to help me. He wants you to be a good, *obedient* monster as well, don't you, Mr. Sloan?"

The guard scowled. "Call me Crusher."

Momentarily distracted from tracing the scars on Tobias's back and his hip, the Director looked up. "No," he said. His nails dug into the bruises he'd left on Tobias's hip the day before, and Tobias gasped and jerked against the chains.

Crusher made an involuntary noise, and Tobias—so close he could count the wrinkles across the Director's forehead—saw the brief flash of a smile before the Director's hand reached the raw nail marks on his inner thigh and clamped down. Tobias writhed harder, and Crusher gasped like he did when Tobias knew he was about to be on his knees. But he wasn't, because it was the Director that had tied him up today, the Director who was hurting him now.

"Is that a problem, Mr. Sloan, with me using your proper name, giving you the respect you are entitled as a real human being and a guard at FREACS? Or do you want to leave and wallow with the other monsters?"

Crusher didn't answer for a second. Tobias could hear him breathing, and it almost matched his own for raggedness, panic. Then the Director's hand jerked, Tobias choked, and Crusher took a desperate breath. "No," he said.

The Director's voice snapped like a whip. "Show me some respect! No, *what?*"

"No, *sir.*"

The Director pulled out another noise from Tobias, and then he gentled his voice. "You want to be useful, don't you? To help me make this little piece of shit an obedient, useful monster, don't you, Mr. Sloan?"

"Yes," Crusher gasped. "God, yes. Fuck, yeah, let me—"

The Director slid his fingers beneath Tobias's collar and pulled him closer, pushed him away, made him sway. "Use proper words, Mr. Sloan."

Crusher took a shuddering breath. "Yes, sir, I want that. Director Dixon, sir."

The Director smiled again, so that only Tobias could see it, and walked to the table with his instruments. He handed an electric prod to Crusher. "When I tell you to, Mr. Sloan," he said, and then picked up a riding crop before turning to Tobias.

"Let's see what you know," the Director said, swinging the riding crop casually in his hand. He brought it up and rested it on Tobias's neck below the collar. "I have one question for you, 89UI6703. What are you?"

Tobias had been called a thousand things, had been told he was so many dirty things, but he had tried to forget them, tried to block them from his mind. Now, between the crop and the electric prod, he dragged out the names and curses. Eventually he found it easier to remember them.

"Enough," the Director said at last, when Tobias had been reduced to blindness, stuttering incomprehensibly from pain and fear, shoulders burning from jerking at the chain, wrists one massive bruise from holding his weight when his legs gave out. The Director—looking satisfied, as though a project had just begun to show promise—stepped back to the small table with his instruments and began carefully cleaning the head of the crop.

"You see how well he responds?" he said conversationally, even though Crusher looked too absorbed in the way Tobias's body shuddered to pay attention. "How thorough and creative he can be? It shows a decent level of intelligence and observation, but really says almost nothing about the freak's true level of understanding. Even a moderately trained animal can produce rote responses to avoid pain. My goal—*our* goal—is to instill belief and understanding where previously there was only memorization. Do you understand me, Mr. Sloan?"

Crusher snapped his attention to the Director's face, clearly struggling to recall the question. "He can't just say the words. He has to mean them."

The Director's mouth quirked in a small smile. "Exactly. Very good, Mr. Sloan."

Tobias could do very little but hang and sob. Compared with

interrogations he had had in the past, the pain had been relatively light. Even compared with a hard whipping, the damage was minimal.

But it was worse, so much worse, because Tobias hadn't been able to go away. He had to stay there, thinking, searching his mind for every degrading thing he had ever been called, for everything he had ever been told a monster was. He could have just given in, stayed silent, retreated, but the difference in pain between the crop and the prod was so vast that he *couldn't*. He couldn't retreat when there was a way, *any way* that the pain could be less.

Usually after a while, the guards and hunters didn't give a damn what he was saying. They never had more than a handful of questions for him, questions he never had an answer to, and when he degenerated into mindless sounds and begging, it was what they had really wanted from the beginning.

The first time a "No, *please*," left his lips, the Director paused, grabbed him by the collar, and pulled him until his feet left the floor. Tobias noted absently, as he gasped from the pressure on his neck, that the Director's arm didn't so much as tremble from supporting his weight.

"Did I give you permission to beg?" he asked.

"N-n-no, sir."

"That's what I thought." The Director pushed him away and glanced at Crusher. "Twice. Space them out. Long shocks."

Tobias tried desperately after that not to beg, to keep answering the Director's single, horrible question, but pleading had been trained into him for so long he couldn't stop *please don't* and *no, God* from slipping out. And every time the Director gave his tight little nod, and Crusher jabbed the prod into his skin.

The first time he had said *God*—he wasn't sure he believed in any kind of god, it was just a word that monsters used when they were in pain, though he knew some religious theory from his reading—the Director had whipped him hard, three or four times, then dragged him off his feet again.

"God doesn't exist," he said. "And he never listens to monsters." Then he had given Crusher the nod.

Now, even when it seemed potentially over, Tobias couldn't expect anything. Time and time again, the Director did things that Tobias hadn't expected, and every time there was pain at the end.

While the Director cleaned the crop, Crusher smiled nastily and shifted the prod from hand to hand, snapping the button to send electricity shooting between the points. When he stepped closer, Tobias tried to brace himself again for the volts.

"Perhaps you should take your annual physical examination early, Mr. Sloan." For the first time that evening, the Director's voice carried a hint of anger.

Crusher hesitated. "Sir?"

"Or perhaps it is your attention and not your hearing that is lacking." The Director placed the crop precisely on the little table, drawing attention to every instrument he hadn't used. "Punishment ends when I say and begins when I say. If you have a problem with that, Mr. Sloan, I'm sure I can find someone"—his tone said *something*—"capable of performing your duties."

The Director held the guard's eyes for a long minute, and Crusher glanced down first. "No . . . sir. Yes, sir."

"Good." The Director glanced at the prod in Crusher's hand. "You can clean that and put it in the charger. It's in the Administration resource room."

After one last hungry glance at Tobias's suspended body, Crusher retreated.

The Director smiled when he left the room. "Good boy," he murmured. Then he walked to Tobias and kicked the stool toward his feet. "Stand on that. Release your hands."

He watched expressionlessly while Tobias struggled to move his aching feet and his arms—numb until he moved them, and then began to burn so badly he panted from the pain. It took him three tries before he could coordinate to get his bound hands off the hook.

Tobias collapsed on the stool and slid to the floor. The Director neither moved to catch him nor to avoid his fall. He stared down at Tobias, considering something that Tobias wasn't sure was about him. After Tobias had caught his breath, the Director tipped his head toward the corner. "Put your clothes back on."

Tobias stumbled up and to his clothes. His hands shook as he pulled the shirt over his head, and he knew it would be agony again when he next took it off. Over the night the crop marks would scab into the fabric, retearing the half-healed wounds when he removed the shirt.

It was as though the Director could read his thoughts. But only monsters could do that. "You will shower after every session," he said. "Not the showers in Administration. They are for humans exclusively, so as long as you aren't bleeding all over the floor, I expect you to use the facilities set aside for monsters. Do you have questions?"

Tobias hesitated, one pant leg on. The Director hadn't told him to remove the tight underwear, so he hadn't.

The man's expression hardened. "89UI, while generally I will expect you to obey, respond, and submit without question, complaint, or excessive noise, when I do give you the opportunity to ask questions, it is because I will not repeat myself, and I expect perfect compliance with my expectations. Whether or not you *know* those expectations is, in this instance, completely upon your shoulders. While I consider this the early stages of training—and thus your mistakes will be punished with more leniency than I would otherwise allow—that does not mean you can expect me to cater to your freakish inconsistency, weakness, deception, and malicious guile. I have no intention of placing my species in jeopardy because I ignored a single mistake. Permitting you to ask, even, when I should let you fail and then be punished, is a kindness. If you are too lazy and stupid to make use of my kindness, you will cease to deserve it."

Tobias took a shaky breath. "Sir, sh-showers are usually locked after dinner. H-How do I get access?"

"I have already informed the guards that you are to be permitted to shower. The facilities will then be cleaned for the evening, possibly by you, and then locked." The Director stopped and waited.

Tobias licked his lips, and then choked out the question. "And if I'm bleeding on the floor, sir?"

"Ask me *clear questions*, 89UI. Don't be stupid and sloppy."

"S-s-sir, how do I sh-shower if I c-can't walk or f-function due to b-blood loss or injury?"

A small smile. "I will have you cleaned."

The door opened, and Crusher reentered the room. Tobias pulled his pants up hastily and stood, shaking, eyes down.

"Ah, good. I trust that all your equipment is properly put away?" the Director asked.

Crusher glanced at Tobias and looked sullen. He was still hard, visibly stiff against his pants, though Tobias had half expected him to jerk himself off while he was out of the Director's sight. But all he said was, "Yes, sir."

"Good," the Director said. "89UI6703, you will report to me every Wednesday at 6:30 p.m. from now on. The staff in Administration knows that you are expected at this time and will not stop you, though if you try to abuse that privilege by entering the building without permission at other times, I will have your hands broken. I expect you to report promptly and without fail. I do not believe I need to waste a guard's time making sure you arrive. If you are more than five minutes early, I will have you beaten. Do not be late. I also expect you to shower beforehand. Do you have any questions?"

"What . . . what happens, sir, if I ar-r-rive late?"

The Director frowned. "I realize that as an ungrateful piece of shit, you find it hard to appreciate what I am doing for you, but if you waste even a second of my time, I will take that as an indication that you are even more of a lost cause than I already know you to be. Don't disappoint me."

Tobias made a small noise, Crusher shifted uncomfortably, and the Director smiled for a second. Then he turned to the guard. "Mr. Sloan, as you have requested this duty, you may naturally arrive at the same time, or earlier, than the freak. I would ask that if you are not able to make it, or are going to be late, you inform me as soon as possible."

"Yes, sir." Crusher nodded. "And thank you, sir, for this . . . opportunity, sir, and . . . honor."

The Director's mouth quirked. "It's good to work with a man of your enthusiasm and experience. If you like, you may escort the freak to the showers."

Crusher's eyes brightened. "Thank you, sir. Freak! Come!"

Tobias followed Crusher out of the room, and when the guard pushed him to his knees in the showers, it was almost a relief, both to be off his shaking feet and to know what he was supposed to do, exactly what was expected, and what would get him hurt.

When he could finally stumble into the barracks—clothes clean, back and chest still raw—he barely heard the other monsters as they swore at him. He fell into his bunk and curled up tight, still shaking.

Usually, before he fell asleep, he thought about Jake. Often it wasn't safe to think about him at any other part of the day. But when he was able to push down every disgusting thing that he had done and that had been done to him and just think about Jake's smile, about the touch of his hand, it kept him going. Some nights he would think, *Maybe he'll come. Maybe he'll come next week*, and it was probably something he didn't deserve to think, something he didn't deserve to hope for, but without that, he had no reason to keep going. And he had to keep going, because he knew that anything else would disappoint Jake.

Even after Leon Hawthorne had told him that Jake was never coming back *(You're going to get him killed)*, Tobias had held on to the hope that Jake would still come for him. Because Jake had said he would, and Tobias had seen that Jake was so brave, so strong, that he would even stand up to his father.

It had been over a month since Jake had visited, and Tobias had still hoped. But tonight, curling up the only way he could to avoid his raw wounds, Tobias closed his eyes and knew he couldn't think about Jake. Every time he breathed he felt the pain of the crop, and he remembered what he was.

Freak, whore, slut, filth, monster.

Jake shouldn't come back. Jake should stay as far away from Freak Camp and Tobias as he possibly could, because Tobias was worthless, Tobias was worse than worthless, and if Jake came to him, he would be contaminated just as surely, he would fall prey to something and it would be Tobias's fault, all Tobias's fault, because that was the kind of monster he was.

Tobias knew this. Tobias had had it beaten into his worthless monster skin, tonight and nights before, but he still wanted Jake back. Somewhere in his black monster heart, he wanted Jake so badly that if Crusher or anyone else said they could make it happen, then Tobias would bend over, Tobias would beg. He'd hope that the promise came true, hope that Jake would come back—if only long enough to look at him in disgust, to put a bullet through his head, even though a fast death was too much to hope for when Tobias had fucked himself up so badly.

Tobias wanted Jake and Tobias was an evil monster, a worthless whore, and he couldn't help but hurt the things he wanted. So he tried not to think about Jake, Jake who wasn't coming back, Jake who must never know how dirty and disgusting Tobias was.

Thinking about Jake wasn't safe anymore. It just reminded Tobias how much of a monster he really was.

LIGHTS HAD BEEN out for a couple of hours when the door swung open. Several monsters jumped in their bunks, Kayla included, but it was only Tobias who staggered through. Kayla exhaled soundlessly against her blanket. She had seen Victor yank Tobias out of the mess hall and heard some talk about the Director. The Director almost never personally requested a monster, and it was even rarer that they walked out of Administration afterward.

Tobias didn't look like he was in much more than one piece, though. He had all his limbs, and his face hadn't been beaten in, but something that made him Tobias was missing. He paused for a moment with his hand on the doorframe before shuffling forward. He didn't manage more than a couple of steps before stumbling against one of the bunks and nearly falling on a monster.

Several monsters snarled. The monster in the bunk kicked out, and Tobias took it—swaying back dangerously—and then more monsters were growling throughout the barracks, wordless ferocious sounds with clear meaning: *shut up and keep down.* They all had been whipped two months ago for after-dark altercations, and no one wanted a repeat, or for the guards to decide that they deserved something harsher.

Tobias ignored them when he usually would have snarled back. He looked like it took every last ounce of strength in his body just to stay upright. His labored breathing was audible even to Kayla halfway across the room. He lurched on unsteadily to his bunk, more than once looking like he was going to collapse in the aisle, but he made it before his knees buckled.

Kayla's hands unclenched from the edge of her blanket, and she rolled to face the other way. Tobias had gotten back to his own bunk. Of course he was okay. Roughed up, sure, but he was used to that—more than any other monster still around. He'd be fine in the morning.

But Tobias didn't get up in the morning.

The buzzer blared in the corner, summoning them outside for roll call. The monsters rolled out of their bunks with muttered curses, jostling each other without vehemence. No one had energy for that first thing in the morning when a fight wouldn't help a monster's supply of blankets or food.

Kayla had already snarled her way into the line when she glanced back and saw one motionless body still in its bunk. She was about to shrug and turn away, thinking *Unlucky bastard,* when she realized it was Tobias.

She dodged out of the line and kept her head down while the other monsters exited. No one looked to her. They probably thought she was going to try to roll the unconscious monster, and they didn't think that being late for the attendance call would be worth whatever food or trinkets the victim might have secreted away. She would've thought the same thing if it hadn't been Tobias.

Once the last monster in line stepped outside, she crouched down before Tobias's bunk. His eyes were closed, and he hadn't stirred at all.

Very slowly Kayla brought her fingers below Tobias's nostrils, close enough to feel the small puffs of warm air on her knuckles. Still alive, then.

She poked him hard in the shoulder.

Tobias's eyes flickered open and moved over her face, but without recognition or focus. He didn't even twitch. His face was blank, emptier than she had ever seen, even when Crusher had him pinned.

So he'd finally been fucked. By the Director, no less. Kayla wondered if that was anything like getting fucked by Crusher. She'd never seen the Director herself, but she'd heard enough, and she'd never believed he had any particular restraint with monsters.

Hawthorne waited too long, she thought to herself with the disgust she had for hunters, as well as something of the burning rage she felt toward the guards. She'd always hated Hawthorne for this: he'd fucked Tobias up in every way besides the one he was supposed to. He'd broken through all of Tobias's rules, even the ones Tobias had taught her. He had made Tobias hope for something he'd never get. Especially not now.

She watched Tobias's face for a little longer, but it never changed, never showed any awareness of her. She couldn't make him get up, and there wasn't any point if he wouldn't do it himself. Survival in Freak Camp was all about willpower (and luck), and until today she would have said that Tobias had the strongest will of anyone there. Maybe he still did. Maybe his luck had just run out.

She went to attendance call and breakfast, and when she snuck back into the barracks afterward with half of a small, dry roll, Tobias hadn't moved.

Kayla dropped the roll onto his cot, before his face. Tobias's eyes blinked open, then flickered to her face. She had just begun to wonder if he knew her yet, when his expression twisted like someone was stabbing a hot iron into his back. The agonized grimace remained fixed for almost a minute, muscles in his back tense and bowed, and then he looked at her again. His eyes were hopeless, sad, resigned, but the knot in Kayla's chest eased, because this was familiar. This was how she knew him.

Tobias sat up, swaying until he braced himself on the edge of the bunk. "You shouldn't have." He nodded to the roll. His voice was hoarse, a little ragged from screams and abuse, but that wasn't unfamiliar either.

She shrugged, uneasy. "I'll eat it, you don't want it."

He thought about it. He thought about it a hell of a lot longer than he should have, since he had given her extra food more than once, and she knew that he hadn't eaten much at dinner the night before either. He waited long enough for her stomach to twist up, and for her to think about shoving it down his throat so he would stay here and not go wherever in his head he went when he didn't want to feel anything at all. It was the same place she'd learned to rely on, and for how well each of them knew it, they could never be there together.

Then he picked the roll up and ate it in two quick bites. He stood up and limped out of the barracks without another word.

She counted to twenty so they wouldn't be seen together and followed him out.

CHAPTER TWELVE

JUNE 2000

SESSIONS with the Director quickly became one of the most predictable and least secure parts of Tobias's life.

Every Wednesday he walked into the Director's office and looked down from the man's cold, thoughtful gaze. Every Wednesday, they worked to make him an *obedient* monster. Mistakes were always punished, and Tobias always failed.

But that was where the predictability ended. Sessions could take any shape, from punishments for his mistakes to recitations of hunting lore and how to incapacitate other monsters, to Tobias sitting—absolutely silent, absolutely still—in a corner of the office while the Director read reports or signed papers at his desk. Not even the pain was consistent, though whippings and beatings were common. Sometimes the Director punished him just because he was a monster and that was what he deserved.

Ultimately, the only thing that Tobias could rely on was that sessions would take place on Wednesdays and that he wouldn't be able to rely on anything. Behavior that had been complimented or ignored one day could have him strung up in the interrogation room on another. Some Wednesdays nothing truly bad happened, and those left him just as shaken, just as terrified.

Only the Director was constant. He had taken a personal interest, and he took great pains to reinforce how grateful Tobias should be that a busy man, the Director of the ASC, a *real* human being, was interested in his education. He was always there, explaining why Tobias had failed this week; listening, crop in hand, while Tobias fumbled his way through an unfamiliar Latin exorcism; filling out forms silently as Tobias kept his eyes toward the carpet while staying aware of the Director's hands every second.

Tobias became utterly convinced that the Director knew everything. He knew what Tobias ate, who he had blown during the week, and how well he slept. He knew when Crusher made a face behind his back, and he knew if Tobias so much as breathed wrong in his presence.

Part of that, of course, was the cameras placed everywhere in the Director's office, hidden behind reflective surfaces and in the dark wood paneling. But part of it was just who the Director was.

After two months of training, the Director began assigning Tobias to wait on him at dinner whenever he stayed over at the camp on a day that wasn't Wednesday.

"You should be grateful that I am allowing you the opportunity to be instructed outside of the usual sessions," he told Tobias. "Perhaps with these additional hours, you will learn more quickly how to stop being a useless freak."

Tobias was grateful for the extra time with the Director. He was grateful for anything that would stop the pain.

During the second week of dinners with the Director, Tobias knelt at the side of the long conference table, face angled toward the Director's feet while his eyes watched for any sign or direction. The Director sat at the head of the table eating messily, a second, empty place setting beside him.

Tobias had learned early on that he was not the one sitting at that second place. Not that he really would have expected to eat with the *Director,* but the first time he had made even tentative movements toward that second chair, Karl had knocked him to the ground and beaten him until there wasn't an inch of his back that wasn't black and blue the next day.

That first dinner had been almost as bad as a Wednesday session. But after he learned what was expected, for once the perfection the Director demanded was possible. As long as he knelt silently, responded instantly to the smallest indication of an order, kept the Director's water glass full, he was generally safe.

It wouldn't have been bad at all, except for the hunger. They had put the camp on half rations again, something about negative behavior. Two rock-hard pieces of bread and one bowl of watery soup for the last two days left him feeling hollowed out and faint, like his body was consuming everything inside him.

Worst of all, when the Director was done with his meal—for a painstakingly deliberate, precise man, he ate like a monster, scraps everywhere, bits of food scattered across the napkin he tucked fastidiously into the top of his shirt—he would dump everything left into the garbage bag Tobias brought him. Every time, Tobias tried not to flinch to see juicy, pristine pieces of meat, potato, and vegetables that he couldn't name, but which scented the air with flavors he could just barely imagine, disappear into a black plastic bag.

Tonight the Director glanced at him in between bites. It made Tobias's mouth dry with fear, but he didn't move.

"Hungry?" the Director asked.

Tobias froze. There was no good answer to that. But that didn't mean he could lie. The Director would know. "Yes, sir."

The Director smiled, and another piece of meat fell off his fork and onto the table beside his plate. "The scraps from the children's dinner," he murmured. Then he deliberately brushed the meat off the table and onto the floor. "If you are hungry, eat."

Cautiously, sensing the trick but unsure how to avoid it, Tobias reached forward. He shouldn't be doing this, he knew it, but he could *not* look at that scrap, hear the invitation, and ignore it.

When his fingers were over the meat, the Director kicked him in the head.

Tobias fell away, pretending to be hit harder than he was, even though the Director probably knew to the ounce of pressure how hard he had actually kicked. Tobias curled up to protect his head and kept watching the Director, waiting for the next blow, but the Director didn't look angry. "Eat it properly," he said, "for what you are."

Tobias understood what he meant immediately. Some deep part inside him was terrified at how easy it was to understand. But that was not the part of him that kept him alive. *It's true, you are,* he thought. *Just do it.*

He rolled back to his knees, leaned forward, and picked the meat off the floor with his teeth. When he glanced up, the Director was smiling. He deliberately pushed another piece of food off the table.

"Good boy," he said. "Smart boy."

That Wednesday, the Director had Crusher punish Tobias because he had not thanked him for the meal.

THE DIRECTOR'S sessions generally lasted two hours, but even that wasn't certain. One session only took enough time for Tobias to recite a Latin exorcism—he knew he had done it right because the demon chained in the Director's interrogation room had writhed, flowed out of its host's mouth, and vanished through the drain—while another session had gone past midnight, and Crusher had hosed him down in the interrogation room instead of Tobias trying to make it to the showers.

Every Wednesday, Tobias learned how he had failed to live up to the Director's expectations, studied how they could work together to make Tobias a less useless monster, and which punishments would best achieve that goal. Sometimes lessons came before pain, sometimes after, sometimes during, and the lessons ranged from general knowledge of supernatural vulnerabilities to knife work.

Tobias absorbed the lessons quickly. His memory had always been good, and now it was a survival skill. He couldn't hesitate, he couldn't be distracted. He had to correctly interpret every single cue the Director gave him and perform the task swiftly and without error, or he would receive one of the Director's punishments, which were unlike any interrogation he'd endured before.

If Tobias was lucky, the Director would give him the instructions, step by step, and let him ask questions. Other times, he would simply tell Tobias to repeat what he did three Wednesdays ago. Mistakes or hesitations were punished. The Director showed him a picture of a sigil once for exactly ten seconds, then told him to reproduce it in chalk on the floor. He watched Tobias fumble over the details, then had him repeat each piece until he got it right, this time as Crusher applied hot coals to the back of his calves.

The next week, Tobias drew it perfectly the first time. Then he was given another task.

After three months of Wednesdays, when Tobias walked in after hearing the Director's curt "Enter," he saw another man sitting at the table across from the Director. The man had a beer and the remains of a good meal in front of him—Tobias felt his stomach twist a little, but breakfast had been edible, and soon enough he wouldn't want anything in his stomach anyway—while the Director drank his iced tea.

Tobias stepped to his usual position at the side of the door. He didn't know if this was a test or if their session would be delayed, but it was best to behave as though it were a test. If it wasn't yet, the Director could make it one at any time.

The Director might drink alcohol when he was home, but Tobias never saw him drink anything but tea or water. The Director believed that imbibing any kind of influence while working with monsters was tantamount to walking in naked, lying on your back, and baring your neck. If a guard failed a Breathalyzer test at the beginning of his shift, he was immediately terminated.

The guest at the table looked Tobias over and snorted. He was a large man, his suit pristine, and his watch and rings flashed gold. "So this is the monster? So well-trained you could snap and he'd do anything you wanted?"

The Director smiled. Tobias saw the expression in his peripheral vision, but he kept his eyes on the Director's hands. As the Director had explained, he was often too busy to waste time speaking to filth like Tobias when a gesture could suffice. Tobias saw the two-fingered twitch, and he knelt gracefully.

Tobias had wondered distantly how the man had the balls to sneer at the Director. Even guards who called him a teetotalling prude were careful to say it behind his back (so far behind his back that they wouldn't even say it in front of Tobias anymore, afraid he might spill something during an interrogation that would get them a private session of their own)—but now the man's head snapped to Tobias, and then he looked back at the Director.

"Did you tell him to do that?"

"I did. With some work, 89UI6703 has become reliable in several ways."

"Make him . . . make him do something else."

Tobias saw the *come here* flick, but not coupled with the slight raise that would mean *get up first,* so he crawled. He crawled on his hands and knees and kept his head down until he was about two feet away from the Director and then stopped, sitting back on his heels. That was as close as he could come toward a real without further permission.

He didn't look at the stranger's face, but he could hear the amazement and something more in his voice with his next words. Tobias let his eyes flicker sideways to where Crusher stood, one hand holding a cutting whip, the other clenched at his side. Crusher was, predictably, hard, and he had the familiar brutal lust in his eyes.

Maybe I can get a sandwich out of him later, Tobias thought idly, before returning his gaze to the Director's hand.

"How are you doing that? When you said you were training the freaks to be useful, I thought you were either unhinged or bullshitting us, Jonah, but that . . . that was something. My wife's dog doesn't obey like that, and she's taken it to more schools than a PhD dropout."

"He's a freak, Senator," the Director answered dryly. "Much as I hate to admit it, he's quite a bit smarter than a dog. I use gestures when I don't want to bother vocalizing basic instructions. Granted, this one has taken to the training rather better than most, but just kneeling and crawling is not that impressive. He can do quite a bit more than that, can't he, Mr. Sloan?"

Crusher started to attention and nodded. "Yes, sir. Pre—the freak's . . . good at a lot of things, sir."

"What—" The senator put down his beer. "What kinds of things?"

Of all the men in the room, only the Director was completely calm, at ease. Tobias couldn't stop his heart rate from picking up. He doubted the senator cared about the history of wendigos in North America.

The Director considered, eyes steady on him, before they flickered to Crusher, moved to Tobias, and then back to the senator. "By all reports, he's quite skilled with his mouth. Would you like to see for yourself, Senator?"

"His . . . mouth? You mean . . . ?" The senator leaned back, wiping his greasy fingers on the napkin on his lap.

"Quite so," the Director said. "Mr. Sloan can corroborate."

"Yeah," Crusher said. "He's . . . yeah. I . . . yeah. Sir."

"Would you be interested, Senator?" The Director lifted the pitcher and poured himself another glass.

The man stared.

"Sir," Crusher said, stepping forward. "If Pr—if the freak's sucking him off, can I—"

"No, Mr. Sloan." The Director's tone made Tobias wince, grateful it wasn't directed toward him. "No, you may not."

"But, sir—"

The Director turned in his chair to look directly at the guard. "You will control yourself and do your job, Mr. Sloan, or you will leave this room, do you understand?"

The guard retreated to the wall. "Yes, sir."

"Well." The senator coughed. Tobias could just see his fingers nervously twitching over his knees. "If you're offering a, a demonstration—I'd better accept it myself, just so I know you aren't blowing smoke—or, y'know what I mean."

The Director gave a short, clipped laugh without humor. "Yes, I do." He jerked his head at Tobias and made another gesture.

Tobias did as he was told. It was easier than usual, since the man never released his death grip on the arms of his chair and couldn't seem to do anything but make sharp, high-pitched whines.

Afterward, as Tobias slid back the required two feet, the senator wheezed, "Holy shit."

"I take it he performed well?" The Director sipped his tea.

"He, uh, you could say that."

"You can help me, then, with your opinion. Did he perform

well enough that I should waive the usual punishment for touching a real human without asking for permission?"

Tobias froze, unable to breathe, to feel anything beneath the pounding in his ears. How could he have been so stupid? There was always a test, always more under the Director's commands, and he should have fucking known better than to assume that it would be all right just because he was clearly not the only one the Director was training today.

Touching a real without explicit permission or orders, even when they had said yes to the blowjob, even when they clearly wanted it, or were touching him, was equivalent to hitting a guard. Monsters routinely lost limbs or disappeared into Special Research for even implying that they might fight back.

It took all his self-control not to panic, not to throw himself on his stomach and beg and apologize, not to run and hope that Crusher accidentally killed him. Because this too was a test, and Crusher would never kill him, would never step that far out of line, unless the Director said he could.

And begging wouldn't help. It never had helped unless that was what the Director had told him to do. Then, sometimes, if he did it well enough, if he repeated enough of what the Director had told him about how worthless he was, about how much he deserved the pain, if he created new ways to say that he was sorry, then the Director would stop the pain, because Tobias understood his lessons.

But he had to truly understand. He couldn't just say the words. The Director knew the difference.

"He . . . he had to ask permission?" the senator asked.

"Of course. He's just a freak. You could have made him beg for the privilege, or told him exactly what he should do with his tongue."

The senator took a hard breath. "Maybe . . . maybe next time?"

The Director smiled. "Yes, next time. I'm still waiting for your opinion on the punishment."

"I think he was good enough that this time . . . this time . . ."

"This time only," the Director said smoothly. "That sounds reasonable. But a bit too merciful. Would you mind if I altered that a bit, disciplined him lightly?"

The senator huffed a shaky laugh. "Well, you're the boss here. You sure seem to know what you're doing."

"Thank you." The Director looked at Tobias. "Tonight you will stay on your knees in the corner, remain silent unless I speak to you, as though you are bound and gagged. If you move, if you make any noise, you will be restrained and I will do what is necessary to educate you. Do you understand?"

"Yes, sir."

The Director nodded and turned back to the senator.

"The next time you want to threaten the ASC budget, Senator, I want you to remember two things. One"—he gestured at Tobias—"the good work we do here confining, controlling, and training supernaturals to useful tasks. And two"—he pointed toward the ceiling—"that I have video of you with your cock down a monster's throat."

Every corner in Freak Camp had its own video camera. Tobias knew that the ones in the Director's offices were strictly private.

Stupid man, even if he is a real, he thought as the senator gaped at the Director. *Fighting only gets you hurt.*

JAKE TURNED SOUTH AT TUCSON, finally getting the sun out of his eyes, easing the dull ache in his head. He was supposed to leave Roger's that morning, but last night he'd gone into Las Cruces to, for lack of a better excuse, blow off steam. He hadn't made it back until close to noon, and Roger had bitched him out again about how he'd be no use to Tobias if he smashed up his car and himself on the side of the highway. That was also why days ago Roger had locked up his own liquor and confiscated Jake's hunting duffel, after the last disastrous attempt at a solo hunt nearly got Jake chewed up by the tiniest werewolf pup he'd ever seen.

Jake knew Roger was right. He was extremely fucked up, and two weeks at Roger's hadn't much helped him find his footing. None of that was Roger's fault. He knew how to kick Jake's ass better than anyone (well, not as good as—but Jake wasn't going there).

Twenty minutes later down the highway, he took the exit for Sahuarita. At a gas station, he asked for directions for Iglesia de Gracia y Fe. He stood for a few extra minutes in front of the cooler section, wondering how Alejandra Rodriguez would react to him showing up with a six-pack—then shook himself and turned back to the Eldorado.

When he pulled into the single-story church's parking lot, there were a few cars already parked. He took the spot closest to the road and exit, then slowly got out of the car, taking an extra moment to stretch and roll his neck while studying the church. It didn't look like much with its sun-stained adobe walls, lined with scrubby bushes.

He and Leon had never been churchgoers, except to access whatever holy water and other equipment needed to take down whatever demonic ass was giving them trouble that week. Jake only remembered going to a Sunday service a couple of times when Dad had left him with a babysitter whose grandkids were annoying as hell and inclined to snitch.

As he stood staring, a side door opened and a Hispanic woman appeared in the doorway, waving him closer. "You must be Jake."

He winced, then nodded and slowly crossed the gravel lot to the church.

Alejandra was short and solidly built, a little over five feet, her long black hair pulled back in a smooth ponytail. She wore no makeup, and it was hard to tell her age, apart from the laugh lines creasing the corners of her eyes.

"Call me Alex." She shook his hand, grip strong and sure, then held the door open wider for him to follow her inside.

She led him to a dining room with several round tables. Crossing to another door, she called, "What can I get you to drink? Iced tea, coffee?"

"Coffee sounds good." Jake surveyed the room with its mismatched chairs and walls pinned with children's Sunday school drawings.

She returned with a mug of coffee and a dish of sugars and half-and-half containers, and he shook his head. She lifted her eyebrows. "All right, but it's bitter as sin, just so you know." She gestured for him to take a seat at one of the round tables.

Jake took a big swallow and, thanks to his years of intensive training as a hunter, barely avoided making a face. At least not much of a face, as he caught Alex's grin before she turned back to the kitchen.

She returned with her own coffee mug and set to breaking open and stirring in the half-and-halfs. Jake watched her, blinked, and realized he was close to dozing off. He really should've slept more and drank less the night before. Maybe the next few weeks. He took another drink of the coffee and did not wince at all.

He had talked to Alex briefly on the phone back at Roger's, an awkward get-to-know-you conversation before she agreed to maybe help. Roger had told him she was as solid as they come and had no love for the ASC or organized anything, so he'd told her his real name. Out of years of habit, he'd done it the James Bond way—*it's Hawthorne. Jake Hawthorne*—and realized in the next second he never wanted to say it that way again.

She'd played it pretty cool, and he thought now, sitting

across the table from her, that she didn't need to play anything cool.

"So," she began. "I appreciate what you told me on the phone and for coming out all this way to talk some more before I see how much I can help with this paperwork. Has Roger told you much about me?"

Jake shrugged. "Only that he'd want you at his back in any hunt. And you, uh, got this church."

She laughed, her eyes wrinkling at the corners. "According to some, I do. Others disagree, but they ain't managed to kick me out of the building yet. People come here on Sundays if they want to."

"You . . . preach?"

"I try. I get up there and talk and read Scripture and tell everyone how I messed up but aim to do better tomorrow. I don't go on as long as some, and I think that helps."

"I don't believe in God." Jake hadn't meant to say that, but something about her calm, matter-of-fact demeanor moved him to tell her the truth. "I was never part of any church, but we visited them often enough for the holy water and blessed silver and whatever. There's some reason why those things work against werewolves and shapeshifters, but why does salt melt a slug? Nothing I've seen has convinced me there's a god managing everything behind the scenes. If there is, he's got a bad sense of humor."

Alex nodded, unperturbed. "I see plenty of reason for that. It takes a lot to have faith and not much to lose it. I wouldn't blame anyone for that. And it's not my job to make people believe something they don't want to. I try to be here for those who want to ask questions, who can't make sense of all the hurt the world brings—why everything's so goddamn unfair."

Jake caught his breath. He hadn't expected to hear that, or for her to look straight at him as she spoke. Like she already knew about Toby, about how angry Jake felt all the time. Life had been a bitch to her too.

He took a minute before speaking. "Well, I did come here with one question, and that's if you can help me get a friend out of a place that's going to kill him any day now."

Her brows drew together, and she leaned forward on the table, clasping the mug between her hands. "I'll do what I can. I'm no miracle worker, but I take God at his word that my faith can move mountains. We just gotta target the right mountains. Now." She smiled at him, sitting back. "Tell me about Tobias."

THE DIRECTOR TOOK a last bite of his steak, removed the gravy-stained napkin from his neck, and leaned back in satisfaction. "The cook here is truly excellent. I'm surprised he's not in New York, the things he can do with a basic sirloin."

He wasn't talking to Tobias and thus wouldn't expect a response. Tobias, on his knees beside the conference table, kept his eyes locked on the area of the Director's hands, his breathing perfectly even, his expression empty but alert, and did his best not to smell the food, not to look at it, not to think about it.

Then his stomach growled.

He couldn't stop his breath from hitching with the sudden surge of terror. *Wait wait wait,* he told himself, fingernails digging into his palms to give himself a focus for the panic. Moving now would just make it worse. Begging before he was given permission would just make it worse.

When the Director pushed his plate over the side of the table, crashing the cheap ceramic against the wooden floor and scattering food everywhere, Tobias couldn't help flinching. But he managed not to make a sound.

The Director sat back. "Clean it up . . . any way you want. As long as you remember what you are."

Tobias crawled forward, head down, words spilling out automatically, requiring little conscious thought. "Thank you, sir. Thank you for the food, sir." He lowered his mouth to the steak bits and lukewarm potatoes and ate as quickly as he could without making noise.

He flinched involuntarily when he felt the Director's hand in his hair, but the Director made the noise that meant Tobias should continue doing exactly what he had been doing, so he continued eating, expecting any second for the Director to jerk his head up or kick him away. But there was no pain and no blow. Instead he ate while the Director petted his hair.

Tobias was exhausted. Hollowed out, hungry, and exhausted from not enough sleep and not enough food. Wednesday hadn't been bad as far as Wednesdays went, but it was always dangerous to sleep, to let his guard down even a little on Thursdays, even when he knew Kayla would watch his back, at least as far as making noise if someone tried to sneak up on him.

Now it was Friday, and he was kneeling silently against the wall, eyes locked on the Director's hands as he had his dinner.

Crusher stood in the corner, slowly smacking his club against his thigh while he watched Tobias.

After a few minutes, the Director put down his fork and turned to Crusher. "Would you stop that? I'm having dinner. Water."

That last was for Tobias. Quickly and silently he rose, retrieved the pitcher of filtered ice water from the tray farther down the table, and refilled the Director's glass. He concentrated hard on keeping his hand steady. He couldn't let a single drop spill.

"I don't like it, sir," Crusher said.

If the Director had looked at Tobias that way, he would have dropped, but Crusher just looked uneasy. "You are under no obligation to guard me, Mr. Sloan."

"Not that, sir." Crusher jerked his head at Tobias. "It's just . . . you've said the progress has been good, but the little freak's still . . ."

"Unbroken in the only way that matters to you?"

"Unidentified, sir."

The sneer on the Director's face faded, and he looked thoughtful. "True." He looked at Tobias, and even though he didn't look nearly as irritated as before, Tobias couldn't stop the slight tremors in his hands. "What did you have in mind? Bear in mind the restrictions I've put in place."

Crusher shrugged, trying to look casual, but Tobias could see how the muscles had tensed in his arms, his hips rocking forward. "Just a little rough interrogation, sir. One more, just to be sure the freak's not hiding something nasty behind that pretty face."

The Director considered. Tobias found himself counting every soft click of the great clock set in the bookshelves, trying to bring his heartbeat down.

"I think that's reasonable," the Director said, slowly. "But remember the restrictions."

Crusher grinned, and Tobias lost control of his breathing. "Yes, sir," he said. "I can do that, sir."

THEY HADN'T ASKED Tobias what kind of freak he was in a long time. Tobias supposed that when he was Hawthorne's pet monster, or the guards' whore, or the Director's project, it didn't really matter what kind of freak he was.

This time was different. Terrifyingly different. There were five or seven men—Tobias couldn't keep track, they seemed to change, and they kept a blindfold on him half the time—and they pushed him around, each taking a turn doing whatever they could to him, anything that wouldn't mark him up too bad, lose him a limb, or scar his face.

After the blindfold went on—as well as the muzzle that kept his mouth open so he couldn't bite down, even by accident—they started pushing him to his knees. Voices he knew, voices he didn't still asked the question, taunting him to *show them he was a freak* even though at that point he didn't think they expected anything.

If he had any gift, any power, he wished it would come now. He wished he could kill them all. Or that it could be over faster. Sometimes he just wanted it to be over, all over, that they'd push him past the point of feeling anything ever again and there would be nothing left to do but throw him in the incinerator.

By the time they got to waterboarding, Tobias wasn't sure how he was still breathing. They had tried not to hit him hard enough to break anything, but he was pretty sure he had a couple of cracked ribs. And it was hard, so hard when they shoved his head into a dirty bucket, or pressed a wet cloth to his face, to wait until there was air to fill his aching lungs.

Why don't you just fucking breathe, whispered the little voice that wasn't numb and far away. *It would be so easy. They would never notice. You might die anyway.*

That sparked the old reminders. Jake. He had to stay alive, he had to keep gasping air through his abraded throat, raw from screaming and gagging. Jake had promised, and even though Tobias didn't think he was coming back, knew he didn't deserve Jake to come back, he couldn't give up. That would be like saying he didn't believe in Jake.

He was weeping, choking, breaking down, the thin numb edges in his mind dissolving and sliding toward blessed unconsciousness and even more blessed death (*I'm sorry, Jake. I tried, I really did, but I can't stop them*), when Crusher pulled his head close.

"You want it to stop?" His fingers dug into Tobias's throat under his collar. "I can make it all end."

Tobias looked at him. It was just a movement of his eyes—motor function seemed to have cut out a while ago, and they had been passing him back and forth like a rag doll—but Crusher saw. He leaned so close that Tobias could feel his hot breath on his ear.

"Let me fuck you," he breathed. "Just say yes, freak. He can't touch me if you say yes."

Tobias had thought he was past fear. Fear had slid away hours ago into numbness, into nothing at all. Now there was a rush of pure terror, of the sudden need to fight, to scream. But he couldn't move his mouth quite right (fuck, did they break his jaw?), and all he could think was *No, no, no, that's Jake's, only Jake, no no no.*

Somehow he managed the word, the only word he wanted. "No."

Crusher snarled into his face, his hand tightening around Tobias's throat before he threw him back into another guard's arms.

"Dump him again," he said. "He can't even fucking answer a question right."

And every time after that Tobias still answered no until he couldn't hear the questions anymore.

WHEN TOBIAS OPENED his eyes and the shadowy infirmary room came into focus, he had no idea who the gray-clothed monster sitting in the chair staring at him was. Then he remembered Kayla had taken on a new, uglier face recently.

"I heard them say you're as dumb as a dog," she said, monotone voice as flat as ever. "But it's not true. You're even dumber."

Tobias blinked twice, wondering if this would make any sense if he hadn't been kicked in the head so many times.

She continued to stare at him, face as expressionless as the blank white wall behind her. Maybe shapeshifters had to get used to showing emotion on new faces, or maybe this was just Kayla. "Even dogs know when to roll over and die. Every stupid animal does. Why don't you, Tobias?"

He closed his eyes, but she kept talking.

"You stupid—lucky—*stupid* son of a bitch. If they gave me just *one* chance, I'd've jumped on it. I'd've gone through the incinerator by now, whoosh, where none of them could ever touch me again. Why don't *you,* Tobias? Is it true, then, do you *like* what they do to you?"

At that, Tobias mustered what was left of his voice, shredded from screams. "No." It hurt, coming out.

"Then why don't you *die,* you stupid whore." Kayla didn't raise her voice, but it came out in a furious, contorted hiss. That might have been emotion, he thought distantly. "Give up. Just give up already. You've been here longer than any of us, it's time for you to *go.*"

Tobias shook his head, eyes still closed.

Now Kayla's voice rose in pitch, though she still kept it low enough that none of the guards outside would hear. "Why? Why the fuck *not?* What is *wrong* with you?" He offered no answer, and after a moment her voice dropped back down to the monotone. "It's that hunter boy, isn't it? You're waiting for him. Because he said—"

Tobias didn't answer. Didn't move.

Kayla made a strange sound, almost like a cough. It might have been her attempt at a laugh. The chair legs squeaked back as she stood up. "You really are dumb as shit. He's fucking you over like every other hunter, like every other real. He's *not* coming for you, Tobias. He'd probably be laughing right now if he knew how much you believed him."

Tobias rolled over, away from her, even though his ribs and head nearly made him scream. "Go away, Kayla."

After a moment, he heard soft footsteps across the floor and the door swing shut.

He promised. Jake promised. And he's always kept his promises.

Tobias had no belief that he would survive until Jake came for him. If he was honest with himself, he had more faith in his own death than for Jake taking him out of the facility in time.

He wouldn't court death. He wouldn't ask them for it. He wouldn't be the one who broke Jake's promise. But he could feel death over his shoulder, closer every week, more surely than Jake's promise had ever been.

He didn't even have the strength to hate himself for giving up.

WHEN TOBIAS LIMPED NEXT into the Director's office, head down, the Director was as he always was: a cool, cold-eyed presence. But there was a different set to his expression tonight, something else on his mind compressing his lips into a tight line.

The guard in the corner was new. New to Freak Camp, not just to the Director's sessions. Tobias looked at him a little longer than he should have. It hurt to move, hurt to breathe, and that slowed his reaction times, slowed them dangerously. He knew he had to ignore the pain—they wouldn't keep him in the infirmary much longer—but it was hard.

The Director saw the look. He saw everything. Tobias couldn't find the energy to be more afraid. He had felt numb since the interrogation. Blank. He was torn between terror of this hollow feeling and hoping that it would stay until he died. It wouldn't be that long now, not with how little he could care about his self-preservation.

"Mr. Sloan is on suspension, as is Mr. Gomez. Though I suspect for this stunt Mr. Sloan will be out for a good bit longer, and he will not be rejoining us for our little conversations." The Director smiled, but it was not a happy smile. "He did not have proper authorization for the damage he inflicted."

The Director was pissed, but not at Tobias. Tobias wondered if it would still hurt.

But instead of teaching Tobias how he had fucked up that week (and the week before, when he had been in the infirmary), the Director told him to get him a glass of water before returning to his paperwork.

That Wednesday, for the first Wednesday in a long time, Tobias had a quiet hour without any new pain, and afterward he went back to the infirmary where he didn't have to be afraid of the other monsters in the dark.

He didn't think it would last, but for now, he curled up, hid his eyes, and slept as deeply as he could.

CHAPTER THIRTEEN

JULY 2000

ANOTHER WEDNESDAY FOUND Tobias kneeling against the wall of the Director's office. He was still numb, hollow, stiff from the night that almost killed him, but he could feel that wearing off, and that terrified him more than anything else. The Director could have him beaten—he had done that last week because Tobias had hesitated too long before responding to one of the senator's commands during another visit—but nothing could hurt more than the return to feeling.

Still, some of his survival skills were returning, and he supposed he should be grateful, even if he wasn't—though if the Director asked, he would say so and mean it. He didn't need to look at more of the Director than his hands, and Tobias was no longer consciously aware of watching his hands. Each long finger was buried deep into his brain, locked into his spine where all the nerve impulses radiated out, and any twitch of his finger, any snap of his wrist could make Tobias act without conscious thought. *Come here, pick it up, stop, sit, kneel, crawl,* and Tobias would find himself moving.

Tobias would have felt relief at that if he felt anything at all. Responses so ingrained as to be instinct were responses that wouldn't earn him a beating, responses that would keep him alive without requiring him to feel, think, or process.

Victor stood stiffly next to the door. True to the Director's word, Crusher had never joined their sessions again, and other guards learned quickly what the Director liked, what he wanted, what his little nods and gestures meant. Today, the Director sat at his desk scrawling his elaborate signature over a pile of pale red forms. He used a dark fountain pen that gave his *J*'s a particular swooping look and bled through the sheets onto the plain white paper he kept beneath them.

Tobias recognized the color of the papers. He had been assigned sometimes to sort piles of ASC paperwork, and execution permission requests were always that shade. He had been grateful, at the time, not to come across his or Kayla's numbers on the papers. Now he wondered dully who was going to die in the next few days and if they had been in Special Research for very long already, or if part of what the forms authorized was their induction there.

The Director let Tobias kneel for a while, the scratch of his pen the only sound in the office, and then he glanced up and made a tiny scooping, jerky motion with his left hand. *Stand and come here.*

Tobias stood and walked forward. He stopped when the Director's hand told him to stop.

The small table that usually held the Director's interrogation tools stood in the middle of the room; a black handgun rested on top of the pristine white sheet. Tobias didn't look at it, didn't let his hands stray.

The Director signed the last sheet with a flourish and dotted an *I* with enough force to punch a hole in the paper. Tobias flinched—he had scrubbed the Director's desk once, trying to get those little black dots out of the hardwood—but otherwise gave no reaction.

"Good," the Director said. "That's done." He turned the full force of his brown eyes on Tobias, and Tobias felt a throb of terror beneath the hollow and numbness. The Director's eyes flickered to the gun and then back to Tobias's face. "Pick it up."

Eyes locked on the clawed feet of the Director's desk, Tobias picked up the gun. His hands were shaking slightly. He willed them to stop.

"Take the safety off, put it to your head, and pull the trigger."

It was an awkward angle, and Tobias couldn't manage it as smoothly as he should have. The fumbling gave him time, too much fucking time, and thoughts tumbled like hail pounding on the aluminum roofs of the barracks, like broken bodies thrown out of a black van.

Was this really it, the moment of death, the moment of release? Should he angle the blast so that brain matter flew more toward the less expensive—and easier to clean—area around the conference table, or move it to be sure that Victor wouldn't catch any of the gore? What would Kayla do when she learned? Would it hurt? Would he still be numb in hell? Oh God, would the Director really make it this easy? Would Jake know that he was dead? Would he care? Had he asked that Tobias be put down because he couldn't come get him after all?

Did the Director wait until he signed my execution form to give the order? was Tobias's last thought before he pulled the trigger.

The empty click of the chamber was loud in the room, and the hammer vibrated through his skull. He clenched his eyes shut—they had been open, fixed on the Director's desk, locked onto the Director's hands—and fought to keep any other reaction off his face, any sound coming from his mouth.

Of course the Director would never make it that easy. He would have done it in the yard or in his interrogation room, not in his office. Tobias had been a stupid freak even to guess, to wonder, to hope.

He should have known better from the start than to wish the gun was or wasn't loaded. That was the lesson.

He forced his eyes open again, homing in on the Director's hand. He kept the cold barrel of the gun pressed against his temple and hoped his expression gave away nothing, even though the Director knew it all.

"Clean it. Put it back. Get out," the Director said.

Tobias quickly and silently used the plain white sheet to rub down the gun—get the filthy monster fingerprints off the shiny black—placed it back in the middle of the table, turned, and left. He didn't change his pace as he walked out of Administration, across the yard, and into the showers. He made his movements there as methodical, impersonal, and obedient as they had been cleaning the gun.

IN THE LIBRARY, Tobias hunched over the massive spell book, occasionally checking that the notes in his notebook were still legible, in spite of how his hand had been cramping the entire day. He took a moment to close his eyes and massage his right hand, ignoring how the healing flesh screamed at him. He was off computers for the week since he had failed to report a possible demon sighting. The Director didn't want him back on the electronics until his hands healed enough to be decently fast on the keyboard.

"Why did you not report the weather changes?" the dry voice asked him once he had gotten the involuntary whimpering under control.

Tobias gasped against the thin cords that bound him to the chair, his hands palm up on the table. "There w-wasn't enough data to conclusively prove any kind of s-supernatural activity. It was a micro-irregularity and had not been confirmed with nonweather data, or even confirmed as something other than a m-mechanical malfunction."

"You don't have the qualification to make that call," the Director

said. He nodded at the guard, a new one, who pushed the electric prod into Tobias's shoulder again.

After he stopped shaking, the Director moved closer and laid a thin switch over his wrist. "89UI6703, you have no right, no ability, to accurately judge what is and is not important. You find a sign like that, you report it. I don't care if it's supported. I think you thought that you were doing what you had been told, but you didn't. The next time you allow a sign like this to go unreported, I will assume you are protecting the enemy, and your punishments will reflect that fact. Do you understand?"

Tobias dragged in a ragged breath. "Yes, sir. It was an accident, sir. I will report everything, sir."

"Good." The Director handed the switch off to the guard. "I'm pleased that you understand your failings. Because this was simply about your stupidity, your punishment will be light." He nodded to the guard. "Beat his hands like I told you. Make sure the damage isn't permanent. And muzzle him first."

Tobias wouldn't be on a computer for another week, but that didn't mean he couldn't continue to research.

He still liked the smell of the library, the musty paper and bindings, and sometimes he could almost hear Becca's voice in his ear. He hid it better now. He kept the same blank expression whether the Director said he was serving him dinner, or Victor was giving him a choice, or they sent him to the library. He thought that it worked. The beatings had become fewer since he stopped . . . wanting this room, the feel of the pages under his fingers, the silent reliability of the words. He wasn't sure why he hadn't given it up completely, hadn't truly let it go—like he had long ago stopped hoping that the Wednesdays would stop, or that his stomach would ever feel full—unless it was because this was the one place and time that he could pretend that Jake would still come back, that his life was just like it had been before the Director.

A dangerous illusion, but one that kept him going. Though he wasn't certain anymore why he wanted to keep going.

The other reason he liked the library was that he was often alone. Not that that would keep him safe, but the camera in the corner wouldn't catch him closing his eyes, rubbing his hands, or taking the time to think of nothing at all. As long as he got the work done, no one caught him not working.

When the door opened, he didn't flinch.

"Freak, you're going!" Lonny stood at the door and smacked his billy club against his thigh. "The Director says put everything away, you're not coming back."

Tobias's jaw clenched. That could mean anything from *He doesn't need what you were researching* to *You're not ever coming back to the library.* Or worse.

But he didn't let it show on his face. He closed his books and replaced them on the shelves, mentally filing away the page numbers and notes in case the Director asked. He closed his notebook and set it on the shelf with the rest of the research documents.

The first inkling Tobias got that his luck had run out was when Lonny took a heavy lead line from his belt and snapped one end onto his collar.

Tobias froze, too shocked and horrified to not let it show.

The guard grinned at him. "I told you, freak, you're *going*," and he jerked the line down hard, sending Tobias crashing to the floor.

He caught himself on his knees, but what was the point of keeping himself together when his luck was gone? Eleven years of surviving, eleven years of clawing onto nebulous hopes, and here was the ultimate outcome.

You're going.

There was only one place Tobias could possibly be going. It was where witches went for their executions, where monsters went when they couldn't behave. It was the place freaks went so that hunters could study them until the freaks left in the salted smoke of the incinerators.

Stumbling after the guard down the stairs, Tobias couldn't stop shaking. What did it matter? What the fuck did it matter anymore? He could feel everything in him shutting down, trying to brace for . . . the end. He'd wished for death so often in the last six months, but since the Director had had him put the gun to his own head, he'd understood that was something too good for him to be granted easily.

Instead of taking the door out into the yard, Lonny turned toward Reception. When Tobias tripped again, sheer terror making him unsteady, the guard pulled him up by the collar. Tobias welcomed the more normal form of pain. He had been here before. He had walked this way to interrogations and those brief, lightning-flash moments with Jake.

Lonny stopped outside the resource room, ducked in, and emerged with a short stack of clothes that he shoved into Tobias's arms. Then he towed Tobias deeper into the dark corridors. Other hallways in Reception were for the important visitors, the ones through which senators and civilians walked; scratched, fluorescent-flickering halls like this were for freaks and guards. *Paperwork*, Tobias thought. *Monster comes in, monster goes out, you have to have the right forms with the right numbers.*

At the last door in the hallway, a heavy metal one with sigils keeping demons and other malevolent spirits from crossing the threshold, the guard turned to Tobias and dropped the lead line. "Clothes off."

Tobias couldn't tell what he wanted, fast obedience or a show—Lonny could go either way, depending on the day and his mood—so he compromised by going fast but facing him.

When he was naked and shivering under the fluorescents, old gray clothes neatly folded in one pile, the guard pointed his club at the second set Tobias had carried. "Put those on."

Silently, Tobias crouched for the new clothes. The boxers

and jeans—like a hunter wore, like a *fucking hunter* wore, just the thought made his hands shake—were like his usual pants, until he got to the buttons and zippers. He'd opened enough flies that he knew the theory, but doing it to himself was different, his hands stumbling. The shirt's buttons took a long time to open and then meticulously hook together again, but the guard gave no indication that he would start hitting Tobias with the club he tapped against his thigh.

When Tobias was dressed, head down, hands still, Lonny turned to the door with a grunt and punched a string of numbers into the key box. He waited a few minutes, muttered something into the intercom, and then the red light above the huge iron door turned green. Tobias only half listened. He could probably remember both the password and the number sequence if he had to—lately anything he saw went straight to long-term memory, a Director-induced survival skill—but at the moment he couldn't care less about what Lonny was doing.

He didn't know what sick game they were playing with the clothes. Maybe they were dressing him up as a hunter, preparing to beat him to death for the audacity of pretending to be a real person. That would at least be better than being formally studied in Special Research.

Becca had told him never to fear death, to look forward to it as something that would bring him to an infinitely better place where none of the guards would be able to touch him, but Tobias had stopped believing that sometime while Crusher had used the hot irons according to the Director's cool direction. It was too much to hope for, and he had learned well her other lesson: it was better not to believe in anything that sounded good. Death sounded too nice. He didn't expect that transition into peace and darkness. Much more likely was the hell of Special Research sliding seamlessly into the hell after life. He doubted there could be much difference.

But when Lonny grabbed the lead line again and jerked

Tobias through the open door, everything he had expected shattered into a vast and uncertain lightness.

Standing in the bare white room beyond the door, face in profile, hands in his jean pockets, was *Jake*.

And Tobias could not imagine death, or hell, or true pain, if Jake were there.

WHEN THE GUARD came in with Tobias trailing him on the leash, Jake almost reeled in shock.

It hadn't occurred to him that he had never seen Toby in anything but the gray shirt and pants provided by the facility. In jeans and one of Jake's button-up shirts, Toby appeared like a person Jake had never seen before, one with the look of a long-term survivor who didn't have the resources to survive much longer. Jake's shirt on him was baggy, several sizes too big for Toby's skin-and-bones frame.

"Here you go, Hawthorne," the guard called as he shoved the door closed. He carried Tobias's leash like it was just another weapon, like the club he also held. "Dressed up and pretty like you wanted. Madison get that paperwork to you yet?"

"Not yet," Jake said.

"Can't leave until you get that." The guard grinned. "Always better to inspect the merchandise before you sign the contract. 'Specially secondhand goods." He slapped Tobias on the shoulder, and Tobias winced and swayed.

Jake swallowed hard, his hands clenched. He wanted to get a look at Toby, a good look. He looked rail-thin and pale, like he hadn't gotten as much sun as he used to, and there was something else about him, something brittle that Jake hadn't seen the last time he saw him six fucking months ago. Jake wanted to put his finger on the difference, but first he needed this asshole to go away. Otherwise he would never get Toby to look at him, wouldn't be able to see if Toby could forgive him for taking so goddamned long, for not even telling him where Jake had gone. He was getting Toby out, that wasn't a question, but whether or not Toby would stay with him . . . that was up to Toby.

"Can you leave us?" Jake asked. "Maybe check on where the forms are?"

Lonny's grin faded, but only slightly. "Yeah. Sure. Hey!" He extended the leash. "You want this, or should I check it on the wall?"

Jake felt his jaw jump, and the guard must have seen some of the rage on his face, because he backed up to the door, ran the leash through the hook on the wall, and left through another set of doors to the Reception desk behind the bulletproof glass. Tobias's head followed the lead, his body leaning back toward the door, but he didn't move his feet, didn't move in any way that wasn't necessary.

Jake waited until the door shut behind the guard before he moved forward. Toby cringed away from his hands, a slight movement that Jake might not have noticed if he weren't looking, but he couldn't balk or hesitate now. He caught Toby's face between his palms and pushed him back with the same movement, moving him closer to the wall so that the leash wasn't twisting his head around.

"Toby, you okay?" *You okay?* Seriously, that was the best he could do when he had just *left him*? But Jake had nothing better.

Toby stared at him, some kind of shock in his face, and then he almost smiled. It was a slight flicker in his mouth, in his eyes, gone in an instant, but even that softening notched Jake's tension down. But then his eyes fell from Jake's to his shoulders. "Jake."

Jake figured that was about the best he was going to get. "Let's get this fucking rope off you." He reached under Toby's chin for where the line connected to the collar.

Toby took a deep, shaky breath, but tipped his head up, eyes closed, while Jake's hands fumbled with the clips. When he got the head of the leash off Toby's collar, Jake threw the fucking thing as hard as he could against the wall.

When Toby jumped, Jake laid a hand on his shoulder and smiled at him. "You never have to wear one of those fucking things again, Toby. I promise."

Toby nodded and then smoothly stepped away from him, out from under his hand, when the door opened to let in the first guard, Madison, and an older man with his hair fading to gray at his temples and a small smile not quite reaching his eyes.

TOBIAS DIDN'T KNOW the woman—pretty, well-fed, dressed in a business jacket and skirt, carrying a pile of papers—but with the Director *and Jake* in the same room, he had a hard time breathing.

It had been easy to forget, if just for a second, what he was and what he could expect when Jake was touching him, sliding his hand beneath Tobias's chin, resting his hand on his shoulder —not to restrain him but, as far as Tobias could tell, for the contact alone. He had been able to forget the next logical step after a hand on his shoulder—the fist in his gut, the order to go to his knees—and he let the small voice in his head say Jake's name over and over again, the shock, the *joy* so overwhelming that it squeezed his lungs.

Oh my God, you're seeing Jake again. Even one more time was more than he had any hope left for.

But now: impossible, unthinkable, to forget anything with the Director in the room.

Jake looked at the other real humans, tension in the line of his neck, but not the stark panic that Tobias felt. Jake looked ready for a fight, a fight he knew he would win. It was the same brash confidence Tobias had seen from the first day they met, and the first time that Jake had smiled at him and made him feel almost like a real person.

The woman hung back, eyeing Tobias warily, but the Director strode forward. It was everything Tobias could do not to run, not to call attention to himself. He had already pulled away from Jake—the Director hurt everything he loved, Tobias couldn't risk Jake being too close to him—but it was hard not to drop to the floor or to fumble the leash back around his neck to prove that he hadn't meant to pretend to be something he wasn't.

To Tobias's relief, the Director ignored him completely. To his tight-throated horror, the Director reached out a hand to Jake, smiling, and Jake took it, still tense even without realizing who it was he was touching, not realizing how close he was to pain, death, and a calm voice directing the whip.

"Jake Hawthorne," the Director said, shaking Jake's hand and never dropping the smile. "It's a pleasure to meet you at last. I've heard good things about you. Sally's son, of course." When Jake stiffened, the Director's face fell into the clear lines of sympathy, mouth down, eyes sad. "I'm sorry, that was callous of me. Jonah Dixon, Director of the FREACS facility and the ASC. May I call you Jake?"

Jake nodded. "Sure, Mr. Dixon."

The Director laughed, and Tobias shuddered. "Please, call me Jonah. Though most around here just call me Director. It seems I gave up first names when I stepped into Uncle Elijah's shoes." The Director's smile invited Jake into the joke, shared with him the pressures of responsibility. "Some days I wish I could just get back out there where the worst I had to worry about was a mated pair of wendigos and no backup. Now I have to deal with politicians and law enforcement."

The more the Director talked in that bright, conversational tone he reserved for reals he wanted something from, the more Tobias had to fight the urge to flinch or whimper, but the words seemed to loosen something in Jake, easing a line of tension in his shoulders.

"Cops," Jake snorted.

Tobias wanted to scream at Jake to run, not to believe a single word said in that cold, smooth voice, but he was afraid of breaking the illusion the Director was creating. He didn't give a damn what happened to him, but what if Jake did something that made the Director see him as a threat? Jake was strong and had fought monsters tougher than Tobias would ever be, but there was no way that he could defeat the Director. Tobias lowered his head and focused on giving no sign that he knew the false cheer and charm was a lie.

"Indeed." The Director changed tones smoothly. Tobias recognized the new one as one that asked questions, that looked for the right answer. Any other answer ended in pain. "You can imagine I don't have much time anymore for hands-on work, but when I heard you were requesting a permanent removal of one of our inmates, I showed a special interest. Did you know this is the first one we've approved in over two years?"

"I do now," Jake said. "But everyone hears rumors they get out all the time for bait permits."

"Not at all. Well, I assure you there should be no problems with your new charge from our end, but if there are, know that we can always take him back or give you support. At any time, if the monster proves to be unmanageable, we will take him back. Just because you are signing for permanent responsibility for his actions doesn't mean that we aren't here for you, Jake."

Tobias didn't dare look up to see Jake's reaction, and his voice betrayed nothing. He could have been anything from angry at the suggestion to honestly grateful. "I appreciate the thought, Jonah."

"Good." The Director sounded less than pleased, but he waved the woman forward. "Then I'll leave the rest of the details to Madison, who is so much better at keeping the forms together than I am. Without her and the rest of the staff, this organization would combust faster than a salted ghost. If you have any more questions, don't hesitate to contact me through anyone here or at headquarters. Good luck."

With that the Director squeezed Jake's hand for one last friendly shake, and then turned to leave through the door.

Only then did Tobias realize that Jake wasn't just there for a visit. Jake was taking him away.

It was true. The Director had talked to Jake, the Director was walking away, and Tobias still stood near Jake, not leashed, not dragged back through the doors to Special Research. The Director hadn't said a thing about Tobias to make it clear to Jake just how much of a waste of time he was, how much of a disobedient, useless dog.

Jake was signing papers. Jake was taking him away. It was real, all real, not a fantasy or hallucination. Jake was taking Tobias away.

Tobias closed his eyes, dizzy and breathless and so afraid he would show everything he felt, everything he had never expected to feel. Only distantly did he notice the Director pulling Lonny over, whispering a few words before he left. Only vaguely did he see the frightened glances the woman kept shooting him as she handed Jake page after page to sign. Every time she took the signed document and placed it back in the folder, Tobias felt lighter and lighter. He was dizzy imagining days upon days with Jake, every day a good day where only one person could hurt him (Jake never had, but he could and Tobias wouldn't care), only one person he had to please, and being willing and happy to give that person any fucking thing he wanted.

Tobias kept from passing out only by taking a deep breath and reminding himself that this wouldn't be forever. He was, after all, worthless—he knew that, it had been made abundantly clear—with few assets or abilities that would hold the interest of a man like Jake. But even a year, a month, a week, *any* moment spent with Jake would be a time he could hold on to for the rest of his miserable, short life. It was even easy to believe in death, in peace and contentment, when heaven had come for him.

Jake and the secretary moved to one of the tables to finish the paperwork, but Tobias stayed where he was, watching Jake from under his hair, overwhelmed that Jake's promise was coming true, that Jake had come back. What would Kayla say if she could see him now? He hoped she'd find out, that she would know he hadn't just gone to Special Research. He could almost imagine her face (well, one of her faces) if she saw that Jake really had come for him.

He didn't notice Lonny coming up next to him until he grabbed Tobias's collar and pulled Tobias's ear to his mouth.

"Don't fool yourself that Hawthorne's gonna make you a pampered pet," he whispered. "He's a hunter, and he'll treat you exactly like you deserve—pimping you out to his dogs. And when you stop being a good little bitch, you'll end up right back here."

Tobias didn't flinch. He knew that Lonny was just trying to rattle him, and it wasn't going to work. He knew this wasn't forever, he knew he wasn't good enough for Jake to keep, but he wasn't going to be thrown off by a threat that wasn't true. Unless something big had changed in the last six months, he knew that Jake didn't even own dogs.

Finally, the last paper was signed, and the woman put on the last seal and gave Jake a tense, hopeful smile. "That's it, Mr —Jake."

"We free to go now?" Jake asked, glancing back at Tobias.

She nodded, marking something down on the edge of one form.

Jake smiled at her. "Good. Come on, Tobias."

Tobias hurried to Jake's side, and they kept a steady pace through the last hall.

Leaving Freak Camp and taking those first steps outside the facility were so unreal that Tobias had trouble putting one foot in front of the other. When the last door swung shut behind them, Tobias had to fight to keep his eyes down on the loose gravel under his feet. The sky seemed bluer, the dry desert air fresher, though he knew it was the same air, the same sky, that he had known his entire life.

He would have known the Eldorado anywhere from Jake's loving descriptions and photos, but the sleek black car looked bigger, more dangerous and alive, when the real thing gleamed before him in the sunlight.

He saw Jake's smile out of the corner of his eye. He liked Tobias's reaction. That meant Tobias was safe showing that he was happy. Just the idea of it being *safe* to be happy felt so fucking good. "I'm really glad you get to see her at last," Jake whispered.

When they stopped next to the Eldorado, Tobias closed his eyes and took a deep breath. Being able to show happiness was one thing, but this feeling, this rush . . . he was still close to passing out, and Jake hadn't done a fucking thing to him but smile.

Jake was leaning against the Eldorado, arms crossed, grinning at him, when he opened his eyes again. "Well, Tobias. I did it. I got you out. Sorry it took so long."

"It's okay," Tobias managed to say past the lump in his throat, the lightness in his body. "You came back."

He loved to see Jake smile. He couldn't believe that he was here, outside Freak Camp, standing beside Jake's car, staring at Jake without fear because the guards were back behind the razor wire and he was all Jake's now.

Jake couldn't seem to stop smiling either. Then his eyes flickered down, and he frowned and pushed himself up from the car. "Hey, we should hit the road, but before we put this shithole in our rearview mirror, there's something we gotta take care of."

He opened the trunk and withdrew a pair of heavy-duty wire cutters as long as his forearm. Tobias's brain immediately shut down as it braced him for pain. Not a new reaction or one he could help—it was the same automatic response he had when he saw the electric prod or the Director handling a whip. He was about to lose . . . a finger? Maybe. Probably not his nose, Jake wouldn't want him to look any more of a freak. He briefly considered his genitals—he'd been told often enough he didn't need them to be useful, in every way, to a hunter—but everything he knew about Jake told him he wouldn't cut something off Tobias just because it wasn't useful to him, just because it would hurt. He wasn't like the guards.

Probably just an ear, then. That was likely. Even assuming that Jake cut into the ear canal and damaged something internal instead of just taking off the outer skin, Tobias would still be able to hear orders fine with the one left. Even better, this might mean Jake wanted him for more than just a couple of weeks' hard ride, wanted to mark Tobias as his. And *that* was more than okay. If he was Jake's, Jake was much more likely to salt and burn him somewhere when he got tired of him than to let an old possession get passed around back in FREACS.

Tobias could deal with losing any body parts right now if it was something Jake was doing to claim him as his own. And even if he was too hopeful, if Jake had no problem dumping him back at Freak Camp after he'd had his use of him, at least it would be a reminder that he had once been Jake's.

Tobias's thought process had lasted just a couple of seconds. By the time Jake stepped up to him, Tobias's heart rate was back down, and he watched Jake and the wire cutters almost hopefully, trying not to let his daydreams fly away with him.

"Tilt your head up," Jake said. "I want to get a good angle so I don't hurt you."

The last sentence didn't make any fucking sense, and it almost shattered the edge of Tobias's happy calm, but he obediently closed his eyes and tilted his head up, hoping Jake hadn't noticed how the blood beat harder in his jugular.

The slide of the wire cutters' cold metal against his throat and the sharp *snap* next to his ear made him clench his jaw. The lack of pain nearly made him panic because *oh God, what happened that I can't even feel it?*

Then something hit the ground. Something that sounded too heavy to be an ear.

Tobias opened his eyes, and Jake was smiling at him, the smile that always made Tobias's heart race in a way that had nothing to do with pain or fear. Jake tossed the wire cutters back into the trunk and reached toward Tobias, making him flinch slightly, and rested a hand against his neck. His bare neck.

Tobias looked down, Jake's hand warm and gentle against the naked skin of his neck, and saw the collar in the dirt by his feet. Slowly, hardly believing that he wouldn't touch blood and bone, he reached for his neck on the side opposite of where Jake's hand rested, brushing his own fingers over the exposed skin.

He looked up, so filled with emotions he couldn't even name —was this shock, terror, wonder?—that he stared straight into Jake's eyes, incapable of hiding himself, of not looking and looking his fill. He couldn't read Jake's face, but what Jake saw in Tobias's expression made his eyes flicker with something that Tobias couldn't put a name to, that made him nervous without being afraid.

Then Jake enfolded Tobias in his arms, pulling him to his chest in a grip that was warm and secure but strangely not confining. Tobias felt warmth unlike anything he'd ever known spreading through his body, leaving him weak-kneed. He let his eyes close. Jake was so close that when he took a breath, Tobias felt his own chest lift. It was a sensation—like electricity buzzing through his body, but without pain—that made him understand a feeling he'd never known before.

It felt like safety.

Jake held him, anchoring them together, and Tobias could think of nothing else that there would be in heaven.

It ended. Of course it ended, and it left Tobias shaky but smiling, not afraid to open his eyes and smile. Jake smiled back.

"Come on, Toby," he said, sliding around him and opening the passenger door of the Eldorado. "Let's blow this joint."

Tobias got in, clumsy in the unfamiliar space, and he couldn't keep a grin off his face. And he didn't care. While Jake walked around to the driver's side, Tobias ran both hands down the leather seats savoring the smell of Jake's car, the feel of Jake's life beneath his hands, the knowledge that Jake had come back for him, had taken him away from hell. He had kept his promise.

No matter how long it would last, no matter what happened to him after this moment, Tobias didn't think anyone could take that joy, that peace, away from him.

THE END

The story continues with Book 2 (FEAR), available now!

Thank you for reading Freak Camp!

It would mean so much to me if you would consider leaving a review on a site like Amazon or Goodreads. I love to read every one.

Do you want advance access to the next book, extra stories, and other exclusive Freak Camp content? Sign up for the monthly Freak Camp newsletter at **freakcamp.com**

ACKNOWLEDGEMENTS FROM LAURA

This story would have never been written without my BFF of fifteen-plus years, Bailey R. Hansen, who took this plunge with me back in October 2010. We knew from that very first night it could really be something, but I am still astounded at the magnitude of what we created together.

Enormous thanks to Mackenzie Walton for editing this story. I am incredibly grateful to have had her expertise and guidance from this start of my publishing journey and with such a weird hybrid story like Freak Camp. Thank you as well to my copy editor, Adam Mongaya, who did a brilliant job. All remaining errors are my own persistent ones.

Thank you so much to Christine Griffin, the brilliant illustrator and designer of this book's gorgeous cover art, who also has supported this story for so many years. Your illustrations and enthusiasm helped make its potential so much more real to me.

I'm also so grateful to Kate Rudolph and Melanie Greene, fantastic romance authors, for letting me pester them so often about how to do this whole publishing thing professionally. I don't know where I'd be without you both, Quell and Mel (and my whole slack family. I appreciate you guys and bitches so much.).

Many more thanks go to all my beta readers, especially those who've put in years of dedication to the Freak Camp story—I'm talking to you, Carole M. Stokes! Thank you also to Abbe M. Longman, Amanda Stenson, Birgit, CarolAnn Grafe, Casey679, Dai U, Elphie Dickinson, Jayce Chow, Lightning's Daughter, Lily McGlaughlin, Meghan Parsons, Rachel Willhoite, Rebecca Res, Rebekah JJW, Rita Hattori, Shea Brannen, Sumbul Danish, Tammy Berlin, and many more.

Thank you to Angela James and her community From Written to Recommended, which gave me so many of the tools and confidence to really finish this story with a bang and do it justice.

I also want to shout out my Creative Writing professors at the University of Evansville for building the foundation for my success: Paul Bone, Rob Griffith, Margaret McMullan, Mark Cirino, and Arthur Brown.

And thank you, thank you, thank you to whereupon, who has also been here from the story's conception in 2010 to the present day. The whole Freak Camp world would not exist in its many hues of brilliant-colored glory without you, and I would be a poorer writer. You've taught me so much about writing and living, and I can only hope one day the world will also have the gift of your life-changing stories.

Finally, thanks to my mother who is the best and most cinnamon roll of all mothers, and also to Jud, for joining our family with true Viking spirit during some of the hardest years. It makes me so happy to see you both happy.

ACKNOWLEDGEMENTS FROM BAILEY

When we first started writing Freak Camp, I could have never imagined how big it would grow or how many lives it would touch. I am humbled and honored, and so profoundly grateful for Laura Rye. While this Monster was a mutual labor of love for a very long time, in recent years she has done literally everything to get this book into your hands. She is the best friend and co-author a girl could want.

Thanks also to Mom and Dad, who have encouraged, commented, and critiqued my writing through the years. You are my rock and I'm so glad to have you as parents.

Writing a book takes a village (or at least writing and publishing a good book does!) and Laura has already done a great job of calling out the many people who made this work better along the way. I want to add a profound thank you to the many first readers of this story whose love kept us writing. This book would not exist without you.

ABOUT THE AUTHORS

Laura Rye grew up in the bustling cosmopolitan city of Houston, Texas. After falling in love with the mountains and the sea and every single tree in the Pacific Northwest, she now lives in Portland, Oregon. She graduated from the University of Evansville with a Bachelor of Fine Arts in Creative Writing and now does the boring writing by day and the fun kind at night. One day very soon the fun kind will be her full-time job. FREAK CAMP is her debut novel.

Stay in touch with Laura at **freakcamp.com** and on Instagram: @lauraryewrites

Bailey R. Hansen spent her unconventional childhood traveling the continental United States with a clown and a clarinetist (aka her parents). She graduated from the University of Evansville with a BFA in Creative Writing, lived for a few years in Spain, and has since settled in Wisconsin. A technical consultant by day, she happily writes at any time for both love and money. FREAK CAMP is her debut novel.

Read more of Bailey's fiction and other projects at **baileyrhansen.com**

Made in the USA
Middletown, DE
25 June 2024